HUNTED:
THE IMMORTAL'S KISS

E.L. SUMMERS
L.N. FROST

HUNTED:

The Immortal's Kiss

By
E.L Summers & L.N Frost

Printed in the United States of America

First Printing, 2019

Enchanting Tales Publishing

Baltimore, MD 21221

https://enchantingtales2019.wordpress.com/?theme_preview=true&iframe=true&frame-nonce=f93903abf4

Acknowledgements

Thank you to Brooke Bognanni for always encouraging us and supporting our dreams of bringing our creativity to life.

Table of Contents

Prologue

The gentle warm October air scattered the fallen red and brown foliage around the outskirts of the park's entrance. A wooden post with a metal link held a sign that read, Greenwood Park. Blue spruce trees outlined the park with cobblestone paths with wooden benches leading to a wooden pier overlooking the lake and abandoned toolshed.

Teens strolled through the park with arms linked, clothed in pastel sweaters and earth-toned scarves, sipping coffee. Perched on one bench sat a tall man appearing to be in his late twenties. His shoulder-length black hair swept over his left side, held back with gel. His round amber eyes studied the passing strangers carefully. He crossed his long elegant arms over the middle of his black jacket, feeling his abdomen muscles clenched with hunger.

His long slender white fingers swept a stray red leaf from his black dress pants, glancing up to meet the wandering gaze of a passing young blonde woman in her early twenties. He flashed her a wry grin watching her round cheeks redden in embarrassment. The pain in his chest returned, causing him to bite on his bottom lip to subdue the ache. *Food was easier to come by back than when times were simpler; women flocked to me,* he thought, thinking of the evening of his transformation.

September 6, 1966

London, United Kingdom

The streets of London were barren, with the air thick with smog turning the city skyline into a murky fog. A layer of ash dusted over the city streets covering the surfaces of cars, buses, and buildings adding a layer of grime to the luscious city. Numerous trash cans were ablaze to keep the homeless warm in the rigid September nights. A young man in his late twenties climbed a charred fire escape leading to the roof of what was once a red granite apartment complex.

A thud reached his ears as a cloth bag fell from his hands landing at his feet. Inside the bag were a few newspaper clippings of London and a faded black and white photograph of him and his family, his father dressed in a military uniform, his mother and younger sister both wearing evening gowns in shades of green and purple. Like those below him, he had no home and was admiring the night sky, his hands resting at the nape of his neck with his fingers intertwined nestled against his shoulder-length black hair. Lost in surveying the city beneath him, he couldn't see the shadowland behind him studying his movements.

"What a lovely sight, is it not? Mother nature cleaning herself of the parasites that live in ignorance. If only the fires could spread to other parts of the world instead of staying here," a male voice called, making Simon jump, startled by the stranger's sudden appearance. "At ease, I merely wish to share the view I have no intention of harming you, Simon. Even if I did, I wouldn't be polite about it," Damion noted, chucking inhaling the sweat trickling down the man's neck.

Strange, I never told him my name? he thought, puzzled by the mystery. "Who are you?" Simon asked, taking in the man's appearance. The man's light brown hair hidden underneath a top hat. His grey eyes held cold mirth in them along with a purgatory grin.

Damien smirked, seeing the mortal's fear replaced with curiosity. "Damien Lemire, a native like yourself once upon a time. I'm bored, so I decided to wander around and find myself some entertainment. Would you like to join me? I guarantee you won't regret it?" he asked, moving to stand beside Simon with his hand outstretched towards Simon.

Chapter One

The throbbing ache resurfaced snapping him out of his thoughts, coughing to disguise the moan of agony escaping his lips. The girl glanced at him in concern and he smiled watching her stumble shaking her blonde curls out of her blue eyes. He outstretched one hand, beckoning her toward him seeing the sky darkening from the corner of his eyes. The pink horizon darkened, turning amethyst elongating the shadows from the towering trees surrounding them.

He could smell the sweet crimson liquid flowing through her veins as she drew nearer. Her hands fidgeted with the hen of her blue sweater dress. He waited for her blue almond eyes to meet his in a fleeting glance holding it as he reached out to grasp her warm hand in his cold fingers. A slight gasp escaped her lips allowing him to pull her to the bench to sit beside him.

"Hello, my name is Rose—" she stammered, not prying her gaze from him parting her dry lips with his own, not allowing her to finish her statement.

She tried turning her head feeling him reach out with his other hand gripping her chin preventing her from turning her gaze away. She leaned closer, inhaling the warm leather, feeling his fingers tangling in her hair. He extended his arm, resting it behind her back and removing his fingers from her hair to caress her cheek gently.

She tilted her head, rubbing her cheek against his touch feeling tingles spread through her skin at his touch. He leaned forward, brushing his lips gently against hers once more. She returned the kiss, running her fingers through his hair. His kisses trailed to her neck, trailing along her collarbone. She reached up to pull off the soft cotton sweater, eagerly exposing more of her pink flesh to his lips.

A moan escaped the girl's lips as her breathing quickened, arching her back in pleasure. His lips brushed against her neck before his fangs slid forth and sank deep into the soft porcelain skin. Her eyes glossed over with delight, her cries growing louder. He drew in the warm nectar greedily trying to subdue the painful hunger. The fresh blood stained his lips, yet the limp body remained nestled in his arms.

Rising to his feet, he shoved the corpse away from him in disgust. Drops of blood stained the collar of his white button-up dress shirt underneath his jacket. The warmth spread throughout his body, silencing the ravishing hunger. *I should flee before the vultures and scavengers flock to my newest victim, attracting the media and police to clean up the mess that I have left for them*, he thought, exiting the park as the sirens grew louder.

Chapter Two

The wind picked up as the purple sky darkened to a deep indigo. The sound of footsteps pounding the dirt path leading up to the park's entrance drowned out in the twirling fallen leaves. A yellow glow illuminated the empty park cast from several lamp posts positioned beside each bench. The figure's silhouette cast a shadow over the wooden sign. She extracted a pair of earbuds from her ears, shaking the blonde curls out of her face.

Her labored breathing slowed her beating heart before reaching for the black hair tie around her wrist, pulling her shoulder-length blonde curls into a messy ponytail. Hearing two deep tenor voices startled her, gaining her attention flickering her almond green eyes to her right sweeping her surroundings. She covered her mouth with her arm, inhaling the strong odor of sulfur. One police officer had their back to her, placing the body in a black duffle bag.

An arm rested on her forearm gently, startling her before she turned to face the older gentleman. His blue and white police uniform stretched over his round stomach. His gray eyes were red with fatigue. He shoved a bright flashlight in her eyes, staring accusingly. The woman flinched, taking a step back and diverting her eyes from the blinding white light. He swept the flashlight past to see his partner zipping up a black nylon bag by his feet.

"Sorry, miss. I'm going to have to ask you to leave," he pleaded, moving his calloused hand, gripping her arm tighter and trying to pull her around him to the park's entrance. She twisted her body to one side, digging the heels of her black boots into the hard soil, and swatted his hand away. An exasperated sigh escaped his pale lips, reaching for the set of silver handcuffs from his right pocket.

She noted his movement as he took a step toward, her narrowing the distance between them.

"Hey, Scarlett. There you are. You ran ahead of me?" a soft bass voice called, racing toward her his chin-length auburn red hair blowing in his brown eyes. Loose strands stuck to his forehead damp with sweat. He offered the police officer a gentle smile positioning himself in between the two of them.

"You should listen to your boyfriend, miss, and go home," the cop pleaded, turning his back to her, and walking toward his partner. A smart escaped her lips taking a step after the officer before a tan hand gripped her arm gently. He released her arm, wiping the sweat from his brow before wiping it on the thigh of his blue denim jeans.

Scarlett opened her mouth to protest before a tan hand covered her mouth. A wry smile stretched out over his tan face seeing her eyes narrow in anger. She waited for the two men to pick up the duffle bag carrying it back to the black sedan parked across from the park's entrance.

He removed his hand hearing her teeth clench, pretending to bite his fingers.

"I had this under control, Andrew. I didn't need your help," she sneered, spitting at his feet tasting the sweat on her pink lips.

A deep laugh bellowed from his lungs amused by her reaction. His brown eyes followed the red and blue lights of the police cruiser until it disappeared around the corner.

Scarlett rolled her eyes, following the red cobblestone path to the wooden pier. She heard him following her before reaching the end of the pier. She unzipped the black cotton hooded sweatshirt, placing it on the wooden planks before sitting down on it. Her long legs dangled over the edge of the pier, overlooking the glossy dark emerald water.

Andrew took a seat beside her, resting his calloused hands on the knees of his denim jeans. He placed the gray messenger bag in his lap and reached inside, extracting a black camcorder. "I know you're mad at me for letting the officer's remark slide—" he pleaded, offering her a wry grin laughing at feeling her hand smack his shoulder. "Let me finish," he warned, hitting a switch on the side panel before placing it in her hands.

Scarlett arched an eyebrow, feeling the cold metal nestled in the palm of her hand, staring down at the small screen curiously. The left corner of the screen marked Friday, October 24, 2018. Parents were ushering their children out of the park as dusk approached. She watched what appeared to be an intimate couple publicly displaying their affection for one another.

The wailing police sirens prevented her from overhearing their conversation. The blonde laid limp in the man's arms before he climbed to his feet, laying the lifeless corpse on the wooden bench with her face against the wooden bench. Blood trailed down her collarbone before the man removed a black scarf and tied it around her neck before fleeing the scene.

Scarlett turned the device off before handing it back to Andrew. He placed the camcorder away before removing a leather-bound notebook. When he opened it up a map of downtown Denver with circles noted with dates and locations to mark where the creature had struck. "It's been two months since the first encounter with the vampire. It's odd to see one without a nest nearby," he remarked, adding the date and location of the recent victim.

He frowned at seeing all the victims were young women with blonde hair in their mid-twenties. "With this fourth victim it's clear he has a type," he added, closing the notebook, and meeting her gaze. His lips narrowed making a kissing sound earning another punch in his shoulder.

Scarlett rolled her eyes glancing out at the water, hearing Latin music from a yacht across the lake. Its white lights illuminated the dark sky. "Well without any details on our vampire our hands are tied," she announced, her eyes lingering in the direction of the yacht watching the foam dance across the waves.

Andrew laughed seeing the plan forming in her head. He rested a warm hand on her shoulder redirecting her attention. He tucked a loose strand of her hair behind her left ear. "I see the lustful look in your eyes. You see a party going on and you want to join," he teased, brushing her cheek with his knuckles.

Scarlett felt the warm caress despite the chilly air biting her lower lip feeling her cheeks flush. She climbed to her feet watching Andrew do the same. He reached for her hand trying to pull her against him. The scent of sea salt and leather filled her senses reminding her of the last time they were alone together.

July 1, 2017

Cave of the Winds Mountain Park

Colorado Springs Denver, Colorado

The sun hung high in the blue sky with puffy white clouds dotted the horizon. Scarlett and Andrew followed the tour guide through the granite pathways, leading to a series of granite stairs descending into a cavern illuminated by the LED lantern. Scarlett reached for the yellow ruffled sweater tied around her waist, hit by the draft blowing up from the cavern floors.

Andrew reached for her hand, ensuring that she wouldn't stumble while her eyes adjusted to the dim lighting. The tour guide's excited tenor voice echoed in the underground terrain ushering the group deeper into the cave. "Thanks for checking this out with me, Scar. Usually people aren't interested in it," he noted, walking beside her keeping his fingers intertwined with hers. His warm palms warmed her cold fingers, catching her rolling her eyes at his comment.

She tried taking a step forward to catch up with the group, feeling Andrew tug her hand, lightly drawing her against his chest. She shook her loose curls out of her eyes, staring up at him quizzically. He released her hand, reaching up to tuck a loose strand of her hair behind one ear. A wry grin flashed across his face, his cheeks flushing.

Before she could say anything, he brushed his lips against hers. Scarlett tried turning her head away, pushing against his bare chest. He wrapped one arm around her waist, deepening the kiss, grazing her lower lip with his teeth, a low growl emitting in his chest.

Scarlett lashed out with her fist, grazing his cheek with the silver rose ring on her finger. He hissed, baring his teeth at her, but took a step back in alarm, shoving her backward. She stumbled, slipping on the dirt floor, and falling on her back. Crying out in pain made the tour guide pause in his historical speech, circling back to the two of them, asking if she was all right. She accepted the hand of a woman in her forties, flashing her a fake smile before dusting the dirt from her clothes. She kept her distance from Andrew the remainder of the tour before driving back to the manor.

Chapter Three

Scarlett's eyes widened in alarm, lashing both hands out trying to push against him. He stepped closer wrapping one arm around her waist. His lips brushed against her cheek, reaching up for the hair tie and freeing her wavy blonde curls to cascade down both sides of her face. She tried ducking to slip out of his grip and took a step back, feeling her heel slip on the edge of the wooden plank.

Andrew reached out for her wrist, trying to pull her close again, but she swatted it away, causing her to tumble backward falling into the icy water. Her lungs burned as they filled with salty water/ She kicked her legs desperately, breaking the surface. She coughed, spitting out the salty water from her lungs while her wet curls clung to her forehead.

Her green eyes stung from the salt, straining to find a way out of the water. She felt the weight of the water drag her back under before a warm pair of arms circled around her waist and pulled her back above the surface. She groaned, noticing the matted red hair, dragging her to the sandy shoreline. A small patch of sand met the grassy hill, leading back into the woods.

"I'm sorry—" he whispered, seeing her coil her arms around her waist, shivering from the cold.

"You said you'd never try that again," she whispered, coughing, and turning her head to spit out the water lodged in her lungs. She pulled her wet hair into a loose braid, tucking her knees up to her chest. She closed her eyes, focusing on inhaling the chilly night air.

Andrew opened his mouth but closed it seeing the silent tears trailing down her cheeks. He climbed to his feet, dusting the wet sand from his hands, and outstretched one to her. "Come on, let me at least take you home?" he pleaded, waiting for her eyes to reopen.

She wiped the tears with the back of her palm and climbed to her feet. She wiped the sand on her wet jeans, gesturing for him to lead the way up the grassy hill to the parking lot where his silver Jeep sat.

The sound of their footsteps pressing against the dirt trail filled the silence between them. He stuffed his hands in his pockets, sneaking a glance at Scarlett, watching her remove the silver necklace and clenching it in her hands. The silver cross dangled in between her fingers.

"Scar—" he pleaded, flinching at watching the silver chain swing in his direction brushing against his arm.

"Just let it go, Andrew," she sneered, smirking at noticing the welt left on his forearm from the silver. She was the first to reach the Jeep, waiting for Andrew to catch up and unlock the driver's side door before leaning over to unlock the passenger side door. Scarlett climbed into the passenger's side, resting the necklace in her lap before reaching her arm behind the seat finding a soft red blanket. She wrapped it around her shaking body before buckling the seatbelt across her lap.

Andrew took a seat behind the steering wheel, fishing the keys out of his pocket. He inserted the key into the ignition and turned on the heat. "I just wanted to say, I was sorry," he replied, feeling the warm air blow up from the vent.

Scarlett pulled her hands from under the blanket rubbing them over the warm air. Andrew glanced in the rearview mirror slowly backing out of the parking spot. He slumped his shoulders, getting no answer from Scarlett before maneuvering his way out of the parking lot and onto the highway.

Scarlett picked up the silver chain, fidgeting with it restlessly.

"Scarlett?" he pleaded, keeping his eyes on the road ahead of them trying to get a reply from her after a long uncomfortable silence had fallen between them.

The only sounds were the heated air emitting from the vents and the tapping of his fingers on the steering wheel. Scarlett's hands stopped fidgeting with the chain, gripping it in both hands. Her gaze drifted out the window, watching the other cars pass by. Andrew opened his mouth to press her but shook his head, letting out an aggravated sigh.

As they turned off the highway after ten minutes of driving, the tires crunched over a dirt road. Peach trees and cherry trees were abundant on both sides, leading up to a three-story Tudor manor in grey granite stone with an adjoining garage. An iron fence surrounded the property secured with an electronic keypad.

"I guess the silent treatment will continue?" Andrew groaned, rolling down the window to reach over to enter the six-digit code.

The gate buzzed before it parted, lasting five minutes before closing with a click behind him.

Huh, he figured that out all on his own? she thought, waiting for him to drive into the garage before removing the key from the ignition. Scarlett slipped the necklace once more around her neck and threw the blanket behind her on the backseat. She opened the passenger side door eager to escape his company.

Andrew reached out his hand ready to stop her but flinched, hearing the car door slam shut. He closed his eyes, hearing the door leading to the garage slam shut behind scurried feet. He hung his head, taking in a deep breath before opening his eyes and exiting the Jeep, placing the keys in his pocket.

His footsteps were muted by the plush coffee-colored carpet leading to the foyer. The smell of onions and Cajun spices lingered in the air, causing a small smile to flicker across his face. He turned right, descending the hallway decorated with various Greek paintings to arrive at his room.

Andrew entered his room with one wall taken up by a metal desk with a laptop and two monitors. His four-poster bed and another desk covered with notebooks occupied another wall. The third wall had an entertainment system, and the last had a large bookshelf filled with thick novels, comic books, and cyclopedias, taking up the corner next to his closet. His walls were painted in shades of crimson and black decorated with large sketches of dragons fighting one another.

He tossed the duffle bag on his bed, colliding with the silhouette stretched out on the green moss-colored comforter. He draped his jacket over the back of the chair and collapsed into the leather chair in front of his computer. He glanced away from the stack of papers, hearing a gagging sound emitting from the bed.

A young woman laid there with her legs crossed at the ankles propped up by one elbow flipping through a leather tomb of the history of magic. Her green eyes scanned the page yet paused to wrinkle her nose in disgust flipping her long wavy chestnut hair over her shoulders letting it reach her tailbone. A loose strand rested over the patch of bare skin from the cleavage of the red heart scoop neck corset.

"Ugh, what smells like wet dog?" she exclaimed, covering her nose with both hands causing the book to fall off the bed.

Andrew rolled his eyes, crossing the room to his dresser to pull out a gray short-sleeved shirt and black denim jeans, keeping his back to her. He tugged the shirt up and over his head, tossing it into a corner and moving to tug down his pants, revealing the black briefs underneath. A cry of disgust filled the room before the thick tome flew, hitting him between his shoulder blades. The book fell on its spine, spilling back open by his feet.

"Ouch! What was that for, Raven?" he demanded, getting dressed and turned to face her seeing an arm draped over her eyes. He let out a deep chuckle, bending down to pick up the book before placing it on the desk. He collapsed in the black swivel computer chair, spinning around to face her. "You can open your eyes now, I'm dressed," he teased, laughing at hearing a sigh of relief escape her lips. "Why are you even in here, what did you do?" he pressed, spinning back to face the desk, and turned on the computer.

Raven chuckled, climbing off the bed to grab another comic book from the black marble shelf. "I figured this was a safe place to hide. No one would ever suspect I'd be in the nerd cave," she teased, perched on the edge of the bed the skirt to her long-sleeved purple dress spread out over the plush comforter matching the light purple tights she wore underneath. Andrew snorted, shaking his head waiting for the computer to finish booting up before plugging in the camcorder and downloading the file he had shared with Scarlett. "Where is your partner in crime?" she pressed, after not getting a retort from him.

"Good idea. Come to the one-room Matt is known to avoid. Speaking of our fearless leader, is he in the garage?" he asked, seeing her shrug her shoulders in response. "Very helpful. If you're going to stay in here don't snoop through my things," he demanded, grabbing one of the notebooks climbing to his feet.

He heard a bitter laugh come from Raven; her eyes glued to the page in the Marvel comic book. He exited the room descending the hallway, making his way back to the garage and pushed open another doorway to his right that sectioned the massive garage into two rooms.

The soundproof interior lined with shelves with mechanical pieces for cars and motorcycles. In one corner of the orange painted room sat a long oval wooden desk with a laptop set up with papers scattered around it. The sound of a screw tightening drew Andrew's eyes to the back wall where a motorcycle was leaning against it.

Snow-white hair peeked out from a black bandana, yet the rest of his long hair rested in the middle of his back. Hearing footsteps approaching, he glanced up from the engine he was tinkering with wiping his greasy hands on his black jeans. Red eyes regarded Andrew in annoyance. The red muscle tank top hugged his muscular frame covered with specks of grease. He wrinkled his nose in disgust setting the wrench on the shelf beside him. "Whatever favor you want, maybe you want to consider taking a shower first?" he teased, ignoring the low growl emitting from Andrew's chest-baring his teeth in annoyance. "Very funny, Matt. Raven said the same lame joke," he sneered, crossing his arms over his chest. He opened the notebook clutching the pen in his right hand. "I dove into Lake Greenwood to prevent Scarlett from drowning," he protested, watching the smile fade from the other man's pale lips. "Just answer my questions and I'll tell you what happened," he added, seeing the white eyebrows knit together in concern.

Matt closed the engine up before grabbing the gray tarp to trap over the motorcycle. "A steep price for an annoying mutt who has nothing to offer," he hissed, heading toward the door finished with their conversation.

Andrew stepped close reaching out to grab the back of Matt's shirt stopping him in his tracks.

A wry grin flashed across Matt's face, resting both hands over Andrew's. "I won't repeat myself, Andrew. If you have nothing to offer me, then I can't help you," he replied, gripping Andrew's wrist adding slight pressure forcing Andrew to release his shirt before turning his back to him, entering the manor.

Andrew stormed into the manor after him, closing the distance between them once more and grabbed Matt's forearm, preventing him from entering the kitchen. "I wasn't finished talking to you. I guess I shouldn't have been surprised you refused to help me. No one gets anything from you for free," Andrew shouted, not seeing a tall, willowy girl enter the foyer overhearing his protest.

She wore a pair of blue jeans, brown Mary James boots, and a light red flannel long-sleeved shirt. Her long platinum blonde hair hung down her back in a braid. She placed her hand over Andrew's, startling him, causing him to glance in her direction.

"I know what you want, Andrew. My answer is still no. I only require something in exchange not out of greed but to make the pain of calling on the spirits worth it," Matt replied, smirking at seeing the girl hugging her purse to her chest afraid to say anything.

A sly grin crept on her face twinkling her blue eyes before reaching into the black sequin tote bag finding a bottle of cinnamon apple scented perfume before spraying Andrew with it. Matt chuckled seeing Andrew flinch in alarm. "Dawn, was that necessary? I just want a name. Name your price—" he pleaded, hoping that Matt had changed his mind.

Matt let out a sigh of frustration, closing his eyes and taking in a deep breath before opening them back up. Seeing Matt's red eyes darken, Dawn let out a cry of alarm before fleeing to her room. Andrew arched an eyebrow not seeing what had frightened her. "Dawn was smart not to evaluate my patience, I'd advise you to do the same Andrew," he warned, seeing Andrew open his mouth but close it is thinking over his statement.

"I just want to help Scarlett. I messed up today and I want to make it up to her by giving her a lead to go on," he persisted, deciding to play his last card seeing Matt regard the request carefully.

Matt laughed amused by Andrew's predicament, heading back to the garage. Andrew tried reaching for his arm again but was shooed back by a blast of frigid wind. Matt shoved Andrew against the wall, sliding down the wall falling on his butt. He watched Matt disappear into the garage before the motorcycle's engine roared to life. Staggering to his feet, Andrew retreated to his room hoping in time Matt would change his mind.

Chapter Four

The two-story black granite building towered over the smaller businesses in Downtown Denver. Dusk settled and the red letters of *Sângele Vampirului* (Blood of the Vampire) lit the purple sky. Simon's footsteps crept past the throng of people lining outside the bar's entrance. He smirked hearing the catcalls thrown in his direction from a tall brunette who was the last to enter the staggering line of men and women in their late twenties and early thirties. He ignored the lustful stares from the redhead wiping down the bar.

An exasperated sigh escaped her red lips, watching him pass to climb the spiraling staircase to the second level. The interior of the bar featured crimson cotton carpeting, dark espresso colored wooden tables with matching chairs, French bay windows lined the far away with weathered wooden accents overlooking the city. The main bar featured black iron cast gargoyles. The lobby adjoining the bar featured a black leather sofa and recliner with gothic paintings by Simone Martini hung over the dark amber walls.

Upon reaching the landing, Simon flinched, hearing out of tune bass notes humming in delight to the guitar solo of "One" from Metallica's *...And Justice for All*, before screaming the lyrics. Approaching the nearest bedroom, he was greeted by a tall slim figure swaying side to side clutching a plastic guitar in both hands. His short shaggy amber hair fell freely over both shoulders to the black t-shirt covered in white skulls. Hearing the soft chuckles, he craned his neck over his shoulder noticing the figure standing in the doorway. He finished the song, raising the plastic guitar in the air triumphantly before setting it aside.

He crossed the dimly lit room to the ornate dresser, reaching for the glass of blood. His dark eyes softened back to amber, wiping his mouth with the back of his palm before wiping it on his blue jeans. The room, like all others in the estate, featured dark wooden walls, a king-sized bed, a desk beside the bed, a walk-in closet, and a wide-screen television mounted to the wall.

"Am I in trouble?" he inquired, seeing Simon glancing toward the window taking in the purple sky.

An annoyed sigh escaped Simon's lips. "No, you twit. I'm here to see your elder brother, Donovan. Is he here?" Simon sneered, watching the other man pout shrugging his shoulders.

Michael turned to stick his tongue out in response. "Forgive me for thinking you'd want to spend time with me. No one ever wants to play with me," Michael whined, peering at the hallway waiting to see if Donovan would join them.

Simon let out a bitter laugh. "Any sensible person would rather have their eyelids nailed shut or spend an eternity entombed in the catacombs of a church," he sneered, smiling at seeing Michael recoil in disgust.

"A bit morbid, Simon. Self-affliction is not a theme I thought you of all people would be into. I know my brother can be a bit imperious, but there's no motive for giving into temptations," a deep voice warned, passing Simon to enter the room taking a seat at the desk. He watched Michael return to stand in front of the television screen picking the guitar up once more. Donovan wore a midnight blue dress shirt with black velvet pants, his navy trench coat over his broad shoulders. His hair was a dark auburn with his bangs worn at an angle covering his deep brown eyes.

Simon let out a bitter laugh lingering in the doorway. "My apologies, should I have addressed him as an irrational; baboon instead?" he jeered, catching the small television remote thrown in his direction in Michael's anger.

Donovan chuckled hearing the remote hit the wooden wall before falling to the ground shattering in pieces from the impact. "Your arrival is flavored with a sense of desperation. Must I once again save you from your own mistakes?" he pressed, hearing Michael snicker in delight lost in his game.

"Do not be quick to pass judgment on matters that don't concern you—" Simon protested, balling his hands into fists at his side.

"Not judgement, merely a theory based on your hostile reaction. Now, inform me on why you linger upon my domain?" Donovan added, resting his hands in his lap watching Simon warily.

Simon was quiet crossing the room to the closet finding a wooden panel that slid to one side revealing a hook. He entered the closet retrieving a dartboard and hanging the string on the hook. Clutching a dart in one hand he took a few steps back. Donovan climbed to his feet moving to block his path. A sly grin danced across Simon's lips tossing the dart watching it sail through the air toward Donovan's face. Donovan caught the dart with ease, an annoyed expression on his face.

Simon regarded his response, collecting another dart from the bag by his feet. "I was trying to satiate my thirst—" he confessed, hurling the dart in frustration watching Donovan step to the left allowing the dart to fly past him and striking the center of the board.

Donovan laughed amused by the statement. "Being sloppy with your leftovers doesn't excuse your actions. Now I must wonder if my establishment will be infested by mortals seeking our demise," he hissed, glaring in Michael's direction at hearing him snicker amused to hear his brother lecturing Simon.

"No, not any mortal just the slayers," Simon corrected, throwing another dart watching it sail through the air before embedding itself in Michael's left calf.

Michael yelped in pain, dropping the guitar to tug the dart free. He wiped the dart clean of blood before hurling it at the dartboard. *Hopefully leaving a mess for the slayers to clean up will lure them into my trap*, he thought, watching the dart hit the bottom of the board.

Donovan placed two fingertips on his temples rubbing them in agony overhearing both Michael and Simon's thoughts simultaneously. "You will lose them here despite not asking for permission first? Very well play your pathetic game so long as I'm left out of it." Donovan explained, climbing to his feet to exit the room. He stood against the black iron banister staring down at the empty dance floor beneath them.

"Ah, but why bother with boring formalities when the meat bags are flocking here anyway?" Simon teased, following Donovan out into the hallway.

Donovan watched the staff setting up the bar for the festivities blocking out the tirade of thoughts in Simo's head. "Your pea size mind has trouble understanding a dismissal. Now, leave us. I am no longer in the mood to play host," Donovan snapped, ushering Simon to leave the bar.

Simon laughed amused by Donovan's anger. He bowed in mockery to Donovan before descending the stairs leaving the bar from the kitchen to avoid the line of mortals waiting to enter the bar. Donovan disappeared to his room seeing that Michael lost in his game.

Chapter Five

Earlier that evening, Scarlett raced up the marble staircase to the third floor, inhaling the sweet aroma of white lilies in the blue-tinted glass vase on the end table outside of her room. Humming to herself, she fished in her pocket for a set of keys to unlock the door. Entering the room, she flicked a light switch to flood the room in yellow light. The rose gold wallpaper welcomed her, matching the amber furniture.

Scarlett stared at the note in bewilderment reading the note over once more before climbing to her feet crossing the hallway. *Matt will have some good news for me*, she thought, knocking on the door across the hallway from her own. Frowning at hearing no answer she returned to her room grabbing her phone from the glass coffee table and dialed Matt's number.

Matt cruised down the highway feeling the bitter wind push against him blowing the white tendrils of hair exposed from underneath the black helmet behind him. He turned off the main highway away from the city and toward the mountains, picking up speed. His tires sailed over dirt roads causing a dust cloud to form behind him. Peering through the clear visor of the helmet, he couldn't help but smile, admiring the violet sky.

Feeling his phone vibrating from his pant pocket, he pulled over to the side of the road, cutting the engine. Matt's smile broadened seeing Scarlett's name on the screen. He removed his helmet placing it on the handlebars before pressing the phone up to his ear. "Hey, small fry," he answered, staring up at the horizon watching the sun dip behind the puffy white clouds.

Scarlett climbed to her feet, keeping her phone pressed to her ear, crossing the room to where a mini fridge was stationed beside a bookshelf full of thick tombs and magazines. She selected a water bottle before collapsing once more in the recliner. Her eyes landed on the note hesitating to ask him about it. "I just wanted to hear your voice, it's been a long day," she groaned, taking a sip of the freezing water.

"Wow, don't I feel lucky knowing that my voice is the only thing keeping you from going over the edge," he teased, hearing the strain in her voice.

Scarlett laughed, nearly choking on her water, and wiped her mouth with the back of her hand. "I need a leash on him after the stunt he pulled today," she confessed, suffering at recalling the close encounter.

"No, I was referring to another matter. Why, what did the mutt do this time?" Matt asked, hearing her let out a sigh of annoyance.

Scarlett took in a deep breath trying to control her anger. She let the breath out slowly. "The mongrel wanted a reward for showing me stolen footage of the park," she started to explain, clenching her fists unaware that she was squeezing the water bottle until some of the water splashed on her leg spilling on the carpet in front of her.

"I take it that you came across the most recent victim?" he inquired, aware that she had gone to Greenwood Park to investigate police reports of a young woman who they believed to be attacked by a wild animal.

"Yes, he tried making a move on me. He can't take no for an answer," she added, hearing Matt cough trying to cover up laughter. "It's not funny! I tried getting away from him and fell in the lake," she replied, climbing to her feet to throw the empty water bottle in a metal trash can in one corner hearing Matt emit a cat whistle in response. "Remind me again why I thought it would make me feel better talking to you?" she snapped, placing the phone on speaker and sitting it on the dresser searching for a towel to wipe up the damp puddle on the carpet.

Matt stopped laughing seeing that it had upset her. "I'm sorry, I know how scary open waters can be for you. That explains his insistent demand of my services on your behalf," He noted, drumming his free hand on one of the handlebars.

"Don't let the mutt talk you into helping him. There's nothing he can offer me to apologize for what he did," she warned, tossing the wet towel in a white wicker basket full of dirty clothes.

"It would be nice to capture the vampire before more lives are added to the list. Besides, my price is too steep for the mutt to afford—" he teased, trying to cheer her up.

"It would be nice to rub it in Andrews's face that we solved the mystery. Care to meet me at *Sângele Vampirului*? It's a new nightclub that opened downtown. We can discuss whatever the spirits offer you about our vamp,"

"I have a few errands to run first. I'll let you know if I can't make it," he replied, placing his phone on speaker to put his helmet back on.

"I know I'm looking forward to it. Stay out of trouble until then if that's even possible," she teased, before hanging up the phone removing the wet clothes changing into black dress pants and a shimmery blue tunic that hung off her shoulders. She slipped out of her room making her way to the basement to kill some time before the club opened.

Matt hung up the phone placing it back in his pocket before turning the engine back on. Amongst the woods leading up to the mountains nestled a wooden cabin that Matt owned that was isolated. He used it for opening a channel to the other side knowing that he wouldn't be distracted or interrupted by other slayers.

Chapter Six

Scarlett surveyed the hallway, not seeing any other slayers before descending the basement stairs, greeted by the wafting scent of pine hearing muttered verses of Latin before an explosion went off, filling the room with green smoke. Scarlett was quick to cover her mouth with one arm, swatting at the gas with the other.

"If you're here for a weapon tune-up, you'll have to wait your turn," an annoyed voice yelled, chopping herbs on a cutting board keeping their back to Scarlett.

"What if we just wanted to keep you company? Do we get something anyway?" Scarlett teased, reaching the landing stepping onto a blue oriental rug etched with white runes.

Underneath the rug was granite stone with a magic circle carved into the stone with Celtic cymbals marking where each element lived. Scarlett took a seat in a brown leather loveseat facing one wall lined with guns, rifles, swords, daggers, bags of ammunition, and bones of grenades. Beside the loveseat was a desk littered with papers, books on runes and herbs, vials filled with different colored liquids, with printed blueprinted tapered to a cork board above it.

"Everyone always wants something from me except you, or Matt," she muttered, not glancing up from the black cauldron adding the chopped herbs to the simmering pot. Scarlett frowned, climbing to her feet, closing the distance between them. Scarlett rested her hands gently on the girl's shoulder prying her away from the table. Blue eyes blinked offering Scarlett a weak smile.

She allowed Scarlett to lead her over to a black computer chair stationed in front of another desk with a laptop and more books on the lore of monsters. Ari reached for the bottle of iced tea taking a long sip of it. "Sorry, I didn't mean to lash out at you," she mused, running a hand through her waist-length wavy black hair streaked with blue highlights. She removed a blue satin hair tie from her wrist pulling it up in a loose bun letting the long bangs from her face.

"It's been a rough day for everyone. Maybe I should extend the invite out to you as well?" Scarlett teased, noticing the blue silk cloak draped over the back of the chair. The various shades of blue matched the long-sleeved bell-sleeved shirt she wore with black jeans.

"A distraction sounds tempting seeing how the other girls were so generous to point out my lack of social skills. I would love to, but I have too much on my plate to ignore," she replied, reaching for one of the books in front of her, studying the weathered pages with a frown.

"I can tell. You're wearing the same clothes from the night before. Ari, did you get any sleep? Surely whatever you're working on can wait?" Scarlett pressed, seeing the bags under her friend's eyes.

Ari rubbed her eyes, closing the book in frustration. She reached in one of the desk drawers retrieving a pair of blue-rimmed glasses. "Who can sleep when one's on the edge of a scientific breakthrough? I almost have the formula figured out. I just need to figure out how to keep an ingredient from self-destruction," she confessed, staring at the cauldron ignoring Scarlett's concerned notion of sleep.

"Maybe tinkering with one of the weapons will take your mind off it and help you refocus?" Scarlett suggested, aware that the problem would annoy Ari until she solved it. Ari nodded in agreement reaching for a plastic bin underneath the desk finding pistols in pieces. In another bin laid a tool belt fashioned with wrenches, bolts, pliers, and other tools. "What kind of potion were you brewing?" she asked, watching Ari dismantle a pistol, emptying the barrel to clean it before refilling it with silver bullets.

Ari climbed to her feet placing the pistol on the shelf along with the other weapons before returning to her seat. "At first, it was to create an updated version of tear gas aimed at vampires. I thought rose petals would be a good part, only to realize the chemical difference when crushed, losing the texture that makes them a threat against the bloodsuckers. I tried garlic and despite its improvement, the vapors are weak, taking too much time to cause a reaction," she explained, smirking at seeing the dazed expression on Scarlett's face.

"I'm now trying to use formulas to create small sun spheres but creating miniature suns with herbs is proving quite difficult. I need a more scientific solution," Ari muttered more to herself glancing at the blackboard covered in formulas and spells.

"Andrew thinks I owe him… for what? Sharing with me something I could have discovered myself," Scarlett mumbled, glancing up to see Ari raising an eyebrow at her quizzically. "Sorry, I guess I'm still upset about what he did earlier," she confessed, watching Ari push her chair closer to Scarlett reaching for her hand squeezing it lightly.

"He tried making a move on you again?" Ari guessed, smiling at hearing the gagging sound from Scarlett. "To be fair, he sees himself as your knight in shining armor," Ari mused, hearing a groan from Scarlett.

"Matt let me stay here when I had nowhere else to go," Scarlett protested, annoyed that Andrew saw her as a damsel in distress.

"Andrew is the one that brought you to us," Ari remarked, seeing Scarlett staring at her blankly. "Andrew told us that he found you after he killed a female vampire that was trying to protect you—" she started to explain, seeing Scarlett shake her head failing to believe the tale.

"Why would a vampire protect me? That seems a bit farfetched even coming from Andrew," Scarlett protested, seeing Ari shrug her shoulders.

"It could have been a clan that fed on animal blood. They're rare but some do still exist. You'll have to ask Andrew for the full story," Ari suggested, seeing Scarlett hang her head in her hands.

If what Ari said is true, then Andrew thinks he saved my life that day, but what really happened? she thought, hearing a low chime from a grandfather clock emit from the floor above them marking the top of the next hour.

"I almost forgot I have a date with Matt," Scarlett announced, hearing Ari swoon playfully. "Good luck with the potion. Try to get some rest, maybe then it'll come to you," she suggested, climbing to her feet waving to Ari before heading back up the stairs.

Chapter Seven

Simon sat perched in one of the wooden bar stools at Sângele Vampirului, watching the bar filled with humans, their voices a dull chorus of syllables rang in his ears. He clutched a wine glass in his right hand, filled three-quarters full of blood. The crimson liquid was a warm and bittersweet taste of roasted honey lingered on his lips.

How revolting, forced to drink blood from a glass, masquerading my thirst instead of enjoying mortal's sweet nectar the way it's intended, Simon thought, taking another sip from the glass. His eyes landed on Donovan, seeing him approach the bar, stepping behind it and carrying a box of wine glasses lining the wooden shelves. The red-headed bartender was beside him wiping the glasses down before prepping the garnish station, cutting slices of lemons and limes.

Donovan chuckled softly earning a puzzled glance from the girl not hearing what was so funny. Donovan sat the box on the floor and reached across the bar for Simon's glass to refill it adding animal blood to the wine. "Your suffering is caused by your own decrees. You know how I run my establishment, yet you remain to wait for your prey to arrive," he whispered, offering the glass to Simon with a small grin.

"Oh, Donavon, when will you learn that we are gods among mortals? We should be flooding the streets with their sweet nectar, yet you refuse and insist I follow you and your delusional rules and drink toxic animal blood," he sneered, taking a sip of the drink before spitting it out in disgust. He shot a dirty look in the bartender's direction hearing her laugh at his expense.

Donovan laughed, taking the glass from Simon's hand before taking a long sip before offering the empty glass back to the bartender. "Don't insult the help, Simon. You were the one foolish enough to believe the food would satisfy your palate," he suggested, trying to hide his amusement allowing the barmaid to clean up the mess.

A look of revulsion flickered on Simon's face at the idea of drinking animal blood. He opened his mouth to protest wanting to wipe the smug grin off Donovan's face.

"I don't appreciate you talking about my master as though they're feeble insects. They allowed you to use their club for your selfish endeavors, so the least you can do is show him some respect," she snapped, bowing her head unaware that she had spoken her thoughts out loud. Her hands fidgeted with the hem of her V-neck A-line satin cocktail dress embroidered with red roses.

"Shiva, don't rise to his banter, why don't you take a break before the festivities begin?" Donovan replied, resting a hand on her shoulder feeling the tension build in her shoulder.

How sweet, Donovan is trying to shelter his sheep from the wolves, Simon thought, noticing the black tribal band tattoo around her neck. "Shiva De Grace? A covetous sex slave sold to the highest bidder?" Simon sneered, smirking at watching her hands clutch into fists glaring at him as she passed slipping out from behind the bar.

Donovan watched her flee toward the lounge anxious to distance herself from Simon. "That was childish. Any sign of your prey?" Don asked, gaining Simon's attention. Donovan grabbed a wine glass filling it with blood from a bag fetched from a blue cooler underneath the bar.

Simon wrinkled his nose at the rustic smell emitting from the red liquid in Donovan's wine glass. "Sadly, not yet, probably waiting to make a grand entrance. The offer still stands for you to taste the sweet nectar and feast like the gods we are," Simon insisted, grimacing at watching Donovan take a sip of his drink. "Think of the endless possibilities, you can finally get revenge for the loss of your family—" he protested, hearing glass shatter from Donovan's clenched fingers. Donovan leaped over the bar closing the distance between them. Gripping Simon by the collar of his shirt and shoved him up against the bar. Simon's drink fell from his hand spilling red liquid all over the bar and the plush carpet. Donovan's nails dug into Simon's shoulders, tearing through the fabric of his shirt drawing fresh blood.

"Remember, Simon, you are here because I alone allowed it. Mock me again and the slayers won't be your only concern," Donovan sneered, releasing his grip before disappearing into the crowd of people dancing behind them.

Simon reached for a napkin wiping the specks of blood from his shoulders once the small wound closed. He unbuttoned the vest admiring the torn sleeves of the white button-down shirt he wore underneath it. He tore the shredded fabric before resting the vest on the back of his barstool. *How amusing, Donovan tried intimidating me. To think, he tried to enforce this revolting lifestyle without considering my own,* he thought, taking his seat once more groaning in annoyance upon spotting Michael approach him from the corner of his eye, taking the empty seat to his right.

Michael had stood at the entrance of the lounge watching Donovan slam Simon up against the wall overhearing their conversation. He waited for his brother to walk away dissevering into the incoming throng of people taking a seat beside Simon. He smiled waving over a blonde waitress wearing the same V-neck A-line satin cocktail dress as Shiva. He ordered in sălbatic roşu (wild red wine) which was code for preparing animal blood or blood bags into a wine glass mixed with red wine.

"I was starting to think the night would be boring, yet it's always fun watching my brother kick your ass," he jeered, thanking the woman for his drink. "What did you do to piss him off?" Michael asked, ignoring Simon wrinkling his nose in disgust as the drink offered to Michael before taking a sip from his drink.

Simon ordered a new glass of red wine watching Michael pull out a leather wallet extracting a crisp five-dollar bill to tip their bartender. "Simply, the truth, that drinking from humans instead of revolting animals will provide him with the strength required to avenge the family he has lost," he added, taking a sip of his drink, using the reflective glass to scan the room behind his seat.

Michael blinked confused by the statement, *Wait, I thought I was Don's only family?* He thought watching Simon carefully wondering if Simon's victim had already arrived. "We're all entitled to our opinion, even if they're wrong," he replied, ignoring the bitter laughter from Simon. Michael turned in his chair scanning the mass of faces, trying to figure out who Simon was searching for. "Any idea what your slayer looks like?" Michael asked, not bothered by Simon's reaction to his statement.

"Why, so you can become her valiant knight in shining armor in the redemption of your desperate attempts for attention?" Simon sneered, denying the fact he had no clue who he was searching for, yet continued to scan the room. *The fool has a point; I have no clue what she looks like. I wonder if I feed out in the open will it draw her out?* he thought, taking another sip of his drink.

"I'm not desperate, I'm a true gentleman. Besides, it beats being an arrogant asshole," Michael snapped, finishing his drink before climbing to his feet and disappeared into the throng of dancing people. *A witty retort for the baboon, as usual*, Simon thought, reconsidering his plot to draw the slayer out.

Chapter Eight

Each block of Downtown Denver decorated with streetlamps illuminating the darkened city block in yellow streaks of light. Some of the metal poles of the street limos were decorated with purple or orange paper garland in the spirit of Halloween. Soft blues music soiled out from the open door guarded by a bouncer checking identification to the line of people waiting outside the doors to *Sângele Vampirului* enduring the brutal ten-degree winds. Scarlett glanced down at her phone for the third time since reaching the club. *Still no word from Matt. I just hope he doesn't stand me up*, she thought, hugging the black jacket tighter to keep warm feeling the wind whip against her cheeks.

She stepped forward in line approaching the towering brute shaven older man clearly in his late forties dressed in black slacks and a collared black dress shirt that constricted over his wide muscular chest. She removed her hands from her coat pockets fishing in her purse for her wallet for her license flashing him a wide smile.

The bouncer nodded, waving her into the club. She had received a ticket checking her jacket before stepping through the lounge and into the bar. Her green eyes scanned the room adjusting to the soft orange lights pulsing in time with the music. She crossed the room, pushing through the throng of dancers trying to reach the bar.

Donovan slipped through the crowd of dancers trying to head upstairs, still enraged by his conversation with Simon. The patron's thoughts buzzed in his head like infuriating flies, thwarting his ability to concentrate on his surroundings. A warm body collided with him, scattering the whispers in his head. He reached both arms out, resting them on the girl's shoulders to steady her, seeing her stumble back a step.

"My apologies," he announced, speaking loudly over the mix of voices and swing music. He leaned in closer to speak in her ear. "Due to a distracted mind, I lost focus on my surroundings," he apologized, bowing curtly amused to see her roll her eyes in response. "It appears I miscalculated on the success of my bar's premiere," Donovan remarked, smiling as her eyes lit up upon taking in the interior of the club.

Scarlett smiled accepting his apology. "There's no need for you to apologize I should have been more aware of my surroundings. Are you the club's owner?" she inquired, taken aback by how polite he seemed.

"Yes, but it appears that my presence is needed elsewhere for the moment," he replied, bowing to her once more. "Enjoy your experience this evening, Miss Blackwater," Donovan whispered, walking past her heading for the stairs to the second wanting an overview of the bar.

Scarlett watched him effortlessly maneuver past the other dancers toward the winding stair. She blinked baffled by his words wondering if her name had been present on her ticket to her jacket. She fished in her pocket for the receipt seeing that her name wasn't present anywhere and that she was given a number.

That's odd, I never gave him my name, nor have I ever met him before. she thought, shuffling through the crowd to the bar leaning over to shout over the music. "Hey, can I get a Bloody Mary?" she asked, screaming over the loud music.

Michael had seen the exchange between the girl and his brother and had followed her back to the bar. He ordered the same as her placing another crisp five-dollar bill into the plastic tip jar. He had changed resembling the same outfit as the bouncer outlining his thin muscular frame.

He thanked the bartender offering Scarlett her drink turning in his seat to face her. "Well, hello there beautiful. My name's Michael. What's yours?" he demanded, handing her the drink from the bartender.

Scarlett smiled, nodding her head in thanks before taking a sip of the cool, tart liquid. She pulled out her phone, staring at the screen expectantly, only seeing the dragon screensaver showing the time marking an hour had passed since her arrival. She flinched, nearly knocking her martini glass over at feeling a cold hand resting on her bare shoulder. Fighting down her frustration she offered him a polite smile. "It's Scarlett, though thanks for the drink, I'm waiting for my date," she confessed, thinking back to the mysterious note she had received thinking it was a better response than to lie and say she was waiting for a friend.

"May I keep you company while you wait?" he pressed, offering a sly smile, and meeting her gaze as his hand shifted to her thigh. Scarlett gripped his wrist tightly with one hand, adding slight pressure while prying it away from her thigh.

"There are plenty of pretty women out on the dance floor. Why don't you ask them to dance with you?" she suggested, shooing him away in annoyance.

Michael's smile faded, climbing to his feet, feeling rejected. He finished his drink before following her advice slipping into the dance floor to find a woman to dance with. Scarlett sighed in relief finishing her drink also before climbing to her feet heading toward the opposite side of the bar to dance hoping to avoid the creep.

Simon chuckled softly watching Michael flirt with the girl before shooting him away like a swarming fly. *Poor fool, he never stood a chance. I wonder if she could be my slayer. Donovan surely seemed smitten with her*, he thought, watching the girl sway in tune with the fast-paced jazz music.

Chapter Nine

Another hour had passed before Scarlett headed back to the bar, pushing damp wisps of her hair from her forehead, ordering a glass of water. She pulled out a hand mirror from her purse, removing the blue headband from her hair. She ran her fingers through her messy curls before replacing it wiping the sweat from her brow with a damp napkin. The music had slowed to a classical blues number forcing couples to sway side by side together.

"Is it just me or does it seem like every guy in town showed up tonight hoping to score?" she remarked, finishing the water before ordering another Bloody Mary.

Shiva had taken cover behind the bar to keep watch over the girl, noticing both Simon and Donovan's careful eye. They both seemed interested in the girl, which put Shiva on guard. She prepared the drink, adding salt to the rim of the glass before pouring the red liquid into a martini glass and adding a lemon wedge and lime wedge for garnish.

She placed a stack of napkins in front of Scarlett and a tall pint glass full of ice water. "I know what you mean; usually when a new club opens, you expect more women to show up than men, but maybe all these guys thought they were going to get laid," Shiva replied, having overheard Scarlett's comment.

Scarlett nodded in thanks, emptying her glass of water in three big gulps before pushing the empty glass aside. She removed the lemon and lime wedges, placing them on a napkin and reaching for her phone again. Despite the late hour, she didn't see any messages from Matt. *I guess he's not coming after all,* she thought, taking a sip of her drink. "And to think, I got all dolled up for my date only to get stood up. Even worse, every creep in here wants me," she admitted, staring toward the exit tempted to leave.

"The night's not over yet. He might still show, though most men only have a one-track mind. They think that all women are good for is one thing, and don't care how they get it. Even here at Sângele Vampirului, men treat women like their nothing more than mindless slaves," Shiva explained, thinking of how men looked at her.

"You make it sound as though you know from experience. At least the drinks here are good otherwise I might have left already," Scarlett answered, taking another sip of her cocktail, spotting a gentleman taking the empty seat beside her and ordering a glass of wine.

"Rough night, I take it? I couldn't help but overhear your conversation—" Simon noted, watching Scarlett with her drink.

"Let me guess, you want to buy me a drink too?" she hissed, taking another sip of her drink. She wiped her mouth with one of the napkins, anxious to finish her drink and leave.

"Of course not. I am a chivalrous man. I believe that a beautiful woman, such as yourself, should be allowed to enjoy her evening how she truly desires," Simon replied, glaring at Shiva, hearing her snort in response as she fetched a shot of Tequila for the man beside Simon.

Scarlett arched an eyebrow, surprised by his statement. *I thought chivalry was dead*, she thought, resting her elbow in one hand. "Then why are you still here? To keep the creeps at bay?" she inquired, thinking that he was trying to impress her.

"Yes, if I only watch from afar, I can't fend off the desperate mongrels that beg for your attention. Offering them false illusions of success won't swat them away. I'm sure the last suitor will return to make another attempt," he advised, turning to face her, showing interest in the conversation.

"You saw that? I thought it was amusing to see how easy it was to reject him, though I can't help but ask if you've been watching me all night? What made you decide to break your silence and talk to me?" she asked, taking another sip of her drink.

"I was afraid if I kept afar, you'd leave having a bad impression of the place," he replied, meeting her gaze, and resting his hand on her shoulder brushing away a strand lock of her hair. "Do you believe there's any truth behind the meaning of Sângele Vampirului?" he asked, watching her blink, started by the question, tearing her gaze away from him.

"Sângele Vampirului roughly translates to the blood of the vampires in Romanian, but I doubt the other patrons here are aware of it," Scarlett answered, staring down at her drink, fidgeting with the straw.

"A random entity to name your establishment under... Miss—" he added; aware he had never gotten her name.

"Scarlett Blackwater, though who are we to question the passions of the bar's owner?" she protested, resting her hand on his forearm, feeling the warmth from alcohol race through her starting to feel buzzed.

"A fair argument, Miss Blackwater. I became so captivated by your company that I forgot to introduce myself. My name is Simon Revlon, and I would love to know more about you," he pleaded, smiling at seeing her cheeks flush, becoming ensnared to his charms

Scarlett opened her mouth, ready to reply, when she noticed the owner approaching them. "I'm sorry to interfere with what was an amusing conversation, Simon. I need to discuss a matter of immense importance with you in private," Donovan explained, standing behind Simon studying the girl ensuring she was all right.

Chapter Ten

Simon followed Donovan's quick strides toward the back of the bar. "I hope the matter is dire, Donovan. Otherwise, you'll just wind up wasting my time," Simon sneered, following Donovan into the empty office. He heard the door close shut behind them, tapping his foot impatiently.

"I should have known a dimwit such as yourself could never produce just a simple plan. What a pity and here I thought I would have the luxury of staying out of your affairs for once." Donovan remarked, grimacing at the onslaught of thoughts coming from Simon.

"I don't know from where I was standing it seemed as though it was going quite well. Is there another reason behind your hostility?" he noted, wondering why his charms hadn't worked on her as quickly as it had on others. His eyes widened as realization dawned on him.

"Amusing, I gather you have an attachment to this human? I guess I'll have to discover for myself what was worth proctoring her over the rest of your clan," Simon replied, reaching for the door behind him, anxious to return to the girl. He recoiled his hand, darting to the side, seeing Donovan lunge toward him, closing the distance between them.

"Sister by marriage. If you have a lick of intelligence you will leave her alone," Donovan snapped, turning to lunge at Simon once more.

Simon tried once more to race toward the door grabbed by Donovan. Donovan's sharp nails dug into Simon's shoulder hurling him across the room and onto the wooden desk filled with papers. Simon lashed out raking his nails through Donovan's arm drawing blood staining the papers underneath him.

Simon tried staggering to his feet, ducking to avoid the chair hurled at him by Donovan. He heard it clatter beside him, crackling and breaking in pieces from the force. Simon reached for a broken slab of wood from the chair, lunging at Donovan, and thrust with the piece of wood.

He drove it into Donovan's chest pushing him across the room and into the wall closest to the door. "Admit it, you failed to protect your slayer. I will relish biting into her beautiful delicate neck," he announced, grabbing two more slabs of wood clutching one in each hand to stab Donovan with.

"Only a fool celebrates before achieving victory," Donovan snarled, feeling the paint of the wall fleck behind him before placing one hand around the shaft of wood. He grimaced, tugging it free, feeling blood trickle underneath his shirt from the hole the wood had caused.

"Ah, but it is? With you out of the way, there's no one to stop me from claiming my prize. You think you can beat me, yet you can barely keep up with me," he jeered, hearing the volume of the music in the bar increase to drown out their fight.

"Our altercation isn't complete. This is the time you bow down and beg for mercy," Donovan muttered, bending the wood to break it in half before lunging at Simon, catching him off guard.

Simon had succeeded in batting one of the pieces of wood out of Donovan's hand with his own, yet the second one slammed into his shoulder. He grabbed Donovan's wrist bending it until the bones snapped under the pressure. He kicked Donavan back a step to extract the piece of wood from his shoulder.

"Ah, but I have an ace up my sleeve no amount of superiority can defeat," he noted, amused to see the puzzled look on Donovan's face. He heard the music turn off before an alarm went off. sending the patrons into a panic. *Surely, a slayer can't refuse to help a civilian even in an intoxicated state*, he thought, falling to his knees raising his arms over his head before yelling for help.

Chapter Eleven

Thirty minutes had passed without Simon returning, making Scarlett worry. She finished her drink and climbed to her feet. The jazz music shut off before a loud siren scratched through the bar, sending the other guests to panic, running toward the exit.

"There's a drunk arguing with the owner in the back office," a waitress yelled, removing the cash from the tip jar, placing it in the cash register and locking it before following the crowd toward the exit.

Scarlett pushed through the panicked crowd hearing the desperate cry for help. "Help, there's a monster trying to kill me," Simon screamed, hearing the approach of footsteps before the office door swung open.

Simon watched her scan the room, seeing the bloody stains on the desk and along the hardwood floor. Adracalin rushed through her senses before she reached in her back drawing a silver dagger.

"Scarlett! Thank god you're here. You have to help me, he's a vampire!" Simon cried, stumbling toward her before falling to his knees beside her.

Donovan let out a sigh of annoyance, slowly approaching them. "It seems even here idiotic morons can be found. You, sir, came into my establishment and attacked me. You cry out vampire, yet you lack proof of such ridiculous conclusions?" Donovan asked, offering Scarlett an apologetic smile, watching her place the dagger back in her bag.

Mortals are weak and easily manipulated, I will prove it by pinning your precious human against you, Simon thought, meeting Scarlett's skeptical gaze. "I'm sorry, the dim lighting played tricks on me. I mistook red wine for blood. Our conversation thus far hasn't led you to believe I'm crazy?" he pleaded, seeing Scarlett shake her head no, offering him her hand helping him to his feet.

"False accusations shouldn't be taken lightly. Are you going to press charges, mister?" Scarlett pressed, realizing she had never gotten his name.

"Donovan Vaslie, and no. The police shall remain out of my affairs. No harm was done, even if the man took a leap with his superstitions," he replied, seeing her smile in relief. "A moment to refresh myself and then I shall offer you a drink on the house to show no ill will?" he suggested, wanting to change into clothing that wasn't soaked in blood.

"I will keep you company until Donavan joins us," Simon suggested, offering Scarlett his arm.

Scarlett stared at him skeptically, wondering if it was safe to be alone with him.

"I guess I wanted to be right about this place, and now I feel like a fool," he confessed, watching her sigh, reaching for his hand, and squeezing it gently.

She followed his lead back to the empty bar. Scarlett took a seat at the bar ordering a glass of ice water with a wedge of lemon seeing Shiva wiping down the bar listening to their conversation.

Scarlett removed the lemon wedge from her glass, squeezing it into her water before fidgeting with the straw, not sure what to say to him. *I have a knack for picking the crazy ones*, she thought, taking a sip of her drink, feeling his eyes watching her fidget with her drink.

Five long minutes of silence had passed between them before Scarlett coughed, trying to break the awkwardness. "Earlier you asked if I believed there was any merit to the lore behind the meaning of the bar's name?" she drawled, choosing her words carefully, seeing the hopeful look in his eyes.

"I take it that it should have been a warning sign that I'm crazy?" he teased, seeing her avert his gaze, glancing behind them, anxiously waiting for Donovan to join them.

"No, not crazy, just desperate for attention," Shiva mused, under her breath, watching Donovan approach the bar to join them, ordering three shots of Tequila for them. Shiva rolled her eyes at the dirty look sent by Simon adding a few drops of holy water to his shot glass before placing the glasses in front of them. "Maybe you should ask Donovan about his choice for the name?" she suggested, watching Donovan take a seat next to Scarlett.

Scarlett turned to glance at Donovan, expectedly curious to hear his answer. "I thought it was an effective way to attract patrons. A reminder of home and a ploy that they would be lured in by the lore," he explained, nodding his head in thanks, seeing the blue-tinted shot glass placed in front of him. He raised his glass in salute to Simon, waiting for him to do the same before inhaling the juniper flavored liquid.

Simon snickered upon hearing Donavon's answer. *A fascinating take, yet I'm the villain for filling her head with lies?* he thought, saluting Donovan, and raising his glass as well before drinking it. His eyes darkened, feeling the sweet-bitter burn his throat, causing him to drop his glass. His eyes turned black coughing loudly, clawing at his throat in pain, trying to spit out the vile liquid.

Scarlett glanced at Simon in concern, seeing his eyes turn to black, baring his fangs at Shiva in anger. She stumbled from her seat, knocking her glass over, spilling the clear liquid on the bar in front of her. She fished in her bag, retrieving the dagger once more, trying to steady her breathing and racing heart. Donovan grimaced, clutching at his skill in pain, hearing Shiva's thoughts as well as Scarlett's.

Donovan climbed to his feet to stand beside Scarlett, placing his hand on her shoulder making her jump. "I see that the snake finally bared its fangs. Please calm yourself, Scarlett, I will ensure no harm comes to you," Donovan pleaded, moving to stand in front of her seeing that Shiva had hidden behind the bar.

Simon glared at Donovan, trying to dart around him to get at Scarlett grabbed by his throat and tossed to the ground. Simon laughed, watching the girl stare at Donovan in awe, startled by his actions. "How do you intend to protect the lamb from the wolves? Shall we inform

Scarlett of the true intent behind your protection?" Simon sneered, seeing the girl's shocked expression.

Donovan glared at Simon standing between her and Simon grasping his head in pain. "Cease your games, Simon. I will clear up this misunderstanding she has about me once you leave our presence," he growled, grabbing Scarlett's glass half full of gin before tossing the liquid in Simon's face.

Simon swatted the glass away in annoyance, hearing the glass hit the ground before shattering upon impact. Shiva jumped to her feet, grabbing the bottle of holy water, and throwing it at his face. He howled in pain, feeling the liquid burn his flesh. It sizzled in his ears, disorienting him, distracting him from hearing Donovan scoop up the girl and flee to the second floor.

"You have won this round, Donovan, but you can't protect the little lamb from the wolves forever," he warned, baring his fangs once more before exiting the bar.

Chapter Twelve

Simon's threat lingered in Scarlett's ears before strong arms slipped around her waist. In a blur, she arrived at the top of the swirling staircase, reaching the second story, seeing over the balcony to the main floor below. Donovan leads her into the closest room setting her on the edge of the bed taking a seat beside her.

"I take it you're a vampire as well?" she whispered, mystified by his kind nature, trying to rationalize the intent behind his actions.

Donovan let out a low groan in pain, rubbing once more at his temples. "I would appreciate it if you stopped grouping me in with Simon. Unlike that fiend, my meals do not derive from humans. Be at ease that no harm will find you here while in my care," Donovan explained, hearing the girl's neurotic thoughts subside.

Scarlett glanced at her hands, feeling her knuckles turn white from the tight grip she had on the dagger's handle. She relaxed her grip, sensing the hurt tone in his voice. "It would be foolish to let my guard down around you, I was trained never to trust your kind," she remarked, twirling the dagger in her hand anxiously feeling his eyes linger on her hands. *Is this another trick? Should I call for backup? What would Matt do in my situation?* she thought, hearing him grimace in pain gaining her attention.

"You may think what you wish, though quiet your thoughts please. I take it Matt's your leader. I was under the impression you were with the beast that stole you from my care." Donovan explained, annoyed that the girl feared him.

Scarlett let out a bitter laugh, amused by his statement. "Nice try, but I already fell for the sad story once tonight and look where that got me," she snapped, rising to her feet, and heading toward the door. *I should just call Matt and tell him I got a lead on our vamp*, she thought, annoyed to see Donovan leap to his feet, blocking her path.

"You could leave now and risk the chance of never learning more about your past," he mused, seeing that she was determined to share what had happened with the other slayers.

What could he know about my past, we just met, she thought, skeptical of his statement, stepping around him, startled to feel his arm reach out grasping her hand gently. The cold caress startled her, making her pause in her steps.

"A moment of your time is all I'm asking for. If you wish to leave afterwards, I won't prevent you from doing so," he pleaded, sensing her hesitation in her thoughts. "I know a great deal about your past and wish to share it with you if you're willing to listen," he added, taking a seat on the bed, closing his eyes, taking in a deep breath trying to ignore the pain in his temples.

Scarlett arched an eyebrow, ready to voice her thoughts aloud, leaning against the doorway keeping her distance from him. She glanced down at her purse perplexed if she should call Matt afraid to trust her judgment. She couldn't help but think of how badly she had misjudged Simon.

Donovan opened his eyes, surprised to see she was still standing in the doorway. "Your doubts are valid, Scarlett, but I speak only the truth. I was gifted with the rare ability to hear people's thoughts after my rebirth," he noted, laughing at hearing a rapid string of thoughts as to how it worked.

Scarlett felt her face flush, feeling his gaze in her direction, seeing her thoughts cease in fear. He sighed, wondering how many more times he would have to repeat his words for her to believe him. He waited, listening to her weigh the pros and cons of his gift before moving to perch on the edge of the bed.

Scarlett placed her hands at her side, smoothing out the wrinkles in the plush comforter, trying to control her nerves and wishing that she had another drink.

Donovan rested his hand over hers, smirking at seeing her flinch once more. "I do not blame you for questioning my intentions when you believe that all vampires are alike. Just like mortals, we are each unique in personality, aside from our gifts," he remarked, understanding that she feared he would deceive her just as Simon had. Sighing, he left the room before quickly returning with a bag of blood marked as deer.

"Additional proof that you need not fear me. Drinking the blood of animals satisfies my thirst, leaving me with no motive to harm you," he added, returning the bag back to the bar downstairs before returning to the room to sit beside her. "Perhaps now that your fears are laid to rest, you are ready to hear what I have to say regarding your life prior to joining the slayers?" he pleaded, gritting his teeth trying to ignore the buzzing thoughts coming from her, Shiva, and Michael.

"The story I was told was that on a mission, one of the slayers, a werewolf, slew a group of vampires and found me bathed in their blood. I was splashed with holy water and, not seeing any signs of a bite, he took me in," she stated, seeing him thinking over his response, glancing down at a bronze ring on his left hand twisting it self-consciously.

He glanced up feeling her eyes drawn to him nodding in agreement to her story. "I see. that explains your disappearance. My nest and I were traveling in search of a haven. My beloved feared your safety. She wanted to prevent harm from occurring to her sister," he answered, seeing her roll her eyes, laughing bitterly in disbelief.

Scarlett understood that he had lost his wife but did not believe she had a sibling. "You're lying! Matt has never lied to me, and I'm sure me having a sibling is something he might have mentioned," she snapped, surprised by his somber expression. He removed the ring offering it to her to examine it more closely.

Etched into the bronze was a pair of dragon wings with the inscription dragostea mea veșnică (to my eternal love) I.C.B. "Isabel

Cynthia Backwater," he noted, hearing her surprise. He thought that the woman had the name of their mother and the same last name as her.

"We were married after I turned her, to save her life. Your village attacked hers one night when I wasn't there to protect her. The werewolf killed them all in cold blood, including her. Isabel died protecting you," he sneered, placing the ring back on his finger. His fangs bared thinking of the painful memory.

"I'm sorry for bringing up painful memories—" she replied, surprised to see him show such human emotions. *Is he a dhampir? That would explain his humanistic tendencies. He has yet to prove how this woman is related to me*, she thought, catching him offering her a weak smile.

Donovan laughed, forcing his fangs back, amused by her thoughts, not surprised that she was trying to rationalize his behavior. "If I was a dhampir I wouldn't have been a match for Simon," he replied, recalling the box of mementos he had saved belonging to Isabel. "Wait here, I may have something that will help you believe my story," he added, climbing to his feet to exit the room, and entering the hallway.

Scarlett climbed to her feet, following him out to the hallway, watching Donovan standing in front of a painting mounted on the wall in front of the top of the stairwell. It was a backdrop of the night sky adorned with a full moon overlooking a meadow. Clusters of white moonflowers with some of their petals floating in the emerald water were at the center of the meadow. He lifted the portrait, revealing a bronze metal safe. He punched in a sequence of four numbers before it clicked, swinging it open to collect the wooden box inside before closing the safe and placing the painting back over it.

Michael had ensured Shiva had cleaned up the mess in the office before showing her to her room. "Hey, big brother. What do you get there? Is it a preset for me?" he pressed, watching his brother sliding a painting into place after closing a safe. Still lingering in the doorway, Scarlett laughed overhearing Michael's persistent questions. Donovan motioned for Scarlett to follow him back into the bedroom setting the box on the bed.

Donovan sighed in annoyance overhearing Michael's questions yet had decided to ignore him hearing them repeated in Michael's head. "Michael be silent. The box is for Scarlett. It holds items left to her from her sister, Isabel," he replied, watching Scarlett perch on the edge of the bed reaching out for the wooden box examining the carved runes on the lid.

Michael glared at Donovan crossing his arms over his chest pouting studying Scarlett, sensing that she was waiting for him to leave before opening the box. "I believe Scarlett would like some alone time brother though don't take it to heart. Not every girl will become smitten with you," Donovan added, watching Michael lingering in the room anxious to learn what the box held.

That's fine, just keep more secrets from me, Michael thought, turning to leave aware that his presence wasn't wanted. Donovan groaned hearing the distaste in Michael's thoughts aware that he would have to explain how Scarlett was related to Isabel.

Scarlett glanced up from the box hearing a door slam at the end of the hallway. "Will he be okay? I thought I was being gentle when I rejected him earlier," she replied, sliding the box open caressing the soft velvet that lined the inside. Inside the box, there was a worn beige leather journal stacked on top of a pile of photos wrapped together in a gold chain. Scarlett carefully untangled the chain noticing the pendant. It was a pair of bronze dragon's wings clutching an oval-shaped amethyst jewel.

Donovan watched her examine the necklace carefully in awe marveled at the beautiful structure remarking that it held her birthstone. "In time, he's not used to women saying no to him," he replied, reaching into the box to extract a black and white photograph. It brought a somber smile to his lips. Scarlett noticed the smile flicker across his face and leaned to peer at the photo in his hands. A smiling brunette was glancing at the camera holding a blonde baby girl.

Scarlett smiled, slipping the chain around her neck, lifting the hair out of the way, comforted by the cold metal brushing against her skin. She noticed a few photos of a rustic cottage surrounded by trees and cornfields. "She's beautiful, I can see what attracted you to her. If she was once human how did you two met?" she asked, smiling at a photo of herself as a toddler waving at the camera with a gap missing in her front teeth with pigtails dressed in a purple romper.

Donovan laughed seeing what picture had caught Scarlett's attention watching her turning the photo over to examine the date. *It seems like such a long time ago*, she thought, setting the picture aside inhaling the faint scent of sage.

"I had collapsed in the neighboring woods from starvation when your sister discovered me. She was a healer and nursed me back to health. I figured it was only polite to remain and pay off my debt to her," he explained, glancing toward the window focusing on her fluttering thoughts than the painful memories.

Scarlett glanced back over the picture of her and Isabel struggling to remember her. "I wish I could remember her, yet it seems like such a long time ago," she noted, aware that he was studying her wary of her reaction. "What did she think she was healing you from?" she asked, after a moment of silence had fallen between them.

Donovan closed his eyes aware of the question that was coming. "Bear in mind our paths crossed long after I was turned," he started to explain, his voice somber with heartache.

June 21, 1501

Bran, Romania

The sun hung low in the city square, as a young man passed the grassy hillside entering a cabin. Nestled against the base of the mountains leading up to Bran Castle. His long dark hair clung to his fair skin slick with sweat. His breathing labored dragging a rapier with one hand, while his other rested close to his chest bound in gauze. A heavy sigh escaped his lips, kicking the door to his chambers behind him leaning against the ornate door.

He gulped in the chilly air catching his breath before crossing the dark room resting the sword against a wooden dresser. The searing hot pain in his shoulder radiated down his arm. *I should remind Mother why it's foolish to train with real swords,* he thought, feeling the glass vial shift in his pocket full of green liquid. The elder of their village was a gifted healer. He had recommended Donovan to stay and rest, yet the various herbs had made him nauseous.

He perched on the edge of the cot filled with gray wool quilts to remove his boots and blue tunic. He placed the glass vial on the nightstand beside his bed and stretched out, staring up at the ceiling. He tried closing his brown eyes to block out the pain, yet he was failing miserably. He caved, reaching for the vial and drank it in one large gulp, grimacing, forcing down the bitter minty taste. Fatigue consumed him as he stretched back out letting the drugs lure him to sleep.

He awoke from dreamless sleep wondering if his younger brother Michael was in the room. Each night, Michael would crawl into his bed in tears, frightened by nightmares of their father's passing. His eyes blinked open sweeping the room, seeing a shadow at the foot of his bed. He noticed the long lacerations marring his skin leading up to his shoulder, wondering how the bandages had disappeared.

"Mother?" he called, his voice cracking before using his other arm to push himself into a seated position.

The figure rose to light a wax lantern set in the wall before moving back to the bed. The small oval gold clasp that held her long chestnut curls on top of her head glimmered in the dim candlelight. She sat beside him reaching up to sweep his damp bangs from his sweaty forehead. "Go back to sleep, my dragon, it will help lessen your pain," she soothed, trying to push him back down.

She shook her head in dismay at his disobedience. Her green eyes watched him admiring the wounds on his arm. "Your instructor informed me of the injury, and I wanted to ensure you were all right. I took the bandages off to clean them and was about to replace them with clean ones," she whispered, licking the drop of blood from her lips.

Donovan closed his eyes, believing her words, startled by a white-hot pain flaring back up his arm. His eyes flashed open in alarm, seeing fresh blood dripping from the wound staining her long white fingers. Bracing his injured arm against his chest, he rolled away from her falling on the floor. He gritted his teeth staggering to his feet and picked up his sword.

"You're not my mother. What type of fiend wears her face??" he hissed, pointing the sword in her direction. Blood continued to run down his arm dripping onto the carpet filling the silence that had fallen between them.

The woman bared her fangs once she turned to face him rising from the bed. "How rude, of course, I'm your mother. You should allow me to heal you or at least clean up your mess," she demanded, moving toward him, only to hiss in pain feeling the blade brush against her skin.

Donovan took a step back, alarmed by how fast she had moved. "No, you can't fool me twice, demon. Was it that noblemen you were eloping with? Was he the cause for your demonic transformation?" he sneered, keeping the blade between them.

His mother lunged at him again, feeling the rapier plunge into her shoulder. In anger, she shoved Donovan away causing him to slam back into the wall behind him. She tugged the blade free with one hand and discarded it, tossing it across the room behind her. Ignoring the open wound, she lunged at Donovan before he could climb to his feet. She clamped her mouth around his open wound, sinking her teeth into his flesh. He tried pushing her away, feeling her teeth slide down his arm scraping his flesh, feeling a slight pain across his abdomen.

Donovan didn't see the shadow appear behind his mother prying her off him. As his strength weakened, his thoughts turned to Michael. He wondered if his brother would be next. His vision started to fade, with his last sights his mother's demonic form and a strange man before he lost consciousness.

Chapter Thirteen

Scarlett listened to Donovan's tale seeing the distant expression on his face. She waited until he finished, expecting an answer to her earlier question. Donovan bilked at hearing the quiet thought, snapped out of his memories. "Forgive me, your question sparked past trauma," he noted, in apology.

"I was traveling to America, and food was scarce. I became unconscious and I awoke to your sister tending to me. She informed the town that I was suffering from a severe illness and was under her protection. That was when I decided to change my food source," he explained, seeing the shocked expression flicker across her face.

"The more you share about Isabel, the more I fear I can never measure up to her," she replied, finding another photo of Isabel standing in front of a blonde middle-aged woman holding a young baby. *We both resemble this woman; she must have been our mother. I wonder whatever happened to those who raised us*, she thought. still mulling over the facts of his story.

Donovan glanced over her shoulder, smiling at the picture grasped in Scarlett's hands. He reached out wiping a stray tear from her cheek making her flinch, startled by the gentle caress. "She would be honored seeing the woman you have become in her absence and you remind me of her. Trying to help those in need despite their outwards appearance," he whispered, seeing a weak smile, finding a dried moonflower pressed into one of the photos of Isabel.

"Your sister was a kind and gentle soul; your dwelling became a haven for me, and I fell in love with her. On the eve of your seventh birthday, she ordered me to take you into the woods to watch the moonflowers bloom as a present. Upon our arrival home, your sister was discovered on the porch dying. The town attacked the house, hoping to destroy the monster and its protector. In an act of weakness, I turned her, and we left the town taking you with us," Donovan explained, grimacing in pain once more hearing her whirlwind of thoughts after processing the latest information.

Scarlett glanced down at the jewel resting against the top of her chest. *They both came from two separate worlds, yet they were able to make things work*, she thought, reaching up to trace the intricate details of the wings.

"Did something in my tale resonate with you?" he asked, perplexed by her thoughts.

Scarlett stopped fidgeting with the necklace and smiled. aware that she was still anxious around him. "I was just processing how a vampire could fall for a human, both your world views are different—" she explained, clenching both hands in her lap growing frustrated to ensure how to explain what was troubling her.

Donovan placed both hands over hers forcing them to uncurl caused by a fleeting thought. "I see, my story makes you second guess your own fate with your lover," he noted, seeing her cheeks flush slightly shaking her head in denial. "You don't need to convince me—" he warned, chuckling seeing her cover her face with both hands in embarrassment.

Scarlett collected the photos before carefully placing them in her purse excited to share them with Matthew. "Things between us are complicated. I keep getting mixed signals from him," she replied, finding a picture of her and Matt sitting outside the manor on her phone before showing it to him.

Donovan studied the picture with a smile. "Our paths have crossed a few times after I had settled here. He's an honorable hunter few would allow a monster to plead their case. Most would just kill them on sight. I take it you two were meeting tonight though I'm sure something of importance had occurred to prevent him from your engagement," he explained, recalling his amusement knowing that her relationship was an area he should leave alone.

Scarlett sighed in relief having noted the late hour. "He could have told me that and I wouldn't have wasted my time waiting for him," she mused, confused on whether to be mad at Matt or thank him for creating the chance encounter.

"I understand your frustration, give him my thanks. His absence allows us a chance to meet. I believe the night is growing late, though I will grant you one more question," he replied, climbing to his feet, outstretching his hand to her. Scarlett nodded in agreement to his claim and accepted his hand.

"You're right, the night wasn't a total loss, I got to meet you and found the answers I was searching for," she replied, letting him pull her to her feet and followed him back downstairs to the main foyer. "Was any of this explained to you prior to being sired or did you learn from the experience?" Scarlett added, grateful to have her questions answered.

"My mother taught me the basics though her methods were distasteful. When I was able, I fled and made my way to America hoping to disappear. The rest of my knowledge comes from experience," he explained, amused by the new questions forming in her head after hearing his answer.

Scarlett stood beside him at the club's entrance trying to peer through the darkened window for Simon. "Fear not, Simon will need time to lick his wounds before returning. My door will always be open to you," he added, trying to reassure her fears seeing her trying to sweep the exterior outside the bar.

Scarlett's shoulders slumped in relief before wrapping her arms around Donovan's chest, feeling him flinch in surprise before reluctantly returning the embrace. "Thank you," she whispered, letting him open the door holding it open for her.

"You're welcome. Would you like me to accompany you home?" he asked, gaining a negative head shake from Scarlett. He watched her leave descending the street before locking the bar up for the night.

Chapter Fourteen

Stepping out of the bar, Scarlett scanned her surroundings warily. She pulled her jacket tighter against her frame to fight against the frigid air. She glanced down at the pendant around her neck once more, comforted by the thought of her sister being with her. *To think, all this time, I thought I was alone*, she thought, glancing up watching a shadow dart from the corner of her eyes. Scarlett fished into her purse for the dagger catching the blue light from the phone emit from the bottom of the bag, resting against the journal and the photos Donovan had given her.

A mass of shadows gathered beneath the closet streetlamp causing the bulb to shatter making Scarlett jump. The darkened street caused the hair on the back of her neck to rise. She reached for her phone with her free hand turning on its flashlight sweeping it around her. She tried taking a step back to retreat into the bar for safety before icy tendrils snaked around her ankle pulling her to the ground. A cackle rang through her ears watching the light from the phone dim once it sailed through the air and landed on the concrete with a crunch.

Scarlett tried kicking the force away, lashing out with the dagger in her hands. A shadow stepped on her wrist, causing pain to shoot up her arm causing her to drop the dagger. Another cackle rang through her ears before kicking the dagger away as the metal bounced against the concrete cut through the eerie silence.

Scarlett gritted her teeth cradling her bruised wrist against her chest trying to push herself up on the other arm. The icy wind brushed her cheeks as another shadow towered over her grabbing her arm raking her arm with its black talons.

She hissed in pain straining to see in the darkness searching for the glint of silver in the night. Two tendrils coiled around her ankles drawing her toward the mass of shadowy figures with their red eyes staring at her in hunger. Their talons clawed into the gashes on her arms digging into her flesh lapping up the blood greedily. Scarlett screamed trying to squirm out of their grasp weakened from the loss of the steady blood flow running down both arms. Darkness enveloped her as the pain intensified, feeling a chunk of flesh being torn from her shoulder before blacking out unaware of the howling wind building in speed around her.

Chapter Fifteen

Matt glanced down at his phone noting the late hour climbing off his bike, parking his motorcycle across the street from the bar. Hearing the piercing scream, he dropped the helmet and ran across the street. Struck by the dark wave of shades crowding the body face down on the concrete, he drew closer recognizing the mop of blonde curls and the purple flames inked on her back, where the shades had torn the fabric away to tear at her flesh. A low growl emitted from his chest before a gust of wind gathered around him thrust toward the mass of shades.

The shades paused in their pursuit shrieking in agony as flurries began to fall from the sky, blanketing the area in white powder. Matt lunged at the closest shade; his nails elongated turning into claws before ripping the shade into confetti. A howl escaped his lungs while his red eyes turned black, the falling snowflakes quickened in speed turning to hail bounding against the concrete. He towered over Scarlett letting the storm whip around them in a white dome. Watching the shades turn to icicles before shattering from the strong gale of wind, Matt turned to examine Scarlett's limp form.

He shook the layer of powder from his jacket kneeling to swaddle it around Scarlett, scoping her up in his arms. He noticed the black leather handbag nestled beneath her and picked it up as well. The speed of the falling snowflakes softened landing in her hair. He brushed his lips over her forehead, watching the cold caress jar her awake moaning in agony.

Scarlett felt an icy kiss brush against her skin. Her eyes opened wide in fear blinking the snowflakes from her eyelashes. The scent of motor oil and leather soothed her senses before she hissed in pain closing her eyes once more.

"I'm sorry, maybe if I had come sooner, this all could have been avoided," he whispered, holding her closer to his chest feeling her shiver, trying to fight the cold. Scarlett smiled resting her cheek against the warm leather focusing on the smell trying to ignore the ache in her shoulder.

Matt smirked watching her trying to drift off to sleep to ignore the pain caused by her injuries. Blood trailed down both cheeks from the corners of his eyes as well as his nostrils, an effect from continuing the blizzard swirling around them marking their trail with white powder and the billowing gusts of icy wind. Upon approaching the gate to the entrance, he shifted Scarlett over his shoulder, noticing the purple rings marring her flesh, to free one hand to press the numbers on the keypad to open the gate.

The gate closed shut behind them with a loud click he reverted to his human form. His nails returned to normal, nearly dropping Scarlett, exhausted from the effort of summoning the storm. He shifted her once more, waking Scarlett once more causing her to groan in pain.

"Thank you again, for rescuing me," she whispered, her throat hoarse from the frigid air. She gritted her teeth feeling the pain flare in her shoulder once more. He noticed her staring at his face in concern wiping the dried blood from his face with the back of his hand before wiping it on his pant leg.

Matt swiftly carried her through the garage entrance before climbing up the stairs to her room. "There's no need to thank me. I should have been there sooner," he soothed, taking a seat beside her on the edge of the bed. Her hand reached out for his, intertwining her fingers with his.

Scarlett squeezed his hand seeing the worried lines in his brow trying to ignore the burning ache in her shoulder. "Do you think the one who sent those things is the one responsible for the recent murders?" she inquired, closing her eyes shifting her weight to try and rest her shoulder on the pillows underneath her. She hissed gritting her teeth, feeling the shooting pain shoot up her arm.

Matt rose to his feet, slipping his hand out of hers to help prop more pillows underneath her injured shoulder. "Rest now, we can discuss the matter later. I'll get Jet to tend to your injuries and give you something for the pain," he replied, bending down to brush his lips against her forehead before exiting the room.

Scarlett could hear whistling from the hallway, making her groan, pulling the comforter over her head. A tall willowy man in his early twenties entered the room carrying a blue nylon bag in his hands. The whistling ceased seeing the covers over the lump on the bed.

He perched on the edge of the bed, scanning the room with round blue eyes. "That's strange, I was sent to treat a patient, yet there's no one here," he mused, setting the bag on the floor in front of him. His brows knitted in thought drumming one hand on the knee of his gray jeans matching the green long-sleeved shirt flecked with dirt and grass stains.

The whistling resumed, reaching into the bag to retrieve a bag of wooden incense sticks, a lighter, and long metal cylinders. He placed the cylinder on the windowsill filling it with a handful of the incense after lighting each one. A light smoky smell filled the room before pocketing the lighter taking a seat once more on the bed. He reached for the comforter gently pulling it away noticing the small dark stain in concern. He pulled out gauze, bandages, a wooden bowl, a wooden spoon, a vial of ginger oil, and a bag full of green eucalyptus leaves.

Clusters of small bruises resembling fingers along the length of her arms and legs. He dumped the leaves into the bowl grinding it into dust before mixing in the ginger oil to make a paste. "This may sting a bit but at least it won't stink like last time," he replied, seeing her eyes open, watching him carefully. A smug smile danced on his lips reaching for the Swiss army knife on his belt to cut away at her shirt revealing the black satin bra underneath.

Scarlett inhaled the smoky scent of the hops incense taking in a deep breath before letting it back out. "Another long session with Ari?" she asked, noting the dirt and grass stains on his grey jeans. He nodded in agreement putting the knife away before applying the paste to the lacerations on her arms. She gritted her teeth feeling the soft white gauze layered on secured in place with a bandage.

"Yes, we were out in the garden gathering herbs when she taught me a new tea for pain remedies," he replied, studying the puncture wound on her shoulder. He reached in the bag grabbing the bottle of water to flush out the wound hearing Scarlett whimper in pain. "I'm sorry, but we want to ensure it doesn't get infected," he noted, covering it with the paste before applying the gauze over it with a bandage. "I'll be back. I'm going to get the tea I mentioned. It'll help with the pain," he reassured her, seeing the tears well in the corner of her eyes.

Jet placed the items back in his bag shaking the light brown bangs that fell over his blue eyes while climbing to his feet. He raced downstairs to collect the cup of tea from Ari nodding his head in thanks before returning to the room. He concentrated on her breathing. Her eyes opened smelling ginger and honey. Jet crossed the room handing her the cup while wrapping his arms around her waist to help her sit up. She grimaced her hands shaking but managed to take a few sips of the warm sandy colored liquid. Jet waited for her to finish drinking the tea before taking the empty cup from her hands and lowering her back onto the pillow. "Is Matt going to be okay?" she whispered, feeling the warmth spread over her body.

Jet smiled hearing a yawn escape her lips while the tea kicked in. "He just needs some rest. The snowstorm he crafted took a lot out of him," he reassured her, pulling the comforter back over her chest, finally noticing the strange necklace around her neck. He waited for her eyes to close before removing it and placing it on the nightstand beside her bed. He slipped out of the room turning off the lights and closing the door behind him.

Chapter Sixteen

Matt returned to the landing of the third-floor, hearing Jet teasing to Scarlett before entering his room. Upon entering the room, he flipped the switch on the wall, turning on the air-conditioning, hearing the fan buzz from the window. He closed the door behind him, letting his eyes adjust to the darkness. Crossing the room to the four-poster bed he collapsed reaching up and over his head for the satin blue cord pulling down the sheer canopy. The velvet navy blue comforter matched the blue snowflakes that matched the walls bare of any paintings or pictures. In one corner, was a metal display case holding small ice statues resembling memories from his past.

A yawn escaped his lips, exhausted from creating the storm. He ran a hand through his hair, ensuring he had kept his demonic side at bay. *If I had pushed myself any further the demon would have consumed me*, he thought, pulling the covers up to his chest and closing his eyes.

"What's wrong with doing whatever it takes to save your mate?" a deep voice argued, earning a moan of annoyance from Matt, too tired to argue with the demon.

"Scarlett isn't my mate. I did what I would for any other slayer," he protested, hearing the demon laugh in his head.

"Keep lying to yourself if you must, just remember you can't lie to me," it taunted, seeing the memory of the last time Matt had lost control to save a woman. "Don't let the past repeat itself," it warned, replaying the night's events in Matt's head until sleep plagued him. An hour had passed before Matt jarred awake hearing soft raping from the other side of the door. He groaned pulling the comforter over his face to block out the beam of light spilling in from the hallway from the open door.

"Mathew? Are you awake?" a girl asked, standing in the doorway, she shivered feeling the arctic air from the air conditioner brush against her face. Her almond blue eyes tried peering into the darkened room unable to see if he was awake or not. Her blonde hair fell over dark skin trailing over her shoulder. She wrapped her bare arms tighter around her waist glancing down at the white tank top with green anchors and matching cotton shorts she had decided to wear to bed. "I couldn't sleep and figured you could help," she pressed, hearing the bed shift as he turned in the bed, keeping his eyes closed as his hand searched the bedside table for his shades.

"I was asleep until you knocked on the door. Come in and get under the covers before you freeze. Why aren't you asleep like the others?" he asked, giving up his search, keeping his eyes closed as he moved on the bed, making room for her.

Dawn followed his orders pulling the plush comfort around her shoulders. "I had a bad dream. Usually I can confide to Raven, but she went on a run to meet up with Andrew. I figured you might still be awake and could help," she confessed, hoping that he could help.

"Usually, but I just got back from saving Scarlett, a vampire got the drop on her and my ability saved her. What was your nightmare about? Wait, what are they up to at such a late hour?" Matt noted, gritting his teeth pushing himself into a seated position. He rubbed the sleep from his eyes before switching the air conditioner to fan, so it would be warmer in the room for Dawn.

Dawn shrugged her shoulders at his remark repeating what Raven had told her, that she was going out to meet up with Andrew. She twirled a strand of her hair around her finger. She felt Matt's eyes lingering on her expecting an answer. "I was out in the fields and was with Raven. We were trying to fight off a banshee and it got the drop on Raven. I froze, watching helplessly it ripped Raven to shreds," she whispered, her hands shaking before her eyes welling up with tears.

Matt reached out drawing Dawn close to his chest wrapping his arms around her in a hug. "Those spirits are dangerous. I would never allow you to face one on your own. Those belong in the area that myself or Andrew would complete not you girls. What created the nightmare, were you reading Ari's records again?" Matt asked, gently lifting a hand up to wipe her tears away.

Dawn felt her cheeks flush in embarrassment nodding her head yes in agreement. "I'm sorry, I couldn't help myself. Before coming here, I knew nothing about the paranormal world aside from fairy tales, and I never want to be that ignorant again," she admitted, relieved that she would never be forced to face them.

"You mean before I made you aware of what my intentions were when I rented this manor from your parents? I'm not mad that you read them Dawn, just understand that just because they are on file, doesn't mean you will be forced to face them. You know that if you have any questions you can come to me or Ari, right?" he asked, wondering what other paranormal beings she had read about not recalling what was kept in the files.

Dawn nodded in agreement, taking in a deep breath. Dawn offered him a weak smile, grateful that he had taken the time to hear her fears. "I received a letter from my folks asking about you. I might have slipped that you finally summoned the courage to ask a girl out," she teased, not wanting to burden them with her questions.

Matt sighed having an idea who she was hinting at. "If you have questions just ask them, I promise to do my best to answer them," Matt offered, seeing her hesitate. He could hear his demon laughing in amusement mentally telling him to shut up as the wind picked up around them. "I'm sorry, I didn't mean to lose control, though. Is it really that obvious between me and Scar?" he asked, forcing the wind back to a gentle breeze.

Dawn flinched startled by the sudden gust of wind knocking into her chest, knocking the wind from her before Matt reigned it in. She laughed, nodding her head in agreement. "Were you born with your abilities or is it the demon's power?" she asked, thinking that he had never talked about it. She let him think over her question sharing what she had overheard. "Scarlett seemed excited to meet you last night, but that's obvious. You smile more when she's around and you think no one is watching," she admitted, wondering if he was aware, he did it.

"Born with them but they didn't awaken until I was of age, taking a life in the process. Until then, my parents assumed I was born with a rare disease, making my internal body temperature below what is considered normal. I don't mind my powers; it's the parasite I wish I could rid myself of. I admit I enjoy my private time with her, I never noticed that I was acting out of the norm around her," he admitted, running a hand through his hair wiping away sweat. He grabbed the bottom of his shirt yanking it off before tossing it into a corner of his room.

Dawn let out a low whistle not expecting him to remove his shirt staring at his bare chest. "I think it's cute that you two share a special bond. I don't believe you that you were oblivious to how you act around her," she teased, seeing his hair stuck to his shoulders in sweat. "Are you okay, do you need me to leave?" she asked.

"No, I knew I just feared getting close to her. I don't want to hurt her or worse scare her when she sees me at my full power. I'll be all right. It's just a bit warm in here, but you don't have to leave. I know after having a nightmare the last thing you want is to be alone," he admitted, wondering if she wanted to spend the night instead of going back to her room.

Dawn sighed in relief, thinking she had caused him to get overheated. "Would it be okay if I stayed? I don't know when Raven will get back, and you're right I don't want to be alone," she confessed, hearing a yawn escape her lips stretching out on the bed.

"No, you can stay if it will put you at ease, though here put this on, I'm not the warmest person to sleep next to," he warned, grabbing a sweater from the floor before offering it to her. Once she had it on, he turned the air conditioner back on putting it on low not wanting the room to get too cold for her. He took off his pants laying on the bed beside her.

Dawn glanced down at the sweater pulling it on over her shirt before pulling the covers back over herself. "Thank you, you should give Scarlett more credit. She seems stronger than she looks," she whispered, trying to rest his fears before drifting off to sleep.

Matt watched her fall asleep thinking over her comment. He closed his eyes allowing his body to give into exhaustion falling into a fitful sleep the room still too warm for his liking.

Chapter Seventeen

Golden rays peeked out from the blinds as Scarlett groaned whimpering pain. Her eyes widened in alarm scanning the room antically before the familiar scent of leather and motor oil wafted in her nose. She rubbed her tired eyes feeling the aches from the night prior return. She ran a shaky hand through her messy curls stuck to her forehead from the cold sweat. Noticing the rays of sun filtering in the room. She glanced toward the window peering through the purple lace curtains.

The amber sky lightened, turning pink as dawn had broken before a yawn escaped her lips. *What time is it?* she thought, reaching for her phone resting on the end table beside her bed. The motion caused a shooting pain to trace up to her arm, startling her to fall out of bed. She cursed loudly, staring up at the ceiling in too much pain to move. She swept one hand out finding her phone and seeing that it was five minutes after six in the morning. Reaching out her other hand she pulled the comforter on top of her covering her face thinking sleep would help her escape the pain.

Scarlett didn't hear the appeasing footsteps before a gentle knock came from the other side of the door. Getting no answer from Scarlett, they opened the door and poked their head inside, flicking the light switch. Soft baritone laughter wafted into the room upon seeing the lump huddled underneath the comforter on the carpeted floor.

The tall figure knelt beside Scarlett gently pulling the comforter back noticing the dark bloodstain through the gauze around her shoulder. His green eyes noted the other injuries before he slipped both arms around her waist lifting her up and placing her on the bed. The movement caused Scarlett to moan in pain blinking her eyes open.

"Good morning, sleeping beauty," he teased, crossing the room to retrieve the first aid kit from the top of her dresser before taking a seat beside her on the edge of the bed.

"Hey, sorry for waking you. I fell out of bed trying to reach for my phone. Now that you're here—" she inquired, hearing the bed creak under his weight, taking a seat beside her.

"Was it a booty call, unable to wait for Matt to make the first move?" he teased, hearing her cough trying to suppress a laugh. He opened the first-aid kit taking out fresh gauze and bandages seeing her nod in agreement. "You would think, with being rescued by Prince Charming, it would give you pleasant dreams," he added, smirking at seeing her cheeks flush lightly. He peeled away the damp bandages over the lacerations on her arms. He noticed the smile falter fighting the pain while he wiped the areas with an antiseptic wipe before applying new gauze and bandages.

"Thank you, Vincent," she mumbled, her face still pressed against the pillow brushing her damp cheek against the pillowcase hiding the tears. She took in a shaken breath holding it in for a few minutes before letting it out slowly. Scarlett outstretched her hand accepting his help to roll back onto her side.

Feeling the chilly breeze rift across her bare chest, her cheeks flushed, glancing down, unaware that nothing was covering the lacy black bra. Vincent crossed the room, picking up a blue silk robe hanging on the back of the door. He helped her to her feet, pulling her injured arm through one sleeve before watching her tie it.

"I thought that the striptease was my compensation for a job well done?" he teased, letting her swat him in the shoulder lightly before leading the way downstairs.

Scarlett followed him tying her messy hair up in a loose bun. The smell of basil wafted in from the open window as they drew near the kitchen, with light pooling in from the open window naturally lighting the room. A wooden box lined with other herbs along with basil sat in the windowsill above the kitchen sink. The white ceramic tile matched the sandy wallpaper lining the kitchen walls decorated with floral paintings.

Scarlett took a set at the sandy-colored bar clapping her hands excitedly by the cup of coffee placed in front of her. She wrapped both hands around the warm glass inhaling the familiar hazelnut aroma.

Vincent snickered hearing her sigh in delight before placing a mason jar full of sugar and a gallon of almond milk in front of her. "Now that I've successfully bribed you with coffee, do you mind telling me what happened last night?" he pressed, pouring himself a cup of coffee leaning against the counter.

Scarlett grimaced at watching him drink black coffee before glancing down at her drink. She glanced up hearing him clear his throat impatiently waiting for her answer. Her hand instinctively reached for the necklace, panicking when she didn't feel the foamier cold metal of the chain. "It's nothing pressing that can't wait until everyone is here," she whispered, her eyes shifting to the fresh bandages on both arms. She shifted in her seat craning her neck to glance over her shoulder, hearing footsteps approaching.

Dawn skipped into the kitchen, still in a white tank top with green anchors and matching cotton shorts with her blonde hair bound in pigtails. She sat the black paperback book on the bar before passing Vincent to get to the fridge. Her blue eyes scanned the interior of the fridge before grabbing an apple and the jug of orange juice. She nodded her head in thanks to the offered glass from Vincent, filling it to the brim with orange liquid before taking a seat beside Scarlett.

Scarlett glanced down at the book's cover in disgust before sweeping it off the bar's countertop and onto the floor. Dawn gasped, setting her drink aside to bend over to pick the book up from the floor. "How many times are you going to read that trash?" Scarlett asked, disgusted, seeing Dawn clutch the book to her chest protectively.

Dawn stuck her tongue out at Scarlett in protest, taking a sip of her drink. "It's not trash. It's a romantic story of two worlds coming together," she protested, hearing a loud groan come from the foyer before Raven entered the kitchen. Her hair was fastened in a low ponytail resting over her shoulders wearing purple shorts and a white camisole tank top.

"It's unrealistic, on top of poor writing, targeted at naïve hopeless romantics," Raven sneered, staggering toward the coffee pot nodding in greeting to Vincent seeing him offer her a white ceramic coffee mug.

Vincent arched an eyebrow noting the bags under her eyes.

"Vincent, do you mind cooking up some pancakes?" she pleaded, watching him study her critically. She poured herself a cup of coffee adding cream to it before carrying it over to the kitchen table not wanting to sit at the bar next to Scarlett or Dawn.

Vincent continued to drink his coffee pretending that he hadn't heard her request. "Vincent, weren't you listening to me?" Raven pressed, sighing in annoyance at seeing him shaking his head no. "I wanted you to make us breakfast," she demanded, glancing at the kitchen door hearing it swing open before Jet entered the kitchen to wash the dirt from his hands.

"Better give the highness what she wants otherwise it might get ugly," Jet whispered, still wearing the clothes from the night prior. Vincent sighed, shaking his head before finishing his coffee. "I'll give you a hand to spare her icy wrath," he added, watching Vincent tuck the silver chain with a pendant of a golden snake swallowing its tail underneath his shirt helping Jet cook breakfast.

Dawn opened her book before tapping Scarlett's shoulder impatiently. Scarlett glanced at the book wondering what Dawn wanted to show her. "To disprove Raven's harsh words, I wanted to show you a section from my favorite chapter," she gushed, reading the quote out loud, "Don't be self-conscious, if I could dream at all, it would be about you. And I'm not ashamed of it." (*Twilight*, Stephanie Meyer). Scarlett rolled her eyes grabbing the front half of the book to slam it shut nearly shutting it in Dawn's hand.

"Ouch!" Dawn cried, shaking her hand trying to fight back the tears hearing the soft chuckles drifting from the foyer. "That wasn't funny,

Scarlett," she spat, clutching the book before moving to the kitchen table taking a seat next to Raven.

Andrew entered the kitchen moving to take a seat beside Dawn. He grabbed her left hand and brought it to his lips tenderly. Dawn's cheeks blushed, patting his hand lightly. "Thank you, Andrew," she whispered, climbing to her feet kissing his cheek before pouring him a cup of orange juice.

He offered her a sly grin accepting the glass with a nod glancing down at the book. His smile faded, shaking his messy hair out of his face. "I like a romantic take as next as the next person, but Meyers made werewolves so aggressive," he protested, fidgeting with the drawstring of the blue cargo shorts matching the navy muscle tank.

Ari slipped past Andrew pouring herself a cup of coffee as well before refilling the pot, still wearing the clothes from the night before. "She should be lucky you didn't offer to use the pages for kindling," Ari whispered, taking the empty seat beside Scarlett, making her chuckle.

Vincent placed the stack of banana pancakes on a plate on the bar before moving to cook eggs and bacon. He noticed Matt dragging his feet toward the kitchen in nothing but black cotton shorts. "Good morning, Matt. You look worse than Scarlett. Just have a seat and I'll hook you up," he noted, adding eggs and bacon on a plate sitting it on the bar before adding a cup of black coffee.

Hearing Matt's name, Scarlett turned in her chair, her eyes flickering to his bare muscled chest. A small smile danced on her lips, studying the mass of white scars covering his chest and back. Ari snickered seeing what Scarlett saw, letting out a catcall. Raven whistled in appreciation of the view.

Vincent shook his head, grabbing his red muscle tank top from the back of one of the bar stools and tossed it at Matt. "Matt, if you wanted to hove Scarlett a strip show, at least ask us to leave first," he teased, fixing himself a plate before joining the others at the kitchen table.

Jet laughed grabbing a water bottle from the fringe before hopping onto the clean counter. He noticed Matt's slouched position wondering if he had yet to recover from the night before.

Matt caught the tank top not wanting to put it on the room was too warm it felt hot and stuffy, yet he knew it would put the other men at ease. He tugged it on before pushing the plate and coffee away from himself in disinterest. "Very funny, Vincent. I'll need to recover further before trying a stunt like that," he replied, hearing Scarlett nearly choke on her coffee.

She reached for the napkin beside her glass wiping the coffee from her chin nearly spilling it on her robe. "Good morning, Mathew. I take it you didn't sleep well?" Scarlett asked, seeing the dark shades covering his eyes.

"I wanted to thank you again for last night—" Scarlett whispered, seeing Matt wave his hand dismissively. Scarlett reached for his free hand patting it lightly. "I know it took a grave toll using your power like that," she pressed, aware that the sunglasses were worn to protect his sensitive eyes.

"It was nothing, I would have done the same if any of the others were in danger. I'll be all right. I just need some time to rest and recover. Last night my mind was restless with thoughts on the current situation," he admitted, taking the glass of ice water Ari placed in front of him taking a sip to gather his thoughts. "I take it some of you have heard about the events that occurred last night?" Matt asked, thinking of the best way to start the conversation.

Andrew stared down at his drink wondering how much Matt would show about the night before. "Yes, please share with us your heroic tale of how you came to Scarlett's rescue," he sneered, jealous that Matt had been the one to save her and not him. Scarlett rolled her eyes wondering how long Andrew would stay jealous before glancing at Matt unsure of what to say.

"I heard that we were hit with an unknown blizzard covering at least a mile or two with ice and snow. I have a feeling Matt was the reason behind this though was it due to the vampire we've been tracking?" Ari asked, surprised to see Matt standing considering the amount of magic it would take to cover such a large area with snow.

"It was the only way to protect her; the vampire can control shades which from what I could tell are an extension of his mind, allowing him to control them. When I found Scarlett, they were attacking her, and I did what I thought was necessary to keep her safe. The vampire used this to his advantage escaping capture," Matt admitted, seeing her shiver out of the corner of his eye trapped in the memory.

Vincent frowned, seeing Scarlett shake thinking of what she had endured. "Don't underestimate Scarlett like that Andrew, Jet and I saw her injuries and it seems she put up a hell of a fight," he warned, aware that Andrew was jealous, seeing him cross his arms over his chest.

Raven frowned seeing that the others were giving Andrew a tough time. "Scarlett shouldn't have been foolish enough to venture out by herself in the first place," she protested, seeing Andrew offer her a weak smile at coming to his defense.

"That's not true, Scarlett had plans to meet up with Matt," Dawn protested, crying out in alarm at feeling Raven lash out kicking her from underneath the table.

"Dawn's right, I was supposed to meet up with Scar for a date only I got held up being forced to turn up late. Don't be childish and believe that this is just another vampire. It took everything I had to keep his shades at bay. Who knows how it would have turned out if their master had been there?" Matt warned. seeing that they were ganging up on Scarlett.

An awkward silence had fallen over the group. "Is the ability he has over these shades a natural gift other vampire might have?" Jet asked, finally breaking the silence. Scarlett shrugged glancing at Ari, aware she had already tried researching it.

"Not that I have discovered. I believe it's a rare gift like hearing thoughts or bending dimensions. His weakness would be any source of light which is why Matt's powers were strong against him. Most vampires have the common elements super strength, speed, a healing factor, and blood lust," Ari explained, going over the common traits they were all aware of.

Vincent arched an eyebrow surprised by her comment. "I would hate to encounter a vampire who can warp dimensions," he noted, wondering if there was a way to harness Matt's ability to weaken Simon.

"I agree. I fear coming across a vampire with that amount of power, yet I don't doubt Ari knowing that she is usually right with her research. Are there any spells or devices we could use to our advantage?" Matt asked, looking at the others for suggestions.

Jet glanced at Ari seeing the wheels turning in her head. "You would need a powerful magical weapon capable of emitting pure sunlight otherwise anything else might stun him, but it wouldn't be enough," he noted, drumming his fingers on the table wondering if there were any spells to replicate sunlight.

"Matt, you said the shades are tied to him. If we hurt them could that be enough to weaken him?" Raven asked, seeing that both Jet and Ari were trying to think of a way to use magic to weaken the vampire.

"I'm not sure, at the time I was more focused on getting Scarlett to safety than discovering his weaknesses. There was one theory confirmed that all the victims including Scarlett had common physical features. I believe that the bodies were bait," Matt admitted, knowing that the group needed to know all the facts.

Scarlett groaned clutching her empty coffee cup tighter. "I had drawn that same conclusion, but I didn't think Scarlett was one of them," Andrew admitted, running a hand through his hair feeling like he had failed to overlook something obvious.

Raven reached out patting Andrew's arm seeing the frustration flicker in his eyes. "Other innocents will be lost trying to lure Scarlett to him, just so he can have his way with her?" she asked, snickering at seeing Vincent grab Scarlett's uninjured arm, as she stumbled to her feet nearly knocking her chair backwards. She clenched her fists at her side trying to pry her arm free from Vincent.

Matt jumped to his feet, wrapping his arms around her waist tightly, careful not to touch her injuries. "We were better off without your comment, Raven, though based on his patterns no one will be lost if we can put an end to him," Matt warned, an arctic wind picking up around him glaring at Raven for hinting that either they lose more lives or worse use Scar as bait.

Scarlett closed her eyes taking in a deep breath before opening them. She rested her hands over his grateful that he was on her side. "I get where Raven is coming from, she thinks that if I offer myself as bait. than innocents will be spared, but what would stop him from going after others once he was through with me?" she argued, smirking at seeing the icy wind push against Raven knocking her out of her chair.

Ari sighed muttered a spell under her breath making the wind come to a standstill. "Can we not enrage our fearless leader when he's in a weakened state and has little control over his powers? I would like not to have a mini blizzard in the kitchen if I can avoid it. Based on his blood lust, we have at least two months before he seeks out another victim. That should give us plenty of time to conduct research and test out innovative ideas," she offered, holding a hand to Raven to help her climb to her feet.

Raven accepted her help, muttering an apology to Scarlett and Matt. "I meant no harm by it, I was just voicing my opinion," she protested, entering the kitchen to refill her glass. She sat back down staring down at her drink in silence.

"What makes you so sure he'll abide by that schedule without trying another trick to lure out Scarlett?" Andrew asked, holding his hands up defensively seeing Matt glare at him. "I'm sorry, but coming from someone that likes Scarlett, they can't take no for an answer," he added, aware Matt had the same fear.

"Are you speaking about the vampire or yourself, Andrew? It's clear you can't take no for an answer either. Even if it's clear his intention is for Scar, it would still take his body the same amount of time, otherwise there would be more bodies," Matt explained, lowering his shades ignoring the pain to lock eyes with Andrew to get his point across for the mutt to back down.

Andrew sighed in exasperation climbing to his feet. He stormed from the room not wanting to upset Ari by starting a fight with Matt. Raven frowned running after him knowing that he had lost the pissing contest over Scarlett again. Dawn glanced at Ari. "What can we do to help?" she asked, trying to lessen the tension lingering in the room.

Ari watched Matt push the shades back up his body, shaking under the strain. "For now, more research needs to be conducted on what is best to use against shades. I'm working on a few weapons that may aid but I still need to conduct tests with them. You can help me or work with Jet there's a list of herbs I need him to gather for me," Ari suggested, thinking it was wise not to comment that Raven had a crush on the werewolf.

"That sounds great. Ari. I appreciate you looking more into it. I think until this vampire is slain no one leaves the manor alone and that we go on lock down in the evening until he's turned into dust. I would hate for any of you to face him alone." Matt warned, squeezing Scarlett's shoulder gently before letting go yet staying within her reach for comfort.

Dawn nodded in agreement climbing to her feet to change. She told Jet she would meet him out in the garden. He waited until Dawn left before turning to Ari. "Why does it feel as though I'm being punished? Did you have nothing else for her to do?" he asked, aware she would bombard him with excerpts from her book.

Scarlett laughed reaching for Matt's hand aware that he needed rest. "You're good with her Jet, and besides, it was either you or Ari," she warned, seeing him sigh after finishing the rest of his drink before carrying his dishes into the kitchen.

"True, but you won't be alone in your suffering, Vincent will be helping you unless he has something better to do? I need someone to keep an eye on her besides Raven. I fear that Dawn will do anything to please Raven, including leaving the manor," Ari explained, turning to face the couple. "You two get some rest, it's clear neither of you have yet to fully recover. There may be a few toys for people to try later once I get all the bugs worked out," Ari admitted, trying to keep a straight face knowing that Scar was about to get a strip show.

Vincent had tried sneaking out of the room sensing that the meeting was over when he heard the request. "Wait, why am I being roped into babysitting duty? You just said Jet was the man for the job?" he whined, knowing how boring the task was.

Jet ran a hand through his hair, biting his lip to stop himself from arguing with Vincent. "If you help get all of the herbs collected, I will spar with you," he suggested, seeing Vincent squeal in delight before running out into the garden. "Let me know when you're ready for our lesson. I may need the distraction afterwards," he added, seeing Ari nod in agreement as he followed Vincent outside. Scarlett wished Ari luck with her project before taking Matt's hand, leading him toward the stairs.

Chapter Eighteen

Scarlett led Matt back to his room letting him collapse on the bed, turning the air conditioner on for him. She let out a low whistle of approval watching him tug off the shirt, tossing it in a corner. The icy air hit her back escaping under the warm blanket. Matt shifted in the bed making more room for Scarlett draping an arm around her waist drawing her closer against his chest. She traced a scar that ran down the front of his chest, feeling his fingers comb through her hair. "Did you ever end up recovering from last night?" she asked, seeing he had yet to remove the sunglasses despite the room being completely dark.

Matt stared up at the ceiling, aware he owed her an explanation. "I didn't get much sleep. Dawn came in here seeking comfort from a nightmare, I didn't want to freeze her from the low temperature," he explained, seeing that she was lost in her thoughts. "You never did explain the events of last night up until I came to help," he answered, hearing a heavy sigh escape her lips, feeling her swat at his chest lightly, feeling his nails tangle in her curls tugging it playfully.

Scarlett cried out in alarm hearing him mutter an apology before resuming to stroke her hair. "I had a long in-depth conversation with Donovan," she answered, aware that he wanted to hear the truth.

"And yet the owner was nowhere to be found when you were being attacked," Matt interjected, flinching at feeling Scarlett lash out smacking him in the chest. "Why be defensive when I'm just speaking the truth?" he pressed, seeing Scarlett bit her lower lip nervously shrugging one shoulder.

"He offered to escort me home, but after the conversation we had, I wanted time to process it all," she answered, hearing him sigh in annoyance. "He gave me some pictures that belonged to my sister…

someone I never believed existed," she replied, sitting up to retrieve the necklace and photos to show Mathew.

He placed his hand on her arm gently pushing her back to lie beside him. "I'm sure being bombarded by something like that left you with lots of questions. We can discuss it later, but for right now we could both use some rest," he stated, slipping his arms around her waist, and pulling her close against his chest.

Scarlett laughed deciding not to resist his request exhausted herself. "A luxury I wish I had, but every time I close my eyes, I'm reminded of what those creatures did to me," she confessed, closing her eyes concentrating on the sound of his heartbeat.

"The shades are an extension of his power and I was able to defeat them, therefore able to weaken their ruler," he noted, a smug grin dancing on his lips.

Scarlett opened her eyes noticing the smug grin on his lips. "I still think he was caught off guard allowing us to discover one of his weaknesses. I should have shared this with the others but until Donovan fought Simon, I thought he was a normal gentleman," she confessed, reaching out for his hand tracing the scars on his palm.

A low growl emitted from his chest at the thought of another man hitting on Scarlett. "Insight into how he lures his victims into his grasp, though we can use his description to gather more research on the vamp," he noted, trying to dismiss the growl his demon had made.

Scarlett poked his chest lightly hearing the possessive growl. "You're not mad at me for falling for his charm? I felt like an idiot, unable to tell that he was a vampire," she pressed, trying to tickle him with little success.

Matt smirked amused by her antics grabbing her hand and bringing it to his lips. "You shouldn't punish yourself for making a mistake. It happens to all of us. Just reflect on what you did wrong and try to prevent it from recurring," he replied, moving his hand to rub her back massaging it in slow circles. A soft moan escaped her lips until she closed her eyes drifting off to sleep. Matt kissed her forehead once she was fast asleep watching her chest rise and fall peacefully.

Chapter Nineteen

Scarlett whimpered, twisting, and turning in her sleep feeling strong arms wrapped around her waist. Feeling the icy caress on her cheek, her eyes blinked open staring at the sunglass lenses. "Hey there, sleeping beauty. I see you managed to get some rest?" Matt teased, kissing the top of her head seeing her skin slick with sweat from the nightmare that had plagued her.

She shook her head no, stretching her arms over her head, reaching up to mess up his hair. "It wasn't long before my mind reminded me of what happened last night," she replied, cringing at hearing her voice crack. The ache in her shoulder flared, struggling to sit up.

Matt shifted in the bed sitting up before helping her sit up resting her against his chest. "Be patient, in time you'll learn to put it behind you. Who knows you may even be up to telling me what Donovan shared with you," he noted, seeing her frown in response, wiping her sweaty palms on her pant legs?

Scarlett climbed off the bed, kissing his cheek gently. "I'd like that. But I think I'm going to go take a shower. I'll let you get some rest. We can discuss it later," she whispered, patting his knee before crossing the hallway to her room taking a shower.

She leaned against the cold tile letting the bathroom fill with steam. *I had the perfect opportunity to confide in him what was bothering me, yet I froze afraid of how he might react if he knew what my sister was,* she thought, shivering from the chilly water before turning it off.

She reached for a fluffy red towel hanging nearby, wrapping it around herself. Her teeth rattled, feeling the burning pain in her shoulder shoot up her arm. *Those shades are more powerful than I thought.*

Mayne Ari will have a clue how to defeat them? she thought, crossing her room to get dressed, not wanting to rely on Matt every time to rescue her. She stared at the oval full-length mirror beside her vanity, transfixed by the streaks of bruises marring her pale skin.

Placing fresh bandages over the scabs and the hole on her shoulder, she pulled on a pair of gray sweatpants and a sleeveless red tank top aware of how warm it was in the basement. She slipped the new necklace around her neck and tied a blue long-sleeved sweatshirt around her waist and ventured down to the basement, leaving her damp curls down over both shoulders.

The mechanical clicking of a keyboard was the first sound that greeted Scarlett upon entering the basement. Ari sat in front of her computer with her glasses resting beside her. A stack of documents scattered beside her filled with rows of equations. "Please tell me you have something to distract me with?" Scarlett pleaded, taking a seat in the chair beside Ari.

Ari shook her head no, her fingers returning to the keyboard and vigorously typing up the long notations neatly scrawled on the papers inside her. Scarlett rose to her feet grabbing the back of the chair pulling Ari away from the computer. A tired sigh escaped her lips, spinning around to face Scarlett. "I was starting to think you had changed your mind and decided to spend some quality time with Matt," she replied, noticing Scarlett fidgeting with the amulet around her neck.

Scarlett saw the puzzled expression on Ari's face upon noticing the necklace. "What? If you're wondering where the necklace came from, it was a gift. After meeting Donovan Vaslie, the owner of *Sângele Vampirului*; he knew more about me than I did," she confessed, watching Ari drum her fingers on her legs, excitedly refraining from asking a million question. "So, what side project were you tinkering with?" Scarlett asked, hoping to change the subject.

Ari laughed amused to see Scarlett attempt to distract her by focusing their conversation on her projects. "Nice try, trying to distract me by asking me to discuss my current project. I was giving you time to recover from last night, but that doesn't mean I'm not curious as to what happened," she replied, seeing Scarlett's shoulders sag in defeat.

"It's a long story, in which there are parts I'm still trying to process," she mused, seeing Ari arch an eyebrow curious to hear more. Scarlett took in a deep breath bracing herself for the onslaught of questions that awaited her. "The vampire that Andrew slew all those years ago, the one he thought he was protecting me from, turned out to be my sister—" she explained, watching Adi raise from her seat.

"Where's Mathew? I think he should be the person you explain this to," she pleaded, trying to cross the room to get to the stairs, only to feel Scarlett rise to her feet to grab her arm, gently halting Ari in her tracks.

"Wait, he's still recovering from last night. I tried explaining it to him when we got back but he was more concerned with treating my injuries," Scarlett noted, seeing Ari frown yet allowing her to guide her back to her seat.

"I understand you're concerned about interfering with Matt's recovery, but you shouldn't keep him in the dark, though aside from keeping me company was there something else you needed?" Ari asked, seeing no sense in pushing Scarlett for details when she was stressed out about it.

Scarlett offered her a small smile grateful to hear the change in conversation despite not fully answering Ari's questions. "I could use a new dagger, seeing as how I lost it last night," she replied, trying to peer at the computer screen, still not making any sense of the long cineplex equations.

Ari noticed the furrowed brow watching Scarlett struggle to understand the mathematical equations listed in the spreadsheet on the computer. "An easy request, though I doubt that's the true reason behind your visit," she mused, reaching in a drawer underneath the desk and handing Scarlett a short dagger.

Scarlett rubbed her temples, trying to chase away the migraine, glaring at Ari, seeing her snicker at the strain the equations were causing her. "Is it that obvious? I just figured if I understood what you were working on, I could help," she lied, hearing Ari laugh while closing the laptop.

"I'll make a deal with you. I'll tell you what the equations mean, then you can tell me what's bothering you?" Ari suggested, waiting for Scarlett to nod in agreement. A smug grin flickered across Ari's face. She placed her glasses back on to study the document closest to her. "I was trying to create some toys using nanite technology to create an artificial light source. Hopefully, if I can get it to work, I can use it against our crafty vampire. Unfortunately, it's not as easy as it sounds," Ari explained, sighing in frustration at a loss for what else to try.

Scarlett stared at Ari in awe understanding now why the equations had been confusing to her.

"Donovan told me when I arrived here, he had sent a journal that belonged to my sister, with a letter explaining how he had met her, but I never received it," she explained, fidgeting with the necklace once more.

"Well, Mathew isn't known for hiding things from us—" Ari protested, watching Scarlett twist the pendant anxiously before letting it rest once more against her chest.

"No, you're right, Matt would have given it to me, but if Andrew ended up with it he might have kept it hidden out of guilt," Scarlett insisted, tying the hilt of the dagger to the waistband of her jeans, eager to use it.

Ari climbed to her feet pushing the chair out of her way. "Well, I could use a break. I say we try interrogating Andrew about the matter?" she suggested, seeing Scarlett nod her head in agreement following Ari out of the basement heading up to the main part of the house.

Scarlett followed Ari down the hallway passing Dawn leaving Raven's room waving to them in passing. They stopped outside of Andrew's bedroom before Ari knocked on the door politely. She waited for Andrew to invite them in, ignoring Scarlett who was tapping her foot impatiently.

Hearing the baritone reply to enter, Ari turned to Scarlett, holding both hands up defensively. "Be polite, he might be forthcoming with the information," Ari whispered, entering the room followed by Scarlett. Scarlett flinched, hearing the door slammed behind her.

Andrew was reclining in his computer chair combing over the footage captured from the street cameras the night prior, yet it was too dark to make out anything. The only thing visible was the blame of white light illuminated from Scarlett's cell phone before it was pitch dark once more. His head jerked up straightening in his seat upon hearing the door slam.

He arched an eyebrow, seeing Scarlett standing behind Ari with her arms crossed over her chest. "Can I help you ladies with something?" he asked, staring at them innocently.

Ari reached out, grabbing Scarlett's arm, preventing her from charging at Andrew. Scarlett shrugged off Ari's arm before crossing her arms once more over her chest. Ari crossed the room to sit on the edge of his bed. "We came to discuss a sensitive matter with you," Ari pressed, holding her hand up to silence Scarlett seeing her open her mouth ready to butt in.

"Look, Scar. If it's about what happened yesterday… I'm sorry—" he protested, watching Scarlett close the distance between them. She pushed his chair up against the wall trying to shove him out of the chair.

"Don't you dare bring that up. I'm trying not to throw up my breakfast," she sneered, reaching for the dagger, resting it against his Adam's apple. "I'm going to give you the opportunity to redeem yourself," she warned, gripping the dagger's hilt tightly in her hand. She smirked watching the smug grin falter with beads of sweat running down the collar of his shirt.

Andrew swallowed feeling the silver singe his hair, feeling the scent of burnt hair in his nostrils. "I'm sorry, I just assumed that was what you were upset about," he pleaded, his mind racing trying to fathom what she was angry at him for.

"Andrew, we learned that you may have something that belongs to Scarlett. She was told you have a journal that belonged to a vampire you slew," Ari examined, seeing the color drain from his face at the silver resting against his throat.

Scarlett breathed in slowly trying to calm herself, not hearing the soft chuckle. Andrew laughed harder before crying out in alarm, the dagger digging deeper in his skin drawing a thin trickle of blood

Andrew gritted his teeth reaching out to grip her wrist digging his nails into her flesh. Startled by the flash of pain, her hand retreated, dropping the dagger. Andrew lashed out with his foot, kicking the dagger across the room. "I'm not sure what you're talking about," he protested, placing his hand over the gash adding pressure to stop it from bleeding.

Scarlett braced her wrist against her chest, glaring at him understanding something clearly at last bruises that marred her flesh. "Don't play games with me, Andrew. Donovan told me—" she tried explaining, cut off by sneering laughter.

"Surely you're not naïve enough to believe him. I know you're desperate to learn about your past, but bloodsuckers will spot out any lie to manipulate you," he sneered, glancing at Ari desperately. "Ari, please talk some sense into her," he pleaded, not hearing the chant under her breath.

He tried taking a step toward Scarlett to comfort her. His eyes widened in alarm upon feeling paralyzed. He glanced over at Ari seeing her eyes closed with her hands placed together concentrating on the spell.

A sly grin stretched out over Scarlett's, face aware that the spell wouldn't last long. She raced toward the desk, pulling each drawer open to search it recklessly dumping items on the floor in her haste. She ignored Andrew's protests of infringing on his privacy. She frowned, not finding anything that could be a journal. Moving to the bookshelf, she started pulling down books, setting them on the bed beside her. She knocked over a wide leather tome, the sound hollow.

She grabbed the book with both hands, prying it open, amused to see a bundle of money stacked on top of an amber dusty journal etched with dragon wings. Scarlett pocketed the money hugging the journal to her chest. Crossing the room to where Ari was, she rested one hand on her shoulder, squeezing it lightly. A cold layer of sweat ran down Ari's neck blinking her eyes open. Ari pushed Scarlett aside before releasing the spell causing a surge of energy to ram into Andrew's chest just as he tried to lunge at Scarlett.

Andrew cried out in alarm feeling a burst of energy knocked him backward. He hit his back against the wall before sliding down it in a daze. Scarlett offered her hand to Ari, helping her climb to her feet, aware of how draining magic was for her. Andrew rested his head in both hands, moaning in agony. Scarlett followed Ari's lead to the door stopping to collect her dagger.

"All that trouble, just for a hunk of junk," Andrew whispered, before cursing as her foot lashed out, kicking him in the ribs.

Chapter Twenty

Scarlett felt Ari grab her arm, guiding her out of the room, pushing the door shut after them. Ari leads them back down into the basement. She threw on her cloak pushing the chairs out of the way to sit in the center of the metal circle to ground herself. Scarlett took a seat in one of the chairs turning the journal over in both hands. Along the right edge, a brass padlock prohibited her from opening it.

How does Andrew know if it's junk if he can't open it? she thought, watching Ari climb to her feet, draping the cloak over the back of her chair.

Ari held out her hand for the book once she sat down beside Scarlett. She noticed the lock as well, seeing Scarlett frowning, lost on what to do. "The lock has the same shape as the jewel on your necklace, maybe it can open it?" Ari suggested, watching Scarlett remove the necklace from around her neck yet hesitated to give it to Ari. "I won't break the necklace, I promise," she reassured her, waiting for Scarlet to cave in and hand her the necklace.

Ari carefully aligned the purple jewel into the crevice. "Why don't you fill me in on what Donovan told you?" Ari pressed, waiting for the jewel to fit into the hole, slowly turning the jewel clockwise. Scarlett bit her lower lip watching Ari tinker with the necklace nervously.

Scarlett sighed in relief hearing the metal click before Ari handed her back the necklace. Slipping the necklace back around her neck, she noticed a piece of yellowed parchment fall to the ground as Ari inspected the interior of the journal. "He explained that he fell for my sister instantly and that they were engaged. He was forced to turn her to save her life but tried to live a normal life," she replied, bending to collect the piece of paper carefully unfolding it.

She started reading the list of herbs aloud before pausing handing it out to Ari. Ari handed her the journal in exchange for the list. Scarlett turned to the first page, eager to read it. Scarlett strained to read the tiny cursive handwriting, noticing the date of her second birthday.

To Scarlett Rosalyn Backwater:

If you are reading this, my little sister, then I have moved on to the next life. I am sorry that I couldn't give you more than this journal to help you move on with your life.

In this journal, I have left behind a record of my life and every spell and herb that I used while I was alive.

If you have not yet met him, find Donovan Vaslie, he is the only family you have left in this world.

You must hate me, knowing that your sister was turned into a monster and couldn't prevent her death. I hope you are happy and well my little dragon, and do not feel sad over my passing.

I have found a family to whom I can turn to in dire circumstances. Please, give the letter enclosed to Donovan and know I'll always be watching over you.

I love you, Scarlett, forevermore,

Isabel Cynthia Backwater

Scarlet glanced up seeing a box of tissues extended to her in silence. She felt the dampness on her cheeks unaware that she had been crying. Scarlett flipped through the worn pages finding a folded piece of parchment placed within the space of the spine. Carefully, she removed it unfolding it slowly inhaling the sweet scent of rose oil.

Upon noticing Donovan's name inscribed at the top of the letter, she refolded it and placed it back inside the journal. *I bet it was a letter to bid farewell to Donovan, much like the book was a farewell to me*, she thought, turning to the first page.

October 1, 1994

Fort Collins, Colorado

A wooden one-story brick cottage sat nestled behind two acres of woods filled with cottonwood trees. A young woman sat on the wooden patch humming softly, her long waist-length raven hair tied back in a braid. The warm august air caused a thin layer of sweat to trickle down the back of her neck causing her loose strands to stick to her pale skin. The pink sky brightened to amber while the young blonde toddler slept soundly in her lap.

Her brown eyes glanced down at the young girl rocking her softly, using the hem of her blue cotton dress to cushion her back. A bird chirped in the distance startling her, waking her with a start and started crying. "Shush, little dragon, it was just a bird tending to her little ones," she coned, bending to kiss her forehead feeling her squirm trying to slip from her arms. Round green eyes glanced up reaching her tiny fingers up to grab at the loose strands tugging them playfully.

"Isabel, bring your sister inside. Breakfast is nearly ready," a deep voice called, coming from inside the cabin. The younger girl jumped to her feet to run inside, her blonde curls bouncing behind her. The elder sibling smiled waiting for her sister to disappear inside before letting the smile falter.

If only I could bring myself to tell Scarlett the truth, though how do you explain to a two-year-old her parents are dead, and the man living with us was sent by the church? She thought, watching the sun hide behind the white billowing clouds hearing Scarlett calling her to stop staring up at the clouds and to join them for breakfast.

Scarlett paused from her reading, turning to the last page of the journal. She smiled, finding a picture of her mother with Isabel. Isabel's hands rested over their mother's hands, as both hands were resting over her huge stomach with their father standing beside them. *This picture must have been taken when my mother was pregnant with me. Isabel looks more like our mother than I do*, she thought, diving back into the journal. The next few pages held sketches of the cabin, the church, and a map of the city.

May 1, 1997

Fort Collins, Colorado

The front of the cabin was decorated in bright blue Salvia flowers, picked daily by Scarlett, and braided into her long golden curls. The church had supplied them with books to teach Scarlett to read and write, while Isabel received private studies in herbology. She had told the pastor that she wanted to study herbal medicine.

The skies were bright despite the chilly weather for May. "Isabel, is it true? Is today your birthday?" Scarlett demanded, placing her hands on her hips, dressed in cotton shorts and a yellow blouse, her hair braided with Salvia flowers.

Isabel nodded laughing at hearing the high squeal of delight before Scarlett threw her arms around her in a tight hug. "Then we should celebrate it. I know, let's go into the woods and collect blackberries. You can show off how smart you are by pointing out each plant?" she suggested, taking Isabel's hand in hers heading off toward the woods.

A year had passed with Scarlett spending more time at the church with the nuns learning to read and write. The man Scarlett thought was their father had grown distant, angered by romantic feelings not returned by Isabel. Isabel was a respected healer by the community helping to make a life for herself. Scarlett sang in the church and helped the nuns set up for communion each morning.

~~*

Scarlett stopped reading, staring at the book in awe, reading the passage again. She coughed to cover up a snicker. *It's odd to have connections to the Church, but I guess when you grew up with it you had no other choice?* she thought, finding testimonials of people her sister had helped heal.

Chapter Twenty-One

October 28. 2000

Fort Collins, Colorado

Isabel wrapped the black wool shawl tighter around her shoulders, trying to fight against the brisk October air. The moon hung low and full in the sky, illuminating her way through the forest, a wicker basket clutched in one hand filled with blackberries. Hearing a branch break around the bend, she followed the path of crushed grass leading to a meadow blanketed with white moonflowers.

Marveled by the beauty of the flowers, Isabel moved to collect some and nearly tripped over the unconscious figure lying face down in the mossy grass. Isabel set her basket aside after placing a few flowers inside and knelt beside the man. His snowy skin frightened her, raising her concern upon turning him over, feeling his forehead. His long brown hair covered his eyes, Isabel recoiled her hand trying to slick back his hair, shocked by his icy skin.

Isabel grabbed both of his arms dragging him forward to a nearby Cottonwood tree to prop him up. Ensuring she held the basket in one hand she bent draping one of his arms over her shoulders. With a grunt of effort, she staggered to her feet dragging him slowly back to the cabin. A weak smile flashed across her face spotting Scarlett sitting on the porch awaiting her sister's return.

Scarlett jumped to her feet launching herself toward Isabel, hugging her tightly before noticing the limp figure dragging beside her. "Oh! You found another patient in need of your healing touch," she exclaimed, taking the wicker basket, and disappeared inside.

"Yes, the man is extremely ill and will require my full attention, little dragon. While don't you place these pretty flowers in some water?" she suggested, pointing to the basket before heading to her room to lie the man on the spare cot. She smiled hearing Scarlett noting how beautiful the flowers were before surveying the man's injuries. She noticed a slow heartbeat despite there being no pulse.

Scriptures claim that those born with a weak heart should drink animal blood to replenish themselves, she thought, rising to her feet, and entering the chicken coop that lived in the back of their cabins. A small brown chicken cried, swept in an old green dress. She closed her hands around the small bird's neck adding pressure until it cracked in her arms going limp. Returning to her room she pushed the cot up against the door. Grabbing a pair of cutting shears she pierced the bird's thin neck and held the dripping bird over the man's mouth.

She watched in horror as warm blood dribbled down the man's neck. She tried pulling the bird away thinking her thoughts were incorrect, only to hear a soft moan before icy fingers clasped around her wrist pushing the bird closer to his lips. His eyes flickered open admiring Isabel with his black eyes before releasing her wrist. He drew his lips closer to the creature drinking in the blood hungrily.

Once satisfied with his meal he wiped his mouth with the back of his hand. "My apologies madam, I'm not accustomed to having an audience while feeding," he drawled, trying to climb to his feet. An annoyed sigh escaped his lip when she gently pushed him back down.

"I advise you take it easy; you were found unconscious in the middle of the Fort Collins woods—" Isabel explained, hearing Scarlett singing from her room. He seemed baffled by the sound. "I brought you here hoping to tend to your injuries," she added, staring down at her hands awkwardly.

"I'm grateful for your hospitality. My name is Donovan Vaslie, where exactly is your dwelling's location?" he asked, hoping that knowing his name may put her at ease.

"A pleasure to meet you, I am Isabel Blackwater, and this is my house shared with my younger sister Scarlett. The hour is late, you may stay here to rest," she instructed, pushing the cot aside to exit the room allowing the man to rest while she slept with her sister. She explained to Scarlett that the man needed time and privacy to recover.

~~*

Isabel was able to see Donovan as a man, instead of a vicious monster. I doubt anyone else would have been that accepting, Scarlett thought, thinking of her first encounter with Matt when she had watched him transform into his demon. She glanced up from the journal seeing Ari immersed in her project. She smiled, seeing the sketches of moonflowers and Donovan before finding the next entry.

April 5, 2001

Fort Collins, Colorado

Six months had passed, and Donovan had moved in with Isabel and Scarlett. He had taken over Scarlett's lessons, teaching her Romanian and how to fight using sticks found in the woods. Donovan had kept his feedings a secret from Scarlett, taking animals into Isabel's room to feed. One evening Isabel had taken Scarlett into the woods to resume her teaching of finding plants. Upon returning to the cabin they heard shouting from inside.

"Papa has returned!" Scarlett exclaimed, running ahead of Isabel into the cabin. She wrapped her arms around the tall elder man, burying her face in his hip, wrinkling his suit, unaware of the sword clasped in his hands. His brown eyes glanced over his shoulder seeing Isabel enter the cabin carrying a basket full of plants and berries.

"What are you doing here, Minister Gregory Montgomery? This is not your dwelling any longer," Isabel sneered, crossing the room to grab Scarlett prying her away from him and pulling Scarlett behind herself.

"I am quite aware of this, Ms. Blackwater, though I was sent by the church to investigate claims that a demon was residing here," he sneered, repulsed to see Isabel kneel beside Donovan seeing the long laceration on his side seeing him standing by her bedroom door.

"Scarlett, go to your room." Isabel pleaded, turning to face her sister, offering her the basket.

Scarlett opened her mouth but saw the fear in her sister's eyes. She took the basket and hugged her sister tightly before fleeing to her room.

"I see the rumors were true, you're risking your sister's life by offering this fiend safe passage—" he claimed, placing the sword back in its sheath tied at his waist. Isabel ignored him placing a hand over the gash, noticing the blood stained on Donovan's clothes.

He offered her a sad smile pushing her hand away. "Don't be alarmed, Isabel. The blood is from the deer I was feeding upon. He interrupted my meal and claimed he was sending a demon back to Hell," he explained, laughing in delight at the outlandish claim. Isabel opened her mouth to protest, feeling Donovan press his lips over hers kissing her tenderly. "Go check on the little butterfly. She will be seeking answers for the disagreement between the two men in her life," he whispered, seeing her nod in agreement rising to her feet and heading toward Scarlett's room.

Minister Montgomery turned, seeing Isabel walk away, and took a step toward her, not seeing Donovan close the distance between them. He grabbed the collar of Gregory's black shirt and pushed him up against the wall. Gregory gasped startled by the speed and strength displayed before him.

"I denied our transgressions to put them at ease but do not mock my show of mercy. Isabel requested your departure. I suggest you heed her request," he growled, before releasing the grip on the man's shirt collar and pushing him aside in disgust.

Minster Montgomery stumbled to his feet running toward the door. "Mark my words, she will regret siding with the Devil. It is only a matter of time before this human facade crumbles," he hissed, fleeing from the cabin.

Isabel waited until she heard the front door slam shut before exiting Scarlett's room. She noticed that the lacerations had healed. "Is he gone?" she asked, watching him nod in agreement moving to pick up the fallen chair in their struggle. "I was able to put Scarlett to sleep despite being worried about you. I just read her the fable of King Arthur," she added, seeing a collection of orange orbs drawing near the lace white curtains draped over the window.

Isabel followed Donovan out onto the porch, baffled by the approaching crowd carrying lanterns led by Minister Montgomery. Many were nuns, priests, and other members of the church followed by citizens of the neighboring village. Some pointed at Donovan jeering at the pale scarecrow beside the one they believed to be their healer. They remained standing behind Minister Montgomery too timid to draw closer.

Donovan turned to face Isabel bringing her hand to his lips kissing it tenderly and tried to step off the porch. Isabel shook her head feeling the tears well in her eyes and reached out for his hand pulling him to her side. Minister Montgomery stood at the base of their porch glancing up at them in disgust.

"Hear me, friends and patrons, I bring you here at this late hour to aid me in my cleanse of this demon. Sister Isabel has been bewitched by this heathen," he screamed, pointing his finger at Donovan hearing the crowd gasp in alarm. Minister Montgomery turned to the nearest person accepting the lantern from them and took a step forward.

Isabel's eyes widened in alarm and stood in front of Donovan. "You're wrong! He came to me when he was ill just like the rest of you and is my friend. Do you all believe his claims that I was put under a spell?" she cried, feeling a hot tear sting her cheeks. She blinked not seeing a branch whirl past her cheek from amongst the crowd aimed at Donovan.

Donovan snapped the branch easily in between his fingers before discharging it to the ground. He reached up to wipe the stray tears from her cheek. "Isabel, head back inside where you'll be safe. I will address the crowd. Clearly, they are foolish to believe the Minister's fabrications," he whispered, gently pushing her back toward the door.

Isabel stumbled back into the house closing the door behind her, her eyes blinding with tears. She faintly made out Donovan's pleads before everything grew silent. The orange glows blinked out in the night blanketing the area in darkness. She heard some praying before running blindly into the woods. When Donovan returned his face splashed with blood. Isabel crossed the room and wrapped her arms around him never questioning what had happened.

Scarlett paused in her passage, trying to fathom what Donovan was feeling. *Minister Montgomery forced him to choose between abandoning his family or proving what a monster, he can be*, she thought, wondering if that night still haunted Donovan. She noticed the clippings of posters in search of the missing monster before she resumed reading.

Chapter Twenty-Two

October 1, 2001

Fort Collins, Colorado

Things have never been the same, all ties to the church severed from Isabel. People feared to pass through the woods, risking chance encounters with the demon that lived there. Isabel still traveled to the neighboring villages to heal the sick, offering other lessons in herbology. Donovan had promised Scarlett, on the eve of her seventh birthday, he would show her the meadow where Isabel and he had met after weeks of begging.

Isabel hugged her sister tying a red velvet cloak over her shoulders wanting her to spend some time with Donovan alone. She kissed Donovan before waving to them seeing her sister climb onto his back. Scarlett waved back, blowing her a kiss before they disappeared into the woods. Isabel slipped back into the house finishing the cake she had made for her sister.

She was humming to herself, not hearing the approaching footsteps outside her door. She cried out in alarm, hearing the door kicked open. She could hear men speaking in thick accents but couldn't understand what they were saying. Fearful of what they wanted, she crawled under the kitchen table holding her breath. She closed her eyes; hearing furniture clatter being turned over and drawers opened dumped onto the hardwood floor.

The men entered the kitchen and flipped the marble table over, laughing upon seeing Isabel trying to crawl away. The tallest one flicked his wrist, sending a leather whip down at the ground, ensnaring her wrist and dragging her toward him. Pain flared up her arm as the thick leather dug into her skin. A long metal cylinder rested in one of his hands as he pointed it at Isabel.

"Tell us where the demon resides and we will spare you, madam," he sneered, firing the weapon above her head. A loud bang rang through the kitchen filling the room with the smell of smoke. Isabel lashed out swinging her legs out starting the man. He fell to the ground in alarm dropping his weapon causing it to fire again.

One man collected the fallen weapon while a second lunged at Isabel with a long dagger. "Foolish wench, you'd risk your hide to protect the demon?" he teased, lunging at her once more pushing her up against the wall. Isabel felt his callused hand coil around her neck shoving her up against the wall.

She smiled, spitting in his face, and getting spittle in his right eye.

The vein in his neck bulged in anger, slicing her cheek with his dagger. "I am willing to overlook your reckless nature if you give up the demon," he pleaded, plunging the dagger into the wood above her shoulder. His hand loosened around her neck while his other hand traveled down her arm.

Her eyes widened in alarm feeling his knee push her legs apart wider, slipping his fingers underneath the hem of her skirt.

Isabel reached above her head pulling the dagger free and plunged it into the man's chest, pushing him backward. He cried out in alarm falling backward, feeling the blood from the wound in his chest slide down his stomach.

The taller man fired the gun at her back before the pair fled from the back door. Isabel felt the impact of a small coil of lead slam into her back causing her to colas to her knees. Blood rushed down the back of her legs before darkness engulfed her.

The alluring sound of horse hooves trotting awoke Isabel from the darkness. Her eyes blinked open, taking in the soft leather interior of a carriage. Scarlett laid nestled in her lap.

Donovan asked her why she had sent him away when he could have protected her, instead of condemning her to this fate. His melancholy tone worried Isabel, making her aware of his gaze transfixed on her neck. Slowly, she caressed the side of her neck finding two small puncture wounds.

Donovan informed Isabel he had returned with a sleeping Scarlett and was worried by the scent of fresh blood. He had found Isabel in a pool of blood in the entryway leading into the cabin. He acted impulsively and fed her his blood knowing that by saving her life, he had condemned her to immortal life.

Donovan informed Isabel that her body was dying and would be reborn as one of the dead. That tomorrow night, when she woke up, he would show her how to hunt and feed on animals instead of humans. Sensing her concern for Scarlett, he reassured her that the person driving the horses was a human friend of his, and his wife would look after Scarlett while the sun was up. Isabel tried asking him more, but he tenderly placed his lips over hers wrapping his arms around her, rocking her into a dreamless sleep.

When Isabel awoke, she noticed that the carriage had stopped in a small village known as Colorado Springs Denver, Colorado. Donovan held Scarlett in his lap telling her that her sister was gravely ill and that the sun was too painful. Scarlett believed him, and when she noticed Isabel was awake, she leaped into her arms hugging her tightly. Scarlett accepted her new family under the assumption that Isabel and Donovan would get married

~~*

Scarlett flipped through the list of spells, reaching for a piece of paper to copy for Ari. Once finished, she closed the journal locking it shut and hugging it to her chest. Ari glanced up from her computer upon hearing the soft metallic click. She wrapped her arms around Scarlett noticing the silent tears streaming down her cheeks.

Scarlett shifted her arms setting the journal on the desk accepting the box of tissues held out to her. "The journal was insightful, but I wish I could remember her. No matter what was going on in her life, she always put me first," she replied, pulling the pictures from her pocket to show Ari, wiping the tears from her face.

Ari took the pictures from Scarlett seeing the resemblance, while Scarlett collected herself. "Most siblings are like that, even if they don't want to admit it. Trying to make up for your parent's mistakes," Ari explained, handing the pictures back to Scarlett avoiding eye contact, pushing memories of her own family aside.

Scarlett arched an eyebrow hearing Ari's voice crack before coughing, trying to cover up her reaction. "You speak from experience, but I thought you were an only child?" she pressed, putting the pictures back in her pocket thinking she knew extraordinarily little of her friend's past.

Chapter Twenty-Three

Ari let out a bitter laugh shaking her head no. She reached for the silver chain resting underneath the collar of her shirt. Attached with an oval locket etched with runes. Ari pried it open revealing a black and white photo of her parents holding her in their arms, while the other side showed Ari standing beside a boy that was her twin. "There's me with my parents and the other picture is my twin brother Adrian," Ari explained, letting Scarlett examine the two pictures before she closed the locket. A distant expression flickered across her face as she thought of her brother.

November 10, 1990

Highway I-70, Denver, Colorado

The humid dessert air gradually dropped to freezing temperatures with the setting sun. A black line crossed the amber horizon as the blazing sun hid behind the clouds. The blackness thickened shifting to a large oval shape before it opened like a door.

A young girl stumbled through, falling on her hands and knees. A male teen gracefully landing behind her, his wool cloak billowing behind him before the portal closed and disappeared. The girl's breath labored glancing over her shoulder annoyed at how much easier the journey had been for him.

"That was close. Couldn't you have held it open for a few minutes longer?" he asked, pulling the cloak underneath him before sitting on the ground. She tried reaching out for the cloak to thwart the cold, yet he swatted her hand away not wanting to rest for too long.

An aggravated groan escaped her lips, shoving her long raven locks out of her face. "Of course, Adrien. The next time I create a portal to another realm I'll ensure it's held open until it reaches your satisfaction," she sneered, feeling the chilly night air pierce through the thin plum sundress with white leaves etched into the hem. "Why are we here anyway?" she asked, wrapping her arms around herself for warmth.

Adrien opened his mouth ready to answer yet praised choosing his words carefully. "A safe place where we won't be hunted by those seeking out your powers," he replied, watching her frown but shake her head, not accepting his answer as the truth. "Now, get up. We need to keep moving, which requires another portal," he snapped, climbing to his feet holding his hand out to her.

She stifled a yawn staring at his outstretched hand in disbelief. "You're kidding me, right?" she pleaded, seeing him shake his head no, tapping his foot impatiently. "That took everything I had, and now you want another one? Why don't you do it while I rest?" she sneered, wishing she had worn leggings and a cloak. *He could at least offer me his cloak. I'm freezing, but sure I can just whip up another portal*, she thought, glancing over the matching dark blue wool pants and a knitted gray tunic covering his form.

Adrien noticed the gooseflesh covering her pale arms and unclasped the navy-blue cloak holding it out to her. "I wish I could, but I can't. Not everyone was born with magic running through their veins," he replied, draping the cloak over her shoulders using the gold leaf clasp to pin it to her dress. "Come on we should walk until your magic returns," he suggested, watching her cling to the cloak yet not climb to her feet.

Ari glanced up from her locket lost in thought. "That's all I remember before waking up here. Matt informed me that my brother was dead and that due to my powers I would be safe staying here. I'm guessing we were close, yet when I look at his picture, I feel sadness and anger that I don't remember him or our parents," she admitted, rubbing her temples feeling a headache from forcing her memories to become clearer.

"Thank you for sharing that with me, I know it wasn't easy," Scarlett whispered, slipping her arms around Ari pulling her into a tight hug. Ari returned the embrace, taking in a deep breath preventing the flood of memories to overwhelm her. Scarlett pulled away seeing the distant expression flicker across Ari's face. "I think I'm going to head to the park to clear my head. It'll give you a chance to do the same," Scarlett replied, seeing Ari smile watching Scarlett collect the journal, placing it in her purse.

Ari nodded her head in thanks, reaching to pick up the dagger offering it to Scarlett. Scarlett accepted the knife tying the sheath to her belt before heading toward the door. "Just be back before dark. Matt doesn't want anyone out alone with Simon on the loose," Ari warned, relieved that Scarlett didn't try to press her for more answers about her brother.

Scarlett nodded her head in agreement before exiting the garage relieved to see the jeep was still running. *I guess Andrew was so focused on our fight, he forgot to take the keys out of the ignition,* she thought, climbing behind the driver's seat and drove toward the park. She was relieved to see the park deserted and approached the swing set. Sitting down on one of the swings, she pulled the journal back out of her purse reading the contents once more.

It was clear talking about her brother was difficult for Ari, but she rarely shares anything with us. I'm glad I learned the truth about my sister even after all this time, she thought, leaning against the swing letting the gentle breeze lull her to sleep. Cold, large raindrops splattered onto her face jarring her awake as the rain increased falling faster dampening her clothes.

Scarlett looked up at the sky noticing the grey sky turning magenta. *Damn it! How long was I asleep? I'm sure Matt is going to bite my head off for being out so late,* she thought, climbing to her feet to head back feeling the raindrops fall faster, matting her damp hair to her forehead.

She threw her purse on the passenger's seat shaking her wet hair out of her face before starting the engine to drive back to the manor.

Chapter Twenty-Four

Donovan leaned against the wall facing the window in his room, he closed his eyes enjoying the soft patter of raindrops hitting the glass outside. He sighed hearing the rambling thoughts of his brother before Michael appeared beside him. "What do you wish of me, Michael?" he demanded, opening his eyes, and turning away from the window. Michael dressed in the usual uniform stained with specks of dirt.

Michael held both hands palms facing up defensively. "I came to check up on you. Don't tell me, you're still sulking over what Simon said to you last night? The smug bastard just wants to tempt you to throw your morals away and be like him," he reassured Don, seeing his brother sigh. *It seems like I was right again. Why does he care what Simon thinks when Don's more mature? We should try to get Simon to be more like us*, he thought, seeing his brother flinch, realizing that his thoughts had gotten too loud in his excitement.

Donovan reached a hand up rubbing his temples. "Quiet your thoughts, Michael, my head already aches without your aid. Simon will never conform to our ideals, so why even entertain the idea?" Donovan asked, turning back to face the window watching the raindrops slide down the panel of glass. "If you must know, I was reminiscing about the past," Donovan confessed, leaning his forehead against the cold glass.

"Simon's focused on targeting the slayers, so what's to stop them from thinking we're responsible?" he suggested, moving to stand beside Donovan staring out the window watching the rainfall. "Why lose yourself walking down memory lane when you can't change the past?" he asked, wondering if Don had considered his life turning out differently.

"Simon's end game is to turn Scarlett and, in the process, get rid of us. He massacred enough humans to have the council come after us because of this territory belonging to us. Why does reminiscing of the past concern you? Am I not allowed to mourn over those I lost in the past and how to prevent such a nightmare from recurring?" Donovan asked, hearing his brother's thoughts whirling around restlessly in response to Donovan's question.

"Why dwell on things you can't change? You want to protect Scarlett, yet you can't protect her if she's not here," he suggested, staring out the window thinking of the night Donovan had saved his life.

January 12, 1601

Paris, France

Donovan let out a weary sigh glancing up at the manor before him. He had caught news of his brother obtaining ownership of the popular establishment Le Chabanais. Donovan had left Romania wanting distance from the woman who had tried to murder him. He arrived at a towering white building isolated from the city streets with a row of white marble one-story houses boarded up with wooden boards nailed over the windows. Laugher billowed out from the brothel, mingling with the howling wind.

He stumbled inside trying hard to ignore the many voices of the woman and the company they kept in their beds. The walls are decorated with lavish paintings and gold candles illuminating the space in soft yellow light. A young woman in her late twenties in a red sequin gown danced on a wooden stage in the center of the room.

He recognized his brother's voice, following the thoughts through a throng of women, descending a long corridor with plush green carpeting to a single bedroom at the end of the hallway. He entered a large bedroom finding his sibling spread out on a king-size bed with satin gold sheets and a woman on either side. Both women were clad in black lace lingerie with black thigh-high boots, stroking his face in admiration.

Donovan stood in the doorway, clearing his throat with his arms crossed over his chest. Michael glanced up from the bed, his cheeks blushing with the soft sheets caressing his bare skin. "Donny! You got my letters and here I thought you were never coming to visit me," Michael exclaimed, trying hard not to laugh at his brethren's discomfort. He climbed off the bed bending to pick up a plush white robe tying it around his waist.

"Yes, your letter hinted that you were in dire distress, yet here you are acting without a care in the world. You have not changed from our last encounter," Donovan muttered, ignoring the women's thoughts desperate for him to leave.

"Why bro, I didn't know you cared," Michael teased, reaching into his pocket tossing a bag of coins to the two women. He smirked watching them both reach for it before fleeing the room. He started laughing before it turned into harsh coughs. He reached for a silk handkerchief, spitting the blood into the cloth before putting it away. "I was afraid you were going to ignore my request or worse disappear again," he explained, sitting on the edge of the bed motioning for Donovan to sit beside him.

Donovan crossed the room to sit beside his brother, smelling the blood staining the cloth. "I would never ignore your cries for help. I did warn you that persuading a nest of vipers would lead to your demise," Donovan replied, taking in his sibling's poor condition.

Michael let out a bitter laugh amused by the statement. "Please, don't say I told you so big brother. You promised if I ever needed your help, that you would help me. I need your help. I have yet to experience the world and you just came back." Michael pleaded, reaching out for his brother's hand.

Donovan sighed, wondering what Michael wanted from him, taking in his brother's weakened form. "All right, I will aid you in escaping death this once. I will make it as painless as I can for you," he whispered, lashing out with his nails to slice his brother's throat.

Donovan bit into his wrist and pushed it to Michael's lips forming the metallic liquid to flood into Michael's mouth. Once finished, with the transformation he picked Michael up in his arms and headed for the door. He had his family back even if his actions would appear selfish to others of his kind.

Chapter Twenty-Five

Donovan sighed, placing a hand over his eyes in annoyance. "I see that night marked the end of your humanity—" Donovan noted, feeling regret for forcing his brother to live in the night.

Michael waved his hand dismissively. "I didn't bring it up to make you feel guilty, bro. I wanted to remind you of how powerful you are," he replied, ignoring the bitter laugh coming from Donovan. "I mean it, we can take the fight to Simon and ambush him before he has the chance to fight back," Michael protested, picturing Donovan beating up Simon with a smug grin.

"Has the memory of the incident already passed from your mind? Simon was victorious in our last encounter, a feat I'm still puzzled over. How was he able to win when he has never accomplished the task before?" He pondered, amused by the visual in his brother's head.

Michael was quiet seeing that the conversation had given his brother a headache. "No, the fight is still fresh in my mind Donnie. Maybe drinking human blood offers him extra strength? He said, drinking from animals made us weak," he advised, seeing Donovan shrug his shoulders unaware of the answer.

"I doubt it, the buffoon sticks to the same tactics. His only chance to beat his opponent is to fight dirty, yet there was no evidence of foul play. Forgive me for being short-tempered with you, I know you're only trying to discuss the situation with me, but I am feeling unwell, another issue to add to the matter at hand," he admitted, hearing the thoughts of concern coming from Michael.

Michael placed a hand on Donovan's shoulder unaware he was ill. "Yes, and unfortunately I can't be of much help. I didn't see your fight; I was helping Shiva escort people out of the bar. Scarlett witnessed some of it, could she help clarify things for you?" he suggested, afraid to ask what his illness was, aware he wouldn't burden him with the truth.

"No, I doubt she could be of aide. I led Simon to the back hoping to dominate him into letting go of his fascination with the girl. Instead, he overpowered me, staking me with a wooden support leg from the nearby table. My actions were slower than normal, and I wasn't at my usual strength," he admitted, at a loss for the cause of his defeat.

Michael frowned, stroking his chin trying to produce a solution. "I don't get it, you're older than Simon, so unless your drink was spiked, you should have been able to crush him like a bug. I had assumed he had used Scarlett as a shield," he admitted, picturing Simon's throat crushed in his brother's hands.

"She arrived at the end and prevented Simon from casting the final blow against me. Tell me, if my drink had been spiked what would the poison be and how long would the effects linger?" he asked, closing his eyes once more feeling exhausted from the conversation.

Oh crap, I wasn't expecting him to follow my rationale. I owe Scarlett a bit of gratitude for intervening when she did, he thought, staring out the window trying to think of a logical answer. "I was just grasping at straws, Donnie. Don't you think if you received drugs, you would have noticed it by now? I can check the surveillance tapes from behind the bar from last night to double check?" he suggested, hoping his brother was okay, not wanting his suspicion to be right.

Donovan arched an eyebrow catching parts of his brother's thoughts. "Why would Scarlett require your thanks? Go ahead and put your theory to work. I'm going to go lay down for a bit. Hopefully, this headache will leave me," Don replied, pushing himself to his feet before collapsing on the bed.

Michael turned watching his brother lie down in his head before leaving the room. *He won't admit it, but his fight with Simon could have killed him. Scarlett intervened and offered Simon a chance to get away. I guess I owe her an apology for how I treated her,* Michael thought, heading downstairs entering the back-storage room. He pulled all the tapes dated from the night before. He sat down in front of the television reviewing the footage trying to figure out if his guess was correct.

Michael noticed Shiva enter the room from the corner of his eye. He was still sifting through the footage looking for proof. She placed a hand on his shoulder leaning down to see what he was doing. "Hey, there you are. I was looking for you to entertain me," she asked, perching on the edge of the chair. She frowned, failing at getting a reaction from her comment. "Is there something specific you're searching for?" she added, wanting to help.

Michael blinked, hearing her second question, before tearing his gaze from the television screen. He pulled her into his lap, brushing his lips tenderly against hers. "Sorry if it seemed I was ignoring you," he noted, brushing her hair out of her face. "Something is wrong with my brother and the footage from the tapes might offer me a clue to what it is," he admitted, glancing back at the screen in boredom.

"I've been sifting through these tapes for twenty minutes and I haven't found anything," he whined, growing frustrated with the project. He drummed his fingers on the desk glancing at Shiva. "Do you recall Simon ordering any drinks for my brother?" he asked, thinking of who might have targeted his brother.

Shiva rested her head against his shoulder, watching the blurred images of the surveillance taps pass by quickly trying to trigger her memory. "I'm not sure you're going to find the answer you're searching for," she whispered, hearing him curse in frustration before reaching for the television remote turning the television off. She reached for his hand kissing it softly. "Hear me out, I may have an answer for you, but you're not going to like it," she warned, climbing to her feet turning to face him.

Michael reached up to caress her cheek seeing the fear flicker in her eyes. "Don't be afraid, there's nothing you can say that will upset me," he whispered, seeing her shaking her head in dispute. He reached out his hand to wipe away a stray tear, only to have her swat his hand away,

"Stop it, your kind words are only making it harder," she stammered, trying to suppress the tears seeing him frown not understanding why she was upset. "I thought I could weaken Simon and depose all our problems. He was alone at the bar—" she explained, seeing realization dawn on Michael's face before he jumped to his feet. "Michael, wait! I never meant for your brother to consume it. It was an accident," she pleaded, grabbing his arm trying to push him back in his seat afraid of Donovan's wrath.

Michael watched her eyes dart toward the door planning her escape. A sly grin spread across his face. Before she could run to the door, he grabbed her waist picking her up and throwing her over his shoulder. Ignoring her protests, he headed up to his brother's room. He entered his brother's room closing the door behind him before placing Shiva down. He leaned against the door preventing her escape. "Hey, Donnie. I found a discovery behind the mystery of how Simon kicked your ass," he announced, seeing Donovan stir before sitting up in bed.

Donovan didn't hear the murmured voices reaching his room until his brother's familiar voice reached his ears. He groaned feeling a dull ache return to his temples at the onslaught of thoughts coming from the pair. He held up a hand seeing Shiva open her mouth ready to argue her case. "I take it she has something to do with it?" he demanded, seeing Michael pout pointing his finger accusingly at Shiva.

"Michael, stop trying to pin the blame on me, I told you it was an accident—" she pleaded, staring at her feet scared of meeting Donovan's gaze.

"Enough! Michael, rein in your toys and tell me what you discovered," Donovan demanded, seeing his brother flinch, and stealing a fleeting glance at Shiva.

"We were reviewing the tapes and discovered what may have offered Simon an advantage over your duel," Michael suggested, nudging Shiva waiting for her to admit to her mistake.

"You made it clear that you hated the man who was visiting, so I put a special mixture into his drink. I didn't know he wouldn't enjoy the mix of animal blood or that you would finish the drink for him," she explained, trying to push past Michael, desperate to escape, seeing the anger flash in Donovan's eyes.

Donovan sighed pinching the bridge of his nose trying to ignore the flood of frantic thoughts coming from Shiva. "Your intent was to poison a customer in my bar? What would have occurred if an innocent bystander had consumed it instead of me? As if I didn't have enough matters to contend with," he groaned, wincing upon hearing the girl's frantic thoughts increase after hearing his response. "Shiva be silent! Go back to your room unless you know of a remedy for your costly mistake?" Donovan asked, seeing the girl shake her head no watching Michael step aside letting her bolt from the room.

Michael watched the door slam shut behind her before he glanced over at his brother in concern. "Any idea of how to create an antidote? What if Simon attacks again, aware that you're still vulnerable?" Michael asked, hesitant to ask about Shiva's punishment not wanting her to be hurt yet he knew he couldn't shelter her from his brother's wrath.

Donovan watched Michael cross the room taking a seat on the edge of the bed. Amused by his brother's concern for the girl. "To be honest, I lack an answer for your question. Another attack seems unlikely yet, he may become desperate in his quest to claim Scarlett. I was going to inquire if the girl knew how long these ailments will inflict me, but it became clear she used a poison she lacks the knowledge of," he noted, glancing over at his desk where a pot of ink, a black feather quill, and pad of parchment lay.

Michael followed his brother's gaze and arched an eyebrow. "Were you writing to the council?" he asked, trying not to laugh, seeing Donovan nod in agreement. "Why? They would only help us if they received something in return," he warned, noting the correspondence at the top of the page.

Donovan sighed, not surprised by his brother's reaction at the mention of the council. "It's common courtesy when one receives a letter brother—" he replied, hearing Michael let out a bitter laugh thinking that the council was useless. "They got wind of Simon's activities and inquired about my actions on the matter. Mother wishes to send two of her lap dogs to clean up the mess since I have yet to rein him in," Don explained, glad he had burned the letter before his brother got his hands on it.

Michael grimaced upon hearing the mention of their mother. "I thought the old bat forgot about us, it's been so long," he mused, easing to his feet, and crossing the room to the desk. He tried looking for the original letter yet didn't find it. *What is Donnie hiding from me now? If they want Simon so badly, just dangle Scarlett in front of him*, he thought, cursing hearing Donovan let out a low growl in warning.

In a flash, Donovan pushed himself from the bed and closed the distance between them. He grabbed Michael's wrist preventing him from opening the desk drawer. "We will not use Scarlett as a ploy to get at Simon. Do not fabricate such ideas. I informed mother that Damon's time to reclaim his fledgling has expired when the first body turned up," Donovan explained, before letting go of Michael's wrist standing beside his brother in the loft.

Michael flinched unaware that his thoughts would enrage his brother. "It was merely a suggestion. I would never wish any actual harm to occur to her," he snapped, pushing Donovan off with ease. Unaware of the strength, he had sent Donovan into the wall near the door, causing the paint to fleck from the wall from the impact. *I don't want to hurt him, but I may never get this chance to teach him a lesson*, Michael thought, hearing laughter from Donovan.

Donovan rolled his eyes beckoning Michael to approach him again. "How pathetic little brother, my weakened state will not give you an advantage in our struggles," he sneered, waiting for Michael to lunge at him once more before throwing him over his shoulder. He ducked low avoiding Michael's fist watching him flail falling over the banister and landing gracefully on the floor beneath them. He smirked watching Michael race up the stairs to launch another punch at his head, only to have it blocked by a roundhouse kick.

Michael sidestepped the second kick aimed at his ribs placing some distance between them. "Nice shot, Donnie. I thought you weren't going to take it easy on me?" he demanded, hearing Donovan sighed in response Donovan lunged at Michael aiming a swing at his ribs. Michael jumped dodging the blow and did a backflip onto the banister's railing. He beckoned Donovan before jumping down once more to the lower level.

Donovan followed his brother's theatrics and closed the distance between them. He swept one foot out waiting for Michael to try jumping to dodge it and lashed up with his other foot kicking Michael in the chest. Michael caught Donovan's foot in both hands before twisting it in an awkward arch, lifting him up hurling Donovan away from him and toward the railing, trying to lung toward Donovan once more.

Donovan flew toward the railing waiting until his outstretched hands hit the railing. He used it to flip behind Michael, punching him square in the back sending him to the ground. "I never said I would take things easy on you, dear brother," Donovan corrected, hearing his brother grunt in alarm at the crack from the force of Donovan's punch. Michael gritted his teeth rolling to get behind Donovan, lashing out with his legs trying to kick Donovan behind the knees and taking his legs out from under him.

Donovan staggered back a step letting Michael pull him to the ground. He took a sidestep back placing dome distance between them to catch his breath. "Impressive, your speed has improved since our last duel, but your arrogance will lead to your defeat," Donovan warned, standing in a fighting stance waiting for the next attack.

Michael grinned upon hearing this taking a step back leaning against the wall. "I'm not as stupid as I look, Donnie," Michael hissed, motioning for Donovan to make the next move.

Donovan rolled his eyes before he disappeared in another flash step appearing in front of Michael. He grabbed Michael's left arm adding pressure until he heard the bone snap. Michael dug his fingernails into his brother's stomach. Donovan hissed out in pain pulling away from his brother, backing up before delivering a kick to Michael's injured limb. Michael merely smiled trying to ignore the pain while he dug his bloody fingernails deeper into Donovan's chest. feeling his piercing the bone.

Donovan cursed staggering back a step placing both hands over the gaping hole. He gritted his teeth waiting for the hole to close ignoring his blood running down his body. He watched Michael clutching the injured arm to his chest waiting for the broken bones to mend. "Ah, for once our little spat lasted longer than usual," Donovan noted, seeing Michael catching his breath.

Michael remained silent retreating to his room not wanting to gloat in his efforts. *I just don't understand how he cares more for her than me, we're both his family*, He thought, heading to Shiva's room, and knocking on the door waiting for her to answer.

Donovan watched Michael leave a frown appearing on his face. "Why do you doubt my love Michael? Scarlett may be family, but you are the one I was born to protect." He muttered softly before returning to his room.

Chapter Twenty-Six

Scarlett returned to the manor as thunder boomed overhead, muffling her steps. The darkened sky illuminated by flashes of lightning making the rainfall faster. She laughed hearing the others bickering in the main dining room before sneaking to her room to change into dry clothes. She pulled her hair back into a tight braid and pulled out a pair of black jeans and a red long-sleeved sweatshirt. Stashing the journal in her top dresser drawer, she tucked the necklace underneath her shirt collar and retreated downstairs. She hid, lingering on the stairs, eavesdropping on their conversation

Vincent sat on the edge of the sofa, his boots wet and muddy from the rain. He stared out the window lustfully watching the rain hitting the glass and rolling down it with flashes of lightning illuminating the room. Raven and Dawn sat across from each other on the floor playing poker. Vincent drummed his fingers on his lap letting out a long-exasperated sight.

Jet entered the dining room placing a bowl of chips on the coffee table. "Vincent, stop pouting. You could always join the girls in cards?" he suggested, taking a seat beside Vincent jabbing him in the ribs lightly.

Vincent rolled his eyes fidgeting with the silver chain around his neck pulling the pendent free from underneath his shirt. Raven let out a bitter laugh earning a dirty look from Vincent. "And risk losing all of our clothing or money in the process?" she rebutted, earning a chuckle from awn in response. "Sorry, Vince, but after the tricks you pulled last time, I don't trust you," she added, shuffling the cards before dealing a new hand. Vincent placed his hand over his heart and leaned back dramatically.

Scarlett opened the closet pulling out a blue foam mallet hurling it at Vincent before grabbing a second one and climbed onto the railing. "We can always invent a new game?" she called, watching the mallet hit Vincent in the face making the others laugh before Jet pointed to her on the railing gaining the other's attention. Vincent arched an eyebrow trying to reach for the mallet, beaten by Jet, who was already on his feet. He bowed to Scarlett twirling the mallet in one hand beckoning her forward.

Vincent climbed to his feet excitedly and climbed onto the coffee table. "Wait, we need to learn of this new game and of the rules," he exclaimed, ignoring Raven's hands trying to grab his leg and shove him off the table.

Dawn giggled, swatting Raven's hand away, curious to hear him finish.

"As the referee, I proclaim this as standard melee and the first to knock the other off the table is the winner," he added, jumping off the table ushering the girls to clear their cards from the table.

Dawn obliged, ignoring the dirty look from Raven, before taking the bowl of chips and moving onto the sofa. She patted the empty seat beside her for Raven, yet Raven shook her head leaving the room heading toward the garage. Vincent took the offered seat instead before grabbing a handful of chips from the bowl. Jet laughed, climbing onto the table before extending his hand to Scarlett. Scarlett followed Jet accepting his offered hand to climb onto the table and bowed to him.

A sly grin crept over her face before swinging at Jet. Jet bowed to her once more before parrying the blow. He swung low aiming for her legs while taking a step forward trying to knock her from the edge. Scarlett jumped avoiding the strike hearing Vincent booing her efforts. She couldn't help but laugh before mimicking his move, using her shoulder to slam into his mallet, knocking it out of his hands. Jet held up both hands defensively but was too late to avoid the blow to his chest.

He tried grabbing the mallet but did not see Scarlett push it deeper into his chest knocking him back a step. He stumbled and jumped down from the table. He grabbed the fallen mallet and offered it to Vincent. "Step in for me Vince? I'm going to go check up on Ari in case that's where Raven headed off to," he explained, hearing Vincent squeal in delight accepting the weapon and bowing to Scarlett.

Jet laughed thinking Scarlett's game was better than sparing out in the rain before heading to the garage. He paused outside the door hearing Ari yelling at Raven before Raven fled from the garage in fear. He knocked on the door before entering. "Should I even ask what just happened?" he called, seeing Ari picking up fallen papers before placing them back in a neat pile beside her laptop. He let out a low whistle seeing the carnage the room was in before moving to pick up one of the benches and placing it back in its right position.

Ari glanced up once she had finished tidying up her desk wiping the sweat from her brow. "Raven came in here searching for a weapon to lure out the vampire hoping to use Scarlett as bait. When I refused to help her, she went on a rampage and I lost it," she confessed, offering him a small smile of gratitude for his help.

"Scarlett saw we were restless and invented a harmless game. I take it Raven got jealous and tried getting even?" he mused, thinking of their morning meeting when she had suggested the idea to Matt. "Knowing you, you have something up your sleeve for punishment?" he asked, picking up the last of the fallen papers and placing them in the drawer of the desk.

Ari sighed, closing the laptop, and climbed to her feet. "No, not a punishment but Scarlett can't keep them distracted not with the storm raging," she mused, reaching for a box of gems, chalk, and a wooden board no larger than the width of her chair and headed toward the exit. Jet arched an eyebrow noticing the runes etched on the bag. "Will you grab the laptop for me and come with me," she asked, seeing him nod his head in agreement before following her with the computer.

Ari entered the living room amused to see what Jet had meant by Scarlett's game. Scarlett was chasing Vincent around the coffee table but stopped when she noticed Ari enter the room. She squealed in amusement letting Vincent tackle her to the sofa unaware of Ari's

E.L. SUMMERS & L.N. FROST

presence. Jet placed the laptop on the coffee table before asking her to fetch Raven. "I'm sure Scarlett is aware of the obstacle course I have created. It seems you could all use something constructive to do?" she asked, hearing the others agree to her statement excitedly.

"I see Ari decided to intervene before me?" Matt inquired, standing on the landing of the staircase with his sunglasses still on. Dawn appeared around him pulling Raven's hand leading her past Matt and off the steps. They watched Ari setting the different colored gems on the surface of the wooden board. Each gem rested on a chalked coordinate.

Ari slipped on her blue silk cloak, aware that the others were awaiting her explanation. The course is a survivor's obstacle course set in various terrain. "The course itself stretches out over two miles. The terrains you may encounter are mountains, woodlands, a cave, and the wetlands," Ari explained, using the chalk to draw a circle in front of her large enough for two people to stand side by side.

Matt watched her add a symbol for the four elements in each quadrant outside of the open circle. He grabbed a crate full of weapons from the top shelf of the closet diverting the group's attention.

Scarlett watched the skeptic look flicker over Dawn's face after hearing Ari's answer. "Are there any special rules for the course?" Dawn asked, hesitating to ask if it was optional to take part in the obstacle course. Andrew had made his way out of his room overhearing the announcement and became intrigued by the concept.

"No, but it offers us a chance to gauge each person's fighting level, but we go in one at a time. Bear in mind, the creatures may seem real, but nothing in the course can harm you," Ari warned, aware that Dawn feared to have to fight a real creature. Dawn sighed in relief watching Raven grab a rapier handing Dawn a small dagger. Dawn glanced at the dagger in fear yet took it holding it awkwardly in both hands.

"It's a test to see what you know and to show me if you need additional training to remain a slayer," Matt explained, watching Vincent pick up a bazooka and a bag full of grenades, jumping up and down excitedly awaiting to test them out.

"How do we decide who gets to go first?" Andrew asked, leaning against the doorway seeing Dawn waving to him beckoning for him to take a seat beside her on the floor.

Jet waited for the others to choose their weapons. He noticed Raven approach the crate a second time grabbing a quarry of arrows and a wooden bow and arrow slinging it over her shoulder. Once the others were finished, Jet grabbed more amino for his guns, watching Matt skeptically, seeing that he wasn't grabbing anything from the pile.

Matt waited for everyone to grab the supplies they needed. "First, I need to know if the course is created yet and Ari's the one running the show, you'll have to ask her," Matt explained, glancing at Ari for confirmation.

"To pick the order, you'll stand in a circle around me and I'll use this to pick the order," Ari explained, pulling out a crystal that tied to a string.

"Are you serious? Couldn't we just pick numbers out of a hat or draw straws instead of allowing Ari to use a rock instead?" Dawn asked, choking, grabbing her throat yet no sound came out.

"There that's better. Don't worry, I'll return it before you start the course, that way everyone can hear you scream. Does anyone else want to mock my method?" Ari demanded, earning a unanimous no not wanting to lose their voice either.

Ari closed her eyes and started to swing the pendant slowly turning around in the circle finally coming to a stop pointed at Link. "Great, here we go again. I'm guessing the entrance is the same as last time. Be warned, if I end up getting attacked by nomads I'm going to come after you Matt for giving her the idea in the first place," Link explained, walking out the door ready to face the course.

"What a wuss. I thought he would enjoy all the attention from a group of women who kill all men. If you're wondering, the entrance is past the portal when you step onto the path in the backyard that leads to the woods," Matt explained, motioning for Ari to swing the pendant again before it landed on Scarlett.

"This should be interesting. I'm guessing that after each terrain we pass the opponent we face will be stronger than the last?" I asked, approaching the portal before stepping through it.

Vincent stood there as the pendent landed on Raven and then Dawn afterward. "Man, when will it be my turn? I want to have some fun?" Vincent whined before the pendent landed on him. He yelled out in joy running for the portal, soon followed by Jet leaving Matt last.

"Are you sure you're up for this? I don't want you to pass out if you depend on your abilities too much. I doubt you've recovered from last night," Ari warned, walking with him towards the portal.

"Don't worry about me, I'll spend time together in the mountains until I'm fully healed. Besides, it's been a while since I got to have some fun," Matt explained, pulling out two sliver blades cut into crescent moons and hung on a metal chain before stepping through the portal.

Ari rolled her eyes at hearing this as she walked over to a board that was lying on the ground. She studied it taking note of where each player had ended up. She noticed that Raven and Scarlett had ended up starting in the woods. She sent a werewolf after Scarlett and a changeling after Raven. She hoped that they would end up fighting each other after their battles were over.

She noticed that Vincent was with Matt, deciding to send a snowman along with some frost giants knowing that the men would enjoy the warm-up. She decided to set up a group of vampires, shadow people, nomads, goblins, water serpents, and a few other creatures to guard the wetlands. Placing a mile of terrain between each group of creatures.

Chapter Twenty-Seven

Scarlett stepped through the portal, greeted by the sweet smell of moss and pine needles from the thicket of trees surrounding her. The brisk chilly air whipped her loose strands of hair in front of her face. A piercing howl filled the woods causing Scarlett's eyes adjusted to the dim lighting before she reached for one of the grenades in her pocket. She pulled the car off and hurled the lit grenade in front of her, interrupting the second howl appearing from the north. She smirked hearing the creature whimper in pain after the flash of light faded.

She took a step back bracing her back against the wide oak tree and jumped up, reaching both hands up over her head to grasp the lowest hanging branch. Gripping the tree branch, she swung herself up, watching the grey wolf race toward her slamming its weight against the trunk of the tree. Scarlett gritted her teeth feeling the ache in her injured shoulder flare from the effort. She reached up with her free hand trying to massage the area, and pulled her dagger from its sheath, and watched the brute slam its weight against the base of the tree once more.

Ensuring she wouldn't drop the dagger; Scarlett grabbed the tree branch she was hanging on and dropped down landing on the wolf's back. She plunged the dagger into the back of its throat and used the momentum to slide the dagger across its throat. She heard it growl in protest grabbing her legs with its claws and throwing her off its back. She rolled to the side avoiding its claws from scratching her face and reached for the second grenade.

Removing the cap, she threw it at the wolf's face hearing it grunting with an effort to remove the dagger lodged in its throat.

Scarlett pulled her head into her chest and covered her face with both hands. The wolf howled ready to pounce before the grenade hit its chest before its gray fur burst into bloody pieces of confetti. Adrenaline coursed through her feeling the slow warm truckle run down her leg. *That was easier than I thought it would be*, Scarlett thought, feeling the rush subside. She glanced down inspecting her legs seeing a small wound from where the wolf had grabbed her.

She placed her hand over the wound waiting for it to stop bleeding and cut a strip of fabric from her shirt tying it tightly around the wound. The ache in her shoulder returned. A familiar voice crying for help sapped her out of her agony. She climbed to her feet, hearing the cry once more from the east direction of the woods. She wrinkled her nose at the growing smell of blood and wet fur and ran toward the screams.

Raven exited the portal and scanned her surroundings. She tied the cardigan tighter around her chest wishing she had worn something warmer than the plum knit floral dress. The hair on the back of her neck stood up at hearing the fierce howl pierce the serene woods. She gripped the bow in her right hand keeping her guard up and started walking south. A jingling bell reached her ears as she traveled deeper into the woods.

A flash of light buzzed past her startling her, making her reach behind to grab an arrow. Feeding the arrow into the quiver and fired at the small white orb. Light laughter reached her ears and a force of wind knocked her to the ground. Another orb of light flickered grabbing a chunk of her hair pulling it before disappearing. Raven waited for the orb to fly near her face and fire again thinking she had hit the creature's wings. It cried out in alarm growing prying the arrow from its wing with ease.

The creature was seven feet in height with long red hair and pointy ears. Her amber eyes studied Raven in amusement wrapping the shaft of the arrow in her olden dress. She snapped the arrow in half laughing with a bell-like jingle. She shook her long slender fingers at Raven in disdain before letting out a low whistle. A sense of dread filled Raven before she started running again colliding with Scarlett. They both fell to the soft ground, their limbs tangling together before the jingle returned.

Scarlett let out a sigh of annoyance pushing Raven off in frustration before climbing on her feet. "Don't tell me, you think I need to be rescued?" Raven demanded, climbing to her feet dismissing Scarlett's extended hand.

Scarlett merely laughed seeing several orbs of light in the trees behind them. "I heard you scream and was curious to see what you were up against," Scarlett replied, grabbing Raven's arm seeing her fitting another arrow into her bow. "What are you doing, fairies are harmless," she added, seeing Raven shake her arm away and fired into the trees.

Raven cursed hearing her arrow embed itself with the oak tree's bark before more laughter followed. Scarlett crossed her arms over her chest waiting for the fey to grow bored with Raven's antics. Another arrow fired causing a shrill wail to fill the pace around them. Scarlett covered her ears with both hands, watching Raven do the same.

The figure fell from the trees its white gossamer wings turned into black moth wings. The long red hair fell to the ground around its bare feet losing the dress as well. The creature's amber eyes blackened and grew. Scarlett watched the creature jump lunging toward Raven, so Scarlett quickly reached for a grenade pilling off the pin and hurled it at the creature. The blast knocked both Scarlett and Raven to the ground before engulfing the creature in flames.

Raven watched the croaking figure try to crawl toward them. She reached for her bow and fired an arrow into its skull. "Eww, what the hell was that?" Raven demanded, watching the flames burn the remains to ash.

"My guess, it's probably a changeling," Scarlett replied, glancing down at her leg ensuring that the wound hadn't started bleeding once more. She glanced up catching Raven watching her and seeing the fleeting look of concern.

"Why would Ari send something after me I've never seen before?" Raven noted, seeing Scarlett shrug in response. "Remind me when we get back to kick her ass," Raven replied, dusting the dirt from her cardigan. Scarlett gestured with her hand to continue walking through the woods. Raven took two steps ahead of Scarlett before the earth crumbled beneath Raven's feet. Scarlett felt a force of wind knock her back a step away from Raven. The soil beneath Raven split, pulling her into the abyss.

Scarlett walked over to where Raven had been standing, tapping the soil gingerly with the edge of her foot. She tried searching for the sunken ground but didn't find any. *That's odd, the earth seems solid with no signs of a sinkhole. Poor fool, she should learn not to underestimate Ari*, Scarlett thought, heading further East to continue with the course.

Chapter Twenty-Eight

Jet exited the portal whistling a merry tune, scanning his surroundings. The humid air made his hair cling to his cheek with sweat. Wiping the sweat with the back of his hand, he glanced up at the clear grey sky. His boots trekked through towering weeds transitioning to muddy grasslands. He stopped whistling, listening to the birds chirping in the distance. He treaded forward approaching a clearing where the mossy grass was dry. *This is nice, but would Ari really make it easy for me?* he thought, hearing a chorus of sopranos singing Celtic music off in the distance.

Curious to what the singing was for, he headed West smelling burning lemongrass. He noticed smoke billowing in the sky confirming what he had smelt. The singing grew louder in pitch noticing the tall group of women dancing with hands clasped around a bonfire. Sticks wrapped in moss and lemongrass were burning in the fire to mask the foul stench emitting from the bone necklaces they were. The women all had long dark hair in braids woven with lilies with loincloths made from sheepskin.

Emitting a long chant in a foreign tongue, the other women stopped singing and turned to face Jet. They started whispering a new chant causing a thick smog to wash over Jet. He pulled the collar of his shirt over his mouth and started coughing. A weight pressed against his shoulders made him collapse to his knees. He reached for his pistols and fired, hearing it sink into the bones of the skull the leader held. The chanting stopped and turned into a wailing scream.

He grunted climbing to his feet hearing the screams continue before they slowly turned to face him. Baring their teeth, they started to approach tossing the bone necklaces they had been wearing into the fire.

The orange flames darkened turning purple. Jet continued to fire shooting each one in the skull, yet all it did was intensify the putrid smell. He placed his pistols back in its hoister and dusted his hands with salt.

He picked up each body and tossed it into the towering pyre gritting his teeth trying to suppress his nausea. He dragged the last body into the pyre before lining the outer ring of the fire with salt. The fire turned blue before he kicked dirt over the smoldering coal putting out the fire. He wiped sweat from his brow and vomited feeling the heavyweight lift. Jet gulped in the clean air to catch his breath before hearing a familiar voice cry out for help. He took off going wet toward the sound racing through the dense collection of maple trees approaching a pond surrounded by lilies.

Dawn exited the portal scanning her surroundings in fear. She clutched her purse to her chest feeling the crisp breeze caress her skin. The grassy plains lead to a small pond surrounded by lilies next to the mouth of the woods. Entranced by the pond's beauty she knelt at the water's edge. She set her purse aside and cupped the water with both hands drinking in the cool refreshing water. *I wish Raven were here with me, that way I wouldn't be afraid*, she thought, failing to see the ripples in the water.

Dawn removed her shoes placing her feet into the water sighing in relief. She flinched feeling a leaf brush against her leg. She let out a nervous laugh before staring up at the grey sky. Something landed in her hair tugging on it dragging her face toward the water. In a panic, she tried shaking her head thinking it was a bug. The creature burrowed deeper into her hair making her cry out in pain. She staggered to her feet kicking at the water's surface splashing her legs.

Seeing Jet running toward her she waved her arms frantically drawing him to her side. "Ouch! Jet am I glad to see you," she exclaimed, bending to collect her purse and fell crying out once more.

Jet bit his tongue offering her his hand helping her to her feet. He noticed the flash of silver and shook his head. "There's a bug in my hair, and I can't get it out," she pleaded, taking his hand, and climbing to her feet.

Jet snickered seeing the fluttering wings tangle in her hair trying to tug free the flower hair clip. "Hold still, it's only a water sprite that wants the clip in your hair," he warned, sliding his fingers in her hair, and removing the clip tossing it into the water. He laughed hearing Dawn shriek, rubbing her scalp in pain. "The bright colors lured the sprite to you, although usually, they are playful creatures," he mused, watching her collect her purse before hugging him.

Realization washed over her contemplating what he was saying. She released her arms from his waist and grabbed his hand excitedly. "You're knowledgeable about these things, how do we lure more out?" she asked, seeing him wince pulling his hand away from her gritting his teeth in pain. "Sorry, I wasn't trying to hurt you. It just seems better than fighting," she added, staring down at her feet.

Jet opened his mouth ready to argue her suggestion. He glanced down at his hand seeing that she had dug one of his rings into the flesh of his finger. "You'd rather take the cowardly way out of the course?" he asked, seeing her nod her head in agreement, unfazed by his statement. He let out a sigh of annoyance thinking of a plan to summon more sprites. He motioned for her to collect some of the wildflowers along the water's edge and braid them into her hair.

Dawn arched an eyebrow but obeyed his request finding a collection of red and white lilies. "They're usually afraid of humans. They only approached you earlier because they wanted something from you," he explained. Seeing her nod eagerly, he moved closer, taking her dagger, and cutting the sleeves from her dress. He cut a section of her midriff tying the extra pieces of fabric around her waist to hold the skirt in place. "Keep dancing and singing to yourself and they'll come," he warned, saying he would hide in the bushes.

Dawn nodded in agreement and started humming softly to herself while shaking her hips side to side. Jet took off hiding in the bushes where the grass was tall enough to hide him from sight. More sprites appeared dancing with Dawn before two satyrs rushed from the other side of the pond. Their skin covered in grass and flowers trying to blend in with their surroundings. The sprites flew away, yet they grabbed Dawn's arms and legs dragging her into the woods. She tried calling out for Jet to rescue her to no avail.

Jet waited until the horned creatures were gone before climbing to his feet. *I hope Ari will appreciate my initiative in preventing Dawn the effortless way out of the course*, he thought dusting the grass from his pants and headed north curious to see what else was ahead.

Chapter Twenty-Nine

Scarlett wandered through a flat dirt terrain growing bored wondering when she would run into another slayer or monster. The terrain gradually changed to tall grass and humid air. She slipped off her sweater revealing the black camisole tank underneath, tying the sweater around her waist. She walked for a mile arriving at a lake with no clear boats or canoes to use to sail across. Oak trees scattered along one side of the dirt paved area.

How am I supposed to get across without drowning? There's no bridge? she thought, approaching the edge of the lake's shoreline. She placed her foot into the water flinching at the icy caress trying to judge how deep the water was. Absorbed in the task, she did not notice the thick green snake coiled around her ankle. Her legs thrashed trying to pry her leg out of its grasp. It let out a low hiss coiling around both legs before dragging her forward into the water.

Scarlett gasped at the icy water washed over her pulling her underwater. Her eyes and nose burned to file with the salty water. She coughed trying to spit out the bitter water trying to keep her head above water. Her vision blurred before she struck out with her fists trying to scratch its scales. She managed to scratch at its eyes causing it to scream tossing her out of the water.

She whimpered in pain landing on her injured shoulder feeling the sand caress her skin. She coughed spitting up the salty water. She reached for her dagger and held her breath seeing the creature lunge at her once more. The dagger sliced its scales off its underbelly causing it to hiss in pain and lashed out coiling around her waist pulling her back into the murky water. In her attempt to escape, she banged her head against a collection of rocks knocking the air out of her lungs, causing them to fill with water once more.

Jet had arrived at the lake after walking half a mile and had heard splashing noticing bubbles forming on the water's surface. He hurled one of the grenades into the water gaining the creature's attention. He waited for the large snake to break the surface, noticing its body coiled around Scarlett's limp form. Jet drew both guns and started firing. The creature cried out in anger moving closer to the shoreline. He waited for it to be within range and tossed a grenade into its gaping mouth.

Jet smirked hearing it cry once more before it exploded. He scanned the shoreline but saw no sign of Scarlett. He removed his shirt and pants before dove into the water searching for her. Spotting her limp form sinking underwater, he grabbed her waist and kicked his legs forcing them above water. He dragged her to shore, lying her on her back. He began compressions on her chest before performing rescue breaths. He sighed in relief at hearing her cough before helping her roll to her side to spit out the water in her lungs.

Scarlett finished pushing the water from her lungs lying back on her back. Her eyes blinked open trying to sit up, feeling gentle hands resting on her chest pushing her back down. "Relax, Scarlett. It's me, Jet. I slew the beast and recused you, though I take it. It took you by surprise and dragged you under," Jet explained, putting his clothes back on, seeing her nod her head yes.

Scarlett coughed a few more times before sitting up pulling her knees to her chest. "As pathetic as it sounds, I can't swim. I was trying to find another way across the lake, and the thing surprised me. Thank you. If it wasn't for your help—" she replied, staring out at the emerald abyss in fear.

Jet sat down beside her resting his hand on her knee drawing her attention away from the lake. "Don't mention it, though it's not pathetic, I know lots of people who can't swim," he teased, hearing her laugh in response.

Scarlett shoved him playfully, making him laugh harder. "Thanks, but that's not comforting. Have you run into anyone else before coming to my aid?" she inquired, fidgeting with her hair seeing that she had lost her sweater and dagger in the struggle.

Jet reached out for her hand squeezing it gently seeing that she was on edge. He reached into his bag and handed her one of his daggers. "I ran into Dawn, but she got on my nerves. I thought it would be fun to make her pretend she was a nymph and lured by satyrs," he explained, amused to hear her laugh in response. She nodded her head in thanks to the dagger glancing once more at the lake.

Jet climbed to his feet offering her his hand. Scarlett placed the dagger in her sheath and reached out for his hand, letting him pull her to her feet. "It seems like you fared better than one," she noted, dusting the wet sand from her jeans. She noticed him raise an eyebrow in response to her statement. "I got to rescue Raven from a changeling," she replied, shuddering at the thought of meeting them again.

Jet scanned their surroundings contemplating how to get across the body of water. "She disrespected Ari, so she forced her out of the course, by causing her to fall through a sinkhole," she added, amused to see him double over laughing before coughing to clear his throat.

Scarlett noticed him looking off at the oak trees surrounding the edge of the lake. "I thought of making a raft to drift across, but a dagger isn't sharp enough to cut through the bark of the tree," Scarlett noted, letting out a sigh of frustration.

Jet let out a soft chuckle seeing the puzzled look on her face. He instructed her to gather thick grass, seaweed, and twine before he headed toward the nearest tree. He heard her calling out to him to explain what he had in mind. Nearing the tree, he went into a lunge and started running.

He jumped hitting the tree and reaching up for the lowest hanging branch. Jet grunted with the effort breaking out in a sweat and paused to catch his breath. He continued to scale the tree finding where the branches were the thinnest and reached for his knife sawing at the bark.

He worked his way back down the tree feeling beads of sweat trickle down the back of his neck.

Scarlett did see various sized branches falling from the tree in front of her. She carried her bundle to the tree and rested it beside the pile of branches. Waiting for Jet to finish she decided to remove her wet clothing, lay it in the grass to dry. She decided to stretch out letting the sun warm her wet skin. Her cheeks flushed hearing Jet let out a whistle at catching her sunbathing in her undergarments.

Jet placed his knife away and jumped down from the tree. He admired his collection hoping it was enough. He smirked noticing the massive tattoo on Scarlett's back of a dragon breathing purple flames. "Hopefully, we can rig a raft big enough to drift across," he replied, removing his shirt and pants to add to her pile hearing her mocking whistle. "Admiring the view as well I see?" he teased, laying the branches out in rows before braiding them together with moss and weeds.

Jet continued with his process adding bundles of grass in between the cracks to tighten the knots. A comfortable silence had fallen between them as the sun disappeared behind the clouds.

"You're more muscular than one may think," she noted, breaking the silence.

Jet glanced up nearly finished with his construction and laughed trying to hide his discomfort.

Scarlett noticed the shameful expression flicker across his face, turning his eyes back down on his task. *His back is a tumbleweed of sizes. No wonder he never takes his shirt off*, she thought, turning her gaze away staring up at the rolling grey clouds. The soft rumble of thunder in the distance, made her reach for her clothes pulling them back on. They were still damp but handed Jet his clothes as well. Jet nodded his head in thanks relieved that she hadn't inquired what had caused the scars on his back, shoulders, and chest.

Jet placed his clothes in his bag handing it to Scarlett, bending to pull on the braided weeds assessing its resistance, smiling with pleasure at the results. "The raft should be sufficient enough to function as a floatation device for you," he instructed, picking the raft-up patting her shoulder patronizingly while passing her.

Scarlett followed him to the shoreline watching him waddle into the icy water until he was knee-deep in the water. He gestured for her to sit on the raft. Scarlett followed his instruction placing the bag in her lap. She watched him grip the side of the raft tying a section of weeds around his wrist. "Just tug on the twine if you see any ripples or shadows in the water," Jet explained, seeing her nod in agreement clutching her dagger in one hand resting it over the bag, and gripping the edge of the raft with the other.

Jet pulled the raft forward walking further on into the lake waiting for it to drift over the water and pushed off against the sandy bottom. Kicking his legs behind him they started gliding across the lake pushing against the gentle breeze.

Chapter Thirty

Scarlett stared out at the water surveying it for monsters. She smiled seeing the flash of silvery wings passing overhead. Reminding her of the fate that befell Dawn made her snicker. She flinched feeling icy raindrops hit her forehead as the wind picked up. The sky turned grey as lightning boomed illuminating the dark sky with short bursts of light.

Noticing the water ripple from the corner of her eye, Scarlett tilted her head straining to hear soft chimes over the howling wind. As they drifted further the chimes grew louder in pitch mimicking a woman's voice. She moved her hands from the side of the raft tugging on the twine.

Feeling a tug on the twine, Jet came to the surface yet before he could ask what was wrong, a vacant expression flickered in his eyes. He glanced toward the soft voice smiling in glee and swam faster. *Shit! I guess that proves what I heard wasn't a fragment of my imagination. The lore is correct, it only draws men under its spell*, Scarlett thought, trying again to rouse Jet from the spell tugging on the twine desperately with no prevail.

Passing a collection of rocks near the adjacent shore, a green tail splashed in the water before the pitch grew louder once more. Scarlett gritted her teeth not seeing the white scaled limbs coil around Jet's waist pulling him into her embrace. Long red curls covered her face like seaweed. She bared her shark teeth at Scarlett before smiling at successfully ensnaring her prey.

Scarlett tied the bag to the raft and the twine around her waist once it had been untethered from Jet's wrist.

Her palms began to sweat before taking in a deep breath and rolled off the side of the raft. The salty water burned her eyes but pressed on seeing Jet's eyes closed in bliss. She reached for the creature's hair using it to close the distance between them. The mermaid snarled its teeth trying to swat her away, but Scarlett plunged the dagger into her throat.

The song turned into gargled bubbles releasing Jet from the spell. His eyes flashed open seeing Scarlett trying to pull herself to the surface, gasping for air choking on the water now burning her lungs. Jet wrapped his arms around her waist and swam up to the surface. Scarlett gulped in the air trying to spit out the water in her lungs. Her eyes were bloodshot feeling Jet pull the raft toward them and pushing her onto it.

Scarlett kept coughing trying to control her breathing seeing Je hang on the edge of the raft rubbing his temples. "Do you think it'll be back?" Jet asked, scanning the water for other shadows. Scarlett shrugged her shoulders. "If it does, I'm sure she'll bring reinforcement," he added, feeling foolish for falling for its spell.

Scarlett heard his frustration in his voice. She wondered if there was a way to negate the sing's effects. "I see the shore up ahead, so we should be in the clear if she returns," she reassured him, hearing him sigh in relief tying the raft to his wrist once more.

He resumed swimming feeling the light drizzle cease with the storm breaking. Upon reaching the shoreline Jet dragged the raft onto the sandy beach seeing the base of the mountains to the East.

Scarlett accepted his hand climbing to her feet offering him the bag. Jet dressed quickly seeing the sky turn amber as Dusk began to set. Jet extracted a green bracelet shaking it before twisting it and slid it over his wrist. Green neon light burst in front of him illuminating his face.

He reached out for Scarlett's hand before casting the light in front of him. Scarlett took his hand reaching for her dagger with the other hand, cautiously entering the mouth of a cavern. The wind howled inside the interior of the case, yet for the moment there seemed to be no monsters lurking in the darkness

~~*

Andrew had exited the portal inhaling the humid air hearing the fast heartbeat of a human twenty miles from his location. He stood on a grassy hill next to a patch of wildflowers and a waterfall. He closed his eyes listening to the rush of the water hitting the rocks below. His eyes flashed open hearing an arrow buzz past his ear nearly missing his neck. Andrew wrinkled his nose distracted by the stench of sweat and bourbon.

He did not see the second arrow sail through the air burrowing into his shoulder. The silver burned his flesh causing him to bare his teeth growling in alarm only to meet laughter in return. Dusk was beginning to set with the sun hiding behind the clouds, casting the hilltop with shadows. He held up his palms, rising them up over his head in warning. Another silver arrow sailed through the air piercing his wrist. Angered, he tore the arrow free from his wrist, gritting his teeth in pain.

Dropping the arrow, he took off running, leaping over the cliff hearing a deep baritone exclaim that they loved a good chase. He heard the heavy footsteps chase after him pausing briefly at the lip of the cliff. Andrew closed his eyes feeling the rush of wind ruffle through his hair before plunging into the icy water. He heard the voice laugh before jumping off the ledge after its prey.

What were they thinking? Surely a drop from that height would kill any human, Andrew thought, climbing out of the water and onto a dry flat plane shaking the water from his hair. A second splash reached his ears, filling him with dread. A childish squeal filled the air followed by clapping. The water had washed the odor, not alerting him to the third arrow, hitting the cartilage underneath his knee causing him to collapse to his knees in agony.

Liquid molten lava spread through his body despite his efforts to ignore his pain. He tore the arrow free. His vision began to blur before rolling onto his side. The laughter grew louder as the shadow approached. He felt a small dart pierce the skin near his Adam's apple making him unconscious. The figure waited for the earth to split open and kicked the werewolf into the hole. Andrew descended into the darkened abyss before the hole closed.

Chapter Thirty-One

Matt exited the portal knocked back a step by the arctic wind. Light snowflakes fell on his eyelashes. His footsteps muffled in the snow contrasted against the violet skyline. Approaching a fallen tree, dusting off the snow and sitting down, surveying his surroundings. Matt removed the dark sunglasses feeling the headache subside. He waited at the base of the mountain hearing a bear roaring in the distance.

Placing his shades in his pant pocket he started walking West. The wind blew stronger, blowing his long hair behind his shoulders like a white cape. Upon reaching the top of the mountain, a bear lunged out of the snow baring its teeth at Matt emitting a long roar. Matt drew both crescent blades from his sheath and charged toward it, letting his blades arch through the air. The silver sliced through its fur pushing through its neck effortlessly. Blood splattered against the white snow before the towering creature collapsed to the ground.

A heavy sigh comes from behind the stack of boulders covered with snow. Vincent jumped up doing a flip in the air before landing in the snow. Matt rolled his eyes seeing the snow kick-up behind him. "You jerk! I wanted to kill it. I've been chasing it since I got here," Vincent whined, bending to pick up a handful of snow, rolling it into a snowball before throwing it at Matt's face.

Matt ducked easily avoiding the snowball, using the hem of his shirt to wipe away the blood. "You should have killed it sooner instead of delaying your move for dramatic effect. There are other areas to explore, so stop pouting," Matt warned, using the hem of his shirt to clean the blood and fur from his blades.

Vincent glared at Matt hearing muffled voices emitting from the cave to their right. "I'll take your advice under advisement, though I wasn't pouting," he sneered, running past Matt to jump off the top of the mountain rolling in the powdery snow. Matt shook his head hearing Vincent squeal in glee.

Matt inspected the cleaning job he did on the blades, placing them back in its sheath. Hearing footsteps approach, he grabbed his blades and started to stride toward the mouth of the cave. He smirked seeing Jet's silhouette in the green neon glow. Scarlett noticed Matt approach them before she placed her weapon away and lunged toward him. Jet laughed, watching her slip on the slippery snow, and falling on top of Matt.

Jet followed her out of the cave amused to see that Marr had caught her fall. He arched an eyebrow seeing Scarlett's face flush before Matt climbed to his feet, extending his hand to her. She accepted the offer stumbling to her feet dusting the snow from her skin. Noticing her shivering, Matt removed his sweatshirt holding it out to her. "Thank you," she mused, pulling the sweatshirt on comforted by the warmth it provided.

Jet noticed the moon peeking out behind the clouds as night fell illuminating the white snow. "I wonder why Ari chose this place when it just gives Matt an advantage?" Scarlett inquired, not seeing Matt glance up at the moon.

"Ari has a reason for everything she does. I'm sure there's a hidden reason for this location," Jet replied, noticing the sigh of relief from Matt. Matt nodded in agreement seeing Scarlet's gaze distracted admiring the blue firelight on the hill to their right.

"Why don't we take a rest and you can both inform me of what you've encountered so far?" Matt suggested, taking Scarlett's hand sensing her apprehension of traveling in the snow. Jet followed Matt's lead trekking up a small hill leading up to a circle of boulders with a fire pit in the center. Jet took a seat on one of the benches carved out of ice.

Jet snickered seeing Scarlett nearly fall in Matt's also taking a seat beside Jet. Mesmerized by the blue flames, Scarlett was surprised by the warmth the fire emitted rubbing her hands to get warm. "Have either one of you encountered any of the other slayers?" Matt asked, amused to see Scarlett entranced by the fire.

"I ran into Raven before crossing paths with Jet and he ran into Dawn. Both learned why it's wise not to piss off Ari," Scarlett replied, laughing at hearing Raven scream when she fell into the chasm. Jet informed Matt of what happened to them both seeing the curious expression on his face. "Wasn't Vincent with you Matt? We heard him laughing down the mountain," she added, swatting Matt's hand seeing him trying to poke her in the ribs.

Matt smirked, reaching for her hand, resting his cold fingers against her arm watching her squirm. "Yes, he seemed to have beaten me up the mountain, then grew impatient that I slew the mobster before he had the chance," he replied, seeing how tired Jet was from the physical strain of the curse.

Jet stared up at the mountains behind them trying to be more aware of his surroundings. "You know a lot about the area. Was this a place you've visited before?" Jet asked, amused to see that he had piqued Scarlett's interest.

Matt sighed, catching Scarlett staring at him waiting to hear his answer. "Jet's assumption is correct. There used to be a small collection of huts at the bottom of this mountain. I was abandoned up here in hopes that the cold elements would kill the monster that plagued the village," he explained, bending to gather a mound of snow in both hands.

Scarlett rested her head on Matt's shoulder, watching him fidget with the snow. "People fear the things they can't understand and, assuming they're capable of monstrous things instead of admitting they could be wrong," Scarlett noted, thinking back on what she had read in Isabel's journal.

Jet watched Matt freeze the powder snow molding it into a crystal star before offering it to Scarlett. She smiled holding the star into the moonlight watching the white light reflect off its clear surface. "Why did the village blame you? Did something happen to make them fear you?" Jet asked, sensing there was more to the story.

Matt clenched his fists in anger thinking of the rim memories. "That's none of your damn business, Jet. If you ask me again, I'll make you face your fear," Matt growled, climbing to his feet walking away from the fire pit. Scarlett stumbled to her feet pocketing the star and chased after Matt.

Scarlett closed the distance between them nearly falling on him once more. She reached for his hand gently grasping it in hers intermingling their fingers. "Matt, wait!" she called, peering over his shoulder down into a stairwell of steps carved out of ice descending down the cliff they were standing at. "I'm sorry. It's obvious that Jet struck a nerve. I want to help, but you need to let me in," she pleaded, reaching up to cup his face moving to brush his hair off his damp cheek.

Matt closed his eyes comforted by the warm caress. "I need to show you something first for it to make sense," he whispered, opening his eyes, and taking in a deep breath. He reached for her hand leading her to the side of the cliff covered in soft snow. He molded the snow into a sleigh and took a seat in the center pulling her onto his lap. He instructed her to cross her legs in an Indian style and wrap her arms around his waist.

Once situated, he used the wind to push away from the hilltop sending them racing down the snowy hill. Matt laughed hearing her cry out in alarm before resting her head against his shoulder screaming in delight. They tumbled in the snow with Matt landing on top of Scarlett at the base of the hill. Her eyes met hers smiling impishly wishing that he would kiss her. "Was this what you had in mind?" she whispered, seeing his face flush before shaking his head no and climbed to his feet.

Matt extended his hand to her helping her to her feet, watching her dust the damp snow from her clothes. "No, I wish it were that simple. I just thought this was faster to get you here than carrying you down the cliff," he teased, catching her roll her eyes in response. He waited for her eyes to land on the twisted metal up ahead of them. He rested his hand on her shoulder diverting her gaze.

"I wanted to show you why I keep my demon locked away. I came here as a punishment for his crimes." Matt explained, leading her toward a small metal cage with bolts buried in the snow. Twisted metal rings tethered to chains twisted beside it.

Scarlett stared at the cage in horror unaware that she was trying to reach the cage, yet Matt stopped her from reaching it. *How barbaric to look up an innocent man as if castrated from his home wasn't bad enough*, she thought, glancing up at Matt. "Unless they proved you killed someone, I don't see why they had to lock you up like a deranged animal," she replied, thinking of how kind Matt had been to her over the years.

"They feared a monster that killed an innocent child. At the time I allowed it because I agreed with them. Even though at the time I was also a child I wanted nothing but endless days of pain. I thought over time it would repay my sin and the brown stuff is blood when it hits the snow," he confessed, trying to keep the bleak memories at bay.

January 17, 1980

Mount Evans, Denver, Colorado

A young teen sat underneath a wide Oak next to other trees lining the entrance to the trail up the mountainside. Snow white hair hung over his shoulders as light red eyes stared up at the clear blue sky lost in thought. A pair of black slacks, black sandals, and a short light blue sleeveless tunic adorned his form. A small smirk crossed his lips amused by the quizzical looks cast his way by those passing him on their way through the trail.

Travelers walking up the trail to the Scenic Bay dressed in heavy layers in shades of dark blue and violet with leather boots, wool capes, and wool caps. A snowball sailed through the air hitting him in the face before a small form ambushed him, throwing their tiny arms around his waist. "Mathew!" a young cheerful voice rang, amused to see she had knocked the air from his lungs. The force had knocked his back against the tree harder shaking free mounds of snow from its branches.

Merriment twinkled in the young girl's emerald eyes, accepting her brother's outstretched handshaking the snow from their clothes. Her round cheeks flushed, shaking the snowflakes from her blonde pigtails. A smug smile adorned her face throwing her arms in the air in triumph. The wool cloak held with a snowflake clasp billowed with her movement. "Admit it, I got you," she demanded, smoothing the wrinkles from the knee-length crimson dress with black leggings and black leather boots.

Matt couldn't help but laugh in response watching her inspect her clothing for any more specks of snow. "Becca, can't you greet me in a unique way?" he groaned, finally regaining his breath dusting the snow from his tunic. She smiled, shaking her head but not before watching the strangers pass by them. "Why aren't you at the house helping mom with the shop?" Matt asked, climbing to his feet and grabbed her pigtails with one hand giving them a light tug.

"Matt don't do that," she squealed, swatting his hand away with her gloved hand. "Mom was dealing with the farmer's wife and you know that she hates children. Sometimes, I wish I could have been like you. She fired you because you froze everything," she muttered, seeing him wince in response releasing her hair from his grasp.

"That was an accident and trust me the whipping isn't worth it," he replied, a bitter note in his voice after thinking of the wretched memory. "You should head back before Dad comes looking for you. If he comes home from work and sees you missing, he'll be worried," he insisted, ignoring her pout trying to shoo her back down the trail.

Rebecca's shoulders sank at the idea of wondering if her comment had upset him. "Can't we at least play for a bit, Mattie?" she pleaded, not wanting to head back to the house and be bored. She frowned seeing him hesitate to give her an answer. "No one will see us, and besides, it will be an hour before Dad gets home," she pleaded, slipping her arms around his west burying her face against his leg.

"Rebecca, I don't know—" Matt protested, afraid of getting her in trouble.

"Please? Just this once?" she pleaded, glancing up at him seeing him contemplating the idea. "I just want to see the pretty snow you create. Everyone says that you're a monster, but I don't agree with them," Rebecca added, tightening her grip around his leg in a hugging embrace.

Matt slipped his arms around her gently returning the kind gesture before sighing in defeat. "Very well, Rebecca, you win," he confessed, smiling at hearing her squeal in delight hugging his leg even tighter. He knelt in front of her, meeting her gaze. "We can't do it here in the open. Let's head to the playhouse and I'll make a snow fort," Matt suggested, watching.

Rebecca clapped her hands together and jumped up and down in joy before running down the trail. Laughing, Matt raced after her arrival at the caves North of the barn and farmhouse at the foot of the trail. He ventured inside finding his sister in the main cavern waiting for him. He created a large ball of snow in both hands hitting Rebecca in the back.

Rebecca shrieked in surprise before laughing as she ran for cover. Matt smirked allowing the wind to pick up around him as snow soon covered the cavern floor in a soft white powdery blanket. A snowball hit his face as he ducked hearing it hit the wall behind him. Matt dropped to his knees before crawling toward his sister for a sneak attack. He ended up having a mound of snow dumped on him, followed by a fit of giggles before Rebecca hid once more.

A half-hour later Matt stood leaning against a wall panting for breath. His clothes stained with sweat as he kept his eyes closed, trying to cool down remembering why he no longer played with his sister in the caves.

"Matt?" Becca called, her voice echoing in the distance as he groaned before heading deeper into the caves hoping to find a colder place to rest.

After walking a quarter mile through the caves, he paused again leaning against the wall. The wind had quickened doing little to cool down his body temperature. A rumble vibrated through his abdomen before he collapsed to his knees.

He opened his eyes trying to spot his sister before his stomach lurched again, omitting the few contents in his stomach. He groaned in agony, weakly calling out for his sister before coughing, trying to spew the vile taste from his lungs.

"You shouldn't get overheated so quickly; heat sickness isn't ideal for you," a deep voice mocked in his head, making Matt growl in annoyance.

"Shut up." Matt hissed, wiping his mouth with the back of his hand, feeling his abdomen muscles constrict painfully as laughter reached his ears.

"Or else what? You'll attack yourself again? You can pretend to be normal all you want, but we both know you're just lying to yourself," it teased, laughing again as silence answered Matt's second call for his sister.

Matt shook his head, placing his hands over his ears, moving up to his scalp digging his nails into the flesh thinking that the pain would keep the voice at bay. "I told you to shut up! You're nothing then a figment of my imagination. A being brought on by stress and nothing more," Matt spat, feeling a new burning pain coming from within.

He groaned feeling a fire burning in his veins. "How amusing, I forget how humans need to keep things simplistic. Never believe that there's something else out there in the universe. My dear host, did you think it was normal to summon Winter by mere thought?" it mused, the wind growing stronger mixing with icy bits of hail.

"Did that whore of a mother never mention your sire or what you truly are? I'm your demon Mathew, the source of your power and true nature," it hissed, growing stronger as Matt's nails lengthened cutting into his scalp, his hair growing longer, and his skin turning a light blue tint.

Rebecca had wandered deeper into the cave before pausing to glance behind her shoulder looking for her brother. The icy wind pierced through her cloak making her shiver. She wrapped the wool cloak tighter around her small form thinking she had heard Matt calling out for her. "Mattie?" she called, struggling to walk through the howling wind. She heard Matt crying out in pain slowly making her way to him.

Her eyes widened in alarm, seeing her brother on his knees in a puddle of vomit rocking back and forth with his hands over his ears. She inched closer to him seeing his transformation and blinked wondering if she was seeing an illusion. "Big brother?" she stammered, shocked by the sight before her.

The howling wind roared in her ears, but she staggered closer holding her hand out to him. "Mattie are you, all right?" she asked, hearing a soft cackle before a burst of energy lashed out at her. The energy caught Rebecca off guard pummeling into her chest, knocking her back several steps before slamming her into the wall behind her. She felt a sharp pain in the back of her head not hearing the stone walls crumble down around her.

Matt groaned slowly coming back to the world. He felt tired and his muscles ached to push himself up into a seated position. Shaking snow and debris from himself, he quickly scanned his surroundings. In the distance, he could hear faint voices calling out for him and Rebecca.

His eyes widened in horror realizing that the cave had collapsed. "Becca?" Matt yelled, panic rising in his voice, wincing at the pain it caused to raise his voice. Receiving no answer, he stumbled to his feet scanning the area around him. He was about to call out a second time when he spotted a piece of black fabric sticking out from under a pile of rocks.

"Oh, God… no," he whispered, running over to the pile of rubble collapsing next to it. He dug his hands through the rocks, hurling them over his shoulders ignoring his own pain. He forced an icy wind to aid him, lifting more of the debris out of the way, ignoring the warm blood running down from his nostrils. He cleared the mound finding his sister's limp corpse. He touched her throat with trembling hands and felt no pulse beneath his fingertips. A sob caught in his throat, yet he picked her up gingerly hugging her close to his chest rocking her back and forth.

When he felt Rebecca torn from his arms, he snapped out of his stupor. "I'm sorry, Becca. Please forgive me," he whispered, tears flooding his eyes before blacking out once more.

~~*

Matt's mind broke from the memory, staring at the broken cage before them. "This was my prison. I stayed here until they forgot about me. I had to escape or else die from starvation. When our parents found us in the cave, I had lost it and to them, it sounded like I had murdered my own sister. At the time, I believed them and took their punishments with no complaints," he confessed, taking a pause before resuming.

"My father was so angry he tore off my shirt and whipped me with his belt while dragging me through town to this prison. Before leaving me here, tied up, to rot outside in the sun. At night, they would have a fire going next to me allowing anyone from town to come by and beat me. I created my own water and ate snow allowing myself to last for a week before my powers gave out on me," he explained, recalling the pain he endured all those years ago.

"When I got free, I ran, swearing I would never let the demon out again. I collapsed in a more civilized place, I received treatment and a family took me in who was related to Dawn. I did odd jobs to repay my debt to them until I found Ari and slowly the rest of you," he explained, turning his back on the cage not wanting to think of the nights hot metal had kept him company.

"I'm sorry, I shouldn't have shown you this. I should have kept it to myself, I just thought that was Ari's way of telling me to share when she created this place from my memories," Matt explained, trying to pull Scarlett away.

Chapter Thirty-Two

Scarlett silently listened to his tale thinking of what she had read in her sister's journal, of the village turning on her in hopes of slaying a monster. She rested her hand under his chin, forcing him to look up at her. She noticed the anger in his eyes from recalling the painful memories. "Thank you, for trusting me with that. I know it wasn't easy," she replied, letting him pull her away from the cage and down a path laden with marble pillars.

Small boulders nestled against the pillars to prevent snow from piling up on their path. Ice statues of ravens, wolves, and gargoyles positioned around an ice gazebo with white marble benches. Matt guided her to one of the benches, seeing her mesmerized by the detail of the statues.

"I was confined to that cell for two years until the guards got careless. I waited for one of the guards to get drunk and pass out lying against the bars. He was close enough that I could pick the keys from him. When they realized I was free they tried to stop me, so I froze them having no intention of going back in the cell," Matt explained, watching her admiring the glossy glass of the statues trying to fathom what he had endured.

"At least you were able to find this refuge, something magnificent to help fight back against the darkness," she replied, at a loss for what else to say after hearing the rest of his story. She rested her head against his shoulder reaching up to toy with his hair, inhaling his familiar scent.

Matt smirked seeing that she had found a way to amuse herself. "I stumbled upon it when I was trying to escape. I had hoped to leave this place in the past, but Ari had other ideas," he noted, aware that she was being quietly comforted by his company. "That's enough about me, wasn't there something you wanted to share with me?" he inquired, grabbing her hand preventing her from fidgeting with his hair.

Scarlett blinked, snapping out of her daze by his question. She bit her lower lip hesitant to burden him with what she had learned. "I learned the truth about my past," she noted, seeing that he was listening quietly. "When Andrew found me, I was in the company of vampires who chose to drink from animals. Andrew saw the human child and assumed to slay the monsters," she admitted, prying her hand free, removing the picture from her pocket offering it to him.

"The vampire he failed to kill was Donovan, who had to watch the woman he loved die. A journal was left to me detailing the events leading up to that day, and that the girl who was cataloging the events was my older sister Isabelle," she confessed, watching him admiring the picture before handing it back to her.

Matt could hear the ache in her voice when talking about her sister. "It looked like you two were close, though if I had known, I would have tried to make a connection between you and Donovan sooner. I'm sorry, you lost your sister but I'm glad you ended up at our door," he confessed, seeing that despite his sweater she was still cold. He removed his trench coat, slipping it over her shoulders revealing his bare muscled chest.

Scarlett smiled, slipping her arms through the jacket trying not to stare at his bare chest. She coughed clearing her throat and glanced at her hands. "The journal helped me get to know her better than I might have otherwise. Still, it must have hurt Donovan remembering the past," she noted, pulling the jacket tighter around herself trying to keep warm.

Matt smirked seeing that her cheeks flushed scarlet. "He knew that since you were alive, he would have the chance to meet you one day and share his memories of your sister with you. I'm sure he has some good memories to share with you of your sister," Matt suggested, speaking of experience failing to admit the real reason he had kept the cage, to remind himself of the danger his other form was capable of.

Scarlett sensed the bitter note to his answer, wondering if it was meant for himself rather than to her. The snow fell silently around them melting in her hair sending a shiver through her spine despite the warmth the jacket provided. "What did you mean when you said you were glad, I ended up with you guys? Do you think our paths wouldn't have crossed if Andrew didn't find me?" she pressed; aware he had sidestepped her question.

Comforted by the silence that had fallen between them, forgetting that they were in the course drafted by Ari. Matt blinked baffled by her question not understanding what she was looking for. Scarlett laughed, tilting her head to glance up at him, her lips inches from his. She arched an eyebrow hearing the soft growl emit from his chest. "Your kind, stubborn, a fast learner, impulsive—" he replied, shocked by feeling her warm lips brush against his.

He deepened the kiss feeling his other half take overgrazing her lower lip with his teeth breaking the skin. Frightened of it taking full control, he pushed Scarlett away knocking her to the ground. Scarlett felt the powdery snow brace her impact but stared up at Matt in confusion. "I'm sorry," he whispered, reaching out for her hand helping her to her feet.

"I should be the one to apologize, I overstepped my boundaries. I thought you felt the same as me," she stated, turning to head back the way they had come. Matt climbed to his feet grabbing her arm and turned her around to face him.

Matt cupped her cheek in his hand brushing away the snowflakes. "At first, I didn't notice it until my demon side came out to protect you. It looks like a wolf form, so it only comes out when it wants to protect someone. It's the other reason I've kept you at arm's length. I could easily lose control and hurt you," he replied, moving his hand to wipe the small drop of blood in the corner of her lower lip.

Scarlett couldn't help but smile still baffled by his confession. "I know you would never hurt me. Maybe if you allowed me to see it, I could help you control it," she suggested, thinking that she had never seen that side of him. She saw the fear flicker once more in his eyes afraid of hurting her.

Matt could hear the demon laughing at the anxiety of letting the demon reign control. He felt Scarlett's hand rest on his shoulder squeezing it lightly. He took in a shaky breath turning his back to her, "I would say no, but since you can't get hurt here," he explained, thinking of the girl's fate of the last person he had presented the demon to in such close proximity

White fur grew to spread out over his arms and legs while his skin turned blue. His teeth sharpened and lengthened turning into a set of canines with a pair of fangs. His eyes turned to a deep shade of reddish-black before his ears curved shaping into canine ears, poking out of his hair. His hands elongated adding blue claws to both his hands and feet. Matt stood there frozen inhaling the fragrant cherries in her hair from her shampoo.

Scarlett noticed his head bend and his arms shaking afraid to turn back and face her. She slipped her arms around his waist feeling him tense up under her touch. "You don't have to worry about frightening me. I'm not going anywhere," she reassured him, turning him to face her moving her arms to coil around his neck. Pulling him towards her, she brushed her lips against his tenderly. A low growl rumbled in his chest, grabbing her hair pressing her lips harder against hers before pushing her onto the snow once more.

Matt's hands moved to grab both of her wrists pinning her beneath him. She moaned softly feeling his teeth graze her neck before meeting her waiting lips again. Her breathing labored feeling his tongue coil with hers. She tried pushing him off to catch her breath feeling his hands shift holding both arms in a cross above her head, while his other hand tugged at her shirt. Her cheeks flushed hissing in pain at straining her injured shoulder, forcing Matt to revert to his human form.

"I'm sorry, sometimes it can be hard to control it," Matt whispered, kissing her forehead before sitting up, pulling her into his lap. Scarlett rested against his chest fixing her shirt, unaware that he had returned the jacket to rest once more around her shoulders.

She smiled, kissing his cheek, seeing the fear in his eyes. "You don't have to apologize. I'm not afraid. I know you would never hurt me," she replied, seeing him frown failing to believe her words.

Matt let out a frustrated sigh seeing that there was no way of changing her mind. He watched new snowflakes fall dusting his bare skin in an icy comfort. "You may not be afraid of it, but I would be a fool not to be. I can't underestimate it and let it wreck any more carnage," he whispered, not informing her that her statement had amused the demon.

Scarlett patted his arm gently aware that he feared the past repeating itself. "We'll just have to be careful and take things one day at a time," she replied, respecting his hesitation not wanting to push things and make him regret his decision.

He nodded in agreement clutching her hand and brushing his lips gently against it. "We have wasted enough time here. We should return or else Jet may come looking for us," he noted, pulling her up with him as he climbed to his feet. He shook the snow from his skin and offered her his hand. Taking his hand, they retreated the path they had taken hearing an owl hoot in the distance.

Scarlett couldn't help but let a sly grin creep onto her face, aside from Ari, she had been able to earn his trust/ She opened her mouth to ask if they should inform the others of their new relationship, but frowned seeing the icy flight of stairs approach. Matt stepped beside her and placed his hands around her waist scooping her up in his arms.

Scarlett slipped her arms around his neck getting him to carry her in a firemen's grasp bounding effortlessly up the stairs. Reaching the top of the hill, Matt placed her down before taking her hand, as they retreated to the fire pit where they had left Jet.

Chapter Thirty-Three

Jet watched them walk off toward the cliffside of the mountain. *I'm sure it'll make Ari happy to see she was able to push them together,* he thought, seeing the blue flames fading to smoldering embers as the sun dipped behind the clouds once Dusk settled. *I wonder if I should press n without them, or wait for them to get back?* He thought, unaware of how much time had passed.

He heard a rustling near the mouth of the cave thinking that he and Scarlett had failed to spot any creatures in the cave. He arched an eyebrow sensing magic emitting from the sound, aware it was trying to gain his attention. Drawing his pistol, he took a few tentative steps toward it, before lowering his weapon making Vincent's shadow. "Oh, it's just you. I felt a strange magic coming from the caves despite having come through them a brief time ago with Scarlett," he confessed, putting his gun back in its hoister no longer feeling a threat.

Vincent snickered amused to hear that despite the course they were in; Jet was willing to lower his guard. Holding one hand behind his back he waved at Jet, clutching the bundle of twine makeshift net. Jet took another step toward Vincent feeling a warm bubble of air wash over him. His eyes glazed over as the magical trance took hold of him, magic pulling his legs like the strings of a puppeteer. The soothing chant that he had been whispering grew into a bellow. Jet freely removed his weapons and moved closer to the net, until Vincent slipped it around Jet.

Vincent found a tree to tie the netting to suspending the net in the air. He stopped the Latin chant shattering the trance. Jet's eyes widened in alarm feeling the magic dissipate as the gentle breeze rocked the netting. Frantic at his situation, he searched his pockets for a knife not finding his dagger.

Hearing laughter to his right Jet cursed seeing Vincent doubled over in a fit of laughter. Jet grasped the netting in both hands trying to tear it, forcing a hole wide enough to slip through. He cursed feeling his skin rub raw causing blisters in the form on his skin. His palms began to sweat in the restricted space. "All right, Vincent. You've had your fun, now let me go!" he demands, feeling his lungs tighten as his heartbeat began to quicken.

Vincent reached for the dagger standing beside the net and staring up at Jet waving the dagger tauntingly. "But I'm having too much fun watching you squirm. I mean isn't the entire point of the course is to assess us against our fears?" he inquired, falling to hear Matt and Scarlett approach.

Jet spat in Vincent's direction aware that he had a point. He closed his eyes fighting back bitter memories of a dark cavern with bright bursts of light from explosions. "Why are you tormenting Jet that way?" Scarlett demanded, stepping around Vincent, and reaching for her dagger. Vincent tried to push her away, halted by Matt.

She sawed through the twine cutting a hole large enough for Jet to fall through. He crashed to the ground accepting Scarlett's offered hand to climb to his feet. His cheeks flushed with shame at falling to free himself. Vincent smiled sheepishly offering him his weapons back, his fun ruined by Scarlett. Jet placed his hoister back around his shoulder securing the pistole to it and lunged at Vincent. He punched him square in the face, giving him a black eye, fueled by anger and humiliation.

Scarlett laughed seeing Vincent clutching his hand over his swollen eye sulking as the pain flared up the side of his face. He glanced at Matt for help seeing Jet's fists clenched tightly at his sides. "Vincent must have been bored, I haven't seen him use that ability in a long time," Matt mused, seeing Scarlett stare at him in confusion.

Vincent regarded Jet cautiously surprised by the violent outburst. "Think of it as a type of compulsion like what vampires possess but on a smaller scale," Vincent recommended, stepping behind Matt, using him as a shield. He was afraid to admit Matt was right and confess the joy he got from tormenting Jet. "I'm surprised Ari didn't train you against that spell," he mused, hearing Jet muttering more curses in his direction.

Matt smirked hearing the curses thrown at Vincent aware that they wouldn't take effect while they were in Ari's course. "I'm afraid Vincent has a point, Jet," he remarked, placing a hand on Jets' shoulder to steady him, seeing him shake with rage. "I merely mean to point out that Ari should offer guidance or a charm against such spells," he added, seeing Jet nod curtly before shaking his hand away.

"I will take your advice under consideration," Jet glared, taking a step toward the cliff to see Scarlett take a step toward him. She was clearly still concerned seeing the stress he had endured while trapped in the net. He held out his hand, causing her to pause. "Just stay with them, Scar. I need some time to myself, although I appreciate the concern," he noted, over his shoulder before quickening his pace to descend down the snowy hillside to reach his last area.

Matt rested his hands around her waist pulling him against his chest, watching her trying to follow Jet with her eyes. "We should respect his decision and let him come to us when he is ready," he whispered, kissing the top of his head aware that she wanted to comfort her friend. "I've learned it's unwise to cross magical users. Vincent is lucky to have Jet just beginning to learn the craft," he added, loud enough for Vincent to hear him.

Vincent let out a nervous laugh more afraid of gaining Ari's wrath while teaching Jet how to enact revenge with magic. He bent over scooping up a mound of snow in one hand and molding it into a small tight puck. He placed it over his swollen eye gesturing for Matt to lead the way. Matt released his grasp on Scarlett's waist and gently turned her to the other hill to their left. He reached for her hand intertwining his fingers with hers. "There's a cave we haven't explored yet on the bottom of the hill. I'm sure Ari has a surprise lurking inside," he advised, letting Vincent run ahead of them.

Scarlett's shoulders tensed at the idea of exploring the unknown area. She stared down at her feet, careful not to trip and take Matt down with her. Sensing her unease Matt squeezed her hand causing her to glance up at him. They slowly descended the side of the hill letting Matt lay more of the soft powder snow over the icy steps.

Matt helped her descend the hill pausing in their tracks. "It seems like Vincent grew impatient to wait for us to join him. Though what's wrong? You seem anxious?" Matt asked, no longer seeing Vincent ahead of them having already embarked through the caves at the base of the hillside.

Scarlett bit her lower lip, shaking her head defiantly. She noticed the flash of lights beyond the caves where it led to a forest. She wondered if that was the marker to end the course. She glanced at her feet sensing Matt waiting or her to answer his question. He placed his fingers underneath her chin tilting her head up to meet his quizzical gaze. "You've survived the worst of the course, so what are you afraid of?" he pressed, sensing she was ashamed of her answer.

Scarlett opened her mouth feeling her cheeks flush with shame. She dusted the snowflakes from her jacket not finding the words to express what she felt. "Ever since that run-in with Simon... I feel powerless. I feel like I can't defeat him on my own," she whispered, closing her eyes, feeling them fill with tears.

Matt placed his arms around her, holding her in a tight embrace kissing the stray tears. "You're not powerless otherwise you wouldn't have made it this far in the course," he reassured her, kissing her cheek seeing her offer him a weak smile. She opened her mouth to protest, met with his lips. "Besides, you won't be facing the caves alone," he added, taking her hand, and approaching the mouth of the nearest cave.

Matt pulled Scarlett behind him watching her reach for her dagger. He removed his twin crescent blades from the sheath on his back taking a tentative step forward. Scarlett followed his lead resting one hand on his shoulder letting her eyes adjust to the darkened cavern. Water dripping from the ceiling echoed in the eerie silence. Matt threw one of the blades in a wide arc, like throwing a frisbee, watching it sail through the shadows before it returned to his open palm.

Once Matt's blade had returned to his hands, the shadow had turned into a solid figure and tried to lunge toward Matt. Matt pushed Scarlett forcing her to roll to her right dodging a second shadow that had appeared. Matt rolled to the left after releasing the blades again. One blade sliced through the shadow embedded into the granite wall behind it. The vampire had pushed the shadow in front of it, using it as a shield, before ducking low avoiding the blade.

It grabbed the blade in both hands howling in pain and used it to fuel its rage. It lunged at Matt ramming into his shoulder pushing him into the wall behind him. Scarlett drew her dagger and lunged at the vampire to parry the attack. She did not see the third shadow appear until it grabbed her leg and threw her over its shoulder. She whimpered out in pain landing on her injured shoulder hearing her arm crack from the pressure breaking in half.

Her vision blurred feeling tears well in her eyes from the pain. She smirked hearing more shadows cry out in pain as Matt's blades sliced through them like butter. Scarlett faintly made out his white hair illuminated in the dark cave. She heard him ask if she was okay after the sound of bones shattering had liberated through the cavern.

Gritting her teeth in pain, she fumbled in her pocket feeling around for the last grenade. Tugging on the ripcord she gave a warning to Matt before throwing it toward his voice. She smirked seeing the flash filling the cave with white light.

Matt rolled to the right upon hearing Scarlett's warning. He smirked hearing the last remaining shades growl in agony burning from the flash of light. Seeing that there were no more shades he closed the distance between them. Placing the blades back in its sheath on his back, he knelt beside Scarlett. "How's your shoulder holding up?" he inquired, resting his hand on her knee.

Scarlett placed her hand over his letting him hoist her to her feet. He slipped his arm around her waist seeing her stagger. "I'm hoping that once we leave the course the pain will pass," she whispered, using the back of her hand to wipe away the ears.

Matt kissed her cheek leading them both out of the cave facing the entrance of the woods. White spruce trees kissed the horizon. "You should be proud of yourself. You were able to push through your fears and the pain from the injury," he noted, seeing her nod in agreement seeing the portal open between two spruce trees. They paused in front of the portal before Matt tilted her chin up capturing her lips in a tender kiss before letting her stumble through the portal. He informed her that he still had an area of the course to explore.

Chapter Thirty-Four

Scarlett exited from the portal, hearing the familiar voices of Raven and Dawn bickering with Andrew. Ari chanting in the Gaelic manta that powered the spell before her vision cleared. She shoved Andrew's hand away realizing that he had his arms around her waist preventing her from falling.

Her nose wrinkled in disgust hearing Raven laughing at Andrew's failed attempt to get on Scarlett's good graces. "I know the smell is revolting. We keep trying to persuade him to take a shower—" Raven replied, interrupted by Dawn swooning.

Dawn patted the empty seat beside her for Andrew to join her aware that Raven was keeping her distance from him. "I think it's sweet, he wanted to wait for Scarlett to return from the course," she addressed, frowning at hearing Scarlett sigh in annoyance. She glanced back down at her new book, *Little Women* by Louisa May Alcott.

Raven smirked seeing the look of revulsion flicker on Scarlett's face before glancing over at the board in front of Ari. "It seems like Matt is the only one left in the course, though I would have thought he'd be the first to complete it," she remarked, seeing Andrew arch an eyebrow in surprise having assumed he had been the first to return as well.

Scarlett noticed that both Raven and Dawn had changed into more comfortable clothing and figured she would do the same. She didn't want to be in range for the pissing contest over her when Matt returned. She started to head toward the staircase to take a shower yet was 0blocked by Andrew standing with his arms crossed. "Can I help you?" she sneered, annoyed that he wasn't letting her pass.

"Don't you want to share with us how it went?" he asked, finally noticing that she was wearing Matt's jacket. She shook her head no and tried to step around him once more, this time trying to use her uninjured shoulder to brush him aside.

Raven could hear the gravel in Andrew's voice as she too noticed the leather jacket draped over Scarlett's shoulders. She poked Dawn's shoulders waiting for her to glance up from her book before pointing over at the pair. "Don't look now, but I think Andrew is about to lose his cool," she whispered, climbing to her feet moving to wedge herself in between them.

Scarlett offered her a nod of thanks watching her grab Andrew's arm and pull him back toward the sofa. "I'm sure Scarlett will share with us what happened when she's ready," she pleaded, hearing him curse under his breath but allowed her to drag him back to the sofa. Scarlett scurried up the stairs anxious to grab a quick shower.

Andrew followed Raven back to the sofa heaving his shoulders shaking with rage. He slapped Raven's arm away and stormed into the kitchen. The force knocked her back forcing her to stumble backwards a few steps catching her foot on the lip of the carpet falling backwards and landing on top of Ari. Dawn rose to her feet offering Raven her hand not seeing the blood pouring from Ari's nose.

Scarlett had climbed the first two steps and nearly fell overwhelmed by the wave of magic that flooded through the manor. Jet raced from his room at the end of the hall and knelt beside Ari. Matt stumbled through the portal with tattered clothing covered in bloodstains. Matt offered Scarlett a weak smile seeing the look of concern at his disheveled appearance.

Jet extracted a handkerchief from his pocket gently dabbing at the blood running down her face feeling the magic in the room fading. Her eyes flew open widening in fear as her breathing labored. She gripped the edges of the board tightly afraid they had lost Matt. Jet rested his hand over hers and squeezed it lightly. "The storm has lifted," he whispered in Latin. raising his voice. "You can relax, we all made it out alive," he added, sweeping his hand over the circle of salt breaking the spell. Relief flooded her face collapsing her head against Jet's shoulder.

The wave of magic had forced Dawn to stumble back onto the sofa. Raven saw that once Jet ensured Ari, she was pressing her forehead to the cool hardwood floor to ground herself, he turned his head away to vomit. Scarlett ran into the kitchen to fetch a mop and bucket hearing Dawn squeal in disgust. Scarlett accepted Matt's help to clean up the mess while she helped Jet to the sofa handing him a glass of water.

Jet's face flushed with embarrassment nodding his head in thanks. He flinched, opening his mouth to warn Raven, seeing her shake Ari's shoulder gently. "Ari, I'm sorry. It was an accident—" she stammered, afraid of earning the girl's wrath aware of what she was capable of.

Shadows flickered across Ari's face runes spreading down her arms, her eyes blank and emotionless. The magic turned toward Raven sending her hurling across the room. Raven cried out in alarm feeling her back slam into the wall Ari stood there frozen allowing the magic to gather around her in a wild wind.

Matt set the mop aside once finished with his task. He sensed magic building in the air as Raven sat huddled against the wall afraid of what to do next. Matt closed the distance between them and stepped in front of Ari to face her. He allowed his magic to create a shield of ice around them having her magic. "Arianna, that's enough! Control yourself, do not make me hurt you to protect the others," he growled, placing his hands on her shoulders allowing the cold touch to snap her out of her trance.

Ari blinked a few times, shivering and shoving Matt's hands off her shoulders, seeing the ice cage around them. "Matt, what's going on? Is the ritual finally over?" she whispered, collapsing while the cage shattered, as Matt was quick to catch her placing her gently on the sofa.

Jet moved to sit on the edge of the sofa beside her, resting his hand on her knee relieved to see that the red runes had left her skin. "What the hell just happened? Why did Matt address you as Arianna?" he pressed, watching Scarlett retrieving the mop to clean up the puddles of water from the shards of melted ice.

Andrew moved to extend his hand to Raven, seeing that she was still huddled leaning against the wall. She accepted his hand climbing to her feet wiping dust from her clothes. "Matt you need to reprimand her for what she did. What I did was an accident, no need for her to turn into a psychopath," she sneered, ensuring that Dawn wasn't hurt seeing that she was still shaken by what happened.

"Raven, not now what Ari did was an accident, a backlash from the ritual being interrupted. She was a vessel for the unchecked magic which wanted to harm the one responsible. You know that Ari has never used her magic against us, so why would she start now," Matt warned, walking over to where Dawn sat placing his hand on her shoulder to calm her nerves.

Ari sat with her head resting in her hands hearing Jet's question. "That's my name though no one has called me it in an exceptionally long time. Why won't anyone answer my question, what is Raven accusing me of?" she asked, not understanding why Raven was mad at her before catching Matt's words. "Wait, does that mean the barrier's down?" she asked, her voice laced with fear before stumbling to her feet realizing they were all in danger with it down.

Jet reached out for her hand gently pulling her back down to the sofa. "There's no indication that the barrier isn't still intact, but the backlash of magic was strong enough to weaken it," he warned, understanding her fear, thinking she managed to ensure their safety.

Dawn patted Matt's hand offering him a weak smile reassuring him that she was fine. "Raven, you didn't want to be punished for your mistake, so why allow Ari to be punished for repeating your actions?" she protested, smiling seeing Raven roll her eyes unwilling to admit that Dawn was right.

"If the barrier is weakened, do we need to reinforce it?" Vincent asked, standing in the doorway thinking it had been Ari's intention to repair the damage that had been done.

Matt sighed seeing that Jet was the only reason Ari was still sitting instead of heading outside. "I think Raven interrupted the ritual and your magic was in the driver's seat, which reminded me why I never piss you off. I know little about the spells used to create the barrier. Ari this is your area of knowledge what must be done?" he asked, squeezing Dawn's shoulder before walking over to Scarlett to stand beside her.

"I don't recall any of that though if I hurt you Raven, then I'm sorry. You should know that I consider this place my home and would never use my gifts in a negative manner," she explained, taking a deep breath to calm her nerves thinking that she would focus later on why her blackout bothered her so much. "We need to remove the remains of the old barrier and build a new one. Jet in my room are bags made in the colors of the four elements, can you go get them for me?" she asked, glancing at Vincent and the girls taking stock of what their next steps would be.

Jet nodded in agreement squeezing her knee gently before climbing to his feet. An awkward silence filled the room as Vincent cracked his knuckles agreeing to Matt's notion of never earning the girl's wrath.

"When Jet returns and I return from the basement we will create two groups. Some will go with Jet, and he'll enchant the bags before being buried in the four corners of the property. They shouldn't be hard to find since the original bags are still there and need to be replaced. The others will be collaborating with me to create the barrier," she explained, turning to face Dawn and Raven. "Neither one of you completed the course and stepping outside will remove any protections. I can offer you items to aid you, or you can stay inside—the choice is yours," she told them, seeing the anger flicker in Raven's eyes.

Raven glared at Ari still not believing the magical whiplash had been entirely an accident. "Be in denial all you want, but you had to know the risks we were vulnerable to when crafting the spell if it was that strong in the first place," she sneered, storming off to her room.

Dawn moved to go after her when she saw Andrew close the distance between them resting his hand on her shoulder. "Stay here and do what you can to help. I'll go check up on her, since I need to go take a shower anyway," he noted, seeing her nod in agreement offering him a weak smile.

She glanced at Ari tucking a loose strand behind her ear. "What kind of items did you have in mind? I want to do what I can to help, not add to your concerns," she admitted, taking in a shaky breath pushing aside her fears.

Jet returned with the bags she had mentioned hearing Dawn's question holding up a black bag he had snared from Ari's room. Inside was a simple talisman of a silver pendant etched with a pentagram. "I figured with working that close to your magic they may need a shield," he admitted, handing one out to Dawn and Scarlett. Scarlett thanked him tying the metal chain around her wrist clutching it tightly in her palm. She watched Dawn turn the pendant around in her hands before placing it around her neck.

Chapter Thirty-Five

Vincent continued to crack his knuckles, cracking his neck, shifting his weight from one foot to the other. He flashed Jet an impish grin hearing him groan in annoyance hoping that Ari would give him his orders growing impatient.

Ari smiled, disappearing before returning wearing her blue cloak the hood pulled up over her head as a small bag was grasped in her left hand. "This should work we have two groups of three though sorry Matt, seeing how Andrew ditched us you'll have to be the mutt that digs up the goods. I figured you, Jet, and Vincent could take care of the corner stones while we go the center and cast the barrier," she explained, knowing that they would keep Jet from harm.

Matt groaned hearing the snickers in the room. He opened his mouth to defend himself only to stop hearing the demon's comment in his head. "How are you not an animal, you turn into a human wolf remember? Just think if you finish the task quick enough your mate will give you a treat though you humans call it sex?" his demon asked Matt Innocently. "That doesn't make me a mutt and no, my interactions with Scar aren't considered as treats," he muttered to himself, not realizing he was speaking aloud.

Dawn couldn't help but laugh seeing Scarlett's face flush darkly. "I'm not even going to ask what that meant," she noted, taking Vincent's hand leading him outside who protested wanting to ask Matt his question. "That's cute, he has a code name for sex," Vincent yelled, letting Dawn drag him outside.

Scarlett covered her face with her hands feeling her cheeks blush brighter. "Please tell me Vince was wrong. I take it your remark was directed at your demon?" she asked, hearing his footsteps move to close the distance between them moving her hands away from her face.

Matt cursed realizing he had spoken aloud. "This is what happens when you're tired and speak without thinking. Yes, it was directed at my parasite and it called it that not me, though I'm never going to live this down," he groaned, seeing Scarlett smile and shake her head no. "Be careful out there and stay close to Dawn and Ari," he warned, kissing her cheek before calling out to Jet that he would be with him throwing the remains of his shirt in Vincent's face to shut him up.

Scarlett nodded hearing Dawn swoon at the gesture entranced by the taunt muscles in his back as he went to catch up to the others. "I'm not worried, I know Ari won't let anything happen to us," Dawn announced, glancing at Scarlett seeing her frown.

"You're not wrong in your assumption Dawn, but as we witnessed Ari's magic can be unpredictable, so it's wise to be alert," Scarlett warned, seeing Dawn bit her lower lip nodding in agreement as they awaited Ari's instructions.

Vincent ducked letting the shirt fall to the ground as they waited for Matt to join them. "Matt, can you sense where the stones are, so we don't waste time digging for them?" Jet asked, hearing Vincent snicker thinking of more jokes to tell them.

Vincent fidgeted with his pendent smirking at hearing the question. "Can't he just sniff them out like a good little doggie?" he teased, his smile fading after receiving the glare from Matt.
"Vincent. shut up unless you want to be buried by accident. We are all drained from the course some of us had to face real monsters not illusions so choose your words carefully," Matt growled, an arctic wind growing around them. He turned his attention to Jet shaking his head no. "I know some things about magic but only those tied to my powers. Aren't the bags created by Ari, so you should be able to sense her magic if not we can just find the four corners of the manor and just take a shot at it," he suggested, not even giving the demon attention glad that no one could hear it but him.

Vincent rolled his eyes, not afraid of Matt's threat. "You say it like you want to show off your canine skills by burying me in the snow," he teased, hearing Jet groan wondering why they were stuck with him.

Jet removed the amulet he wore around his neck ignoring them both closing his eyes. "Gaia, creator of Earth, aid us in our quest. Guide us toward our stones of protection, so that we may eradicate this disease, by your power, so mote it be," he whispered, opening his eyes letting the magic pull him in the right direction hearing Matt and Vincent fall in step behind him.

"No, not bury you. I would turn you into an ice statue first, knowing you can't die from hyperthermia. What will it take to make you stop pestering me?" Matt asked, following Jet keeping an eye out for anything unusual.

Vincent snickered amused by the plan. "You realize eventually the ice would melt and I would break free?" he replied, holding up his hands defensively hearing him emit a low growl in warning. "I'm not trying to piss you off, I'm just bored," he admitted, seeing Jet pause pointing to a section of the garden where it met the orchard trees. "He found one of the stones. Might as well start digging," he advised, biting his lip to stop himself from encouraging him with treats.

"As painful as it is to admit, Vincent is right. The magic here is the strongest it's been," Jet advised, knowing that if Vincent kept pestering Matt he would snap.

Matt sighed seeing them both staring at him. "Fine though there's a shovel next to that orchard tree if you wish to take Vincent with you to search for the next section or are you both expecting me to dig up all four stones?" he asked, allowing his hands to transform.

"What a good little wolf you are, you must really wish for those rewards once you finish doing the dirty work," his demon called out in glee.

"I don't know which one of you is worse. Though unlike Vincent, I can never shut you up." He groaned, whispering the words under his breath, kneeling in the dirt before he started digging up the earth allowing the work to drown out his demon's laughter.

Vincent arched an eyebrow hearing Matt talking to himself. "Are you going to share with us what it said, seeing how amusing his last comment was?" he asked, glaring at Jet hearing him instruct Vincent to retrieve the shovel from the garden shed.

Jet waited for Vincent to roll his eyes and obey walking toward the shed. "Man, the demon sounds more annoying than Vincent. How has it not driven you insane?" Jet asked, trying to focus on the magic to guide them toward the next location as Vincent returned with a shovel.

Matt switched the bags with Jet before placing the dirt back, packing down the Earth to ensure it wasn't disturbed. "Usually it stays silent or I can force it to behave, but when I'm tired or overheated its chain becomes loose enough to bug me. Sometimes it even tries to take control to create its own form of chaos but that's a rare occurrence," he explained, ignoring Vincent's question.

Jet whispered another version of the mantra he had spoken earlier pointing to the front of the house where the gate outlined the perimeter of the manor. He ordered Vincent to run up ahead and start digging. "It seems your earlier hunch of where the stones were hidden was correct, though trying to regain control over the demon seems taxing in itself," he noted, directing Vincent on where to dig, giving Matt a break.

"It can but you know that all forms of magic come with a cost, and this is mine, even if I never asked for it. I'm sure we could all use some rest once this is over. Speaking of magic, there's another reason for the barrier and why Ari never leaves the manor," he explained, thinking that Jet had a right to know.

Jet took the shovel from Vincent to smooth over the pulse of dirt he had dumped over the hole thanking Gaia for her help. He handed the shovel back to Vincent giving him the location of the third stone. He wiped the dirt off his hands on his pants nodding in agreement. "Yeah and sometimes the cost of magic can be too high, though isn't the barrier to protect us from being ambushed by the supernatural?" he asked, walking to the other side of the gate to collect the stone.

Matt picked the bag up, adding it to the first one. "Of course, its main goal is to create a wall to prevent anything with evil intent from entering our home but there's a second key to the wards. Admit it, you're not a bit curious on what occurred earlier when the barrier came down? I wasn't lying when I said magic took a hold of her, I just didn't clarify on the source of magic. What you saw tonight was Arianna with her magical binds removed," Matt explained, ignoring his demon that was telling him to shut up.

Jet frowned thinking that Matt was just confirming his fears. "Wait, so you mean to tell me that the barrier keeps those binds in place? The magic was intense, and it's not something I would wish to experience again," he admitted, tightening his grip on the pendent feeling his hands shake.

Vincent placed his hand on Jet's shoulder seeing that the color had drained from his face. "We only have one more to go, you're doing an excellent job," he pressed, reassuring him, and wondering if Jet was pushing himself too hard, unaware that Matt's words had rattled him.

"Vincent's right, we only have one left. We can finish this Vince if you'd prefer to go clean up or you can go keep an eye on the girls?" Matt suggested, waiting for him to leave. "I wasn't trying to scare you, Jet. I was merely explaining the situation. Ari is from the fey court, which is why I rarely use her full name. She has no memory of this. When you arrived with her an incident occurred and she begged me to bind her powers. I did as she asked, placing the bind in the barrier not knowing that over the years the magic would build within the boundary," Matt explained, following Jet to the last stone digging it up allowing Jet to finish the binding.

Jet listened to Matt's explanation understanding that she hadn't kept it from him but had forgotten it had ever occurred. "My memories of that day are hazy as well, but maybe if I share with her what I can recall it might jar something?" he replied, thinking that she had a right to know following the instructions Ari had given him before packing down the Earth thanking Gaia once more for her guidance and protection.

"You're welcome to try, though it will have to wait until they finish creating the new barrier. Come on, let's get cleaned up and wait for them to finish. You did decent work, I'm sure your teacher will be proud of what you did tonight," Matt praised, patting Jet on the shoulder heading for the house.

Jet ran a hand through his hair placing the amulet around his neck. "I'm glad I was able to help. Were the runes we saw covering her flesh the binds you put in place or her magic?" he asked, falling in step beside Matt following him back to the manor.

"It was a result of her magic lashing out trying to destroy the rest of the binds. Raven was lucky, if Ari didn't have any loyalty towards her, I doubt she would have been able to walk away from the attack. It occurred once before though at the time the bastard deserved it. no one should be used as a weapon," he muttered, rubbing at an old scar on his collarbone lost in thought.

"I'm surprised she has any energy left to perform the spell. Like you, it seems to take a toll trying to restrain that amount of magic," he replied, heading to take a shower seeing that Matt was lost in his own thoughts.

"Sometimes we do what we must to protect those we care about, even at the risks of our own health. The bind helps take the magical pressure off her though I'm unsure if that will remain the case afterwards," Matt muttered, heading up to his room to get cleaned up.

Chapter Thirty-Six

Ari led them to the center of the yard coming to a stop as she motioned for them to take a seat. Pulling out a container of salt she walked slowly around them creating a circle clockwise. She placed four bowls in the corners one full of water, one of incense, one of sand, and the last a red candle which she lit. She stepped inside before closing the circle.

"This may be draining or feel a bit odd and I apologize, but I lack the energy to complete this spell on my own. We will all hold hands while I cast the spell. All you need to do is visualize giant walls rising from the ground. Are there any questions?" she asked, glancing over at Dawn and Scarlett.

Dawn and Scarlett both sat on the ground crossing their legs underneath them. Dawn watched Ari create the circle of salt in awe before asking what the items in the bowls were for. Scarlett coughed trying not to laugh before explaining that the different items symbolized the four elements, which would help empower the spell. "Should we both try to picture the walls made of the same material, would that kind of detail affect the spell?" Scarlett asked, her eyes watching the flame flicker in the wind.

"No, you can create the walls out of any material you desire so long as your intent is behind it. You want the walls to be heavy and indestructible to ensure that there are no weak links in the barrier. You can also think of positive words and energies. It will help cut down the negative vibes," Ari explained, holding her hands palms up on her knees.

Dawn nodded in agreement, closing her eyes, smiling at the images that appeared in her mind. Her smile grew feeling the warm sun wash over her face as bright blue flowers surrounded the field she sat on. She glanced across from where she sat seeing dwarves constructing a massive wall made from cement. The warm breeze tickled her neck listening to the birds chirping nearby. She concentrated on the pleasant sounds seeing the men adding layers of mortar and moss to reinforce the structure.

Scarlett intertwined her fingers with Dawn and Ari seeing the goofy grin cover Dawn's face before closing her eyes focusing on her breathing. She pictured the lake surrounded with moonflowers like the picture she had seen hung at the bar. She laid in the grass glancing up at the star lit sky hearing her sister recount stories of their childhood allowing Donovan to construct the wall. He pulled tall oak trees together forming the base before covering it with molten lead waiting for it to cool reinforcing its structure. Once the lead cooed, he covered it with vines of thorns.

Ari glanced at the two girls deciding it was better not to question what images were dancing through their heads. She held their hands before focusing on the magic building up around them. "An tógálaí cumhachtach, iarraim ar do sheirbhísí chun cabhrú linn an chosaint a bhí againn uair amháin a atógáil. Go dtabharfaidh Gaia agus a clann a neart duit ina chruthaithe. Go gcinntíonn bean na coille nach dtéann coyotes agus shifters isteach inár bhfearann. Iarraim ar an bhfear glas duit do chosaint a thabhairt ar iasacht dúinn. B'fhéidir nach dtiocfaidh aon rún mailíseach chun dochar a dhéanamh dúinn trí rith trí do fhearann. Scriosann tinte Lady Bridgit iad siúd a bhfuil croíthe gránna acu agus cuireann Morgana iad chuig a n-áit scíthe dheiridh. Chun buneilimintí uisce, aeir, talún agus tine. A bandia triple agus an dia adharc, coinnigh do leanaí slán agus tabhair misneach dúinn cath a chur ar aon olc nua a chuirfear iallach orainn aghaidh a thabhairt air. Mar sin, luaigh é," (The mighty builder, I call upon thy services to help us rebuild what was once our protection. May Gaia and her children lend you their strength in his creations. May the lady of the woods ensure that no coyotes and shifters enter our domain. To the green man I ask for you to lend us your protection. May no malicious intent come to harm us by passing through your domain. May Lady Bridgit's fires destroy those with wicked hearts and Morgana sends them to their final resting place. To the elementals of water, air, earth, and fire. To the triple goddess and the horn god, keep your children safe and give us courage to battle any new evil we will be forced to face. So, mote it be) Ari spoke, letting her voice grow in volume before reaching the end of her prayer.

She then started singing songs of the wild watching the energy build seeing a wall of green surround the outskirts of their property stopping once the magic became too intense letting off a bright white light.

Ari leaned over blowing out the candle thanking each element before emptying each bowl before breaking the circle. "Thank you both for your help. I doubt I could have completed the ritual on my own," she admitted, fighting the urge to lay back down on the ground and sleep feeling drained from both spells.

Dawn blinked, opening her eyes, offering Ari a weak smile. She reached over painting Scarlett's knee seeing that despite the spell being over her eyes were still closed. "Scarlett, are you okay?" Dawn asked, glancing at Ari in concern seeing the silent tears that had cascaded down Scarlett's cheeks.

Ari reached over grasping both of Scarlett's hands squeezing them tightly trying to snap Scarlett out of her thoughts. "Scar, you did good, thank you for your help," Ari whispered, relieved to see Scarlett blink her eyes open nodding in agreement. She pulled her hands from Ari's wiping the tears hanging her head in shame.

Scarlett ran a hand through her hair letting out a heavy sigh trying to calm down. "I'm glad we were able to help, though you did warn us the magic would be intense," she whispered, feeling Dawn's hand rest on her shoulder, helping her climb to her feet. She offered Dawn a weak smile before they stood on either side of Ari offering her each a hand seeing her shoulders slumped in exhaustion.

Ari glanced at their hands before groaning realizing she had to stand up grasping their hands. She drained the last of the magic from the runes on her cloak to give her the energy to remain standing knowing she could restore the magic later. "I did but it's clear your mind was elsewhere after the ritual was completed. What upset you?" Ari asked, asking Dawn to collect the bowls for her.

Dawn collected the items before running ahead giving them a chance to talk in private. Scarlett slipped Ari's arm over her shoulders as they started to head back to the manor. "During the ritual, I was with Donovan and my sister. It made me sad realizing that it'll never happen, that I don't even know what her voice sounded like," she admitted, knowing that with her eyes red and her cheeks puffy Matt would also inquire about what had upset her.

Ari closed her eyes thinking of how to cheer her up. "I'm sorry, the last thing I wanted was to remind you of things you have lost. When Andrew returned with you and explained the situation Matt was upset. He wanted Andrew to hunt down a demon not kill an entire clan of vegetarian vampires. If it makes you feel better, Andrew's punishment was to get completely waxed by yours truly," Ari replied, trying to make her laugh seeing that it wasn't working. "To be honest, if you want to see your sister you could always ask Matt to use his special ability for you," she suggested, letting out a tired sigh.

Scarlett offered her a weak smile appreciating the effort of Ari trying to cheer her up. "If only you had recorded his torment, I'm sure with all that hair it took hours?" she asked, helping Ari enter through the garage. "The offer to ask Matt is tempting and I'm sure given the moment we shared in the course, he wouldn't hesitate to do it, I just know it's asking a lot from him," she added, aware of the amount of energy it would take to do it.

"Who's to say I don't have a recording and yes it took a week to complete it, but I enjoyed it and that was the point. I still think you should ask; he will agree but Matt knows his powers meaning he knows the best time to use them," she advised, collapsing on the sofa having no intention of moving.

Matt wandered down the stairs glancing over the two girls arching an eyebrow at Scarlett's red eyes. "Is there something I need to know?" he asked, walking over to where she was standing wrapping his arms around her waist.

Jet appeared from the kitchen carrying a mug full of tea. He frowned hearing Matt's question. "I brewed a pot of coffee thinking some might need it when I heard you guys come back in," he admitted, taking a seat beside Ari placing the mug in her hands. "I figured you might be exhausted from the spell and it's faster to unwind than waiting for your charms to recharge," he added, watching Ari inhale the hot liquid.

Scarlett reached for Matt's hand forcing him to remove them from around her waist. She dragged him into the kitchen pouring herself a cup of coffee seeing that he was patiently waiting for an explanation. "You seem just as tired as Ari, and here I was expecting you to pounce on me upon your return," she teased, referring to his earlier comment that had been directed at his demon.

Matt groaned running a hand over his face. "I was hoping only Vincent would tease me for my lapse in mental judgement. I may take you up on that offer later unless you want to do all the work. Are you sure you're, all right?" he asked, making an iced coffee for himself.

"I take it he teased you about it the entire time?" she asked, laughing softly seeing him nod in agreement. She took a sip of her drink following him to the kitchen table, letting him pull her into his lap. "You had a question for me. Sorry, your comment distracted me," she admitted, feeling her cheeks flush feeling his free arm wrapped around her waist.

Matt placed his cup on the table wrapping both arms around her waist. "I think you just don't want to admit the answer. It's clear you were crying, I just want to know what upset you, so I can try to make things better," he admitted, resting his head on top of hers.

Scarlett frowned, closing her eyes, inhaling his familiar scent. She glanced down at her cup trying not to cry once more. "Ari instructed us on what to focus on while visualizing a strong structure to reconstruct the barrier," she explained, gripping the coffee cup tighter taking in a steadying breath. "There's this painting at Don's bar of a meadow filled with moon flowers symbolizing how they met. Donovan was working on the wall while my sister was recounting fun stories of our childhood, at least the ones recorded in her journal," she admitted, feeling his lips brush against her neck gently.

Matt took in a deep breath moving to place his hands over hers squeezing them gently. "I can see why you were crying. You wish to have that as a memory and not a fantasy. I'm sorry that Andrew killed her knowing that he was rogue in his actions that day, since not all supernatural beings are evil. You know I could try contacting her? It would have to wait until Halloween but I'm willing to do it for you," he offered, not wanting to see her upset.

Scarlett released the grip she had on the cup letting his hands cover hers squeezing them lightly. She shifted turning to the side, reaching up to caress his cheek before brushing her lips over his. "Ari had suggested I ask for the same request when I told her what had upset me, but I've seen what toll communicating with the spirits has on you," she admitted, running her fingers through his hair.

Matt sighed, not surprised by her comment. "True, it does take a toll except on that day since the spirits want to cross the divide to speak to loved ones. I won't push you on it, Scar, just think it over before you decide against it. We should go join the others, we need to discuss what occurred tonight with the training," he suggested, kissing her lips gently.

She returned the kiss climbing to her feet before refilling her glass. She took his hand following him back into the living room. Matt took the recliner pulling her into his lap letting her rest her back against his chest. "Scarlett, you seem to be in better spirits, though should I go fetch the others for a group meeting?" Jet asked, seeing Ari push herself up from the sofa fighting off sleep.

Chapter Thirty-Seven

Ari sat up on the sofa blushing upon realizing she had been using Jet's chest as a pillow. "Of course, she's in better spirits. I would be, too, if I had a personal play toy," she whispered, under her breath watching Jet wonder up the stairs.

Scarlett laughed hearing Ari's comment. "It's not like that, Ari, otherwise we would have disappeared upstairs," she replied, glad to see she had gotten some rest. "Matt proposed what you suggested without me having to ask him," she added, seeing Dawn and Raven follow Jet back downstairs.

"Vincent is taking a shower, though Raven can you go ask Andrew to join us?" Jet asked, taking his seat next to Ari, letting Dawn have the other sofa. Raven rolled her eyes but ventured to Andrew's room to inform him of the meeting.

"Yeah right, says the one using our leader as a pillow. I guess we know what you'll be up to later, that's if Matt can stay awake for you," she teased, resisting the urge to lie on Jet again. Jet smirked seeing her shoulders slump clearly still exhausted, before going into the kitchen to make her another cup of tea.

Scarlett rolled her eyes taking a sip of her coffee deciding not to respond to Ari's remark. Vincent jumped clearing the last three stairs trying to gain some attention, yet only received a slow clap from Andrew following Raven into the living room. Vincent frowned sitting on the steps landing fidgeting with his amulet. "I take it you wanted to discuss what happened earlier?" Andrew asked, letting Raven sit beside Dawn before sitting on the floor resting his back against the sofa.

Matt nodded his head seeing that Dawn was using Andrew's shoulders as a footstool. "I wanted your insight on the course and your thoughts about the matter. I know that Vincent also owes Jet an apology," Matt warned, seeing Ari rest her hands on Jet's shoulders once he returned from the kitchen and took his seat beside her placing the cup of tea on the coffee table.

Vincent opened his mouth to retaliate seeing the dirty look sent in his direction. He raised his hands defensively letting the pendant rest against his chest. "The course was designed to force us to face our fears while evaluating our skills. I assumed with all of his training with Ari, that he'd be prepared to ward off the trance, and if not force him to face his fears," he admitted, watching Jet reach for Ari's hand squeezing it preventing himself from lashing out at Vincent.

Scarlett noticed Jet clenching his jaw resisting the urge to get up and hit him again. "Vincent, that doesn't sound like an apology. Even if you thought you were trying to help Jet, you have to admit you went too far," she warned, seeing him shrug his shoulders causing Jet to rise to his feet halted by Ari grabbing his arm.

Ari caught Jet's arm tugging him back onto the sofa. "You're right, Vincent. The course was to evaluate fears, but phobias are a completely different matter. Maybe if you explained your fear it might help them understand," she whispered. knowing that Vincent wouldn't apologize until he was put in his place.

He sat back down letting out a heavy sigh, he gripped the pendant around his neck, feeling Ari reach for his free hand squeezing it gently. "I hate small places. They remind me of my life before coming here, or of what I can remember. My memory is foggy, but I recall being in the military," he explained, gaining another gentle squeeze from Ari as encouragement to continue.

He closed his eyes unable to meet the expecting gazes of the group. "We were investigating a cave where our superiors claimed some terrorists were hiding. During our search, a cave occurred and I was trapped under the rubble," he explained, both hands shaking as he tightened his grasp on the pendant, mind wandering back to the day.

November 10, 1990

Denver, Colorado

Darkness blanketed his surroundings as his lungs filled with fallen dust. He tried adjusting his eyes to the darkness, yet the thick smog burned his eyes and nose. His chest tightened, struggling to draw in a clear breath of air. Dirt and piles of debris weighed his body in place like a ton of bricks. Wheezing puffs of air escaped his aching lungs, as his hands pawed around himself trying to dig out a tunnel. Dirt filled his cubicles tearing at the flesh before his mind began whirling with racing thoughts.

With his muscles growing weary his mind grew fuzzy drifting in and out of consciousness. Feeling the cold metal of his dog tags with the engraving *Lieutenant Jet Daniels* resting against his neck, pushed him to persevere until he broke free of the mound. He laid there gasping in the damp air. Once his breathing leveled out, he tried calling out to his comrades. He coughed, spitting out the mixture of blood and dirt. "Can anyone hear me? This is Lieutenant Jet Daniels, are there any survivors?" he repeated, his voice cracking as he stumbled to his feet.

Silence answered him as a secondary explosion went off knocking him backwards nearing the entrance of the cave. The light from the full moon illuminated the darkened cavern filling him with dread. The bottom of the cave littered with piles of rocks, dirt, and dismembered body parts. His chest still ached where his ribs were broken, yet he expected it to hurt more. His arms covered with bloody scabs, over his cheeks and eyebrows. Baffled by his condition, he wondered how he had survived.

He glanced up at the stars seeking answers yet unsure what questions to ask. A flash of light shot across the sky filing his body with warmth. The source was calling out to him gently nudging him forward. Lured by the energy he staggered forward, placing one foot in front of the other, a slight limp on his right side, yet moved blindly forward for a few miles.

An hour passed before he reached the highway, seeing two figures turning a corner to move off the highway and into the endless miles of cornfields leading up to the mountain trails. He noticed the smaller figure collapse in the tall grass, as the other kneeled beside them in concern. "Hey, are you, all right?" he called, his voice cracking once more as he stumbled forward closing the distance between them.

Drawing closer to the pair, Jet noticed the girl's lips were blue and her arms were trembling despite the heavy wool cloak. Adrian took in the man's disheveled appearance, noticing that his military uniform was torn and stained with blood. Seeing that the mortal was unarmed, he raised his voice. "Keep walking, this doesn't concern you, mortal," he sneered, turning his back to Jet to tend to his sister.

"I can't ignore an injured citizen. Is there someone I can call for aid?" Jet protested, hearing the man sigh in frustration before pulling a gold sheathed dagger from his waistband.

"I've already warned you, mortal. This matter does not concern you," he hissed, his hand resting on the scabbard of a knife hidden in his waistband.

Jet searched his waistband for his pistols and cursed realizing they were gone. He threw up both hands with his palms out flat. "I don't want to fight you. Clearly your friend needs medical aid—" he protested, watching Adrian unsheathe the dagger and take a step toward Jet.

"She is my sister. Now, be on your way," Adrien hissed, pointing the tip of the dagger at Jet's throat.

Adrian lunged at Jet before a flash of light sparked within the space between them. It knocked both men back causing Jet to fall on his back grunting out in pain. Adrian sliced the palm of his hand trying to use his blood to create a barrier to protect himself from the man, yet another light exploded burning his hand, causing him to drop the dagger.

Jet's eyes flickered back to the girl concerned that her skin was growing paler and may be a victim to hyperthermia. "Can't you put your hatred of me aside? Let me help you. I can take you and your sister to a hospital," Jet pleaded, watching the man wrap his bloody palm in his shirt adding pressure to stop it from bleeding.

Adrien's hand stopped bleeding as he bent to retrieve the dagger. He sheathed it and placed it back in his scabbard and moved to kneel beside his sister. He scooped her up in his arms feeling her thin frame shivering from the cold. *I see, so even in this world magic still exists*, Adrien thought, before sighing in defeat. "Very well, lead the way. If you attack me your ability will not save you," Adrien sneered, gaining a baffled expression from Jet.

Jet sighed in relief watching Adrian hugging the girl tightly against his chest. Jet gritted his teeth staggering to his feet, leading them back to the highway. They walked alongside each other in silence each lost in their own thoughts. A military car pulled up alongside them before an elderly gentleman rolled down the window.

An engine roared behind them as a black military issued Ford GPW truck slowed to a stop before the passenger side window was rolled down. "Lieutenant Jet Daniels, I presume? I was sent to collect you and those in your party," the driver called, as Jet sighed in relief saluting the man in response. He reached for the door handle. Adrien hesitated before climbing into the backseat cradling his sister in his arms. The car pulled off driving for several miles before pulling up to a manor. Jet entered the bathroom cleaning up and upon returning found a man waiting for them with long snow-white hair.

Dawn sat perched on the edge of the sofa focused on his story. "What happened after you came here?" Dawn asked. wondering if that was the end of his story. Jet opened his eyes and shrugged his shoulders at a loss for words. He nodded his head in gratitude seeing that Raven had gotten up to bring him a cup of tea with honey. He gripped the mug with both hands taking a long sip from it, his throat parched from speaking, not caring that it had grown cold. He glanced over at Matt hoping he had an answer that would satisfy her.

"He passed out. his injuries had finally caught up to him. I tended to his wounds along with the others before placing them in rooms. In the morning, Ari's brother was gone and with time she showed me her powers," Matt explained, toying with a lock of Scarlet's hair. She squirmed trying to swat his hand away yet was too exhausted to succeed.

Ari's brows furrowed processing his answer. "Wait, you said he died? So, how do you know he didn't stay here?" Ari asked, arching an eyebrow, taking the empty mug from Jet, setting it on the coffee table before massaging his shoulders to help with his stress. "Unless... did his spirit tell you this?" she asked, a somber note in her voice. thinking that was the only way Matt knew.

Matt nodded his head confirming her conclusion. Scarlett tilted his chin up kissing his cheek, seeing the sadness flicker across his face at confirming her fears. An awkward silence fell over the room before Dawn climbed to her feet. "I think I'm going to turn in. It's been a long day for all of us," she mused, tucking the book under one arm and collected the empty coffee mug to carry into the kitchen.

"Goodnight, Dawn. I will discuss with you and Raven tomorrow about your new training regime. You two didn't complete the course showing that you need more training," Matt suggested, resting his head against Scarlett's shoulder.

Raven rolled her eyes letting out an exasperated sigh. "Do you mean you're going to train us or force Vincent to do it, so that it doesn't take away from your time with Scarlett?" she sneered, hearing Vincent admit that he wouldn't mind helping Matt to train them.

Matt glared in Raven's direction not at all amused by her comment. "Why wouldn't I train you Raven. seeing how you hold no respect for anyone else? Vincent may lend a hand, but I would never put another slayer above the rest of you," he admitted, wondering why Raven was angry with him.

Raven jabbed her finger in Scarlett's direction. "You have yet to reprimand Scarlett for her reckless behavior. You tried to share the blame by failing to meet up with her, yet maybe she needs to brush up on teamwork," she hissed, thinking of how Scarlett had acted toward her while in the course.

Scarlett laughed ignoring the dirty look from Raven. "I'm not sure why you're complaining, I made sure you were safe—" she protested, interrupted by Raven.

"But you took it on by yourself acting like I was bait," Raven hissed, as Vincent rose to sit down beside her resting a hand on her arm.

"Raven. I know it's hard to accept help from others. It makes you question your abilities as a slayer," he pleaded, understanding why she was upset.

"How do you know I haven't reprimanded her Raven, when you have yet to talk to me the last few days? You have been hiding from me or have you forgotten?" Matt asked. wondering why Raven was attacking Scarlett.

"How do you know she was hiding from you and wasn't just hesitant to approach you about the matter? Clearly, she has some issues with Scarlett she needs to work out, but you can't think rationally when it comes to Scar," Andrew protested, amused by the glare sent in his direction for using her nickname.

"Aren't you calling the kettle black mutt, seeing how you're still trying to get into her pants despite her turning you down every single time? Raven if you have a problem just say it, instead of holding on to your anger," Matt advised, seeing that a fight was about to break out.

Andrew clenched his hands tightly at his sides taking in a deep breath. "No, I am willing to admit that my feelings toward Scarlett can be my kryptonite, but you have yet to do the same," he admitted, hearing Vincent sigh wondering why they were trying to start a fight at such a late hour.

"What are you trying to say, Andrew, that unless I act like you and mark her I'm not showing my attraction towards her? How did this become about you when my question was directed towards Raven?" he asked, seeing that Andrew was close to lashing out at him.

"I think it's sweet. Andrew is protecting his new admirer," Ari muttered, under her breath.

Jet laughed, diverting the focus of the argument to him. "I'm sorry, Ari was just stating that Andrew was defending Raven. He hoped by having a pissing contest over Scarlett then you would stop trying to intervene to why Raven was being rude to Scarlett," he replied, aware that he owed the group an explanation for his sudden outburst.

"I think Raven is jealous that Scar has three men fighting over her, including one that we're trying to kill. It's clear Raven has feelings for the werewolf they're just not returned just yet," Ari advised. thinking it was cute.

Scarlett groaned covering her face with both hands. "Trust me, Ari, it's not something I enjoy. Raven, if what Ari said is true, then I'm sorry. I would be relieved to hear that someone cares for Andrew, just not me," she pleaded, slipping her arms around Matt's next pulling him in for a kiss.

Raven sat there speechless wondering how Ari had figured out that she had feelings for Andrew. She blinked hearing Andrew sigh before storming from the room seeing Matt return the kiss. She muttered a goodnight to the others before chasing after him.

"Remind me to never try hiding anything from you, Ari," Scarlett noted, amused to see that she had been correct of Raven having unrequited feelings for Andrew.

Raven followed Andrew out to the garage, reaching out for his arm as he opened the door leading out to the garage. "Andrew, I'm sorry you got dragged into my problems. Don't let the anger consume you—" she pleaded, watching him turn to face her swatting her arm away. "Don't tell me how to feel, Raven. I was trying to have your back, yet they had to use it against me as a big joke," he sneered, entering the garage keeping his back to her.

Raven sighed running to stand in front of him, grabbing his shoulder forcing him to turn and face her. "Did you ever stop to think that they weren't mocking you? That there may have been some truth to what they said," she pleaded, hearing him snort shaking his head in disbelief.

He pressed the button to lift the garage door open greeted by the chilly night air. "I will always have feelings for Scar, that will never change. Don't ruin our friendship by asking me to," he pleaded, turning his back to her and ran toward the manor's front gate. Raven closed the garage door after him questioning her motives for sympathizing with Scarlett before returning to her room.

Scarlett sighed hearing Vincent reassure them that he would try talking to Raven hearing her bedroom door slam. "Why does Andrew always drag me into the middle of every argument?" she groaned, reaching up to toy with his hair feeling a yawn escape her lips.

"It's not your fault that Andrew is stuck in the past and can't move on. I wasn't trying to upset Raven, but I've seen how she's been acting around the mutt and I just wanted to put a stop to it. The love note she left open on her desk was the biggest clue," Ari admitted. seeing that it was just the four of them, moving to lean against Jet inhaling his scent.

Jet tried hard not to laugh wishing he had seen the note as well. "Why not follow in Scarlett's suit and try asking him out to dinner or a drink? Even if he's not interested in her romantically, they can become closer friends," Jet noted, reaching up for the blanket draped over the back of the sofa lying it over Ari.

Ari sighed in content wrapping her arms around his waist closing her eyes in content. Matt chuckled seeing that Andrew wasn't the only one clueless to a love interest.

Jet laughed hearing Scarlett snoring peacefully. He let Ari slide down so that she was sitting in his lap she moved, readjusting before settling once more. "Matt, maybe you should take Scarlett up to her room? It seems like I'll be staying here for a bit longer," he suggested, aware that it had been a long day for everyone.

Matt smirked seeing that Scarlett had fallen asleep curled against his chest. He bid Ari and Jet goodnight before scooping her up in his arms carrying her up to her room. He laid her on the bed lying beside her before pulling the comfort over them both. He kissed her lips tenderly resting his arm over her waist and closed his eyes inhaling her sweet scent.

Chapter Thirty-Eight

Scarlett tossed in her sleep, waking suddenly drenched in sweat. She ran a hand through her damp curls feeling a cold arm draped over her waist. She smiled seeing Matt lying next to her. She glanced out the window seeing the grounds illuminated by the waning moon. Scarlett tried slipping out from the embrace, feeling him reach out grabbing her wrist before his eyes opened.

"I'm sorry, I didn't mean to wake you. Go back to sleep," she pleaded, bringing his hand to her lips.

Matt ignored her request sitting up in bed. He pulled her against his chest running his fingers through her damp hair. He arched an eyebrow noticing her skin drenched in sweat, hearing her sign in relief at his icy caress. "Did you have a bad dream?" he asked, seeing her nod in agreement.

Scarlett took in a shaky breath inhaling his familiar scent nodding in agreement. "Andrew ran off in such a hurry, clearly upset by seeing us together. In my dream, he went after Donovan to get back at me," she whispered, glancing out at the moon once more.

Matt continued to stroke her hair reaching up with his free hand wiping the tears away. "It was just a bad dream—" he pleaded, kissing the top of her head seeing her shake her head vigorously.

Scarlet frowned realizing he was right feeling the familiar weight of the necklace around her neck. She glanced down at it in thought. "Can we go checkup on him and put my delirious thoughts to rest? After the day we had we both could use a drink," she pleaded, hearing him sigh in protest.

Matt let out an exasperated sigh seeing no reason to deny her request. "If I had denied your request you would have tried venturing there on your own?" he groaned, hearing her laugh agreeing to his answer. She turned to face him brushing her lips over his. Matt returned the kiss, feeling her arms slip around his neck deepening the kiss.

Scarlett moved to climb to her feet only to be stopped by Matt. He returned the kiss before grasping her chin gently to gain her attention. "We will check up on the vampire but not tonight. We will go there tomorrow once we've recovered, taking time to rest and restore our energies. You couldn't keep your eyes open and I can barely create a snowball," he pleaded, pulling her against his chest wrapping his arms around her waist ensuring that she couldn't break free.

Scarlett sighed resting her head against his chest stretching her legs out on the bed. "Always the voice of reason, though I'm not sure I can go back to sleep," she confessed, thinking it was wise to wait instead of going when they were vulnerable. "I always knew Ari was more powerful than she let on, given some of the feedback from Jet's training, but tonight was different. It seemed like something else took over her," she added, feeling his fingers stroke her hair kissing her neck gently trying to soothe her.

"It was a backlash from the barrier being broken. Her magic was tied to it being locked away to ensure she never lost control over it. What occurred tonight was her magic in its natural form. We were lucky that she was able to rein it back in," he admitted, seeing that Jet wasn't the only one scared of Ari's power.

Scarlett shuddered, frightened at the idea of seeing Ari release all her power. "Wait, if her magic is tethered to the barrier is that why she can never leave the manor?" she asked, wondering if Ari left would the barrier be at risk for falling again.

"I believed so. I mean how can a person leave when their powers are bound to the place. Now that it's broken there's no guarantee that her powers are bound meaning that she could leave if she wanted to, yet I doubt Ari would venture outside. It's clear that they were running from someone, I mean why leave the fey world and come here?" he muttered, under his breath lost in thought.

Scarlett blinked hearing what he had whispered grasping his hand turning to face him. "What makes you think they came from there? Jet said he came across them on the side of the road?" she asked, confused by his remark.

Matt blinked his eyes realizing he had let it slip while falling back asleep. "When Jet went to clean up, I got to speak with them in private. Adrian wanted to leave demanding that Arianna open another portal. She refused him burying under the mound of blankets I brought her to get warm. That's when I saw the runes and took a guess at their origin. It led to a nasty fight between me and Adrian," he admitted, moving to sit up on the bed to become more awake.

Scarlett shifted, pulling the comfort over her resting her head against his shoulder. "What happened to her brother, I can't imagine the guy had the nerve to argue with you after you took them both in trying to help them," she replied, smirking at hearing the yawn escape his lips seeing that he was still tired.

Matt sighed seeing that she wasn't letting the matter go. "He went berserk claiming that I was sent by the court to capture them. and that I was a monster unable to show acts of kindness without having an internal motive, wanting to use her for my own greedy purposes. He attacked me with a dagger getting in a lucky cut before my demon took control. When I regained control, Adrian was gone, and she was kneeling beside me in her true form. Afterwards I created the bind for her and in doing so removed most of her memories," he explained, wrapping his arms around her waist. "I could always show you those memories along with what occurred to your sister or do you want to keep living in the dark?" his demon inquired as Matt mentally told it to go away.

Scarlett kissed his cheek seeing that he still questioned his actions from the past. "It sounds like you tried doing what was best, though it sounds like your demon scared Adrian away?" she replied, letting a yawn escape her lips slipping her arms around his and closing her eyes hoping that she wouldn't be plagued by any more nightmares.

"Your guess is as good as mine. It wasn't until Halloween that his spirit contacted me, and I discovered his fate. Let's just say even back then Ari was protective of those she saw as innocent even if it meant turning on her own blood. Go to sleep, I'll ensure you have no more nightmares tonight," he whispered, running his fingers down her back to lure her back to sleep. Once Scarlett was asleep, he moved her, so she was more comfortable before joining her in sleep.

Chapter Thirty-Nine

Faint rays of warm light streamed in through the living room windows jarring Jet awake. He blinked his eyes open seeing that Ari had fallen asleep nestled against him. Jet brushed her hair out of her face, shaking her shoulders gently to wake her. "Good morning, I take it you were able to get some rest?" he asked, watching her open her eyes, helping her sit up. He took the blanket and draped it back over the back of the sofa.

Ari yawned, running a hand through her hair to tame it, taking in her surroundings. "It looks that way though you could have moved me instead of sitting there all night. Last night was a bit insane for everyone," she muttered, moving to climb off his lap.

Jet sat up, stretching and wincing as he realized how stuff his muscles were. "I think that was my intention, but I must have dozed off not long after. Breakfast first, then we can talk about last night. I don't think anyone else is awake yet," he suggested, taking her outstretched hand climbing to his feet following her into the kitchen.

Ari saw him wince leading him into the kitchen as she filled the kettle with water setting it on the stove to boil. She pulled out two mugs selecting Chamomile tea to help with muscle aches. "No, everyone is still resting though it is before Noon, so I'm not surprised," she admitted, moving so he could use the stove.

Jet laughed nodding his head in agreement making them a cheese and spinach omelet. "I would argue with you, but given the events of last night, I'm sure they needed time to recover," he noted, thinking that Matt would sleep the rest of the day away. He carried the food to the table letting her fill the two mugs with tea before joining him.

Ari placed a Chamomile tea bag in his mug placing Chai tea and Green tea mix in her own before adding the water from the kettle. "You're probably right seeing how a lot of magic was used and it can be draining if you're not around it a lot. I thought I would be one of them, yet I feel well rested," she admitted, placing his tea next to his plate before joining him.

Jet climbed to his feet fetching a packet of honey to add to his tea. "I wouldn't tell the others that or they may think you're bragging, though I might have to meditate outside if the tea doesn't help. The backlash from your magic was intense, stronger than I've ever experienced," he admitted, taking a sip of his tea hoping she didn't feel guilty for what had happened.

Ari frowned as she took a sip of her tea, adding honey as well. "I'm still at a loss about what occurred. One minute I'm performing the spell that creates the course, and the next Matt's standing in front of me surrounded by ice. It's clear I lost control of my magic, did I hurt anyone?" she asked, fearing the worst.

Jet took a bite of his omelet reaching out to grasp her hand covering it with his. "Raven had disrupted your concentration and you lost control of the portal. The creatures Matt faced were real instead of illusions crafted from your magic, and you scared Raven," he admitted, not wanting to lie to her wondering why she couldn't recall what had happened.

Ari closed her eyes, taking in a deep breath to calm her nerves and squeezing his hand in return. "Don't you mean I scared all of them? I blacked out from magical exhaustion. I'm sure Matt was able to manage it on his own though the course was based on everyone's memories and fears; that's why you entered one at a time. I then used a spell for bringing a storybook to life mixing the two spells together," she explained, taking a bite of her food thinking that Jet would appreciate an explanation of the spell.

Jet listened, impressed with the complexity of the spell. He took another bite of his breakfast understanding why it had drained her. "Channeling two spells intertwined at one followed by fixing the barrier,

I don't see how you're not exhausted from it all," he remarked, taking another sip of his tea baffled by how the rest had recharged her so quickly.

Ari shrugged her shoulders, taking another bite of her food. "I'm at a loss though maybe I just got an energy boost and will crash later. I did use my stones for the barrier, so my magic was only used for the first ritual," she explained, playing with her necklace.

Jet frowned seeing that she was lost in thought, carrying their plates to the sink seeing that they were both finished, refilling his tea. "I was wondering if you felt up to it, to have our lesson. I want to learn defensive magic given what Vincent put me through," he admitted, wanting a way to ward off his magic in case he tried using it again.

Ari winced recalling Jet being angry with her. "I was wondering when that would be brought back up, though in my defense, I knew of Vincent's immortality with his amulet, but what he did to you last night was a first for me. I should have taught you sooner how to deflect magic that acts like a siren's magic," she admitted, finishing her tea before placing her mug in the sink.

Jet finished his tea, also placing his mug in the sink. He rested his hand on her shoulder squeezing it lightly. "I'm no longer upset with you; I was just frustrated last night. I've seen your magic do marvelous things, yet that feeling of being manipulated like a puppet was scary," he admitted, sharing why he had been so angry after returning from the course. "Like he said, he thought he was doing me a favor, forcing me to face my fears, and I failed," he admitted, hanging his head in shame.

Ari placed her hand underneath his chin lifting it up gently. "You didn't fail; it takes a lot for a person to overcome their phobias. What Vincent did go too far. If the goal of the course were to face them then I would have created small caverns and Mathew would have been chained up at one point of the course. The course was to evaluate you, not break you," she advised. understanding his frustration.

Jet offered her a weak smile relieved by her words. He arched an eyebrow in response to her comment about Matt but figured he wouldn't press her. "The positive aspect in all of this, was the course forced Scarlett and Matt together. I thought Andrew wanted to take Matt's head off when he saw them together," he noted, seeing that his comment had made her smile.

"I couldn't resist. I had something planned for Raven and Andrew, but she didn't get to the cave section of the course. I mean the only ones that didn't see it was Matt and Scarlett they just needed a little push. If you're curious about my comment about our fearless leader, you can ask it's not like he's awake to stop me from telling you," she replied, leading him outside.

Jet followed her lead heading to the garden taking a seat on one of the wooden benches. "I feel like it's a story Matt should share with me but would be too proud to admit. If you don't mind sharing it with me, I'd like to hear it," he admitted, curious to learn what she had meant by her comment.

"You're right he would never admit it though I believe he told Scarlett while they were on the course. I couldn't hear conversations. I could only view the actions taking place on the map. That's something I can experiment with in the future. My theory is that when Matt obtained his powers his village rejected him. Where you were sitting on the mountain there's a cage underneath is a cavern. He has all those scars I just assumed he was tortured and would freak if put back in those types of situations," she admitted, knowing she didn't have any proof for her theory as she took the seat next to Jet.

Jet listened to her story thinking that it was a good guess. "That would explain why they seemed closer once the course was over. Sharing something that intimate with those you trust draws you closer," he replied, staring up at the clear blue sky seeing the sun disappear behind the clouds.
"I agree, I feel that sharing subjective experiences help create a more intimate relationship. I would say ask Matt about the scars, but I would hate for him to lash out in anger. You wanted a lesson to learn, correct? I guess we should start off by seeing what you recall about barrier spells," she suggested, thinking that was a good place to start.

Jet nodded in agreement drumming his fingers on his knees lost in thought. "You use an image of a wall or a shield in your mind and empower it with a repeated mantra or ritual to keep it activated," he replied, recollecting on what they had discussed about using shields in spells.

"That's correct, the strongest shields are ones created by an element you feel a connection to. Many see themselves surrounded in a bubble to ensure there's no weak spots in their barriers. Many can create these, but it takes a bit of magic to make them visible to others," she explained, climbing to her feet motioning for Jet to try his hand at creating one.

Jet climbed to his feet reaching for the amulet around his neck closing his eyes. His hands fell resting at his sides focusing on the soil beneath his feet. Jet thought of large, strong oak trees surrounding him, their vines intertwining around him like thorny webs. He opened his eyes to see what he'd created seeing four thin saplings growing from the earth around him. "Why do I have a feeling you're going to show off by demonstrating how it's done?" he asked, offering her a weak smile as he enjoyed watching her perform magic.

"I only show off when you ask me to Jet, you know I would rather encourage your magic then make you feel anger that you failed in comparison. That was a great first attempt, it takes most a month of more to summon any type of physical barrier. There is a drawback with choosing Earth, you'll be encased in a small dome of it. Would you be able to manage it?" she asked, wondering if he had thought of this.

Jet frowned, shaking his head, not understanding her concern. "It's odd that despite my fear, I feel connected to Gaia so that's what I focused on. I thought if I used an external web, like a secondary defense, I could avoid being encased in it," he admitted, taking a seat on the ground considering her advice. "Would that still be an issue if I had chosen a different element?" he asked, thinking it was wise to try working on ways to cope with his phobia.

"That's not a bad idea but it could leave gaps in your defense. All four elements would lead to the same problem though I may have an idea you could use. I think you should stick with Earth though was this what you were trying to create?" she asked, growing a ring of trees around herself as thick vines wrapped around each tree creating a thick webbing showing him the problems with the shield.

Jet smirked, nodding in agreement, watching her craft the spell in awe. "Yes, though I can see where the gaps leading to weakness in the shields strength. Should I try dealing with the phobia before working on crafting a shield?" he asked, wondering what she might suggest he try.

"I wouldn't push yourself into a situation you aren't ready to handle. It will still make a good shield so you can create it and meditate on different defensive measures. Not everyone uses the same method, some use your idea and have another layer of trees on the outside that are animated and react to incoming attacks," she explained, dissolving her spell. Ari paused pulling up the left sleeve of her tunic seeing red runes running down her arm.

Jet noticed the red marks on her arm closing the distance between them. He noticed her recoil when he grabbed her arm gently. He pulled the sleeve of her tunic away seeing that the runes were still present. "Any clue as to what these are? They appeared last night after the barrier was breached. It seems like it's tied to your magic," he noted, seeing her look away unable to meet his puzzled gaze frightened by the runes.

Ari shrugged her shoulders pulling her arm free hiding the runes from sight. "I have no idea; I've never seen them before though I have a few guesses on their creation. It can wait until later. We were working on your magic, remember?" she advised, not wanting to speak her fears aloud.

Jet rested his hands on both of her shoulders gaining her attention. "I know the focus of the lesson was to help me and I appreciate it, but I can tell whatever is on your mind frightened you and with everything that happened last night, you have enough on your plate," he replied, offering her a weak smile before sitting once more on the ground crossing his legs underneath himself pondering over the advice she had given him on the shield.

Ari sat across from him resting her hands on his knees. "You're right, I fear what these runes mean but I'm still your teacher. I can't abandon you just because my own magic took an unexpected turn. My question can wait until Mathew rises from his sleep, until then we will focus on your training," she suggested, thinking that it was a fair compromise.

Jet nodded in agreement resting his hands over hers. "That sounds like a fair compromise since he might still be asleep well after we're finished. He seemed exhausted during our retrieval of the stones," he admitted, thinking that the course had been intense for them all. "Should I keep trying to produce the shield I had proposed with an additional layer of protection?" he asked, focusing back on their lesson.

"You should focus on the first shield you created and try to strengthen it. First. try to create a deeper connection to Gaia so that the trees are fully matured and not saplings. Break it down to simple steps instead of creating it all at once," she advised, closing her eyes to help lead him into meditation.

Jet nodded in agreement watching her relax. "Smart idea to break it down into steps and build on them," he noted, closing his eyes taking in several deep breaths holding them in before letting them out slowly. Jet pulled his hands away from hers resting it in the grass.

He focused on his breathing, picturing the soil washing over his skin starting at his feet and moving slowly up his body. He focused on the sounds of the wind bursting through the trees around them.

Feeling the sun wash over his face as it peeked out once more from the clouds, he was able to summon one red oak tree before opening his eyes, leaning back surprised to feel the strength of the bark press against his back. He offered Ari a weak smile, wiping the sweat from his brow drained from the effort it had taken him to create the tree. He touched his amulet, thanking Gaia for her help.

Ari opened her eyes, watching Jet practice his magic. The tree grew slowly behind him before reaching its full height, casting shade over them. "Congratulations, Jet. That was an impressive feat for your first try. I think it would be wise to take a break and just meditate for the remainder of the day until your magical energies are restored," she suggested, thinking that the tree should stay and act as a focus for his future training.

Jet grinned, elated that she was impressed with what he had accomplished. "I agree, otherwise I'll exert myself trying to summon the other three trees, though I'm willing to listen when you feel ready to tell me what frightened you," he advised, not wanting to push her just reminding her that he was there to listen when she was ready. He stretched his legs out staring up at the tree still baffled that he had managed to create it.

Chapter Fourty

Ari let out a sigh seeing that their lesson was finished meaning she couldn't stall any longer. "I fear that those runes reveal that I'm not an innocent witch that I'm one of the monsters we were trained to hunt down and kill. Those runes are part of the fey language and not of the fun-loving kind, we read about in fairy tales. What if I were trapped here because Matt knew what I would become? What better way to study dark and twisted magic than from a natural source?" she asked, pulling her knees up to her chest.

Jet frowned, moving to scoop her up, returning to the tree letting her back rest against his chest. He slipped his arms around her shoulders leaning against the tree. "Knowing where you magic comes from offers you a way to have more control over it. I've seen your magic do marvelous things and never believed it was from malice intent," he replied, wondering if she would believe him.

Ari sighed closing her eyes letting her head rest against his shoulder taking in his scent of shifted soil and pine. "Thank you, sometimes it helps to have a voice of reason when your mind is swept away with the what if scenarios. I just wish I knew the whole truth instead of wondering if there was a reason my magic was chained. I caused harm to another leading to a loss of my memories," she noted, feeling comfort in his embrace.

Jet smirked, moving his hands to toy with her hair removing a few leaves. "It is very tempting to let your mind wander, going down a dark rabbit hole. I think fatigue was my redeeming quality last night, recalling those memories was intense. I still haven't learned much of my activities leading up to that day," he admitted, understanding her frustration.

"I know. I appreciate you sharing your past with everyone though I have no clues to lend you. Now that we know where my magic comes from, we came through the portal which would explain the light you saw. These are more questions for our leader," she suggested, annoyed that they would have to ask another for questions about their own past.

Jet shrugged his shoulders continuing to stroke her hair seeing that it was relaxing her. "The light led me to you and your brother forcing our paths to cross, so in that regard I'm grateful your brother forced you to come here," he added, offering her a weak smile knowing she had a million questions for Matt.

"I agree. I would hate to never can teach you what I know about magic; you have come a long way since our first lesson. I can still recall that day, you wanted to impress me that you opened your spell book and performed the first spell you came across. To this day, I think Raven still has nightmares about becoming an old hag," she replied, chuckling at the memory.

Jet laughed feeling his cheeks flush in embarrassment at the memory. "It seemed so earnest, trying to impress this impressive witch, hoping to earn her respect by perfecting the first spell I learned. In my defense, the spell worked just not how I envision it," he replied, thinking that the spell had mentioned that it would provide the target with knowledge failing to warn that it would increase their rate of aging.

She laughed at the memory. "On the bright side an aging spell is innocent compared to the other spells that were in my book of shadows. You're not the only one that has made mistakes, the first spell I cast was a light spell. I ended up with a blackout in the manor for a month," she admitted, recalling how upset the others had been without electricity.

Jet laughed surprised to hear that even she had made mistakes. "I had just assumed that you knew magic when you came here, though you made your spell too strong? At least you only caused a blackout and not a fire by creating lightning with it," he replied, relieved to hear that she had made mistakes when starting out.

"Yes, with elemental magic, but when it comes to other versions of spells, I was clueless about them. Through trial and error, I taught myself what I knew with magic and technology though it helps that Matt paid for me to attend online classes," she explained, playing with his amulet.

Jet thought of swatting her hand away but saw that it was distracting her and thought better of it. "That was generous of Matt, but it doesn't surprise me he is a supportive person. Who would think that such a simple trinket like the amulet could keep me grounded? I still have my dog tags from the military but it's too painful to wear," he admitted, wondering why he had kept on it for so long.

"Well it was created by your magic with a little spark from mine, so it makes sense that you would use it as a grounding tool. We all have an item to help us channel magic; you have your pendent and mines my locket. Do you think if you could discover your memories would you wear the tags again?" she asked, letting go of the necklace drawing on his chest seeing that it bothered him.

Jet shrugged, glancing down to watch her tracing rune patterns on the chest of his shirt. He tucked a loose strand out of his eyes pondering her question. "Maybe if there were some good memories associated with it. I feel guilty, it's so peaceful out here. I don't want to go back inside," he admitted, naming each rune she was drawing, wondering if it was a test or if it was absentminded.

"Who said we had to return indoors? The barrier is restored and there's no rush to venture from our resting place. I'm sorry, I'll stop if it's bothering you, I was drawing the first runes that came to mind. Were you trying to draw them?" she asked, closing her eyes, letting her hand rest against his chest.

Jet laughed reaching for her hand intertwining his fingers with hers. He repeated the runes she had drawn in the dirt with his free hand. "It wasn't bothering me; it was just a bit ticklish. I remember when I first started to learn how to draw runes and needed a cheat sheet, and now I can draw them with my eyes closed," he boasted, closing his eyes in content.

Ari laughed, tempted to press her luck, and tickle him. "That sounds like a challenge, Mr. Daniels, would you care to place a little bet on your drawing skills? The winner decides the punishment for the loser?" she offered, poking him in the chest playfully.

Jet arched an eyebrow, intrigued by her proposal. "Addressing me so formally can never lead to anything good, though I accept your challenge. What's the worst that can happen?" he replied, swatting her hand away, seeing that she enjoyed tickling him.

A smirk appeared on Ari's face, seeing that he had accepted her challenge. "The runes I taught you are what the Vikings used on their journey. I could be fair and use those as your test, but what would be the fun in that? I think we will start there and end with the Elder Futhark alphabet," she suggested, thinking it would be a fun challenge.

Jet bit his lower lip, thinking of her challenge. "Two diverse alphabets though I have read about the Elder Futhark alphabet, so I'm not at a total loss. What kind of runes are we drawing?" he asked, hoping that he could accurately recall the letters from what he had read on the Elder Futhark alphabet.

"I was thinking we would take turns, with each selecting a run and seeing if the other can draw it. Unless you don't think that's fair?" she asked, smiling innocently.

"I already accepted the challenge even if you have a higher chance of success, I'm not going to back down," he replied, using his left hand to draw the Occult Symbol Algiz, the Rune of protection.

 She reached her hand over his leg, erasing part of his rune before adding to it. She used his main line to draw Inguz for fertility. "Your runes aren't that bad perhaps we should add some rune carving to your training," she suggested, thinking that he was ready for the next level.

Jet arched an eyebrow, perplexed by her suggestion. "What is rune carving—is it carving runes into objects to fuel them with magic?" he asked, intrigued by the idea, erasing half of her drawing to sketch Wunjo, the rune for love.

"That's exactly what it sounds like learning to carve runes into stones and other objects before infusing them with your power. Many can struggle with it, knowing that they can easily carve a rune, but the challenge is discovering the balance of the magic behind it," she explained, erasing his rune, going for the Elder rune, Jera, for the yearly harvest.

Jet stared at the rune, realizing she had switched to the other rune alphabet. "It sounds as complex as creating the shield, though I welcome the challenge. You win though care to share what the rune was?" he asked, baffled by the drawing, curious to hear what his punishment would be.

"It's the rune for the yearly harvest, though I cheated by going with a rune I know you have yet to learn so does that mean I win or does the victory go to you? Many don't use the elder version because a lot of the runes are complex and have too many to memorize. I think you'll find it easier than the shield since we can just start off by carving," she suggested, thinking it would give him a fun side project.

Jet smiled studying the rune once more before she erased it. "No, you gave me fair warning you might use it and I have researched the Elder Futhark alphabet; I just couldn't remember them all. You'll take it easy on me when deciding my punishment?" he pleaded, excited by the idea of carving wood thinking it was a fun craft to keep his hands busy.

Ari smiled tapping a finger to her lips considering her options. "What's a girl to do, so many ideas I'm not sure which to choose. You have two choices; we can go on an outing as friends or you can create a personalized object for me," she suggested, thinking both would show her something new about him.

"An outing as friends meaning spending time alone together, which is what we're doing now?" he replied, thinking he had an idea in mind to offer her. "I think I'll choose the second option, though it maybe takes me a day or two to craft it," he added, seeing that she was intrigued by his answer.

"That's fine you know that I'm in no hurry to receive it. But a hint as to what you're creating would be nice," she pleaded, laughing at seeing him shake his head no. "Thank you for this morning, I needed the distraction. I've been focused on creating new weapons to create artificial sunlight. I fell into my unhealthy habits ignoring what I needed to try and create it. I just felt that with the threat to Scar, I needed to create it as soon as possible," she explained, sitting up to face Jet.

Jet smiled, happy to hear he was able to recharge her. "It was no big deal; you would have done the same for me if I need it. Artificial sunlight sounds complex, I could see how it could be frustrating. Maybe taking a break before returning to it will help you see it from a new perspective?" he suggested, thinking that after last night they all needed a break.

"You're right, I gave Andrew a prototype and the sun bomb destroyed an entire cave full of vampires. The only drawback is the amount of time it takes to activate it. I used nanite and a computer algorithm to set off the reaction. I want to ensure everyone returns when we finally face the vampire," she explained, moving to climb to her feet, only to laugh as she saw a vine wrap around her ankle, tugging her back down.

Jet held up his hands defensively, seeing her arch an eyebrow at the action and thinking he had done it. "I'm sorry, I think my brain exploded from the mathematical jargon. It sounds like you're on the right path if the prototype worked," he replied, reaching for the locket, curious of what it held inside.

"I see, so your brain exploding causes the vine to act on its own. You have the same reaction Scar had when she asked me about the project, but at least you didn't turn into a zombie afterwards," she mused, kneeling in front of Jet so he could see the locket clearly before opening it.

Jet studied the pictures in the locket, laughing at her comment. "Well your first mistake was trying to explain it to Scarlett. The idea doesn't sound that hard to understand fueling the explosive with nanite technology, I've just never cared for math," he replied, letting her climb to her feet following her dusting the soil from his pants.

"You know that there is math in creating runes. Are you sure you still wish to learn how to carve them? That reminds me. I need to check the runes on the cage, Andrew will be using it tonight," she muttered to herself, closing the locket before tucking it underneath her shirt. She entered the kitchen filling the coffee pot before turning it on thinking that the smell would help wake the others.

"If it's presented in front of me and I can see it I'm good at it, but you're presenting complex mathematics with no visual aide. What kind of math is involved?" Jet asked, following her into the kitchen.

He noticed Dawn seated at the table eating a bowl of cereal with a tablet reading the news to her audibly. "Good morning, Dawn. Did you want me to refill the kettle for tea?" he asked, seeing her wave, holding up her glass of orange juice. "Do you want help with your task Ari?" he asked, wanting to avoid those that were lured by the smell of coffee knowing that they'd demand he cook them breakfast.

Ari laughed, shaking her head no. "Go ahead and hide before they come down the steps seeking out your cooking skills. I think your question would be better answered with an explanation, just know that your math skills will be put to the test," she explained, pulling out a pot thinking she would make chicken and dumplings stew.

Dawn wrinkled her nose, hearing them mention math, pausing the news story she had been listening to. "Raven was up early this morning, she went on a run with Andrew," she explained, carrying her dishes to the sink before returning to her room to get dressed.

Jet made another cup of tea, transferring it into one of the travel mugs. "In that case, I'm going to start on my secret project while taking shelter from the zombies," he informed her, seeing her smile, wanting to know what he was up to.

Ari laughed, pulling out a cutting board and the ingredients she would need. "I would run then, seeing how I hear movement upstairs. I think it's good that Raven and Andrew are spending more time together. I'll work on my own project when I'm finished with the stew," she mused, watching him head for the stairs.

Jet laughed, grabbing a pencil and a pad of stationary from one of the drawers and tucking it underneath his arm. "You're just being mysterious because I won't give away what I'm up to," he replied, heading toward the hallway to retreat to his room waving to Vincent seeing him slowly making his way to the kitchen.

"Perhaps, or maybe I just want to keep it a surprise until you're ready to receive it. Good morning, Vincent. The coffee will be ready in a minute. Would you like me to make you something?" Ari asked, seeing him enter the kitchen as she threw the vegetables into the pot.

He stared at the coffee pot, listening to it brew before realizing she had asked him a question. "Good morning, Ari. I'll make something once I have my coffee, though did Jet leave because of me?" he asked, aware that he owed him a proper apology.

"No, he wanted to disappear before people started demanding food from him, though you do owe him an apology for last night. I'm not going to lecture you on it. I'm only glad you came to that conclusion on your own. Can I ask what made you lock him in a box?" she inquired, getting out what she would need to make the dough for the dumplings.

Vincent shrugged his shoulders, making him feel worse. He sighed in relief, hearing the coffee stop brewing before pouring himself a cup. "I thought I was helping to push him to take on his demons, but if I'm really honest, I think I was just bored. I've never heard why he hated small spaces and thought he had made it up," he admitted, taking a sip of his coffee, and leaning against the counter.

"I guess it's a good thing you don't know the others' fears and phobias. I would hate to see what you would do in your boredom. I think it's only fair you share your fear with Jet to make amends," she suggested, spraying a bowl and placing the ball of dough in it before covering it with a towel and setting it near the window to proof.

Vincent ran a hand through his hair, thinking that it was a good suggestion in theory. "I would take you up on that offer, but I don't have any fears," he admitted, setting his cup down to make a fried egg, placing two slices of bread in the toaster.

Ari cleaned up the counter arching an eyebrow at his comment. "Are you sure about that Vince? I can recall a certain man freaking out because he misplaced his pendent. Isn't that why you wear a fake one to protect it from being destroyed?" she asked, giving the pot a stir, standing beside him.

Vincent shrugged his shoulders, glancing down at the pendant around his neck. "Why wear the real one and risk losing it knowing that my powers are tied to it," he replied, dismissing her comment, and adding a slice of cheese and tomato to his sandwich. He set it on a plate, grabbing his coffee mug, taking them both with him to the table.

Ari rolled her eyes, wondering why she even tried talking sense to him. "Whatever you say, Vincent, though I hope you know I don't believe you. Everyone has fears, including you," she warned, adding chicken stock to the vegetables cleaning up Vincent's mess for him.

Vincent took another sip of his coffee afraid to admit that she was right. "Thanks, Ari, I would have gotten that once I was finished," he noted, taking a bite of his sandwich. "Stating the fear out loud makes it seem like I'm vulnerable," he whispered, glancing out the window seeing the new oak tree near the garden.

"Don't sweat it. I figured it would help keep my hands busy while I was waiting. Admitting your fears doesn't make you vulnerable Vincent. Sometimes saying them aloud can help you to realize what you fear. It can even help you understand them and perhaps overcome them," she advised, turning the fire under the pot on low before joining him at the table with a cup of tea.

Vincent sighed, taking in a deep breath staring down at his hands. "I do fear the pendant being destroyed and not having it as a safety net. I want to have a legacy knowing that the extra time I was given wasn't wasted," he whispered, finishing his sandwich waiting for her advice.

Ari reached out her hand to grasp his gently. "That sounds like a rational fear though that explains why you want to take over the training for Matt, thinking that it would be a way to have a lasting image on those that study under you. I said everyone has a fear including me. I fear what my magic is revealing to me," she admitted, thinking of the runes from her morning training with Jet.

Vincent nodded in agreement squeezing her hand gently. "Matt has enough on his plate without having to train the others. You always know what to say to us, maybe you should take it as a sign that it's trying to reveal something to you that you've forgotten?" he suggested, trying to repay the favor by laying her fears to rest.

Ari gave him a weak smile as thanks for his words. "Perhaps you're right though I may have to wait and see what it will reveal. I wonder if Matt knows it as well. Were the love birds up when you came down?" Ari asked, taking his plate, and placing it in the sink for him.

Vincent finished his coffee refilling his mug, laughing, and shaking his head no. "It was pretty quiet when I left my room not wanting to disturb them. I take it you still want me to talk with Jet despite our heart to heart?" he asked, knowing what her answer may be.

"Why ask a question you already know the answer to? Even though we had a conversation you still owe one with Jet to make amends. He's in his room if you wish to get it over with," she suggested, taking out her phone and sending a text to Matt, knowing that it would wake him.

Vincent groaned, finishing his coffee before rising to his feet. "I was still hoping the answer may be different, Jet has a mean right hook when he's pissed," he admitted, placing his mug in the sink before venturing off to Jet's room.

Chapter Fourty-One

Scarlett stirred hearing the buzz of the phone vibrating on the end table. She groaned pulling the blanket over her face, laughing realizing she had hit Matt with the blanket. She brushed her lips over his resting her head against his chest hearing the phone buzz again.

Matt groaned reaching out his hand blindly searching for the phone silencing it once he had it. "Good morning, Scar. I take it Ari believes we slept long enough?" he mused, returning the kiss before sitting up on the bed chuckling to himself seeing that he had stripped during the night.

Scarlett pushed herself up grinning noticing that he was wearing nothing but his boxers. "Good morning was that her blowing up your phone?" she asked, running her fingers through her hair, feeling her cheeks flush realizing he had caught her staring at his chest.

"Yes, who else would be texting my phone nonstop to get my attention? I'm going to go jump in the shower before heading downstairs. I would ask you to join me. but I don't want you to be tormented just after waking up," he explained, climbing to his feet and heading to his room for some clean clothes.

Scarlett blinked, disregarding his warning, and staggered to her feet, following him to the bathroom. She splashed chilly water over her face, trying to wake up. She turned on the hot water, letting the room fill with steam before stripping and entered the shower. Lost in her task, she did not notice that the steam had disappeared once Matt entered the room.

Matt paused unsure of his next action. "Scar, should I just wait and come back later? You know the water is going to be freezing once I get in there," he warned, using his clothes to cover up, not realizing she would beat him to the shower.

Scarlett laughed, peeking out from the curtain, and laughing even harder. He was using his clothes to cover up his groin. She finished washing her hair, a sly smirk flickering over her lips. She cupped the water in her hands, splashing him with it, ignoring his warning.

Matt groaned, seeing that Scarlett wanted to start a water war. He sighed, dropping his clothes before stepping into the shower. He turned the hot water off, waiting for her reaction.

Scarlett laughed, seeing that she had gotten her way, throwing her arms around his neck kissing his shoulder blades. She screamed, feeling the water drastically shift from hot to icy cold. She moved away from under the facet, admiring his glistening muscles, seeing him smirk in triumph.

Matt laughed, seeing Scarlett stumble away from the water. "What's wrong, Scar, a bit cold for your liking? You didn't seem to mind it last night when we were sharing the bed," he teased reaching out for her arm pulling her back underneath the water.

Scarlett laughed, shaking her head not as she let him pull her under the icy water. She brushed her lips against his reaching up to brush his wet hair out of his face. "Who said I was complaining? I can manage it, otherwise I wouldn't be here," she protested, feeling the chilly water run down her back.

Matt laughed, deciding to compromise, making the water go lukewarm for her. "I'm sorry, is that better? I just wanted to see what your reaction would be. You can go back to a hot shower when I'm done," he offered, returning the kiss before reaching for the body wash, keeping her under the water with him.

Scarlett laughed, taking the body wash from him, squeezing it into her hands and massaging it into his shoulders. "Don't you dare try apologizing, you enjoyed it. The worst is over unless you want to keep tormenting me?" she teased, kissing his jaw seeing him smirk considering the idea.

He laughed, shaking his head in response. "I should be careful. If I make you scream too much, someone may try to come in to see if you're all right. Besides, you could try getting revenge by turning off the chilly water," he advised, taking the bottle from her, using it to draw on her stomach and back before rubbing it in.

Scarlett bit her lower lip, considering the idea and pulled away from him to reach for the shampoo. "A tempting offer if I get cold, though has your hair always been this long?" she asked, lathering the shampoo into his scalp, thinking that the chilly water was good for her injured shoulder.

I went with it. Why do you think I should get it cut? It comes in handy with covering up the scars from the collar," he admitted, standing under the water to watch off the suds.

"No, you've had it that way for so long, so any difference would seem odd," she replied, staring up at her shoulder, aware that she needed to wash it, but feared touching it.

Matt took the washcloth from her as she turned, keeping her back to him.

"Does it look any better?" she asked, squirming feeling his cold fingers trace her tattoo before gently washing the wound on her shoulder.

Matt held her still, being gentle with the cloth. "It's healing the wound is no longer open though I don't think it will leave a scar, but it may still be tender for another week, but Ari's herbs may help with that. Is it still hurting?" he asked, kissing her neck tenderly.

Scarlett sighed, thanking him before reaching for his hand, slipping it around her waist. "It only hurts when I extend my arm or if I end up sleeping on it, but nothing compared to the first night. I think the chilly water helped; I barely felt the washcloth touching it," she admitted, leaning against his chest.

Matt chuckled, washing her hair before letting her rest against his chest. "I'm glad I was able to help though I think I'll step out and allow you a chance to warm up," he admitted, kissing her once more before stepping out of the shower grabbing a towel to dry off with.

Scarlett sighed in delight feeling his fingers comb through her wet curls before letting her stand under the water to rinse. She returned the kiss, waiting for him to exit the shower before turning the hot water back on. She stood underneath the hot water before turning off the shower, taking the towel Matt held out for her. She slipped it around herself, seeing that the room had filled up with steam.

Matt got dressed while Scarlett was finishing, using another towel to dry his hair. "Well I think that was more enjoyable then taking a shower alone huh, Scar? I take it you probably want your coffee once you're dressed?" he offered, tossing the towel in a corner before heading for the door.

A wide grin spread out over her face as she nodded in agreement. "It was fun, and the view wasn't half bad either, though I'll meet you downstairs once I get dressed?" she asked, following him out of the bathroom heading to her room.

Matt nodded his head, heading for the staircase before going downstairs. He entered the kitchen, amused to see two cups of coffee waiting for him on the table. "Thanks, Ari, I'm sure Scar will appreciate it though I take it you've been busy this morning?" he asked, taking the iced coffee before heading toward the fridge.

"You could say that though it seems you and Scarlett are a lot closer than you were yesterday. I was just finishing in here, though we may need to talk later when you get the chance," she admitted, turning the stove off and moving to place the pot on the counter to cool.

Scarlett got dressed running a brush through her wet hair before slipping on a black headband descending the stairs into the kitchen. "Hey, Ari, it smells good in here. What were you cooking?" she asked, noticing the pot on the counter seeing the mug of coffee next to the coffee pot. "Is this cup for me?" she asked, seeing Ari nod in agreement.

"Chicken and dumplings. I was in a good mood so I decided to make a meal everyone could enjoy. Yes, that cup is yours though trust me I know better than to deny you caffeine. I'm going to head downstairs unless you want me to make you guys something to eat?" Ari offered, pouring tea into a travel mug.

Scarlett took her cup to the table taking a sip looking out the window. She looked out the kitchen window seeing the new oak tree. "That's nice of you if it's not too much trouble. Did you spend some time with Jet outside?" she asked, aware that the tree came from their recent lesson.

Ari nudged Matt out of the way pushing him toward the table knowing his cooking skills were poor. "If it was a bother, I wouldn't have offered besides no one wants Matt in the kitchen," Ari teased, taking out the eggs to make them a quick sandwich. "Yes, Jet created the tree we were working on barriers this morning and I was teaching him how to make one that wasn't encased. That's what I wanted to ask you Matt. During our lesson, these weird runes appeared on my arm," Ari explained, cooking the eggs in the frying pan.

Scarlett laughed patting the seat next to her seeing Ari push him out of the way. "That seems like an interesting challenge for him. You wouldn't want any gaps in your barrier to weaken it, but how do you achieve it without making it encase you?" she replied, curious to hear Matt's answer to Ari's question.

"I advise he create a two-wave barrier. The one close to him can have gaps if he has another barrier outside of the first that's animated. He was only to create one tree so far but I'm sure with practice he'll create more." Ari explained toasting the bread before placing the plates in front of them.

"Thanks Ari, though I was wondering when they would be brought up. I know you can read runes so what is it you really want to know?" Matt asked, after taking his seat next to Scarlett. "If it's to ask if your evil you're not, your parents spirits confirmed your only part fey, and no I have no memories of the evening you arrived here except for binding you my demon took control after your brother attacked me," Matt explained, thinking these were the questions on her mind.

Scarlett took a sip of her coffee confused by their conversation. "Wait, Ari is from the fey court, then how did she get here? What would make you think that you're evil?" she asked, thinking that the runes in question had just been to show that her magic had been let loose.

"How can I be from the Unseelie court and not be evil? They see humans as slaves and get enjoyment out of tormenting anyone they come across including their own kin. When Jet told his story last night, I realized the light he was drawn to is a portal being open and the runes revealed the rest to me," Ari explained, seeing Matt sigh in annoyance.

"Ari, you're not evil. If you were, would you be sitting here having a conversation with us? Yes, you were born there but you grew up here the last few years and you have never harmed any of us. Our DNA doesn't define us," he protested, frowning, and realizing that she still doubted him.

Scarlett frowned, seeing that Ari was troubled by what she had learned about herself. "Matt has a point, Ari, you've never demonstrated that you would gain pleasure from hurting any of us, including Andrew," she protested, wondering if Ari would believe anything, they told her. "I've seen you open yourself up more to Jet, and that takes patience and kindness," she added, lost at what else to say.

Ari sighed, running a hand through her hair before climbing to her feet. "I have projects to work on and I still have questions but it's clear I won't be receiving them any time soon." She groaned, before disappearing into the basement.

Matt sighed, watching Ari disappear. "Do you think she believes us? At least she didn't lash out demanding why I didn't tell her sooner," Matt mused, taking a long sip from his coffee before glancing over at Scarlett.

Scarlett climbed to her feet to refill her coffee, placing her sandwich in the microwave to reheat it before coming back to the table. "I think she was just rattled by what she learned about herself. Why did you keep it from her, did you not want her to know afraid she'd react badly?" she asked, knowing he had a good reason for taking so long to tell her the truth.

"I was worried she would react badly to it or worse she would do something reckless to prove that she's not one of them. I mean if her parents haven't confirmed it, I would have doubted it myself. I know once the shock wears off, she's going to demand more answers," he replied, unsure what Ari would do with the information.

Scarlett sat back down beside him, placing her hand over his. "Give her some space to process the information and take it from there. You said that your demon holds some of the answers to her questions, but I have the feeling he won't do you any favors for free?" she warned, seeing that he wanted to help Ari.

"It would only help me out if I were threatened or amused by it. They call it a demon for a reason, Scar, though I'm not so sure she would appreciate its input. Hopefully, her projects and Jet will help her sort through the mess," he suggested, hoping she was right seeing that for the moment it was best to leave Ari alone.

Scarlett nodded in agreement, taking a bite of her sandwich. "Yes, it made that quite clear last night with its comment," she replied, laughing at hearing him groan. "I'm sorry, I thought bringing it up would make you feel better," she protested, pouting at seeing him reaching for her cup of coffee holding it out of her reach in response. "All right, I take it back, just give me back my coffee, please?" she pleaded, batting her eyelashes at him.

"If you were trying to cheer me up you should have mentioned our activities from last night, though I thought you would be sore after our little game," he teased, returning the mug to her before climbing to his feet to get a refill.

Scarlett let out a happy sigh, taking a sip of her coffee. "There aren't that many opportunities where I get to tease you. I was a little sore, but the cold shower seemed to help," she admitted. A blissful smile flickered across her face at the mention of their intimate night together.

Matt chuckled, walking over to refill her mug for her. "I'm glad. I would hate to have caused you any harm. Though we have a few hours before nightfall. I guess I should talk to Dawn, seeing how Raven is hiding again," he replied, at a loss on how to deal with the girl.

Scarlett thanked him, taking another sip of her coffee. "I was able to keep up with you, it wasn't my first rodeo. I thought Raven was trying to spend more time with Andrew, so why would that trouble you about Dawn?" she asked, wondering what was bothering him.

"She's not troubling me. I just need to discuss future training with her. I want to ensure she can manage being a slayer though there are a few new paths she can take instead. Raven is a complete mess every time I can get her alone, she is angry and lashes out on me," he confessed, finishing his coffee before placing his cup in the sink.

Scarlett stared down at her coffee thinking of some of the paths Dawn could pursue. "Has Raven always been hot-headed? We should all be able to defend ourselves and Dawn seems to rely on others to protect her," she admitted, thinking of how Dawn had done with the course.

Matt scratched the back of his neck thinking over her question. "No, not at first she seems really open to working with everyone and then over time she changed. Could have something to do with her becoming a woman I mean don't get mad, but you all seem to act that way during a certain part of the month," Matt observed, knowing he was going to get hit for his comment.

Scarlett rolled her eyes, finishing her coffee before taking the cup to the sink. She slipped her arms around his shoulders tugging his hair lightly. "As amusing as your antidote is, there's another reason you failed to mention. It's clear she likes Andrew, and he may never get over his feelings for me," she advised, wondering if Matt would try talking to Andrew about it.

Matt frowned, trying not to move, seeing that she still had a grip on his hair. "Do you really think the wolf would give me the time of day, seeing how he thinks you could still be his? Andrew has a one-track mind, and nothing will change that," Matt advised, bending down to kiss her wrists, and nipping them playfully.

Scarlett wrinkled her nose in disgust at the notion, pulling his hair out of the way gently, brushing her lips against his neck. "It was just a suggestion hoping you could get through to him, though now you're stuck with me," she teased, laughing, and letting him pull her into his lap.

"I doubt that's a smart idea. I think Andrew would prefer to fight me instead of talking. Taking into consideration our interactions the last few days, I don't mind being stuck with you, Scar, I just find it pointless that I have to continue to fight for you with your ex," he warned, taking a seat at the table before pulling her into his lap, laughing as his hair fell over her.

She groaned at hearing his comment. "Please don't refer to him that way. We never dated, despite him trying to hit on me several times," she protested, swatting his hair away, trying not to pull on it. "And now I have a foul taste in my mouth thinking about it," she added, brushing her lips over his.

Matt returned the kiss, pulling a grey bandanna from his pocket to tie his hair back. "You realize I'm not the one who produced that term? Andrew claims that you guys were a couple and were just on a break for the time being," he replied, pulling her so that she was resting against his shoulder.

She leaned against his shoulder, inhaling his scent as she tried to suppress her frustration. "Thank you for clearing that up for me. Do I get to go kick his ass now for implying that we were an item?" she asked, resting her feet in the other chair.

"I would say yes if it wasn't for the fact tonight's a full moon. You can go kick his ass tomorrow when he's too weak to do anything about it. I could always ask Ari to give him a little trim; she enjoys the task," Matt mused, chuckling at the memory.

Scarlett laughed at the idea, picturing her beating up Andrew in a weakened state. "I forgot tonight was a full moon, though it doesn't seem fair to offer me such an advantage but I'm still going to take it," she admitted, rubbing her hands together in glee. "Good luck with

Dawn. I think I'll try distracting Ari with a fun task," she announced, giving him a kiss climbing to her feet.

Matt chuckled, watching her head to the basement. "Good luck just remember Andrew is off limits until tomorrow. There may be a video of him being tormented in the living room," he called, climbing to his feet before heading to Dawn's bedroom. He knocked on the door, seeing if she was in her room.

Chapter Fourty-Two

Dawn had opened her window, letting in the natural sunlight as she sat at her desk reading a graphic novel Raven had stolen from Andrew. Hearing the knock on her door, she called for them to enter, placing a bookmark in the book before sitting it aside. She smiled when she saw it was Matt, wondering what he needed.

Matt closed the door behind him before taking a seat on her bed. "Hey, Dawn, I hope I'm not interrupting, we need to talk about your performance on the course and the next step in your training," Matt explained, glancing at the novel she was reading.

Dawn sighed, running a hand through her hair, dreading the conversation. "Raven borrowed the book from Andrew, thinking I might like it. It has vampires in it, but they seem weaker than the reports I've read," she admitted, worried about his review. "I know it wasn't my finest hour, but I'm willing to train and improve," she added, hoping it might ease the blow of what he might say.

Matt held his hands up before patting the spot next to him on the bed. "I wish you would talk to me about the reports you read and where you keep finding them. Ari won't let me near them," he admitted, trying to lighten the mood. "I'm not mad, Dawn, I just want to hear your thoughts so that I can help you improve. Your parents made me your guardian while you're here and I would hate for anything to happen to you," he explained, softly trying to ease her fears.

Dawn's cheeks flushed, realizing she wasn't supposed to have them. She opened a drawer underneath her desk, offering a stack of papers to Matt, taking the seat beside him on the bed. "Raven brought them to me, thinking if I was more informed on what you guys faced, I would be better prepared in the field," she confessed, afraid she had gotten Raven in trouble. "I don't seem to have much confidence in my own skills, and end up relying on others for help," she added, staring down at her hands resting in her lap.

Matt sighed, thinking that Raven was lucky he had discovered it and not Ari. "I'm not mad that you have these, just make sure Ari never catches you with them. She's not a fan of people stealing from her. We can go over these if you like and discuss the monsters featured. What do you think your strengths and weaknesses are as a slayer? Depending on others isn't a sad thing, it shows that you have the courage to ask for aid when you need it," Matt advised, letting her hold on to the papers.

Dawn nodded in agreement staring down at the papers. "Is that courage or cowardice using others as a crutch? I like reading and using what I've read to help others, but at the same time I second guess myself, questioning whether or not I can do the task correctly," she confessed, recalling the discussion she had with her parents before leaving that Matt was her guardian and to listen to him while in his care.

Matt stared out the window thinking over her answer. "It's not a crutch you're the youngest among us meaning you still have a long way to go before reaching the same level as the others. If you enjoy reading why not become a researcher? That's the other half of being a slayer reading up on what you're going to face. Is that something you'll be interested in?" Matt asked, thinking the job would suit her.

Dawn grinned flattered by the offer. "I think I would be good at it, but I don't want to be a burden to Ari. She has a lot on her plate. If I took the position on, would I still get to be trained in combat?" she asked, not wanting to disappoint Raven by not being able to spar with her.

"Yes, your training would still continue. I wouldn't stop you from learning how to defend yourself. You wouldn't be a burden you would be helping Ari by taking on a task she usually completes. There will be rules of course anything you read I want you to discuss with either myself or Ari. There may be times we deny you from touching a document or item but listen to our warning there's a good reason behind it. Do you have any questions?" Matt asked, glad that they came to an agreement, knowing that Raven wouldn't be as easy.

Dawn's smile grew relieved that her talents would be useful. "Thank you, it's nice to learn that I can be helpful to Ari. Should I tell her that Raven stole the reports from her? I don't want to get Raven in trouble, but I know it's the right thing to do," she admitted, wondering when she would start helping Ari.

Matt chuckled glancing at the papers. "It's the right thing to do though it may lessen the blow if you explained how Raven stole them. Come on let's go give Ari the news. Do you have any questions about what you read so far?" Matt asked, climbing to his feet.

Dawn climbed to her feet as well shaking her head no to his question. "The reports were very detailed, though is it true that siren's only target men?" she asked, unaware of how Raven had acquired the reports nor that they belonged to Ari.

"They can attack women, but their call only affects men putting them in a lustful daze. Mermen do the same to women and are categorized with succubi. Succubi are demons that feed off the lust of humans," Matt explained, leading Dawn down to the basement.

~~*

Scarlett glanced up hearing footsteps descending into the basement. She had written down the herbs that had been listed in the journal asking Ari to explain what they were used for, while Ari prepared the cage for Andrew. She overheard Matt's comment waiting for them to reach the landing. "Aren't their male succubi as well that also feed on human lust?" she asked, hoping to never encounter one.

"Yes, though females are more common, it's been a long time since I've dealt with one. I take it Ari's in the back with the cage though you may get some entertainment. It seems that Raven has been in Ari's archives," Matt warned, pulling Scarlett in for a kiss.

Scarlett returned the kiss, laughing at hearing Dawn swoon. "Yes, she was nice enough to explain what these herbs are and what they can be used for. My sister used them for healing and had them recorded in the journal," she explained, sighing seeing Dawn arch an eyebrow wanting to ask Scarlett for more details. "I take it your discussion went well?" she asked, feeling bad for Raven knowing it would piss Ari off to learn she had stolen her documents.

"Yes, Dawn has inquired about taking on the task of being a researcher which means she'll be working with Ari. Is she free or in the middle of casting the enchantments?" Matt asked, seeing that Ari had yet to join them.

"I think that's a great idea, Dawn. You're always reading and seem very inquisitive. I believe she is still working on the enchantments," Scarlett answered, seeing Dawn blush in response to the compliment resting the documents on Ari's desk.

Matt placed his hands over Scarlett's eyes telling Dawn to close hers as a bright flash came from the back of the room. Ari entered the room seeing them standing in front of her desk.

"You can open your eyes now; the enchantments are secured though do you guys need anything?" Ari asked, removing a pair of leather gloves from her hands placing them in a drawer.

Dawn stared at her feet unsure of how to announce what had brought her there. "Dawn has something she wants to discuss with you, but first she wanted you to see that she retrieved some documents Raven stole from you," Scarlett replied, seeing that Dawn was scared to state what was on her mind.

Dawn nodded her head in agreement glancing up to see Ari picking up the documents. "I don't know how she obtained them, she claimed it was to help me be more knowledgeable of what we could encounter," she added, hoping that Ari wouldn't be mad at her.

Ari studied the papers a frown appearing on her face. "Dawn was wondering if she could become a researcher under your watchful eyes." Matt suggested, seeing that Dawn was scared to speak up.

"I was wondering when that would be suggested though I see no problem with that however, I'm not happy that Raven stole from me. All you had to do was come ask and I would have lent the documents to you," Ari explained, hoping that papers were the only thing Raven stole.

Dawn smiled, relieved that she wasn't in trouble. "I didn't know that they belonged to you, Raven never said where she got them from. I know I can come to you or Matt with my questions, but I didn't want to be a burden. I guess that's why I was afraid to speak up," she confessed, relieved to hear that Ari had agreed.

"You're not being a burden, Dawn, I'd rather you come ask me instead of jumping to your own conclusions. I think I know how Raven stole them; she was absent when the barrier fell. For her sake, I hope it was only documenting; magical artifacts are attached to the creator and will lash out when stolen," Ari explained, motioning for Dawn to follow her toward the back room.

Dawn nodded in agreement, following Ari to the back of the basement, curious to see what she was working on. "That was reckless to steal from Ari, though I hope she didn't steal a magical weapon thinking it would give her an advantage. The backlash from her magic was bad enough last night, I wouldn't want to experience that again," Scarlett admitted, hearing Ari explain how the cage worked and how she had enchanted it.

"There's a difference between a backlash and being cursed by magic. If Raven were smart, she would return them. The longer you hold on to them the worse it can become. They can drive her insane or worse kill her trying to return to their rightful master," Matt explained, seeing the book in her hands.

"Ari didn't think anything was missing aside from the records, so we can advise Raven on what to do in case she did take something else," she advised, aware Matt would be worried about Raven's safety. She smirked seeing what had caught his eye. "I was keeping Ari busy. She was able to simplify what the herbs are used for but applying them for medical use is outside my expertise," she admitted, aware that she had only recognized a fraction of the herbs listed.

"I'm not surprised herbs aren't your area of expertise though I'm sure Ari will have a use for them. and will write them in a book for you with all their properties included knowing her. I take it this is the journal your sister left behind?" Matt asked, hearing Ari explain the archive system to Dawn.

Scarlett nodded in agreement offering the book for him to look at. "There are a lot of memories recorded in it, though if she hadn't kept a record of it, I may not have ever gotten to know her. I think despite all the time that has passed, it's still too delicate for Donovan to discuss," she admitted, thinking that despite the pictures and their marriage he hadn't shared much with her.

"I'm not surprised he's an immortal to them; time is limitless, and yet he had the woman he loves stolen from him. He knew that you were alive yet couldn't come seek you out knowing that he would be killed trying to cross the barrier. I didn't know you had a sister or a relation to the vampire otherwise I would have helped you meet him sooner," Matt admitted, looking through the book before returning it to her.

Scarlett took the book from him, reaching up to brush her lips over his. "I know, I don't think I would have believed him without proof. At least I made the connection after all this time," she replied, taking his hand, and leading him toward the stairs, seeing that Ari might be busy teaching Dawn the archives for a while.

"Looks like we were able to find a nice distraction for Ari, though should I even try talking to Raven? I'm starting to wonder if Raven will even listen to me seeing how recently she thinks that we're all out to get her," Matt admitted, returning the kiss, heading upstairs after Scarlett.

Scarlett frowned, seeing that he was worried about Raven despite how she had treated him lately. "Knowing you, it will bother you until you get an answer. As much as Raven annoys me, I wouldn't wish the things you described to happen to anyone," she admitted, biting her lower lip, thinking of an idea. "She might not listen to you, but she will listen to Andrew. I don't want to burden Dawn with trying to ask her," she added, aware she would have to persuade Andrew to help them.

Matt shook his head, not liking the idea. 'No, I should at least try talking to her first before passing the responsibility onto someone else. Wish me luck though if you hear screaming you may have to come rescue me," Matt teased, kissing her once more before heading to Raven's room not sure if she was there or in Andrew's room.

Chapter Fourty-Three

Raven was heading back to her room frowning at seeing Matt standing in the hallway. She opened her door motioning for him to join her taking a seat on her bed. "I take it you have something you want to talk to me about?" she asked, opening the bottle of water in her hands taking a sip.

"Yes, a few things actually though are there anything you would like to admit to first? I talked to Dawn earlier and she mentioned you gave her some reading material," Matt explained, taking a seat at her desk.

Raven nodded in agreement, seeing no reason to lie. "She was upset by how she did in the course, so I figured if she read the documents in Ari's archives, she'd be better prepared. She was tricked in the course by receiving false information, so I figured it was fair," she confessed, aware Ari was mad at her.

Matt arched an eyebrow, confused by her response. "What false information are you referring to? Neither one of you are being punished. The course was to show your strengths and weaknesses in areas that you can improve. I need to know Raven, were the documents the only thing you stole?" Matt asked, knowing that Ari would get revenge for Raven's act of thievery.

"Dawn was under the impression that sprites and satyrs are harmless since nothing bad happened to her in the course," she replied, seeing Matt sweep the room looking for anything that belonged to Ari. "I only took the documents and it seems they were returned to Ari, so no harm done," she added, dismissively thinking they were done with their discussion.

"That's not being misinformed all Dawn had to do was ask and we would have told her how they act around humans. I decided to offer her a job as a researcher, knowing her knack for intel. We still need to discuss your future as a slayer though I don't believe you. You had free access to Ari's stash and all you took were a few papers?" Matt asked, ignoring the dismissal.

Raven sighed, not surprised that he didn't believe her. "She felt foolish coming to you to ask her questions unsure if you had the time to explain it. She seemed to like reading the reports, so what harm was done?" she asked, failing to answer Matt's question, not wanting to repeat herself.

"Raven, I don't know what's been bothering you lately but stealing and lying isn't the answer though you have yet to answer my question. You're upset about being forced to have more training, yet your actions make me wonder how I can trust you out in the field. Dawn looks up to you and this is the type of example you wish to set for her? That as long as you get your way it's all right to steal from those that would gladly give them if asked?" Matt growled, not amused by her response.

"I did answer it, you think I stole something other than the records and I didn't, but you don't believe me. You think I would be foolish enough to steal magical artifacts from Ari, especially after the stunt she pulled on me last night?" she snapped, climbing to her feet trying to leave her room. "Ari never shares anything with us unless she's told, otherwise why would the records be locked away?" she demanded, heading toward the door.

An icy wind swept up shutting the door before Raven could reach it. "We're not done here Raven; you can't just walk away every time things don't go your way. If you had asked me instead of sneaking around, you would know that Ari keeps them locked up because she has no place else to store them. You're on house arrest until further notice for stealing," Matt warned, thinking it was a fair punishment.

Raven glared at Matt, standing at the foot of the bed crossing her arms over her chest. "Fine, store them away in an obsessive old filing system, but to lock them away so the rest of us can't access them seems a bit extreme. Now that you've dealt out my punishment, are we done?" she demanded, annoyed that she was being grounded like a child.

"No Raven, we're not done. You want to act like a spoiled brat, I want to know what has gotten into you lately? Why are you so angry with everyone, acting like we're all against you? I have no say in what Ari does with her room; if you had a problem with it then you need to speak up about it not when things don't go your way," Matt warned, moving to walk toward her.

Raven moved to stand by her window, staring out at the garden. "I don't want to talk about it because then it makes it true, let's just say a troubling letter reached me questioning why I'm even here," she admitted, clenching her hands into fists at her sides refusing to let the tears fall down her cheeks. "I mean why did you let me stay here, I had no skills to offer, I was just a homeless teenager trying to prove that the paranormal existed," she whispered, aware that she shouldn't be angry with Matt.

Matt let out a sigh, moving to stand beside Raven, placing a hand gently on her shoulder. "You have skills, Raven, otherwise you wouldn't be here. Everyone has something unique to offer we just haven't found yours yet, but we can work on it. I let you stay here because I could see that you had potential and would be better off here then on the streets. Do you want to talk about it?" Matt offered, giving her shoulder a gentle squeeze.

Raven flinched, feeling his hand squeeze her shoulder but didn't recoil. She wiped the stray tears away, continuing to stare out the window. "My parents were reaching out to me for a handout. My older brother got caught dealing drugs and is in jail. The letter went on to imply that since they hadn't heard from me or that I haven't come home that I was a prostitute," she admitted, sighing in annoyance. "It's not the first time I've received letters like that from my folks, but the course made me feel like a failure and made me question my options, then Dawn came to me in tears and I just reacted without thinking," she added, feeling her shoulders slump, realizing she had never shared her family drama with anyone.

Matt growled; hearing Raven call herself such a fowl word. "Sorry, that wasn't to you it was a reaction to what your parents called you, though if you wish I could call them and persuade them to stop bothering you. I'm sorry I yelled at you. I just want to ensure you knew what you did was wrong. I wanted you to do the course to show what needs to be improved upon, so I know that when persuading the paranormal you'll return home alive. You're still grounded for a week for stealing and you owe Ari an apology," Matt explained, thinking it was a fair punishment.

Raven groaned, realizing that Matt was right—she was simply scared of confronting Ari. "It's fine I did something stupid and then tried defending it instead of just being honest. Ari isn't going to be as patient nor as kind as you were and is going to lash out at me," she admitted, knowing that Ari's punishment would be harsh.

Matt chuckled giving her shoulder a playful pat. "Not if you go and confess it will be worse if you make her come find you. Ari may seem harsh, but her punishments aren't that bad just a bit gross. I wouldn't wear anything nice when completing her task if I were you. Is there anything else you need to get off your chest? I know the course sucked, but we will figure out what you're good at, it will just take time," Matt advised, making a mental note to call the scumbags later.

Raven shook her head, offering him a weak smile. "Thanks for the heads up I think I'll get this over with. I'd be surprised if we discover I have a hidden talent," she noted, following him to the door. She tapped his shoulder, gaining his attention. "Thank you for hearing me out and giving me unlimited chances to be a better person," she added, bracing herself for Ari's wrath.

"You're welcome, just know that I'm here if you need to talk. Don't think that just because I'm busy that I don't have time to listen to you. You may be right, I recall you being adept with a bow, we can give that another look? Just be honest with Ari and stay by her desk in case things go south," he advised, knowing it was a safe place in Ari's room.

Raven followed him out of her room nodding in greeting to Scarlett before heading toward the basement in search of Ari.

"You guys were chatting for a while, I wasn't sure if you needed to be rescued," she teased, poking his ribs lightly seeing that he was lost in his thoughts.

"To be honest, I wasn't so sure things were going smoothly between us, but now that I have the whole story, I'm mad at myself for not making sure she was okay. Her parents were sending her letters asking for money calling Raven nasty names, and with her failure on the course she was lashing out in anger. I forget that not all of us are orphans or want nothing to do with our kin," Matt admitted, thinking over his options.

Scarlett slipped her arms around his waist, giving him a tight hug seeing that the news troubled him. "I wasn't aware she was in contact with her family, though to be honest she doesn't share a lot about her past. At least now you can do something about it instead of wondering if it was something you did," she advised, feeling sorry for Raven.

"Funny. She accused Ari of doing the same thing, keeping everything hidden and to herself. Though I told Raven she had to confess her crime. I only have guardianship over Dawn. Raven was found on the streets and after staying here for a year her social worker came to me. Raven was claimed as a runaway, I was supposed to return her to her house, but I decided on a different course of action. Her parents think she's attending a boarding school for troubled youths," Matt explained, still amused that they believed the lie.

Scarlett reached up tucking a loose strand behind his ear. "A believable lie seeing that the manor is on an isolated property housing that may fit that profile to the public eye," she admitted, thinking no one would question it. "I'm impressed you were able to get through to her, when someone else would have punished her and left it at that," she admitted, brushing her lips against his.

Matt returned this kiss pulling Scarlett closer to him. "That was my intention at first, but then she started crying and I couldn't just leave her without making her happy. What do you think I should do about her parents? I have a few ideas but not all of them are legal," he asked, hearing the demon laugh in glee.

Scarlett shrugged her shoulders thinking that he must have had something in mind. "Clearly, her parents shouldn't be allowed to continue contacting her, but you want to do more?" she asked, wondering what his ideas were if some of them weren't legal.

"I met them once and I told them to never contact Raven otherwise I would be forced to take action. I went the legal route to try removing her from them and lost the battle. I figured if they were claimed to be insane by the state then they would lose custody of her," he explained, ignoring the demon's comment that killing them would be easier.

Scarlett bit her lower lip seeing that he was low on options. "It seems like an extreme course of action, but if it will keep Raven safe, I'd say to go for it though how would you achieve it?" she asked, seeing that he was considering the idea in his head.

"I'm not sure I could use magic and create illusions or give them a private view of my demonic form. I could also invite them here, but I doubt they would leave here in one piece knowing the others. There is another option the demon is offering but I'm not going down that route, even if they are bastards, they are still innocents," Matt explained, brushing her hair out of her face.

Scarlett weighed his options understanding what the demon had proposed. "I think the easiest option is to use magic forcing them to see illusions that aren't there. If you let the demon loose hoping to frighten them, who's to say he won't try to force his plan on you again?" she advised, reaching for his hand squeezing it lightly.

Damn and here I was hoping to give them a new paint job on the house, The demon mused in Matt's head. "I agree, I'll ask Ari to create some chocolates with the potion inside them before delivering them to Raven's parents," he explained, thinking it was a smart plan.

~~*

Raven descended the basement steps fidgeting with her bracelet. She smiled seeing Dawn greet her embracing her in a tight hug. "Don't be mad, but I gave Ari back the reports—" she announced, interrupted by Raven.

"I know, I talked to Matt and he said Ari agreed to teach you to be a researcher. I actually came to speak to Ari about it," she admitted, returning the embrace before following Dawn over to the desk seeing that she was busy reading old reports.

Ari entered the room placing a stack of papers on the desk. "I see the little burglar has returned. Care to try stealing something else or is it only when the barrier's down?" Ari asked, crossing her arms waiting for Raven's response.

Raven took in a shaky breath shaking her head no. "No, I came to return this seeing how Dawn was kind enough to return the reports for me," she admitted, slipping the bangle off her wrist placing it on the desk. "Matt said if I explained my actions and apologized, you might not take my head off. I know what I did was wrong and I'm sorry," she added, staring at her feet, understanding why Ari would be furious with her.

Ari glanced at the bracelet before walking over to Raven, grabbing her wrist, and pulling her arm up to inspect it in the light. "I'm just ensuring that the object didn't curse you or leave a nasty mark in its wake. Your wrist seems fine but I'm giving you an ointment just to be on the safe side. You still have yet to explain why you stole from me,

Raven," Ari explained, walking over to her desk looking for the jar to give to the girl.

Raven thanked her, thinking that if the bracelet had cursed it would have been her own fault. "At the time, I rationalized it with wanting a rush to distract myself from failing the course, but I don't think that was it. I told Matt that I wanted to cheer up Dawn, thinking that her inexperience affected her performance, but I don't think that's the truth entirely," Raven admitted, shifting her weight from one foot to the other. "I had received a nasty letter from my folks and wanted to get revenge. I never did find what I was looking for so I took the reports to give to Dawn and assumed the bracelet was harmless," she added, letting Ari process what she had shared.

Ari ran a hand through her hair, pacing as she thought over Raven's words. "That was very foolish of you, Raven. Magic isn't a toy, it's a wild force with a mind of its own. If I may ask, what were you searching for? I keep things locked for a reason, Raven, not only did you put yourself in danger, but you broke my trust in the process," Ari warned, taking a deep breath pulling her magic back under control.

Raven frowned, expecting Ari to lash out at her. "I'm sorry, I will work at regaining your trust, and if that never happens, I'll understand that too. I guess I was looking for a potion or a spell to make them regret how they treated me," she admitted, aware that Dawn was listening, waiting to ask for more details later when they were alone.

Ari sighed pinching the bridge of her nose. "Dawn take the reports you're currently reading and go to your room please. I wish to continue this conversation in private," Ari asked, waiting for the younger girl to collect the documents and scurry up the stairs. "Raven, take a seat, I'm not going to yell at you but you're right it will take a while for you to regain my trust," Ari explained, taking a seat in her chair before turning to face Raven.

Raven took a seat in the other chair to face Ari, surprised to hear she wouldn't yell at her. "In the heat of the moment, I felt justified in my actions, but I know it was reckless and understand it was wrong. I'm sorry I stole from you and broke your trust," she whispered, resting her hands in her lap.

"Why does everyone assume that magic is a cure for every situation? Magic should never be used in a negative manner; it will lash out at the caster and all those connected to them. You were lucky that what you stole wasn't active, not everything I own is as friendly. You're not off the hook, for the next week you will prepare ingredients for me and trust me they will not be pleasant. During that time, I will be teaching you the basics of magic," Ari explained, picking the bracelet up, twirling it in her fingers, lost in thought.

Raven nodded in agreement, wondering what was so bad about collecting ingredients. "Will the ingredients I'll be collecting found on the grounds? Matt said I was grounded for that period," she admitted, thinking that she was getting more out of the punishment than Ari, getting to learn more about magic.

"No, I will be providing the ingredients your task will be to prepare them for potions and other remedies, though I'll wait for our lesson to reveal the items to you. Before you go, I'll return the bracelet to you, I activated the charms so that in a moment of need it will protect you," Ari offered, a blue glow consuming the bracelet before offering it to Raven.

Raven reached out for the bracelet, surprised by the offer. "Thank you, that was generous of you to enchant it as a way to defend me if I ever need it," she admitted, placing the bracelet around her wrist. "When do you want me to come to get my lessons and prepare the ingredients?" she asked, accepting her punishment without complaint.

"We can start three days from now. Tonight, is the full moon no one is allowed down here until sunrise for everyone's safety against Andrew. Raven understand that I am using this as a learning experience but steal from me again and I will not offer you such an easy outcome. Do I make myself clear?" Ari asked, forgiving a childish action only once.

Raven climbed to her feet nodding in agreement. "I'm not foolish to repeat the same mistake twice. Besides I'm still surprised by how you handled it by willing to work with me," she admitted, thinking she would have to thank Matt for advising her to talk to Ari instead of avoiding her.

"We all make mistakes, Raven, even those of us who seem to have a grasp on life. I would wait and hold your thanks you may not feel the same way once the week is over," Ari warned, recalling Jet's reaction to the punishment.

Raven smiled but thanked her again, relieved that she was given a second chance and a gift. She greeted Jet in passing, reaching the top of the stairs before heading to Dawn's room to explain what had happened.

Chapter Fourty-Four

Jet descended the stairs seeing Ari putting a jar of ointment away. "That was lenient, though she is in for a rude awakening. I wasn't as squeamish as her and I hated that punishment," he announced holding a black gift bag in his hands.

Ari chuckled, collapsing in her chair pulling her hair out of her face. "What was I supposed to do, punish her for acting like a teenager? At least she stole a low-level magical item, otherwise she would have been in worse shape though what did you bring me?" Ari asked, seeing the black gift bag.

Jet laughed, taking a seat beside her, keeping the bag out of her reach. "Vincent explained to me what you guys talked about, and although I'm scared, he'll try it again I was willing to forgive him," he admitted, pulling out a wooden figurine of Branwen the goddess of love and beauty. "I made him help me paint it and etched on the bottom is the rune Ingwaz for creativity," he explained, handing her the sculpture to admire it.

Ari took the figurine from Jet, turning it around in her hands looking at it from all angles. "It's wonderful, Jet. thank you. It will make a fine addition on my altar. The gift was truly kind of you and I'm proud that you gave Vincent forgiveness instead of revenge," Ari explained, leaning over kissing him on the cheek.

Jet grinned, rubbing the back of his neck, watching her place it on her altar. "After he shared his story with me, I felt sorry for him. I recall having that fear of wanting to leave behind a legacy before enlisting in the military. I'm glad you like it. I wanted to remind you that there is beauty and purity in your magic," he admitted, fidgeting with his amulet.

Ari blushed glad that her back was to him. She touched the rose quartz, thinking over his comment. "I think we all wish to leave our mark on the world ensuring that if something happens that we will be remembered. I'm teaching both Raven and Dawn now, do you think can give me a hand with their training? It's clear that your studies are ending," she explained, sitting back down next to him.

Jet smiled, flattered by the offer, unaware their training was near complete. "What are you teaching Dawn? My shields still need work, but I'd be happy to help in any way that I can," he offered, aware that trying to teach them both would overwhelm her.

"Dawn is learning to become a researcher so most of her training will be more with the archives and artifacts I keep locked away from wandering hands. I know you still have much to learn but I figured you could help Raven learn the basics when it comes to magic," Ari explained, reaching out to grasp his hand.

Jet intertwined his fingers with hers, nodding in agreement with her suggestion. "I hope Raven will be willing to listen to me instead of thinking that only you know all the answers," he warned, aware that Raven was stubborn and might not be willing to listen to him.
 Ari chuckled, agreeing with him. "I know, that's why I'm asking for help. I don't even know if she'll listen to me, but we'll have to wait and see. I know you're working on your shields but is there anything else you wish to learn from me?" Ari asked, bringing her hand up to kiss the back of his.

"Why wouldn't she listen to you? Clearly, she's scared of upsetting you. I think Dawn more than Raven," he teased, seeing her roll her eyes in response to his statement. "I'd like to work on creating spells, I've gotten better with runes given our test earlier and am still unsure of how to use them with herbs to work out a spell," he added.

Ari tugged on a strand of hair, thinking over his words. "I don't mean to scare them, I'm just not good being around other people. Spell crafting can be a very tricky concept, one that you need a good shield for. Why don't we add that to the list and focus more on rune carving and your shields for now? Did you start creating a book of shadows?" Ari asked, seeing him frown in disappointment.

Jet nodded in agreement seeing that she had given the answer some thought before sharing it with him. "Yes, it's stored in my desk in my room, stashed inside a hollow book on history," he admitted, thinking that Vincent had seen it in his room and had been discouraged from looking at it. "I usually add to it after our lessons, though I disagree I think it takes you longer to get comfortable around people," he added, brushing a strand of her hair out of her face.

"I'll have to take your word on that since I know what the others think of me. It doesn't bother me though I'm glad to see your keeping yours safe. Mine is behind you hidden with the storage of blueprints; you're welcome to look at it," Ari offered, knowing that it would intrigue him.

Jet grinned excited to look through the book picking up the book. He carefully opened it up, examining the sections of herbs and spells written in small neat handwriting. He smiled, reading some of the spells and chants they had practiced. "There is a wealth of knowledge in here, thank you for letting me look at it," he noted, failing to recognize some of the words in Gaelic.

"You are welcome to look at it anytime you want to learn from it though you may have to ask for a few clarifications. There are also a few spell books, but I don't think you'll be able to read them," Ari mused, watching him glance through the book.

Jet nodded in agreement thinking that the spell books may be in Gaelic. "There were a few pages I wasn't able to read, though the pages I could make out were informative," he admitted, feeling his cheeks flush hearing his stomach growl. "Have you eaten yet, I heard you made a great stew," he noted, offering her his hand.

Ari laughed, shaking her head before climbing to her feet. "In that case perhaps I should create some translations for you. I've been busy dealing with other matters though should we go before your stomach tries to eat itself?" she asked in amusement, motioning for Jet to lead the way.

Jet laughed, heading up the stairs with Ari close behind him. "I didn't mean to add more to your plate, I am just curious to read what you had recorded," he admitted, entering the kitchen making them a pot of tea.

"You're not a bother Jet, otherwise I wouldn't have offered in the first place. Should we call the others or enjoy a meal alone?" Ari asked, pulling the pot out before reheating it on the stove.

Jet waited for the water in the kettle to boil pondering her question. "The idea of sharing a meal with you is tempting, though it seems Matt and Scarlett are in the living room watching a movie," he replied, hearing music from the television from the living room. He smirked seeing Scarlett stretched out on the sofa, using Matt as a pillow. Hearing the kettle whistle, he added a tea bag of Green Tea into two mugs before adding hot water to it.

Ari laughed poking her head into the living room. "Hey love birds, dinner will be ready in a few, care to pause your movie and join us?" Ari called, sending a quick text to the others upstairs.

Scarlett laughed reaching for the remote to pause the movie. She tried sitting up, laughing as Matt pushed her back brushing his lips over hers. She grabbed his hand sitting up blushing at hearing Dawn swoon followed by Raven teasing them to get a room. "Why are we all eating together instead of the two of you eating alone? Did she not like the gift?" Vincent demanded, before Jet smacked him taking a seat at the table.

"I think it was sweet of Ari to make us dinner," Dawn protested, seeing that Andrew was absent from the table. Raven rolled her eyes taking a seat next to her texting Andrew to see if he were joining them.

"I figured it would be a nice gesture seeing how we may be busy the next few days. I did like the gift Vincent. It was kind of Jet to create it for me, and he said you helped in its creation," Ari explained, placing bowls on the table before filling them with stew.

Vincent grinned relieved to see that she liked it. "I helped him paint it, though should we put some of the stew in a dog bowl for Andrew?" he teased, aware that the werewolf wasn't present.

Raven glared at him not amused by the joke. "He said he'll be down in a minute, he was taking a shower," she replied, setting her phone aside grabbing a glass of water.

Matt reached a hand up smacking Vincent on the back of the head. "Be nice, Vincent, even if your comment had some truth to it. What, don't give me that look, Raven; he will turn into a wolf tonight," Matt warned, seeing Ari take a seat next to Jet.

Vincent winced, rubbing the back of his head. "I was just kidding, though don't lie Matt, you thought it was funny," he protested, seeing Andrew enter the room wearing black t-shirt and matching sweatpants.

He took a seat across from Raven, nodding his head in thanks to the bowl offered to him. "I have to disagree, I didn't find the joke amusing Vincent, though nice try." He groaned, taking a bite of the stew.

"It could have been worse; Vincent could have made jokes about sleeping in a cage. You have an hour before moonrise, though I suggest taking your potion once you're finished," Ari offered, placing a vial next to Andrew's drink.

Vincent laughed nearly choking on his drink as Andrew held up his hands defensively. "Is the vial his doggie snack for being a good boy?" Vincent teased, seeing Andrew roll his eyes finishing his meal before digesting the vial. Andrew grimaced, swallowing the bitter liquid carrying his dishes to the sink.

"Nice try, Vincent, but no one finds you funny," Andrew protested, trying to ignore the snicker that had come from Scarlett. "Ari is it okay for me to head down there now and get situated?" he asked, pulling the headphones from his pocket slipping them around his neck.

Ari bit her lower lip trying hard not to laugh. "Yes, go ahead and get situated, I'll be down in a second to lock the cage. I put blankets in the cage in case you decide to strip again," Ari called, watching him head downstairs.

Dawn poked Raven playfully seeing the lustful smile flicker across her face at the mention of Andrew being naked. "You didn't put pillows in it to make his doggie bed more comfortable?" Vincent asked, laughing at hearing Andrew yell for him to shut up.

Matt chuckled seeing that Ari hurried downstairs to avoid answering Vincent. "I take that as a yes, though who knows maybe Ari will let you unlock the cage in the morning, Raven, seeing as how no one else wants to see the wolf naked," Matt suggested, standing up to take his bowl to the sink.

Vincent laughed harder seeing Raven's face flush scarlet, trying to cover her face with her cup. "Damn, Matt, I think you just made her day. I think Ari will be relieved she doesn't have to see a horrible sight," he teased, seeing that the others were finished helping Matt clean up.

"I was speaking the truth; I know Ari hates opening it in the morning. I heard her scream a few times in disgust after the full moon. Come on, it's clear Raven has a thing for him, it's not my fault Andrew is a moron," Matt replied, taking the dishes from Vincent to wash them.

Raven groaned waiting for the space in front of her to be cleared, crossing her arms on the table burying her face against it. "There's no need to be embarrassed, Raven. I'm sorry, he is oblivious to how you feel. I mean if Vincent figured it out, Andrew should have noticed it," Scarlett accused, hearing Raven laugh at Vincent's expense.

"You forget, Vince has only a few brain cells. I don't think you can say the same about Andrew, though they could both be in the same level of intelligence just one was dropped more as a baby." Matt teased, as Ari ran up the stairs slamming the door behind her catching her breath as she activated a charm to seal the door.

Scarlett laughed seeing Vincent give Matt a toothy grin not fazed by his joke. "Thanks for the compliment, Matt. All I hear is that I'm smarter than Andrew," Vincent protested, throwing his fist up in triumph.

Jet glanced at Ari hearing her panting as the door slammed shut behind her. He felt the wave of magic wash through the manor as the charm was triggered. "Is everything all right?" he asked, forcing her to have a seat at the table refilling her cup of tea.

"Everything is fine though I would appreciate it if you guys wait until I have the cage locked before mocking Andrew. His wolf took offense to it and his transformation started before the moonrise. He's inside it now, but I had to seal the cage without protection," Ari explained, wincing as her left hand brushed against the cup.

Jet winced understanding what had happened, climbing to his feet grabbing gauze from the kitchen drawer. He grabbed the topical ointment and sat beside her. Jet took her wrist gingerly applying the ointment over her palm, and gently laying the gauze over it. "I'm sorry, we didn't think it would add a risk to your task." Scarlett apologized, seeing that Ari had injured herself by not having proper protection.

"It's all right I thought it was rather funny, I was putting my gloves on when my magic warned me of the danger, and I was able to react in time. I would rather have a burn from the bars then getting scratched or bitten by Andrew," Ari explained, thanking Jet once he was finished.

Jet patted her arm offering her a small smile. "That should help the burn heal faster, though maybe you should explain what potion was inside the vial you gave Andrew?" he suggested, aware that Raven had been staring at the liquid curiously before Andrew had taken it.

"Sure, though it should take effect by now seeing that moon rise has started. It's a calming draught allowing Andrew to be in control during the transformation. If the potion is strong enough will make him sleep through the entire night. The drawback is the ingredients only react with the moon. He seemed fine until Matt started making comments and then he lost it. I think Andrew's wolf wants a piece of Matt," Ari explained, hearing a sigh coming from their leader.

"I'm sorry, Ari. I was just joking around though it's clear even his wolf side thinks that Scar should be his mate. I guess that means we'll end up fighting eventually, since words don't seem to affect him," Matt groaned, feeling bad that he had put her in danger.

Scarlett made a retching sound at the idea of being near Andrew, getting a glass of water. "Hey, you said I could take a swing at him first," she reminded Matt, pulling the bandana free, letting his hair fall in his face.

Matt chuckled, shaking his hair out of his face. "That's right, I did promise you that you could get the first hit, but that doesn't mean you'll be the only one. Who knows enough hits to the head will knock some common sense into him," Matt suggested, getting a laugh from Ari.

Scarlett set her drink down on the table sitting in Matt's lap, letting him slip his arms around her waist. She frowned seeing that Raven had fled the room with Dawn going after her. "It seems like Raven disagreed with our course of action, though you said Andrew lacked any brain cells," she reminded him, leaning against his chest.

Ari frowned seeing the girls run from the room. "I think Raven is just struggling to get over her first crush. I'm sure it isn't easy for her though Matt may be right. Andrew lacks a brain otherwise he would appreciate what's in front of him," she advised, climbing to her feet to head to her room.

Jet watched Ari retreat to her room blushing realizing that Vincent had caught him. "I'm going out to the gardens to mediate and practice my shields," he announced, wondering if Matt and Scarlett would return to their movie.

Vincent snickered waiting for Jet to leave before making his comment that what he really needed was a cold shower. "I think I'm going to watch a movie in my room, though if you guys are going to have sex, at least take it to your room, there are virgin ears down here," he teased, laughing at seeing Scarlett considering the idea.

Matt chuckled seeing that they had been caught red handed. "We did that last night though I could always go for another round. Demonstrating it would be an effortless way to give them an education on the matter. If you're watching another porno don't forget to charge it to your card and not the manor's," Matt teased, taking Scarlett's hand.

Vincent rolled his eyes letting out a low whistle not surprised that he'd guessed correctly. "For the last time, it only happened one time and it was an accident," he retaliated, heading up for his room.

Scarlett laughed hoping that Vincent was just kidding. "Be prepared for him to ask you a million questions after telling him that we slept together," she warned, brushing her lips against his hand.

"He can try though I can always show him the cable bill that has his dirty movie on it to the others if he gets on my nerves. I doubt you've changed your mind, you still want to visit Donovan, don't you?" Matt asked, hoping she would suggest they go back to their movie and forget about the trip.

Scarlett glanced out the kitchen admiring the full moon peeking out from the clouds. She bit her lower lip debating her answer. "Would you be mad if I said yes? I can't shake the feeling that something might have happened to him and he's too stubborn to tell me," she admitted, hoping that she was worried for nothing.

Matt let out a sigh yet wasn't surprised. "Very well, meet me in the garage in ten minutes and we'll go to the bar and come straight back here. This isn't a smart move Scar, but I know that you're worried about him and would go with or without me," he warned, heading up to his room to grab a few things.

Scarlett frowned heading up to her room to change aware that her fears were irrational. *If he would just call me back then I wouldn't need to go out there*, she thought, staring down at her phone before strapping a dagger to her boots and adding one to her purse, throwing on the jacket Matt had given her before making her way to the garage.

Chapter Forty-Five

Matt waited for Scarlett to join him, handing her the spare helmet for his motorcycle before climbing on extending his hand out to her. She put on the helmet and grabbed his hand slipping behind him placing her arms around his waist tightly.

The garage door opened as Matt sped out into the night, causing the chilly night air to brush against her flesh. She rested her cheek against his shoulder racing onto the highway before approaching the street the bar was on. The neon sign illuminated the deserted street, as Matt killed the engine helping her off the bike taking the helmet from her. He grasped her hand, intertwining it with hers as they approached the bar's entrance.

"Thank you again for bringing me here," she said, letting him hold the door open for her before entering the bar. Matt followed her inside letting the door swing shut behind him.

Matt pulled her close, brushing his lips over hers. "I would do anything to make you happy, though don't let that fool you, I'm not happy being here and exposing you to a threat, but I understand how much Donovan means to you. I'll stay down here and watch the exit while you chat," he explained, seeing that his answer had made her happy.

Scarlett returned the kiss relieved that he wasn't upset. "Thank you, I know you only want to keep me safe. I'm sure I have nothing to worry about and that it was just a bad dream like you said," she replied, heading upstairs, searching for Donovan.

Michael exited the storage room hearing Scarlett's voice startled to see the stranger standing by the bar. "Hey, I'm Michael. I'm Don's younger brother. Can I get you anything?" he asked, moving to stand behind the bar filling a glass with Scotch for himself.

Matt shook his head declining the offer as Michael took a sip of his drink. "I wasn't expecting to see you two here but given what happened maybe it's for the best. He'll take her advice over mine anyway," he groaned, seeing Matt staring at Michael, expecting an explanation. "Donovan didn't summon her here?" he asked, seeing Matt shake his head, surprising him.

"I escorted Scarlett here because she had something that belonged to your brother. Did something happen?" he asked, ordering a glass of water, and taking a seat at the bar. He coughed covering the low growl in his chest, trying to suppress his demon, smelling the faint scent of blood in the air.

"Ah, you sense it to?" Michael mused, emptying his glass before refilling it. "One of our barmaids tried spiking Simon's drink with a poison a few nights ago, and Don ended up drinking it instead," he confessed, seeing no reason to keep it a secret from the man.

Scarlett ventured upstairs toward Donovan's room standing outside the door. She heard wheezing followed by harsh coughing growing concerned, she knocked hard on the door before announcing herself. "Donovan? It's me, Scarlett. Are you all right?" she asked, waiting for him to answer.
Don sat on his bed covering his mouth with his hand feeling another coughing fit consume him. He sighed hearing Scarlett's racing thoughts before she knocked on the door. "Yes, a moment to refresh myself and then I shall join you. I see you brought company, a wise choice given the current situation," Don replied, hearing her wait outside his door. He cleaned himself up before stepping out into the hallway. Scarlett glanced to the stairwell hearing footsteps approach.

Matt's brows knitted together seeing them standing in the hallway. He closed the distance between them reaching for her hand squeezing it lightly. He tried hard not to gag the scent of blood overwhelming from behind the closed door. "Did you give him the letter?" he asked, seeing her shake her head no as Michael led them into one of the guest rooms.

Michael opened the mini fridge offering Scarlett and Matt a bottle of water sitting in one of the armchairs.

Scarlett sat on the edge of the bed joined by Matt as Donovan stood in the doorway. "Donovan, I'd like you to meet Mathew, he was kind enough to esport me here to deliver this to you," she admitted, holding out the letter to him.

Michael noticed the pair holding hands making him think of perverted thoughts. Donovan groaned, clearing his throat. "Matt and I met downstairs, he seems like a cool guy," Michael confessed, rising to his feet before disappearing to his room.

Donovan pinched the bridge of his nose, before placing his arm over his mouth covering up another coughing fit. "I see he had no choice in the matter knowing how stubborn you can be. A wise choice seeing how a monster is seeking your blood," Donovan noted, ignoring the glare sent in his direction from Matt seeing the man was on edge waiting for an attack.

Concerned, Scarlett closed the distance between them slipping her arms around him in a tight embrace. "Your concern is touching, but is not necessary," he pleaded, returning the embrace, placing his index fingers on the side of her neck, using his nails to draw a French cross.

Scarlett flinched, bringing her hand to her neck, feeling the small scratch. Scarlett rolled her eyes taking her seat beside Matt. "I found something that belonged to Isabel addressed to you… I figured it could wait, but after a troubling nightmare I was worried about you," she confessed, wondering why he had scratched her like that.

Matt grasped her hand looking at her neck in concern relieved to see it was a scratch and not a bite. "Not to sound rude, but your brother mentioned you were poisoned by your staff. Care to explain why this place suddenly smells like a blood bath when you claim to only eat animals?" Matt asked, wondering if Simon wasn't the only vampire they had to fight against.

"Wait, is that why you were coughing? Do you know what the poison was or how you were administered it?" she asked, her thoughts racing forcing him to hold up his hand trying to get her thoughts to ease.

"Shiva informed me it was a mixture using blood blossoms, a flower that grows while feasting on demonic blood. I will recover in a few days' my sire entrusted a book to me, which included a cure for the flower," he explained, groaning in annoyance seeing that it had only encouraged more racing thoughts from Scarlett. "I have already performed the removal procedure. I merely just need time to recover." Donovan explained, retrieving a bottle from the fridge. taking a few sips of water to clear his throat.

"The blood you smell Mathew is mine, I performed the ritual in my bedroom and have yet to clean up the mess. A side effect to the poison is being unable to keep blood down while flushing out the toxin. I hope you are unharmed Scarlett, I created a vampire's cross on your neck in case things take a drastic turn," Donovan explained, collapsing in the armchair across from them letting out a groan hearing both their thoughts on the matter.

Scarlett frowned, reaching a hand up to tentatively feel the scratch, aware that it had already scabbed up. "Don't you think you could have done it sooner?" she asked, thinking of the wound on her shoulder, surprised that Matt hadn't lashed out for the mark. "I'm fine just wondering how effective it will be if I am ever in a situation to need it," she added, not wanting to admit to the idea of Simon biting her.

"Forgive me, I didn't consider it last time given everything that occurred during our encounter. I had forgotten its existence. until I came across it in my sire's journal. I didn't sense his shades outside Mathew, do not blame me for his attack. My lapse in security may have been due to the poison, but I would never allow harm to befall Scarlett.

"To answer your question, it will prevent any vampire from biting your throat you and only I can remove it," Don explained, tensing as the air grew colder around them, causing another coughing fit.

"Right, we should just take you on your word and nothing else? You're telling me that you were clueless that a rogue vampire went unnoticed by you? That Simon killed innocents in what I know you blood suckers see as your territory, yet you only step in now instead of after the first bodies were found? How do we know you're not using this illness as an excuse luring Scar into another trap?" Matt growled, as ice fractures crystalized over the windows seeing the vampire double over in pain trying to catch his breath.

Scarlett reached up cupping both of Matt's cheeks forcing him to look at her. "I get that you're angry but causing Donovan pain won't solve anything. Do you honestly think that with all that has happened I wouldn't be more cautious?" she pleaded, brushing her lips over his trying to force Matt to control his anger.

Matt returned the kiss letting go of his power as the room temperature went back to normal. "I'm sorry, just seeing that he knew more than what he was letting on upset me and I lost control. To know that innocents could have been saved and you not being put in danger, I guess I let the demon sway my actions," Matt explained, as Don spat in a nearby trashcan trying to get his breathing under control.

"You should ask questions before attacking someone though now I understand why so many fears you. I read about those bodies in the paper and was unaware of them being slain by a vampire. He approached me a week ago asking to use my establishment for a meeting. When I discovered he was going after Scar, I tried to protect her to the best of my ability. Yes, your thoughts are accurate I should have hunted Simon down before he became a threat, but how successful are you at hunting down a monster that hides in the shadows?" Don asked, understanding the man's anger but that didn't excuse his actions.

Scarlett rested her head against Matt's shoulder understanding why he had been quick to anger. "Maybe he feared if he asked his questions you wouldn't be forthcoming with the answers. Matt already had mixed feelings about you and the mark you gave me, while appreciated, still makes me question how effective it will be," she admitted, recalling the second reason they had come. *It was a mistake to come here, I had to persuade Matt to go against his better judgement, and who knows if Donovan will even want the letter?* She thought, an awkward silence falling between them.

Don sighed. moving to climb to his feet only to pause. seeing the weapon resting in Matt's hand. "I merely wish to collect the letter that Scarlett was kind enough to bring me. I will not harm either one of you though clearly my word means little to you. No one can remove the mark and any that touch it will be burned. It won't leave a scar and by tomorrow it will disappear, but the magic will remain. It was the best I could offer though I wish I could do more," he explained, hiding his bitterness that they were treating him like a wild animal.

Matt took the letter from Scarlett, walking over to the vampire and dropping the letter in his lap. "There is no such thing as an innocent vampire and seeing you covered in blood doesn't help your image. We should go Scar, we have no reason to stay and continue to put you at risk," Matt warned, not caring that he had hurt the vampire's feelings. Don opened the letter reading it to himself catching the flower petals that fell in his lap filling the room with the faint scent of moon flowers.

Scarlett climbed to her feet smiling as the faint scent filled the air once he had opened the letter. Matt tried leading her toward the door, but she pulled her hand away hearing him sigh in annoyance. "I know with what has happened you're worried about me, but just give me a minute, please?" she pleaded, wanting to thank Donovan for what he had done.

Matt gave a simple nod kissing her cheek before heading outside the room deciding to wait for her in the hallway. "You found a good partner and he has cause for concern. I just wish I had been more successful in gaining his trust, but clearly that will never happen. Thank you for bringing me Isabel's goodbyes," Don replied, once they were alone.

Scarlett offered him a weak smile placing her hands in her pockets. "I'm still surprised I was able to talk him into bringing me here after the shades attacked me," she confessed, thinking that because of that Matt may never trust Donovan. "I don't blame you for what happened. You didn't know he possessed that ability and we both thought Simon had fled to lick his wounds," she added, reaching up to feel the mark, wondering if it would hurt Simon if he attacked her.

"Your boyfriend believes I fed you to the wolves though if I had known I would have insisted on you staying here until morning. I was unaware that Simon had any abilities given his sire, but now I know why I could never sense him. What will you do now, return to your manor?" Don asked, folding the letter, and smiling at the memories the letter brought him.

Scarlett closed the distance between them, embracing him in a gentle hug, sensing that, like Matt, he would continue to blame himself for what happened. "Everything is on lockdown until we can find a way to defeat Simon," she admitted, happy that she could bring him some joy with the letter.

"A wise plan though how will you continue to patrol and keep the morals safe behind closed doors? Does your boyfriend have a plan on locating Simon before more bodies are added to the pyre or other monsters decide to accept the opportunity?" Don asked, returning the hug placing a flower in her hair.

Scarlett let out a heavy sigh shrugging her shoulders. She took the flower braiding it in her hair to keep it in place. "That's a question you should ask him, though he may not answer it. I'm sure the dilemma is weighing heavily on his shoulders," she replied, wishing that she had an answer for him.

Don chuckled giving her hand a gentle squeeze. "I'd rather not given how Mathew will attack if I get too close to him. I take no personal offense; I know your safety is his main concern. the same as myself. Be careful out there Scarlett," he warned, hearing Matt's thoughts about what to do to ensure their safety on the way back.

Scarlett sighed knowing that he was right. "When you put it that way, I am fortunate to have you both go through such lengths to keep me safe," she replied, bidding him good night before exiting the room seeing Matt still waiting patiently for her. "I feel guilty, a heavy weight was lifted off my shoulders by coming here, yet it put you on edge," she admitted, fidgeting with the braid.

Matt reached out for her hand trying to put her at ease. "It's all right I know you only wish to help out those you care about. What now, we can either stay here until morning or head home. I'm sorry I was being a jerk, but this whole floor smells of blood and they are vampires," he explained, hoping that she would understand.

Scarlett brought his hand to her lips, kissing it gently. "You could have been nicer to him, but at least you didn't attack him either. The safer option is to stay here until morning, there is plenty of room, but it's up to you," she replied, understanding that the smell had put him on edge.

"It would be smart to stay here until sunrise to ensure we don't run into Simon. I guess we should inform them to see if they have a room we can use," Matt moaned, heading downstairs to the bar to talk to Michael.

Scarlett frowned aware how unsettling the scent had made him. "I feel like once we're safely back at the manor I'm going to be in your debt," she admitted, rolling her eyes at hearing Michael snicker hearing them in the hallway. He vaulted over the railing, meeting them at the bar.

Matt chuckled patting the stool beside him for her to sit on. "I would suggest you repay the favor here, but it may be hard for me to enjoy it. Why is the bar deserted shouldn't you guys be running given the hour?" Matt asked, seeing that the place was deserted.

Michael let out a low whistle dropping the glass he had in his hands, cursing at his clumsiness before going to fetch a broom. Scarlett took the empty seat beside Matt drumming her fingers on the bar. "A tempting offer but it's no fun if you can't enjoy," she replied, seeing Michael sweep up the broken glass before attempting to fill another glass with gin.

Michael took a sip of his drink pretending he hadn't heard her answer. "We told the press we're closed for the next few weeks for renovation. Don didn't want humans to stumble into this and panic," he admitted, making a sweeping motion to the smell of blood filling the bar aware that Matt sensed it.

"Why is the smell in the bar if your brother claimed to be staying in his room? Wouldn't it just remain upstairs? We'll be staying here for the night and leaving at Dawn if that's not a problem," Matt explained, wrapping an arm around Scarlett's waist.

Michael shrugged his shoulders noticing the possessive gesture. "The smell isn't noticeable to humans, but as my brother explained it took a lot of blood to cleanse the toxin from his system. Animal blood is more dilated to us than blood from a human," he explained, refilling his empty glass. "All of the rooms are fully stocked so feel free to choose one. I'll be in my room if you need anything," he added, finishing his drink before heading for the stairs.

Matt watched Michael head upstairs before pulling Scarlett into his lap. "So, care to stay down here or would you rather go check out our room for the night?" Matt asked, kissing her neck softly.

Scarlett let out a soft moan turning to face him. She slipped her arms around his neck brushing her lips against his. "I'm content right here, though we could go up and try and finish our movie?" she suggested, trying to find a way to distract him.

Matt chuckled picking Scarlett up amused by her shout of surprise. He felt her swing her legs around his waist, as he walked up the stairs finding a guest room that was on the opposite end of Donovan's. "Hopefully, this will do, though do you feel better now that you had the chance to check up on him?" Matt asked, placing her on the bed.

Scarlett laughed reaching out for his hand pulling him down beside her. "The letter offered him some peace like the journal did for me. I guess it's why I felt guilty, I got more out of the trip than I anticipated when you were against coming in the first place," she admitted, slipping her arms around his waist resting her head against his chest.

"Only because I didn't want to put you in danger knowing that Simon would come after you. I know you Scar, once you have your mind set on something, there's no way to halt you or change it, so it was just easier to let you have your way," Matt explained, leaning his back against the headboard allowing her to lean against him.

Scarlett swatted his chest lightly. "You're saying that I'm stubborn?" she asked, fidgeting with the necklace, feeling his fingers toy with her hair. "You have a point though I'm sure Simon has his shades nearby expecting us to come back here," she admitted, understanding his hesitation to come.

Matt glanced out the window wondering if she was right. 'Perhaps though a little bit of snow keeps them at bay. I'm sorry for being a jerk to Don. I was just worried. They claim its animal blood but that doesn't put me at ease," he confessed, knowing that his actions had been out of line.

"I'm fortunate not to sense it, at least not to the extent as you. I thought you were both going to come to blows, which given Donovan's current condition wouldn't have been a fair fight," she replied, kissing his shoulder understanding he was worried about her safety.

Matt laughed only to stop when she punched his shoulder. "I'm sorry but it is a bit funny that we're fighting over your protection, yet Don doesn't really have that right. I know he claimed to be married to your sister, but does that excuse not reaching out to you sooner? I mean he has a phone and a computer, it's not like he couldn't contact you," Matt replied, bracing himself for another hit.

Scarlett let out a heavy sigh pushing herself up pulling her knees up to her chest. "That exact thought had crossed my mind a million times, both when I left here after we met and after reading my sister's journal," she whispered, feeling Matt's arms wrap around her waist pulling her against his chest. He ran his fingers through her hair in comfort, at a loss on what to say.

Chapter Fourty-Six

Donovan sat in his room letting out a heavy sigh. He could hear the thoughts of those inside his bar darkening his mood. He stood leaning against the window twirling a gold ring between his fingers allowing his thoughts to distract him ignoring the knock on his door.

Michael knocked once more before entering the room. He frowned seeing his brother staring out at the full moon. He crossed the room to stand beside him resting a hand on Don's shoulder. "Hey, I just wanted to let you know that Scarlett and her guard dog had decided to stay the night," he explained, seeing that his brother was distracted.

Don glanced up giving Michael a weak smile. "I gathered from their thoughts though apparently neither one of them thinks very highly of me. I'm accused of neglecting Scarlett and since I never contacted her, I have no right to try and protect her," Don explained, slipping the ring back on his finger. "I've been lost in memories wondering if perhaps they are right," he admitted, feeling insecure about his relationship with Scarlett and his brother.

Michael frowned resting his hand on his brother's shoulder. "A lot of time passed between losing Isabel and connecting to Scarlett, so she's going to need validation for all that time lost. As painful as it is, you need to share with her memories that weren't in that journal, since it doesn't seem like her boyfriend trusts you," he advised, patting Don's shoulder. "I have no complaints, Donnie, I'm happy with the life I lived and the life I have now," he added, hearing him grimace at the nickname.

Don rolled his eyes at the childish nickname. "Thank you, Michael, your words comfort me though he may have a point. How would you react entering a vampire's den overwhelmed with the scent of blood?

Your idea has merit even if I'm hesitant to follow through with the suggestion. A suggestion on speaking to her without her protector's presence?" Don asked, cursing as a coughing fit tore through him.

Michael patted his brother's back retrieving a bottle of water from the min fridge offering it to him. Michael stroked his chin lost in thought trying to produce a better idea. "You can leave a note for her, that may be easier than stating your thoughts aloud? Why did you allow so much time to pass before telling her who you were?" he asked, knowing she wouldn't believe Don's answer if they were excuses.

Don nodded his head in thanks, taking a sip to clear his throat. "My mind was clouded with grief and anger that I became lost. You were the one to discover the wolf and his hiding place, but he never left the dwelling long enough for my revenge. I thought I had failed Isabel. I promised to keep Scarlett safe, yet she vanished from my sight. I used every method that I had to find her only to turn up empty. It was only when she appeared here did, I realize she was safe and not harmed," Don explained, taking his brother's advice walking over to his desk to write the letter.

Michael frowned remembering the day mentioned. "I had to find the one responsible or remain feeling helpless, though we learned that they had a strong barrier leading into the manor, but without access we didn't know she was there," he replied, surprised Don had taken his advice.

"I know Michael, I too felt helpless with the situation and I have you to thank for getting me through my mourning. Thank you, for coming to check on me and lifting my spirits. Will you slip this under their door for me? I fear that it will be ripped to shreds if the demon catches my scent," Don asked, once he was finished writing the letter.

Michael beamed giving his brother a mocking bow stepping to the side to avoid being smacked. He collected the letter staring at it curiously. "Good call, her boyfriend doesn't like you and would likely destroy the letter. Despite him not trusting you, do you think he's a good match for her?" he asked, twirling the letter in his hands resisting the urge to read it.

"Not that my opinion matters much to Scarlett. but yes, I believe she has found a good match in the half demon. He cares for her and would do anything to protect her. He survived an attack by Simon's shades clearly Simon fears facing him, giving her more protection if Simon tries to attack her again." Don explained, seeing his brother glance at the letter. 'You can read it Michael, it just states what I have already told you," Don added, knowing his brother well.

"In time she may come to trust you more and value your opinion. How do you know he's a demon? With that type of protection hopefully that's enough to keep her safe. I'd hate to see you lose anyone else," Michael replied, trying to picture what Matt's demon looked like.

"I heard a second voice in his head when we were going to blows. Seeing how he caused the snowstorm outside our establishment during Scarlett's attack. That's my best theory though I lack proof to confirm it. My desire is to have that relationship with her despite her boyfriend's placing doubts in her head," Don explained. agreeing that he didn't want to lose someone else that he loved.

Michael smirked pointing to the other letter on his desk still smelling of moon flowers. "Not all hope is lost bro, she did bring you something to remember Isabel of without being asked," he warned, understanding that Donovan wanted to build a stronger relationship with Scarlett to have another reminder of Isabel.

A mournful look passed over his face. "Yes, though I appreciate it knowing the risks she faced. You were mentioned in Isobel's letter. She said that she found your antics endearing and that she will miss you. That you should continue to be your playful self to ensure other's spirits remain lifted," Matt explained, touching the letter with his fingertips inhaling the flower's scent.

Michael rolled his eyes. "What risk does she have with a demon for a shield?" he protested, laughing at hearing the contents of the letter. He threw both hands up in the air triumphantly, careful not to drop the letter. "See even she was encouraging me to be myself to help keep you sane," he replied, heading off to deliver the letter.

"I said he was a half demon Michael, meaning that he has limitations like any mortal and just because Isabel said it doesn't mean everyone enjoys your childish nature," Don called out after him.

Michael rolled his eyes pretending not to hear him. He walked to the other side of the building, pressing his ear against the door. He frowned, hearing silence before sliding the letter underneath the door and heading to his room. *I'm surprised it was all quiet and not wild animal sex*, he thought snickering, knowing his brother would hear his disgusting thoughts.

Matt sat up in the bed moving to head to the door, hearing someone walking toward their room. He noticed a piece of paper appear on the floor as he moved to retrieve it. He sighed seeing that Scar had other intentions tightening her hold on his waist.

Scarlett kissed his shoulder releasing her grip glancing toward the door. "What time is it? Was someone at the door?" she asked, rubbing the sleep from her eyes, wondering what had gained his attention.

"A little after one in the morning. go back to sleep. I think one of the vampires slipped a letter under the door, but I'll take care of it," he announced, moving to climb out of bed once Scarlett had allowed him to move.

Scarlett shook her head dismissing his suggestion sitting up in bed. "A letter for me?" she asked, letting him retrieve the letter holding her hand out wanting to see what it said.

Matt hesitated before sighing, handing the letter to her. "Yes, it appears Donovan is trying to communicate with you, though he was smart if he came to speak to you in person, I would have turned him away." Matt admitted, surprised that the man had intelligence.

Scarlett took the letter from him surprised he didn't just tear it up. She reached for his hand with the other one pulling him back down next to her. "Yes, you made that clear earlier though I'm not holding it against you, you just want to keep me safe," she admitted, opening the letter to read it noticing the neat handwriting.

Matt held his hands up in surrender. "I can respect someone with intelligence and besides as long as he doesn't come into the room, I see no harm in you reading a letter," Matt explained, claiming his spot on the bed before pulling her into his lap to read over her shoulder.

Scarlett rested her head against his chest seeing no harm in Matt reading it. "You should be careful, it almost sounded like you were being nice to him," she teased, continuing to read the letter.

Scarlett,

I would address this with your nickname, but I do not believe your boyfriend would enjoy another man calling you butterfly. I wish to remind you of my special ability and that I know that both you and your boyfriend lack trust in me.

You claim that I never spent time searching for you, but that is a lie. I tried my hardest after being pulled out of my fog of remorse but without a last name or idea of your location my search ended quickly. I owe what I do know about the mongrel due to my brother's actions and not my own.

He found the wolf's home, but we were unable to bypass the wards. I know that too much time has passed, but I wish to try once more to create a relationship with you.

I will be in my room if you wish to speak to me but if you are not allowed, we can continue to speak through letters.

Sincerely,

Donovan

Scarlett let out a heavy sigh clutching the letter to her chest. "Do you believe that what he wrote was sincere? It's clear he loved my sister dearly and cannot imagine the grief he must have felt losing her," she admitted, thinking it was best to follow the advice of writing back at least until Simon was slain.

Matt bit his lip thinking over her question. "I believe he speaks the truth, though what does he mean by special ability? It's clear he loved your sister and if I were to ever lose you, I would be in the same shape," Matt explained, kissing her neck to erase those thoughts from his mind.

Scarlett craned her neck kissing his cheek seeing that the idea of losing her had troubled him. "I'm sorry, I forgot to tell you, but I didn't think you would believe me. He can hear the thoughts of those around him, though I'm not sure how close he has to be for it to work," she admitted, amused by the nickname he had called her in the letter.

Matt sighed having an idea of what the man had been hinting at in the letter. "Clearly not, extremely far seeing him hint at hearing our conversation without being in the room. Otherwise, why give you a letter after speaking to him earlier this evening," Matt replied, not sure what to do about having his thoughts being overheard.

"Learning that his ability was true was unsettling, though are you mad?" she asked, turning to face him seeing that he was processing what the letter had said.

"Mad at what besides the fact that some stranger can hear my thoughts? I'm more concerned about you Scar. What are you planning on doing with the information he offered you?" Matt asked, willing to support her decision.

Scarlett frowned, staring down at the letter. "Are you mad that he can hear our thoughts, though why are you worried about me? He hasn't given me a reason not to trust him," she replied, wondering if he would question her answer. She heard Matt's phone going off making her curious as to who was up at the late hour. "Saved by the bell it seems, though who else other than Ari would still be up at this late hour?" she noted, curious to learn who it was.

Matt pulled his phone free before answering it. "Hey, Raven, what are you doing still up? I figured you would be asleep though is anyone else still up with you?" Matt asked, surprised that she was calling.

Chapter Forty-Seven

Raven had struggled sleeping and ventured into Andrew's room. She grabbed a sweatshirt from the floor, inhaling his scent before taking a seat at his desk. She heard the buzz of the police scanners listening for anything interesting as she played on his computer. An hour or two had passed before an announcement for an ambulance to arrive at the park caught her attention. She listened to the description as the park ranger had called it in. She called Matt wanting to inform him of what she had discovered. "Hey, Matt, I was in Andrew's room because I couldn't sleep and overheard another victim was attacked at the park. Should I tell Ari?" she asked, unsure of what to do.

Matt glanced out the window thinking over his options. "No, Ari needs to stay there in case anything goes wrong. Tell Vincent to meet me at the park and we can go check it out together," Matt explained, hanging up the phone before moving to get off the bed.

Raven agreed wishing them luck and to be safe before hanging up, heading up to Vincent's room to deliver the message. Vincent had been in bed watching a movie but sprang to action when Raven gave him the message taking the spare motorcycle parked in the garage.

Scarlett arched an eyebrow seeing Matt climb off the bed heading toward the door. "Are you going to tell me who that was or what's going om?" she asked, seeing that he was planning his next course of action.

Matt paused by the door slipping on his shoes and jacket. "Raven just called saying that someone was attacked in the park. There's a good possibility it could be Simon. I'm going to meet Vincent there to check it out," Matt explained, thinking that she would stay at the bar until he returned.

Scarlett climbed off the bed gathering her things as well, bracing herself for the argument they would have. "Let me guess, you want me to stay here until you come back?" she asked, knowing he would agree.

Matt paused frowning as he watched her actions. "Yes, what makes you think I'm taking you with me? The whole reason we're staying here is to ensure Simon doesn't find you and now you want to head to his feeding grounds?" Matt asked, trying to stay calm and not lose his temper.

Scarlett took in a deep breath trying to keep calm. "I know the risk is high, but I can't sit idly by and do nothing. I want to help even if you disagree with it," she protested, thinking what better way to evaluate what Donovan had given her by confronting Simon.

"That's not a reason Scar, you forget that I know you and I can see what you'll try if you go with me. We don't know if that mark will protect you and I won't stand by and let you play bait." He protested, moving to stand in front of her.

Scarlett sighed, slipping her arms around his neck brushing her lips over his. "We'll never know if we don't try and it would be nice to throw him off guard. The last time you went up against him it took everything you had," she noted, concerned that he would get hurt.

Matt closed his eyes letting out a bitter sigh. "I won't be alone. Vincent will be there as backup, evening the odds. You put me in a rough position, Scar, I want to keep you safe and taking you with me is going against everything logical in my head," he explained, knowing that he couldn't risk her being taken from him or worse hurt by the blood sucker.

Scarlett frowned sensing how torn he was over the situation. "I know you're worried about my safety, and I don't want to be your distraction, but wasn't the entire point of the training course was to prepare us for such an encounter? Besides what makes you think Simon didn't send his shades to do the job?" she pressed, trying to get him to change his mind.

Matt sighed, running a hand through his hair, and thinking over the matter. He let out a growl of frustration seeing that she had a point. "All right you win, it's clear that you seem to think he will make an appearance and I know saying no just means you'll find another way to get there," Matt groaned, seeing that she had won their argument.

Matt led the way downstairs heading for his park bike before allowing Scarlett to climb on behind him before heading to the park. He was relieved the vampires didn't stop them from leaving as they drove the rest of the way in silence.

Michael heard a knock at the back door of the bar, while restocking cases of beer. *Great more deliveries for me to unload. Why isn't Shiva helping me with this?* he thought, reaching the door, and picked up the parcel. His brow furrowed upon seeing his brother's name scrawled in neat cursive. "The handwriting looks like mother's, though Don would have said if he was expecting anything from her," he mused, carefully breaking the tape with the box cutter.

"Dear Donovan, hopefully this letter reaches you safely. I have enclosed a present in hopes that it may offer a shift in your perspective. Hope to see you and your brother soon. Sincerely, Madame Celestial," Michael read, placing the letter aside finding a transparent glass vial filled with dark liquid wrapped in black tissue paper. He uncorked the vial and inhaled a sweet smell. *How can this change how my brother sees things?* he thought, emptying the vial into his mouth. A warmth surged through him startling him, thus causing him to drop the vial. It shattered at his feet causing his eyes to darken. "Don, I'm headed out to run an errand. I'll be back later," he yelled, rushing out the door headed toward the church.

Simon sat in the shelter of a leather pew inside an abandoned Church; wooden bars nailed over the windows. Biblical scenes were still intact over painted glass barely visible through the gaps in the panels of wood. With his eyes closed, he listened to the shades he had left stationed outside the bar. Interesting, a challenge awaits my attention nearby. This may tip the tides in my favor allowing my pet to be by my side, Simon thoughts, heading toward the door, kicked in by Michael.

"I'm not surprised to see your brother failed to teach you any manners. Care to enlighten me as to why you're annoying me with your presence without straining yourself?" Simon sneered, watching the shades knock Michael to the ground as he tried to lunge at Simon.

Michael used his nails to tear through the shades like tissue paper before closing the distance between them. "Be quiet, Simon. I don't owe you an explanation," he snapped, lunging toward him once more. His nails dug into Simon's throat. punched in the stomach by Simon.

Michael cursed pushed back, slamming into the wall next to him causing two wooden crosses to fall at his feet. "How amusing, you honestly thought you could defeat me? I'm feeling generous and will grant you the opportunity to flee with your tail between your legs," Simon sneered, beckoning Michael toward the exit. He watched Michael grasp a wooden cross in each hand.

Michael hurled the crosses in his left hand, swatted away with ease. He lunged at Simon driving the wooden shaft of the cross into his stomach. "I'm not leaving without knocking you down a few pegs," Michael declared, amused to see the smug smile on Simon's face falter.

"I assumed luck was on your side, otherwise I should have been able to swat you down like the annoying pest you are," he replied, seeing Michael hang his head in shame remaining silent. Simon pried the piece of wood from his stomach and lunged at Michael. He shoved Michael up against the wall and plunged the bloody wooden cross into his right shoulder.

Michael remained silent and tried to push Simon away only for Simon to grab his right arm. Simon crushed it, shattering the bones painfully. "My patience is wearing thin, and soon it shall outweigh my curiosity," he sneered, waiting for an answer.

Michael cried out in pain glaring at Simon. "Our mother sent Donovan a vial containing human blood. I got to the package first and opened it to quench my curiosity. I figured with the strength it granted me I figured I could defeat you," he confessed, watching Simon tilt back his head and laugh.

"An entertaining fantasy your frail mind conjured up, but in a matter of seconds I have demonstrated my strength crushing your feeble attempts. Now, what should I do with you?" he drawled, watching Michael struggle to yank the wooden cross free from his shoulder.

Michael gritted his teeth and pried the wooden cross from his shoulder. Falling to the ground in a crouch. "Don't celebrate your victory just yet, you jerk," he hissed, and lunged at Simon again. He punched Simon in the jaw before Simon gripped his left hand and twisted it until it snapped in his grasp.

"Ah, but why not? Drinking human blood is what allowed you to last this long against me. I should just squash you like the dull cockroach you are," Simon noted, and watched Michael stagger back pain flickering across his face.

"So why prolong a wasteful duel and not get it over with?" he hissed, as he watched Simon reach for a ceremonial dagger at the leather pedestal before the first row of pews.

Simon laughed in response. "I wanted to draw this out to seek some enjoyment from watching you squirm before your demise. Alas, I have a pressing matter to attend to," he replied, closing the distance between them and swung toward his throat. Michael took another step back feeling his back slam up against the wall.

Simon raised his arm aiming for Michael's neck with the blade. Michael tried to raise both arms and deflect the blow. He wasn't fast enough as the blade glided effortlessly across his throat decapitating him. Blood gushed forth from the wound and sprayed Simon's cheeks. The head collapsed to the floor as Simon wiped the blood from his cheeks. He removed his shirt and bent to collect the skull. He wrapped it inside the black silk before he placed it into a cardboard box.

A messy tiring fight indeed, but the blow this delivery shall do to Donovan shall be worth the time and energy wasted, he thought. Entering the back office. He lit a white wax candle and took a seat at the black marble desk. "Enclosed is a memento of the hefty price one mist pays for the choices we make in life," he wrote, taping the note to the front of the box and ordered the shades to deliver it to the bar. He exited the church to head to the park.

Chapter Fourty-Eight

Vincent entered the west end of the park viewing what was lit under the glow of streetlamps. He noticed the park was deserted at the late hour before he pulled out his phone to call Matt. "Hey Mattie, I'm here what am I looking for besides you guys?" Vincent asked, heading for the other park entrance.

Matt helped Scarlett off the motorcycle and offered her his trench coat. He pulled his cell out and noticed the text message. "I told you, I hate that nickname," he groaned, hearing Scarlett laugh. "You're looking for a crime scene or a victim. In case things go south, you'll have an advantage until we can arrive to assist you," he replied, before hanging up the phone.

Vincent laughed glad to see he had struck a nerve. "What body? The park is deserted except for the three of us, but I'll keep up a patrol," he replied, pitting his phone in his pocket. Laughter cut through the silence, forcing Vincent to turn around drawing his gun in the process only to see nothing but shadows.

A group of shades rushed at him knocking the guns out of his hands. Vincent spun and clubbed the two closest with the barrel of the guns. One of the guns fell from his grasp before more shades pummeled toward him, knocking him to the ground. He lost the second gun before hitting the ground. "This isn't even a fair fight," he mused, trying to kick the mass of shades off his legs.

Simon hid in the shadows watching the shades toy with the hunter. He waited for the man to climb to his feet trying to retrieve one of the pistols. Simon snuck up behind him wrapping his cold fingers around Vincent's neck. Simon laughed adding pressure twisting his neck. A satisfying crack broke through the silence. The limp body collapsed to the ground emitting a slow pulse.

"Interesting, somehow this weak human is gifted with immortality to withstand such a striking blow. At least he'll be out of the way and can no longer obstruct me from claiming what is rightfully mine," he mused, collecting both guns venturing further into the park to seek out his prey.

Scarlett smiled innocently seeing the stern look flicker across his face at Vincent's nickname for him as he pockets the phone. "Would you rather he sticks to Mathew?" she replied, glancing over her shoulder, and reached for her dagger. Scarlett studied the trees anxiously and waited to see if her mind was playing tricks on her.

"Yes, anything but Mattie. It sounds like a little kid. What's wrong?" he asked, pulling out his crescent blades glancing around at the line of trees.

She caught another shadow flicker amongst the trees. "I thought I saw something in the trees but wondering if my mind is just playing tricks on me. Did Vincent finish his sweep?" she asked, anxious to be finished.

"I'm not sure, his line has gone silent, which means either he's distracted, or he was taken out by something. Stay close just in case it isn't your imagination," Matt warned, heading toward the trees to investigate.

Simon stood nearby overhearing their conversation masked by the tree's shadows. He laughed beckoning the shades to ambush them. He kept his gaze trained on the demon and bid his time waiting to strike.

Scarlett moved behind Matt relieved to see she was right. "It wasn't my imagination after all. If these creatures are here, he's nearby," she warned, kicking the first shade that approached, and stabbed the shade to her right, keeping her guard up.

Matt gave a simple nod allowing his blades to fly slicing through multiple shades. "Stay in the light, it's clear they can use darkness to create their forms," he noted, and continued to cut the creatures down.

He made the air colder to freeze the ones attacking Scarlett yet held back on his full power seeking their master.

"Wouldn't he want to separate us and pursue me?" she asked, stepping to the right to avoid one of the shades hands, yet its claws still tore at her shirt. Another shade grabbed the torn fabric and tugged her toward the ground. She rolled to the side, avoiding its teeth, but its nails had raked her skin drawing blood.

Matt jumped in front of Scarlett letting out a low growl while his blades turned the shades into ribbons. He noticed the shades circling surrounding Scarlett. He increased the chill in the air emitting a fog. Snowflakes fell from the sky covering the trees and soil in a white dust. "Keep close, the snow will keep them at bay just in case we do get separated," Matt warned, scanning the area once more for Simon.

Scarlett nodded feeling warm blood run down her arm from the wound. "Don't worry about me, we both know you can't hold the storm up for long," she replied, kicking one of the shade's hands and swung with her dagger cutting at its wrist wounding it.

Simon appeared from the shadows watching the snowfall blanketing the park in white. "I see you two were lured here clearly you will come running for a wounded mortal though I must confess I was the one to make the false report. I must say, it's a valiant effort for you to try and thwart my plans, mutt. but I shall collect what's mine; it is just a matter of time," Simon replied, laughing as Matt threw his blades in Simon's direction, yet the vampire disappeared allowing its minions to be cut down instead.

"Yeah right, like I would let you take Scarlett. You're going to wait for me to tire out, then you really are a coward," Matt exclaimed, a chilly wind began blowing the snow around them in a blizzard.

Simon laughed amused by the man's frustration. "Using one's weakness against them doesn't make them a coward; it makes them strategic. You honestly think you can stop me from taking her?" he teased, sending more shades to attack him.

Scarlett bit her lower lip ignoring the sting of the cold against her skin. Snowflakes clung to her hair melting down the back of the trench coat. She clasped the dagger tighter and swung at the next approaching shade. "Don't worry about me, Matt. You need to stop holding back and take the fight to him," she advised, aware that his restraint was for her safety.

Matt sent a glare in Scarlett's direction. "Leaving you alone allows his minions to get the drop on you. I can still fight and stay close to you," he replied, knowing that if he did lose control she wouldn't last long in the storm.

"What are you planning? He's waiting for the storm and the horde of shades to exhaust us both before confronting us," she noted, ducking to parry the shade's hand but dropped her dagger. Shit, the storm is only going to get worse, and my hands are going numb, she thought, extracting another dagger clutching it with both hands.

Matt appeared by Scarlett's side seeing her shivering from the cold. "I'm sorry. You should have stayed behind at the bar," Matt whispered, pulling out a shawl Ari had sewn charms of heat and wrapped it around her shoulders. He allowed his demon to come forth cloaking everything near them in a sheet of ice.

Scarlett wrapped the shawl tighter against her shoulders feeling a layer of warmth wash over her. "You could have given me that sooner, but there's no way I would leave you to fend off Simon and his minions alone," she replied, watching the branches on the trees turn to brittle ice. The weight of the snow caused them to break and collapse on some of the shades.

"I'm sorry, it still has a few bugs to work out and would only work at a certain degree of Celsius," Matt explained, looking at his handiwork. He watches the ice slowly spread outwards making the shades back away from them fearing the ice.

Scarlett noticed the tightness in Matt's jaw panting from the effort it took to keep the blanket of ice up despite the summer heat. "Matt, we need to retreat, this is what Simon wants. He's too much of a coward to face us until you've depleted your strength fighting the shades," she pleaded, hearing laughter emit from the trees in response.

"Your assumption is correct my pet, though I do not hesitate to confront your mutt head on out of fear. I'm biding my time for the right opportunity to strike," he announced, slipping from the shadows. He appeared behind Scarlett pinching her wrist causing her to drop the blade. He pulled both her arms behind her back brushing his lips against her neck making her cringe.

Matt turned around thinking that he had created enough cover to escape only to freeze seeing Simon holding Scarlett at bay. Simon hissed feeling his lips sizzle from the crosses seeing that he had the demon's full attention.

He smirked feeling the air grow colder as Matt held a blade in his hand. "How amusing, Donovan is trying to prevent my advantages. though there are ways around it, though that reminds me, I have a gift from a fellow hunter," Simon replied, using his free hand to withdraw a gun pressing it against Scarlett's temple.

Matt glared at the vampire taking a breath to steel his nerves hesitant to release the blade, afraid of hitting Scarlett if he was off with his calculations. His hand froze seeing Vincent's gun in Simon's hands. "Now we know what occurred to Vincent, though what do you want Simon? You know I won't risk her safety," Matt growled, the snow turning into small orbs of hail.

Scarlett gritted her teeth, her eyes widening at feeling the cold metal caress her skin. "I can pull the trigger and still have the luxury of turning her. Once she loses enough blood Donovan's protection will falter," he replied, smirking at seeing Matt tighten the grip on the blade hesitant to release it.

Matt glared thinking over what he should do. "How do I know you even know how to use it? It's filled with silver bullets meaning you'll hurt yourself in the process," Matt warned, dropping his weapons seeing that it was too great a risk. He closed his eyes hiding from the vampire that he was giving over control to his demon.

Simon frowned, confused by Matt's actions. "Yes, but the sting the metal will leave will be insignificant if it helps seal my victory," he warned, as the howling wind ceased, and the falling snow was slowing down. Simon watched Matt waiting for him to admit defeat.

Save her, I don't care what it takes, just keep her safe. Just this once, I release you to do as you will, Matt thought to the demon ignoring its gleeful laughter. A low growl emitted from Matt's throat his skin turning a pale shade of blue as his nails and hair grew longer. Ice pooled beneath his feet as black eyes stared back at Simon.

He appeared in front of Simon grasping the hand holding the gun using the other to push the girl away, keeping his attention on the vampire. Ice crept up from the gun, covering Simon's arm in a sheet of ice.

Seeing the flicker of movement, Simon released the gun's trigger. The bullet trapped in the thicker wall of ice wrapped around his skin. Rage flared in his eyes at the pain lashing out at Matt, using his useless arm to thrust at his chest trying to fracture the ice to remove the bullet. Scarlett cried out in alarm, pushed to the ground, trying to roll onto her shoulder. Before she could reach for a dagger, one of the shades closed the distance between them biting into her injured shoulder. Pain flared down her arm as she screamed in agony, her vision blurring overwhelmed by the pain. Simon moaned in delight licking his lips, tearing the bullet free feeling the hot metal burn his flesh.

The demon roared in anger unleashing all his power, as a wave of pure winter magic washed over everything in sight. Once the light died down the demon stood over the girl ignoring the blood running down its host face, yet it hesitated to let go unsure if the vampire was dead.

Scarlett watched a blast of white light strike Simon's chest, knocking him to the ground. She smirked, hearing the shades hiss in pain fleeing from the park. Scarlett clutched a handful of snow, placing it over the puncture wound hoping it would stop it from bleeding. She tore fabric from her pant leg, wrapping it around her shoulder and chest before tightening it. "Is it over?" she whispered; her voice hoarse from screaming.

Simon staggered to his feet with his skin covered in blisters, his arms charred flaking dropping specks of blood into the snow from the magic. He closed the distance between them trying to sink his fangs into Scarlett's wrist to recover.

The demon caught the vampire preventing Simon from touching the girl ignoring its host cries of pain from the movements. "You should be dead, why not just give in, no one would mourn your passing," it hissed, tightening his hands around the blackened skin, knowing the pain his actions would cause.

Simon laughed, spitting in the demon's face. "You can thank your little lamb for my miraculous recovery from extinction," he gloated, laughing once more at seeing the girl shudder in revulsion. He gritted his teeth feeling the talons graze his blackened skin before he lashed out kicking the demon in the stomach. "How much longer can your host endure our encounter before exerting all his energy?" he teased, knowing the demon had used up most of its host energy already.

"As long as it takes. He offered me freedom in exchange for her protection," he growled, ignoring the pain in his stomach creating more ice to latch onto Simon's flesh, ignoring the blood splattering the ground beneath his feet.

Simon hissed in pain feeling the ice lick his flesh, as it was slowly starting to heal. "What fate befalls you if he were to perish protecting her?" he asked, biting down on Matt's wrist trying to break free of his grasp.

The demon moved his wrist away from Simon's mouth using both hands to prevent the vampire from biting him holding Simon's neck away from his body. He could feel his body shaking not realizing he was on his knees. the body shutting down despite his efforts.

Simon grinned, seeing the demon's muscles weakening from the strain. Scarlett's eyes widened in alarm seeing that he was struggling to resist Simon. "Stop! Haven't you caused enough carnage?" she cried, trying to pry him away from Matt only to be swatted away like a bug. He pressed his knees into Matt's chest knocking the man to the ground burying his fangs into Matt's neck. The warm blood trailed down his chin lapping up the blood hungrily.

The demon struggled trying to force the vampire off losing control. Matt woke to pain screaming in agony, his body seizing under Simon's weight. Hot pain surged from his neck, his hands weakly grasping Simon's shoulders trying to push the vampire off him.

Scarlett stumbled to her feet seeing the crescent blade at Matt's feet. She reached for the blade digging it into her palm knowing it would gain Simon's attention. "You did all of this to get to me, well here I am," she sneered, holding her hand out for him.

Lust flickered in Simon's eyes as he pulled away from Matt, closing the distance between them bringing her hand to his lips. He closed his eyes lapping up her blood as her eyes flickered to Matt. He released her hand wiping the blood with the back of his hand.

She wrapped her palm in her shirt, adding pressure to stop it from bleeding. She knelt beside Matt, brushing his hair away from his face kissing his forehead. "I'm sorry, I feel like this is my fault," she whispered, feeling tears cascade down her cheeks.

Matt blinked his eyes open struggling to focus on her voice. He held one hand tightly over the open wound on his neck, his other grasping Scarlett's hand. "Don't be, I'm sorry I failed to keep you safe. Do you forgive me Scar?" he asked, knowing that Simon had won.

Scarlett squeezed his hand removing the wrap he had given her. She balled up the fabric placing it underneath his hand helping to stop the bleeding. "You have nothing to apologize for, you risked your life to save mine, when you should have just given him what he wanted," she replied, brushing her lips over his sensing Simon's eyes on her watching their interaction in amusement letting them say their goodbyes seeing that he had won.

"I would never give you to another, you are worth fighting for. You may be leaving with him, but we will come for you. I promise you that. I love you," he whispered, struggling to stay awake.

Scarlett smiled, kissing him once more, seeing Simon grow impatient. "I believe you, just don't do anything reckless. I love you, too," she replied, informing Simon that she was ready feeling him grab her arm dragging her out of the park. She glanced over her shoulder watching Matt close his eyes focusing on his breathing.

Chapter Fourty-Nine

Scarlett studied the passing scenery to map their route. "Don't try distracting yourself with the thought of freedom, my pet. I have no intention of letting you escape. Even Donovan is unaware of the location of my haven," Simon noted, seeing her tracking their movements.

Scarlett ignored his remark seeing their path moving up north. "There aren't too many areas you could keep me isolated as your captive, so it would only be a matter of time for them to find me," she replied, earning laughter in response. Simon dug his fingers tighter around her arm drawing a small whimper of pain from her lips.

"You are quite perceptive my pet, but the time they'll waste searching for you, will buy me more time," he replied, leading them up through a dirt path littered with vines and fallen tree branches.

"Time for what? You can't feed on me without it hurting you. I saw the pain it caused you when you kissed me," she spat, stumbling over a fallen tree branch.

"Yes, thanks to the mark Donovan placed on you, I am unable to turn you, at least for the moment. No worries, there are other things we can do to pass the time," he replied, pulling her against him before turning to enter the cave to their right.

Scarlett blinked waiting for her eyes to adjust to the darkness. The light from the entrance seemed to fade behind them. Man, it's dank in here. I just hope Vincent could find Matt and help him, she thought, seeing the shades gather beside Simon. They grabbed both of Scarlett's arms preventing her from fleeing.

Simon released her arm, the shades clasped both her arms. He grabbed one of the wooden sticks laying on the ground. He grabbed a lighter from his pocket and lit it, emitting the dark cavern in faint yellow light. The shades hissed at the light before placing the torch in the fire pit crafted in the center of the room. He grabbed a long metal chain with shackles bolted to the cavern wall.

He beckoned the shades toward him and placed both of her wrists in the bronze restraints. "I can't risk you trying to escape and alerting the other slayers of where we are until I'm ready for them," he admitted, brushing his lips against hers.

Scarlett felt her back slam against the cold concrete behind her. She cried out in alarm feeling icy bronze handcuffs slip around her wrists and lock into place above her head. Scarlett tried turning her head away from him, yet he gripped her chin in his hands brushing his lips over hers. His teeth grazing her lower lip lapping up the blood from the punctured skin.

Scarlett spat at his feet in revulsion. Simon wiped the spittle from his cheek and lashed out slapping her across the face. He smirked seeing the red handprint from the strike. "The longer you remain defiant the worst your punishment will be," he warned, extracting the dagger from the sheath on her waist. He placed the blade against her left arm following along the bruises his palm had made.

"Don't worry, my pet. I won't kill you. You're too valuable to me alive, but it doesn't mean I can't have my fun either," he whispered, pressing the blade into her skin drawing down from elbow to her wrist. He laughed watching her grit her teeth to block out the pain. He lapped at the blood hungrily before pulling away. He cut away at her shirt tearing at the hem and wrapped it tightly around the wound to stop it from bleeding.

Vincent stirred feeling someone kick his ribs gently. His eyes blinked open noticing the blanket of white melt and turn grey. "Oh hey, Matt. Any luck with the search? Where's Scarlett?" he asked, shaking the snow from his clothes accepting the offered hand climbing to his feet.

"Wrong hunter, Vince. Raven asked me to come out and check on you if you didn't return before dawn. Where is our fearless leader?" Jet asked, helping Vincent to his feet.

"Man, I feel like shit. I guess we should search the park for him. He was on the other end with Scarlett the last time I spoke to him," he replied, falling into step beside Jet.

Jet reached into his pocket for the onyx crystal Ari had given him, letting it swing in the air, guiding their direction west as they resumed walking in silence. Vincent noticed the crystal asking if Ari had given it to him. "Yes, she put a tracking device in everyone's phone in case of emergencies, but with the surge of magic it interferes with intercepting it," he replied, surprised by the massive amount of ice and snow blanketing the park.

"Why were you out here by yourself?" Jet asked, watching Vincent fidget with the amulet around his neck.

"Matt wanted me to scope out this area of the park first; just in case the vampire showed up and got the drop on me," he groaned, rubbing his neck. Hoping to distract himself from the pain, he bent down collecting a mound of snow before hurling it at Jet.

Jet groaned feeling the orb of snow hit him square in the back. "I'm worried, the fact that neither one of them came to check up on you is a bad sign," he noted, shaking the snow from his clothes.

"Damn, Jet. Look over there," Vincent yelled, pointing to his right running over to the large splash of red that had caught his eye. Matt lied beneath the pool of blood unmoving.

Jet knelt beside Matt, gently noticing the bloody scarf pressed against his throat pinned underneath his hand. He fished in his pocket tossing a set of keys to Vincent before guiding him to where he had parked the jeep. "Bring back the first-aid kit from the trunk. I need to patch him up first before we try to move him," he warned, seeing Vincent catch the keys before running in the right direction. He must have put up one hell of a fight, he thought, texting Ari to inform her that they had found Matt but not Scarlett.

Vincent returned offering him the first-aid kit watching him treat the hole in Matt's neck, after checking his pulse relieved to see he was still breathing. He removed the bloody scarf surprised to see it had stopped the bleeding before adding wads of fresh gauze and securing them in place with tape. "It seems Scarlett was able to stabilize the bleeding from the bite wound before disappearing. It probably saved his life," he announced, bandaging up the smaller lacerations before Vincent scooped Matt up in his arms carrying him bridal style back to the jeep.

Jet grabbed a blanket from the trunk letting Vincent lay Matt down on the blanket before strapping him in. Jet let Vincent drive calling Ari to inform her that they were on their way back to the manor. "Judging by the severity of his injuries, I'd say he fought Simon off before he took off with Scarlett. He's in bad shape, Ari. I was afraid we had lost him," he admitted, warning her for what was in store upon their return.

Vincent reached into the glove department, finding the hand-sanitizer, and offering it to Jet. "Was the wound on his neck from being bitten by Simon?" he asked, watching Jet nod in agreement rubbing his hands together after applying the hand-sanitizer.

"Yes, and it might frighten the others to see him in the state he's in. To make matters worse, until he wakes up we have no way of knowing if he is the victim of Simon's manipulation," he warmed, thinking that when one was bitten a vampire could use it to manipulate or control their victim.

Raven and Dawn were waiting for them outside of the manor's entrance. "Hey guys, we have the living room prepared so you don't have to carry him up to his room, though where's Scarlett?" Dawn asked, watching Jet opening the backseat door for Vincent letting him scoop Matt up in his arms. Both girls seem shocked by seeing Matt covered in bandages following Jet and Vincent inside.

"We think Simon took her since she was gone when we arrived. I doubt she would leave Matt alone given his current state. Can someone get some rags and water? Vincent asked, placing Matt on the living room sofa collapsing in the recliner chair.

Vincent sighed rubbing his temples watching Jet take a seat on the edge of the sofa reaching for the first-aid kit stored underneath the coffee table. Taking the fabric scissors, he cut away at Matt's shirt treating the small lacerations on his chest taking note of the large bruises on his ribs. Jet pressed on the areas seeing that a few of Matt's ribs were fractured. He spotted Ari entering the room as she kneeled beside Matt's head.

"Ari can you perform a spell to tell us if he is under Simon's control?" he asked, grabbing the sewing needle and thread to stitch the wound shut. He took the offered bottle from Ari pouring holy water on the wound after removing the gaze. He waited for the wound to stop steaming before grabbing the two flabs of flesh sewing them together.

"There's nothing I can do, at least until Matt wakes up. The lore is based on humans but given Matt's case I'm not sure what will be the result. What were they doing outside at the park. I thought we were on lockdown?" Ari asked, watching Jet applying a fresh strip of gauze securing it over the wound. She touched Matt's skin seeing how clammy his skin was as his skin was warmer than usual. She went to where they kept the medical supplies, grabbing an IV port, a bag of fluids, and O positive blood. She set it up next to Matt before injecting it into his left arm hoping it would help with the blood loss.

Raven stood in the doorway watching Ari work unsure how to answer her question. "I'm not sure where they had ventured off to. I heard them heading toward the garage and left on Matt's motorcycle, but I had just assumed they were going for a night drive. I called to let him know that there was a police report from the park and that he would go check it out." Raven explained moving to enter the room placing the bowl and rag next to Jet.

Jet rolled his eyes helping Ari with the IV taping the needle in place before wrapping it around Matt's arm. "My guess would be that they went to Sângele Vampirului in search of hints to defeat Simon, hoping to use another vampire to get insight?" he suggested, knowing that Scarlett persuaded Matt to take her.

"There was a letter addressed to the owner in the journal Scarlett had perhaps she went to give him the letter and inquired about Simon," Ari suggested, taking a rag and squeezing out the extra water before placing it on Matt's forehead. She walked to where Vincent sat, placing her hands on the back of his neck, massaging it gently to help with the pain.

Vincent closed his eyes thanking Ari for the kind gesture. "I had considered bringing Jet with me but I couldn't risk him getting hurt or not making it back alive, nor would Ari ever forgive me," he admitted, wondering if there had been more of them present would he had been more successful holding Simon off.

"I don't think Matt considered running into Simon; he probably thought it was just a mugging or another creature, though it was wise that only Vincent went otherwise we may have been forced to bury one of our own tonight. I'm glad to see you fear me Vincent, though you should head up and get some rest," Ari suggested, once she was finished.

Vincent nodded in agreement giving her a mock salute climbing to his feet. "Earning a woman's wrath can be scary, but given your cunning nature, they'd never see it coming," he teased, laughing at feeling her swat his shoulder as he disappeared to his room.

Raven shifted her feet from one foot to the other waiting to see if Ari needed anything from her. "Thank you, Raven for informing us of the situation. Why don't you go up and get some rest as well?" Jet advised, seeing her sigh in relief bidding them goodnight before retreating to her room.

Ari watched Raven head upstairs glancing over at Jet. "Why don't you join her? I'll stay up and keep an eye on Matt to ensure he recovers from his injuries," she suggested, seeing that the hour was late close to sunrise.

Jet opened his mouth to argue but sighed hearing a yawn escape his lips. "You're right, though if you need a break don't hesitate to come get me," he advised, bidding her goodnight.

Ari gave a simple nod pulling out the small discs and her tool kit continuing to work on her project to pass the time. She changed the washcloth on his forehead frowning as she could feel his temperature rising to fetch ice hoping it would help. She changed the bags on the pole thinking one more liter would help cover the blood lost during the fight. Yawning she sat in the armchair next to the sofa nodding off with her project nestled in her lap.

Chapter Fifty

As the afternoon sun peeked out from the horizon, Jet stirred, rubbing the sleep from his eyes. The manor was silent indicating that no one else was up yet. He ran a hand through his hair making his way into the kitchen adding water to the kettle. Waiting for the water to boil he slipped into the living room. Both Ari and Matt were still asleep. Careful not to rouse Matt he changed the bandages making sure not to press down on his throat. His eyes flickered to Ari picking up the materials used for her project and placing them on the coffee table, sweeping her hair out of her face before shaking her shoulders gently.

Ari flinched feeling someone shaking her as her eyes shot open filled with magic before realizing who was standing there. "Sorry, I guess I fell asleep watching him, though was I out long?" she asked, yawning as she pulled her magic back allowing the dreams to slip from her mind.

Jet offered her a weak smile wondering if she had gotten any sleep. "I changed the bandages around his neck before waking you," he replied, hearing the kettle whistle. He extended his hand helping her to her feet. "Why don't you make yourself a cup of tea and I'll go check on Andrew. He should have changed back by now," he suggested, seeing that she was still tired.

"He'll be drained recovering from the full moon from the previous night sleeping in his cage. I didn't get a chance to free him. How is Matt holding up? I take it he hasn't woken yet?" Ari asked, taking his hand to climb to her feet glancing down at their leader.

Jet led the way into the kitchen filling two mugs with the hot water and adding English Breakfast tea bags before handing her one of the mugs. "The smaller lacerations on his arms and legs have healed, but the bite wound is healing slowly. The wound has closed but he didn't stir while I was tending to it and when he does, he's going to want to go look for Scarlett," he admitted, worried that their leader would be panicked once he woke up.

She took the mug taking a seat at the table toying with the bag. "I don't know even if he wants to go, I doubt he would get extremely far. He still has broken ribs and the last time I checked; his fever was getting worse meaning his powers are useless now. We still have yet to discover how much the bite affects him until Matt wakes up," Ari replied, taking a sip of her tea.

Jet reached out his hand squeezing hers gently. "I noticed he felt warm to me too and added Motrin to his IV to help reduce his fever. If it doesn't work, we'll have to try an ice bath, you don't want the wound to get infected," he advised, thinking he would ask Vincent to help if he was up to it. "I know you're worried about Matt, but did you get any sleep last night?" he teased, seeing her toy with her mug.

"A few hours, I've been having weird dreams lately. I think they may be memories of something but I'm not sure. When I wake up the runes return and sometimes, I'm casting a spell," she admitted. climbing to her feet walking over to the basement door. She placed her right hand in the middle closing her eyes to trace the spell unlocking the enchantment. "What are we going to tell Andrew? You know he's just as bad as Matt when it comes to Scarlett." She asked, knowing that Andrew would blame Matt.

Jet waited for her to disarm the enchantment thinking over her question. "Maybe try journaling anything you can recall from the dreams or the spells you find yourself casting?" he advised, seeing that she dreaded informing Andrew of what had happened. "We'll just have to be honest with him, he'll find out the truth from Raven if we try lying to him," he advised, following her down into the basement.

Ari sighed, yet knew he was speaking the truth. "You're right, I just fear Andrew going mad with rage and attacking Mathew. Andrew is weak right now but that doesn't mean he'll ignore what we tell him," she admitted, walking to the back of the room where the cage stood. She pricked a finger allowing her blood to land on the lock breaking the barrier and free the werewolf. She turned around quickly remembering that Andrew would be naked.

Jet placed his hand on her shoulder once she had lifted the barrier on the cage. "Why don't you head back up and I'll deal with Andrew? I can handle myself if he gets out of hand," he suggested, moving to grab a blanket before entering the cage, trying to avert his eyes before tossing it over Andrew.

Ari laughed, kissing Jet on the cheek as thanks before running upstairs. She was relieved that she didn't have to confront Andrew as she went to sit with Matt removing the empty bag from the IV holding the pole in one hand before using a levitation spell to take Matt to his room thinking the cold air would help with the fever.

Jet's cheeks flushed hearing her laugh before darting up the steps. He waited for Ari to reach the top of the stairs before kicking Andrew in the ribs stepping out of the way, as Andrew stirred, lashing out with his legs. Feeling the soft blanket covering his naked torso, Andrew wrapped it around himself as his eyes opened. "What a cruel way to wake someone," he groaned, sitting up rubbing the sleep from his eyes.

Jet rolled his eyes relieved that he had covered Andrew with the blanket. "Consider it a warning for what I have to tell you," he warned, seeing Andrew arch an eyebrow motioning him to continue. "Last night, we received a tip that there was another attack in the park, so Vincent met up with Matt and Scarlett to investigate it—" he explained, watching Andrew's hands ball up into fists at his side.

He rose to his feet seeing Jet rise his hands out forcing Andrew to stop. "I don't understand, why was Scar out with them?" he groaned, dropping the blanket chuckling at hearing Jet cry out in disgust using his hands to shield his eyes. "She was out with Matt trying to get intel from her friend and probably persuaded Matt to let her go with them. Matt put up a good fight but was severely injured resulting in Simon capturing her," he admitted, hearing Andrew let out an aggravated sigh bending to collect the blanket. He slipped it around himself before storming out of the cage and up the stairs.

Jet followed him up to the kitchen, collapsing into a chair in the kitchen taking a sip of his tea despite it being cold. "Where's Matt?" Andrew demanded, entering the living room to find it deserted. Andrew placed his arm on Ari's seeing she was returning to the kitchen. "I'm not going to hurt him, I just want to talk to him," he pleaded, before Ari sighed informing him that Matt was in his room. Andrew nodded his head in thanks before racing up the stairs tackling Vincent over. Vincent offered him a mock salute in greeting before descending the stairs entering the kitchen for a cup of coffee.

Andrew arrived at Matt's room barging into the room feeling the icy blast of the air conditioner hit his chest. He fastened the blanket around his waist before approaching the bed seeing that Matt was asleep. He perched himself on the edge of the bed, shaking Matt's shoulders trying to wake him.

A cry of pain tore from Matt's lips, his eyes squeezed tight, trying to take a breath to scream. His back arched from him subconsciously trying to get away from the person shaking him. He turned to the side throwing up before his body showed dark crimson orbs glaring up at the wolf. "What do you want mongrel? What is so dire that I couldn't wait until I woke up on my own?" the demon hissed, taking over seeing that his host was in no condition to communicate.

Andrew wrinkled his nose in disgust smelling the vomit on the floor mixed with the scent of blood. Andrew removed his hands afraid that he had hurt Matt. "Jet told me what happened last night, and it doesn't make sense. Why would you take Scarlett away from the safety of the manor, couldn't you retrieve the information without her?" he demanded, wondering if he loved Scar, why jeopardize her safety to please her?

"What's wrong wolf, are you mad because you couldn't get a treat from her for being such a good boy? It was all Scarlett's idea she wanted to see the vamp and they were staying at the bar until a phone call was received. There was an attack in the park and of course we had to go off and play hero. The girl made a deal she would run if Simon were there but that was a lie. Clearly, she knows the right things to say to get her way," Yerdin explained, glad the wolf had stopped shaking him.

Andrew growled annoyed at the joke but then blinked caught off guard by the different tone of speech. "You're the demon that grants Matt his powers?" he noted, rolling his eyes at hearing the mocking slow applause. "He let his feelings for her cloud his judgement and sustained those injuries. What happened to Scar, did the vamp take her with him?" he demanded, hoping that she was still alive.

"Wow, you have some brain cells after all and yes I'm the demon named Yerdin even though my host likes to call me it. Emotions had nothing to do with it; do you know how hard it is to take on a high-level vampire, a horde of shades, and heat working against your powers? Add in protecting a mortal who was supposed to run off and how would you have managed the fight? I used my full power and should have killed the bastard. Turns out if a shade feeds then the vamp gets the blood instead. The girl went with him and no Matt couldn't stop him, it was the only way to stop Simon from draining him dry," he growled, not amused by being judged by the werewolf.

Andrew raised his hands defensively seeing that the battle was more intense than he had assumed. "I'm sorry, I know Matt combated Simon before and almost won if he hadn't had to shield Scar from him," he remarked, dismissing the question not wanting to admit he feared not being strong enough unless powered by the full moon. "We knew that the shades were an extension of his will but wouldn't have thought that he could recover through their feedings," he marveled, wondering if there was a way to sever the bond the shades had with Simon.

"No, the first time it was the shades this was his first encounter with the vampire. and he put everything into the fight even letting me out of the cage to have a bit of fun. Simon recovered from Scarlett's blood while Matt's body was shutting down allowing an all you can eat buffet on a silver platter. What happened to you being all emo and out for blood lose your spark?" he asked. seeing that the wolf was no longer acting in a blind rage.

Andrew glared at him punching him in the shoulder seeing that it was trying to provoke him. "My feud is with Mathew not you, since I doubt you hold any romantic feelings toward Scarlett?" he replied, enjoying his conversation with Verdin wondering why Matt kept him locked away.

"Emotions are a mortal trait. I could care less if any of you enjoy my presence. The only one I must keep happy is my host. You do realize that the girl has already picked an alpha. Why keep wasting energy chasing her? There's a perfect cub that will be an omega soon, why not go after her?" Yerdin asked, not understanding human behavior.

Andrew arched any eyebrow confused by his contradictory statement. "I'm confused, if emotions are fleeting then why worry over what Matt thinks, aren't you two connected by a binding?" he asked, trying to recall what he had read about demons. "At any rate, I'm not sure who you're talking about?" he protested, wondering if he was referring to one of the other slayers.

"It's not a binding if it were, I would be long gone by now. His sire passed down a part of his powers creating me. Think of me as a parasite as Matt enjoys calling me when I get on his nerves. I was using a wolf hierarchy system to make it easier on a brain such as yours. Matt's the alpha who Scarlett has chosen by having a mating rite with him two nights ago. I was referring to one of the younger females seeing how once they reach adulthood; they would be low ranking in power with the leaders," Yerdin explained, wondering if he needed to water down his words.

Andrew grinded his teeth, clenching his jaw, startled by the news. "It all makes sense now. Scar has Matt wrapped around her finger because she threw herself at him?" he growled, his hands balling into fists in his lap. Hearing Yerdin laugh, he glared at him climbing to his feet seeing that he would get nowhere with the demon.

"Aww is the wolf mad that he was denied getting a chance to lay with her. If it makes you feel any better Mathew really enjoyed himself in the moment," Yerdin teased, wincing as he felt his host starting to take control.

Andrew growled and lashed out, kicking the bed frame nearly tipping it over before storming out of the room to head into the bathroom to take a shower. His thoughts raced of what the demon had said to him.

The bed fully tilted, throwing Matt on the floor as he rolled before hitting the wall behind him. He screamed in agony wondering why he woke up in pain curling in on himself trying to block out the pain. He tried to use his powers to ice his ribs only to cry out again seeing that his magic had yet to recover.

Chapter Fifty-One

Vincent was halfway up the stairs carrying a second cup of coffee in his hands when he heard the screams from Matt's room. He entered the room wincing seeing Matt curled in a fetal position on the floor.

Vincent set his cup on the dresser and kneeled beside Mathew. "How did you end up down here?" he mused, informing Matt that he was going to pick him up carrying him back to the bed. "Can I get you anything?" he asked, retrieving his cup of coffee sitting on the edge of the bed.

Matt stayed curled up biting his lip hard to keep from crying out as Vincent moved him. "I don't know. I woke up to someone kicking my bed before leaving the room. Can you get Ari or Jet for me?" he asked, the pain still intense despite being on the bed instead of the floor.

Vincent nodded in agreement wishing there were more he could do. "I think Andrew was in here demanding answers about last night," he explained, fishing his phone out of his pocket asking Jet to come up to Matt's room. "Jet is on his way up," he announced, smelling the foul odor noticing the dried puddle between the bed and the wall. He waited for Jet to arrive before getting a washcloth from the bathroom to clean up the mess.

Jet had brought up an ice pack positioning the IV beside the bed seeing that it had been knocked over beside his bed. "I guess Andrew did one thing right in helping you wake up, though you're probably still in a lot of pain," he noted, setting up the IV into his arm before resting the ice pack against his ribs. "The IV should help with the pain, though do you recall anything from last night?" he asked, changing the gauze around his neck relieved to see that the wound was healing.

"That would explain the person shaking me though he seems really pissed even though I didn't talk to him. I don't remember much, Scar, and I went to the bar to talk to Donovan only to discover that he was poisoned making the entire place reek of blood. We were staying there until Raven called saying that someone was being attacked at the park," he explained, closing his eyes to help recall the previous events. "Simon appeared and we fought before he bit me, and Scarlett left with him to save me," Matt added, before realizing that she was with the monster as he bolted into an upright position ignoring the pain, realizing that they needed to go out and search for her.

Jet placed his hand on Matt's chest forcing him to lay back down. Vincent moved to help hold Matt down until he relaxed. "Calm down, Matt, or we'll get Ari to help chain you to the bed," Vincent warned, hearing Jet sigh in annoyance at having to inject the IV once more, taping it against Matt's arm.

"Vincent is right, you need time to rest and recover before you do anything. We will conduct a team and search the area for Scarlett. I think Andrew blames you for what happened because he wasn't able to help given it was a full moon," he admitted, understanding Andrew's frustration.

Vincent snorted at the statement gaining Jet's attention. "Even if Andrew had fought him in his wolf state, he wouldn't be a match for him. If it weren't for my immortality, I wouldn't have made it back alive," he admitted, feeling responsible for Scarlett getting taken.

Matt struggled before giving in seeing that he wasn't strong enough to fight them off. "It's not your fault Vin even I underestimated the vampire. I thought I could take him after destroying his shades but clearly, I was wrong. I'm surprised the rest of you don't feel the same way Andrew does," Matt muttered, knowing that it was his fault Scarlett was gone.

Jet frowned wishing he had stopped Andrew from bothering Matt making him feel guilty for not being able to defeat Simon. "Andrew's feelings are irrational; he believes if he were out there with you then you would have won. You risked your life protecting her as you would have done for the rest of us," Jet replied, seeing Vincent nod in agreement.

Matt sighed reaching a hand up to wipe away the sweat on his forehead. "I guess I'll take your word for now even if I don't fully agree with it. Do you think Andrew will do something stupid to prove his strength?" Matt asked, hoping that the werewolf would leave him alone until he recovered.

Jet reached up touching Matt's forehead seeing Matt sweating. "Most likely but he'll have to get past us to try it. Vincent can you carry Matt into the bathroom. His fever isn't going down, and I don't want it to cause the wound to become infected," he asked, apologizing as he removed the IV.

Vincent helped remove Matt's shirt and pants leaving his boxers on and slipped his arms underneath Matt's hips. lifting him up in a fireman's carry entering the bathroom. He let Jet turn the water on letting the tub fill with chilly water. He added Lavender oil for pain motioning for Vincent to lower Matt into the tub.

Matt tried to assist seeing Vincent carry him into the bathroom before being lowered into the bathtub. A sigh escaped his lips as he leaned his head against the wall behind him enjoying the chilly water, an arm subconsciously wrapping around his injured ribs. "Thanks guys, I owe you one for this." Matt groaned, having no intention of moving.

Vincent chuckled, relieved to see that he was able to help. "You should thank Jet, it was his idea, though just call if you need me. I'm going to have a chat with Andrew," he admitted, rubbing his hands together in glee before leaving the room.

Jet laughed wishing Vincent luck taking a seat on the floor resting his back against the outer side of the tub. "You said you woke up as Andrew was leaving, though it's clear he learned of something that upset him. Do you think your demon shared something with him?" he asked, relieved to see that the icy water had relaxed Mathew.

Matt shrugged, thinking over the question. "It's possible it could also explain why it's silent now instead of being its usual annoying self.

I recall waking once to Andrew shaking me and feeling a rib shift wrong causing me severe pain. I was sick and then blacked out waking a second time when Andrew was leaving. It's possible the demon was in control though I'm clueless about what was shared though knowing it he probably revealed my sex life with Scar," he admitted, knowing that was the only thing that would send the werewolf into a blind rage.

Jet chuckled, surprised that Andrew hadn't destroyed the room in anger. "Man, I remember you saying the demon was cruel, but that must have been hard for Andrew to hear, that the woman he wished was his had been that intimate with you," he replied, climbing to his feet to sit on the edge of the tub. He rested his hand over Matt's forehead relieved to see the skin was cool to the touch.

"Yes, and he left me to deal with Andrew's wrath though we did try to tell the man to move on but he's still in denial when it comes to Scar. What about you, are you just as clueless to the opposite sex?" Matt teased, opening his eyes to watch Jet's movements.

Jet laughed adding more Lavender oil to the bath before turning on the chilly water to ensure it stayed cold. "Yes, it's not obvious that Raven has feelings for him, though as angry as the news made him, it might have been what he needed to hear," he suggested, shrugging his shoulders in response to Matt's question. "I guess I'm just as bad since I'm not sure what you're asking," he admitted, blushing hearing Matt laugh in response.

Matt dunked his head under before coming back up shoving wet hair out of his face. "You mean it will get Andrew to notice another woman, fat chance on that one. I doubt he'll ever get over his crush. Are you telling me you haven't noticed anything different with your tutor?" Matt teased, referring to Ari.

Jet rubbed the back of his neck feeling his cheeks flush. "We have grown closer and there may have been some flirting, but it hasn't turned into anything else that I'm aware of," he admitted, wondering what he was doing wrong.

"I see was the flirting done on your part or hers? At least you notice that there is something there most guys are naive when a girl is interested in him. Ari just discovered she's half dark fey and doesn't have much confidence in herself now. I wouldn't rush anything. I was simply curious if you had noticed," Matt admitted, knowing that Ari didn't react well to pressure.

Jet laughed in agreement thinking over the question unsure of the answer. "Up until she got the news she was doing most of the flirting, but like you said the news shook her and I don't want to pressure her to act on it," he admitted, thinking of how she had reacted to his gift.

"Stick to what's working for you seeing how you both seem content and trust me Ari is not someone you want to piss off, not that she would ever be mad with you. Right now, she's lost and to her you're the one good thing in her life that she doesn't want to lose," Matt admitted, closing his eyes hearing someone walking in his room.

Chapter Fifty-Two

Ari entered the bathroom letting out a low whistle at the view. "Well this is an interesting sight, how's he doing?" she asked, coming up behind Jet placing her hand on his shoulder.

Jet's smile widened at hearing her voice laughing at her reaction to seeing Matt in the tub. "His fever had spiked, so I asked Vincent to help carry him in here. It seems to have helped as his fever went down," he admitted, wondering if now she could cast the spell to test how much damage the bite had done.

"I feared as much. His body is struggling to cool itself down until his magic can restore itself. He seems peaceful. I take it you put a lot of lavender in the water to help him relax?" she teased, perching on the edge of the tub near Matt's head. She placed one hand on the wound the other on his heart as a light red glow covered her hands. Faint chanting filled the air before she stopped frowning at what she discovered.

Jet nodded in agreement to her observation seeing that it was helping to ease his pain. He watched the red glow cover her hands before it disappeared. He reached out, grasping her hand with his squeezing it gently. "What's wrong, what did you discover?" he pressed, wondering what she had learned from the spell.

Ari bit her lip glancing down at Matt seeing him dozing in the water. "I cast the spell we use on all victims of a vampire bite and the taint is there. It's not strong enough for Matt to become a puppet and attack us now, but if he got close to Simon he would be turned into a weapon. His demonic side is trying to expel the toxins but given his weakened state it's not working. I'll make a few potions to see if it helps," she explained, running a hand through her hair, thinking over what she should do.

A sly grin slipped on Jet's face as he scooped up some of the chilly water splashing her with it. "Once he fully recovers the demon may be able to rid the rest of the toxin from the bite, seeing how Matt will insist to go with anyone that is sent to search for Scarlett," he noted, not wanting to see Matt being turned against them.

Ari cried out startled by how cold the water was. A smirk appeared on her face as an orange sized orb of water rose from the tub breaking over Jet's head. "Two can play at this game though should we get him out or leave him in there?" Ari asked, laughing at Jet's wet appearance.

Jet laughed, shaking his wet hair in her direction amused by the scream he had earned for his trouble. "He seems content, I'd hate to move him and cause him more pain. How long can we leave him in there?" he asked, scooping up another handful of water hitting her chest amused to see that it had soaked her shirt.

"Jet! Did you have to aim there, of all places?" Ari asked, pulling off her wet shirt revealing a light blue tank top underneath. "I'm not sure I would say another hour, but he seems content, and the water is keeping his fever at bay. I guess go with your instinct on the matter," she replied, splashing Jet's pants with the water.

Jet laughed, throwing his hands in the air triumphantly before feeling the chilly water splash his pants. "No areas are off limits in a water fight," he protested, kicking off his pants as an idea occurred to him. He removed his shirt folding it up like a net dumping it in the tub before tossing it in her direction laughing in glee.

Ari threw up a shield making the shirt swing back and hit him in the face. "You didn't say magic wasn't allowed either, though I'm enjoying the view," she teased, taking in his bare chest.

Jet laughed moving to reach for the towel to dry his face. "I bet you are, seeing as how I'm almost naked," he replied, picking up his soaked shirt ringing it out in her lap trying again to get her wet.

Ari laughed watching the water hit him once more. "You may want to try a different tactic though you're right I am enjoying the show. All you need is your shorts to come off and we'll be set," she teased, amused by his action.

"Please don't Jet, the last thing I want to see is your bare ass in my face though if you want her shield to drop, Ari is ticklish in the ribs," Matt offered, waking up during their water war and decided to watch the game.

Jet grinned lunging forward reaching for her rubs with both hands knocking her off her perch. He laughed continuing his assault before trying for the third time to strike out with the wet shirt hitting her in the face. "It seems that our water fight woke him, though are you up to being transported back to your bed?" he asked, wondering if their game had woken him.

Ari cried out laughing too hard to cast a spell. She doubled over before taking Jet and herself into the bathtub. "All right you win, though sorry Matt that Jet had to act like a child," Ari replied, bushing as she realized she had landed in Matt's lap quickly climbing out of the tub.

Matt laughed seeing Ari cast a spell to dry herself off not turning to face them. "Yeah I think so, though your fight didn't wake me I sense magic and was scared Ari was up to no good," Matt teased. seeing that Jet had landed on his legs.

Jet laughed climbing out of the tub reaching for the metal chain to drain the tub. He pointed his finger at Ari despite laughing. "Don't lie you know you enjoyed it, though should I go ask Vincent for help?" he asked, draping the towel around his waist.

Ari shook her head, pulling her hair up into a bun. "I can lift him out though I'm relieved you guys didn't put him in the water naked," Ari noted, casting a levitation spell making Matt rise slowly out of the water. She turned to head into the bedroom to place him on the bed.

Jet laughed, tightening the towel around his waist following her lead. "We didn't want to embarrass Matt, nor is that something either one of us wanted to see," he protested, hearing Matt laugh watching Jet insert the IV once more resting the ice pack against his ribs.

Ari cast a light drying spell on Matt pulling the blanket over him as she placed his phone next to him on the bed. "Text if you need anything though I'm sorry about Andrew, I'll ensure the next time he tries to come up here to have hot wax waiting for him," Ari warned, getting a laugh for Matt as she left the room.

Jet winced at hearing her threat for Andrew if he tried hurting Matt. He turned the air conditioner on placing it on high before walking toward the door. "Try to get some rest, I'll be back to check on you later," he explained, closing the door behind him retreating to his room to change into dry clothes.

Ari headed to the ground floor hearing shouting coming from Andrew's room and decided to ignore it thinking that the jerk deserved Vincent's wrath. She entered the kitchen grabbing her cauldron from a floor cabinet before placing it on the counter filling it with water. She went to fetch her book of spells flipping through the pages not realizing that the girls had joined her in the kitchen.

Raven had followed Dawn into the kitchen wanting to escape her room before getting dragged into Andrew's argument. "Look there's Ari, I bet she'll tell you I was right. When your man is in trouble you stand by him," Dawn protested, seeing Raven roll her eyes.

"Just because you like someone doesn't mean you get to excuse their stupidity. You heard Vincent, Andrew let his emotions get the best of him and hurt Matt," she replied, watching Ari adding herbs and other ingredients into the cauldron. "Hey, Ari, what are you working on?" she asked, curious to learn what potion she was brewing.

"Raven's right, Dawn, you never take a fall for a man even if you have a crush on him and besides Andrew caused his own problems, it would be stupid for Raven to take any punishment for him," Ari warned, hearing their conversation. "An energy restoration potion, I'm preparing it for Matt. He's still in bad shape and Andrew only made his condition worse," she explained, finding the page prospering her book open on the counter.

Dawn frowned, taking a seat at the table aware that Ari was right but wanted Andrew to be redeemed. "Dawn is a hopeless romantic, but Ari is right. Andrew's actions were reckless prolonging Matt's recovery, it makes me question if he'll ever get over Scarlett," she groaned, taking a seat beside Dawn.

"I know she is, but there comes a point where logic overrules the heart. Andrew blames Matt for what occurred, but it was an accident. They went to help an innocent none of them knew that Simon would be in the park and I know Scarlett. She was too worried about Matt to leave him," she explained, running a finger down the list checking what ingredients she would need.

Raven arched an eyebrow confused by Ari's statement regarding Scarlett. "What do you mean? Did Matt and Scarlett try taking on Simon by themselves?" she asked, understanding that Scarlett did what she could to protect Matt.

Ari sighed, grabbing a cutting board to set up her station. "We were giving Matt a bath to lower his fever and he told us what happened. Simon appeared and attacked him with a horde of shades. Matt used all his power but one of the shades fed on Scarlett giving the blood to Simon turning the battle in the vampire's favor. Scarlett went with Simon to spare Matt's life," she explained, chopping lavender and rosemary adding it to the water.

Dawn shuddered wrapping her arms around herself watching Ari chopping herbs. "It sounds like Scarlett made the right call even if it was a scary one. Once Matt recovers are you guys going out to search for her?" she asked, curious to learn what the next step was.

Ari paused choosing her words carefully. "We will head out during the day to search for her, but Matt won't be coming with us. He may be our leader but now he's the victim of a vampire bite meaning that until the poison clears from the bite, he's too high a risk to take with us," she explained, putting the cauldron on the stove before lighting it.

Raven frowned feeling sorry for Matt. "Good luck getting Matt to abide by that order even if it's for his safety. No offense to Matt, but he can be stubborn when he wants something," she remarked, wondering if they'd have to restrain him to his bed.

"Poor Matt, I'm sure he wants to rescue Scarlett, especially when he feels like he failed protecting her," Dawn added, watching Ari stirring the contents in the cauldron.

Ari laughed opening a few bottles adding different amounts of each ingredient before taking a step back as a burst of plum smoke hit the air. "I agree, Matt will insist on going with, but we don't have time to wait for him to recover nor can we risk him becoming a puppet for Simon. If it comes down to it. I will drug him to ensure he behaves," she noted, turning the heat down to allow it to simmer.

Jet entered the kitchen wearing a grey long-sleeved shirt and black jeans passing Ari to grab a bottle of water. "I know the potion is important but you could have let Raven help, compared to some of the other potions you had me brew, that one is simplistic," he advised, seeing that the potion was nearly finished.

"Hey, Jet, why is your hair wet? I didn't hear the shower." Dawn asked, seeing an impish grin appear on his face glancing at Ari.

"I needed something to distract my mind with and besides, I had all the ingredients already prepared, though perhaps when I make another batch, she can lend a hand. I warned Jet that bathrooms can be dangerous for someone as clumsy as him," she teased, poking him in the ribs.

Jet laughed, swatting her hand away before taking a sip of his water. "Yes, and now I know to be more cautious, though it seemed to amuse you and put you in better spirits, so I'm not upset by it," he protested, glancing in her cauldron seeing that the potion was simmering. "Matt is asleep though we need to have a meeting to discuss our next course of action," he whispered, wondering if she would take the lead for Matt.

Ari gave a simple nod glancing down the hallway to Andrew's bedroom. "You know a certain person will try to take over the role as leader thinking that he knows best? Let me finish this first before we gather the morons," she replied, knowing that they would all look to her for guidance.

Jet laughed setting his water bottle on the counter moving behind her. He tugged on her hair lightly before moving to the fridge making a cheese and fruit tray. "I heard you let Vincent teach Andrew a lesson for his reckless action against Matt?" he asked, knowing that Vincent would want praise.

"I didn't have much of a choice. Vincent was already in there when I came downstairs though I did leave a little present by the door in case Vincent needed any help. I doubt it will do him any good, Andrew has a thick head," she replied, feeling Jet tug her bun free letting her hair fall around her shoulders.

Jet grinned holding his hands up defensively seeing that he had undone the bun in her hair. "Sorry, I couldn't help it. Your hair looks better down," he confessed, seeing her blush at the compliment.

Dawn giggled watching their interaction before leaning over to whisper in Raven's ear. "Is it just me or are they flirting with each other?" she asked, seeing Raven nod in agreement.

Jet placed the snack on the table overhearing what Dawn had asked Raven. "You know it's rude to whisper about people in their presence, and even dangerous when they can use magic," he warned, laughing at seeing Dawn flinch muttering an apology.

Ari smacked the back of Jet's head hearing the threat. "Be nice, it's harmless when it's simple gossip. Finish this up for me Jet, I'm going to go ruin Vin's fun," she explained, heading for the bedroom. She knocked on the door once before entering it seeing that both men were still in the room.

Jet laughed, rubbing the back of his head. He pulled out an empty vial from a drawer uncorking it and filling it with the potion replacing the cork and putting it aside. He joined the girls at the table reinforcing that he had been kidding, warning Raven never to use magic for malice.

Vincent and Andrew were still wrestling, failing to hear the knock at the door or acknowledge Ari was standing in the doorway. Vincent had finally managed to pin Andrew underneath him. "Are you going to apologize to Matt for what you did?" he demanded, refusing to get off him until Andrew agreed.

Andrew growled in annoyance trying to throw Vincent off him despite him being coiled around his legs. "For the last time, I didn't mean to hurt him, but I lost my temper. You can't punish me for expressing how I felt," he protested, tired of Vincent repeating the same request since he barged into the room and tackled him to the ground.

Ari sighed, shooting an orb of magic into a corner of the room making a loud boom go off to gain their attention. "Vincent, how many times must I tell you Andrew never apologizes for anything, even when he knows what he did was wrong. The best you can hope for is to give him a punishment he'll never forget and move on. Can I expect you two boys to act civil and come join us for a meeting?" she asked, staying by the door. She kept her distance from Andrew; she hadn't admitted that after the narrow escape in the basement she had mistrust with the werewolf.

Vincent punched Andrew in the gut as he climbed to his feet stumbling as Andrew lashed out with his legs tripping him. "I don't think I had much luck in punishing him, though I'll leave that up to you," he suggested, laughing at hearing Andrew wince following them down the hall and into the kitchen.

"I think Ari should start with an update on Matt when you're ready," Vincent suggested, thinking that they were worried about Matt.

"The potion you prepared for Matt is ready if you want me to administer it to him before you start?" Jet asked, seeing Andrew standing in the doorway with his arms crossed over his chest.

"No, it can wait. I would rather he sleep some more instead of waking him to take it, though I guess we should get started, though sit down Andrew I don't want a fight breaking out," Ari demanded, pointing to the chair between Dawn and Raven. She ran a hand through her hair trying to settle her emotions knowing that her magic was itching to be let loose. "I was able to replace the amount of blood he lost from the fight but there was damage done both by Simon and Andrew.

Besides the deep bite mark on his neck he also suffered a few fractured ribs. Andrew broke one or two of them causing a small tear in his lung, but his magic was able to heal the damage. He's still extremely weak and is struggling with his core body temperature causing a fever. He also has the taint from the bite and I'm unsure if he can remove it from his system," she explained, sitting next to Jet.

Andrew complied with the command, listening to Ari's report, ignoring the dirty looks he received for the damage he had caused. "That's a lot of injuries, will he recover from the bite?" Dawn asked, surprised that Andrew didn't seem to have any remorse for the extra injuries he had caused.

Jet placed his hand over Ari's once she had taken the seat next to him. "In time, his magic will be restored, and he can recover from his injuries at a faster rate, but we have another matter to discuss—" he explained, interrupted by Andrew.

"We need to go out and search for Scarlett," he protested, seeing Jet hold up his hand stopping Andrew from ranting.

"Yes, Scarlett volunteered to go with Simon in exchange for Matt's life, but we need to be smart about it. We can start our search in the day, searching for clues from the park where she was last seen," Jet announced, seeing Andrew nod in agreement.

"We will return here at dusk to ensure no one gets attacked by Simon though I doubt he will leave and risk Scarlett getting loose. I'll be heading to the park to see if I can find a magical trail to help us with our search. Someone will have to stay here to keep an eye on Matt," she explained, holding Jet's hand using it to ground herself.

Dawn raised her hand, gaining Ari's attention. "I volunteer to stay and look after Matt," she volunteered, seeing Raven nod in agreement with the suggestion.

Andrew seemed surprised by Ari's plan. "I thought you never left the manor; will the barrier stay intact if you venture outside the grounds?" he asked, seeing Vincent glare at him thinking Andrew had asked a stupid question.

"That was before the barrier was taken down and my powers were bound. That is no longer the cause my powers created the barrier so I can come and go without affecting it. Thank you for offering to stay, you two. I'll ensure there's things for you to do while staying here." She offered smiling gently at them glancing around the table to see if there were any other questions.

Raven smiled, happy to help. "I would feel better knowing someone is here to help keep Dawn company," she replied, laughing as Dawn thanked her. "I gather the search will start tomorrow or are we waiting for Matt to recover more?" she asked, aware that Andrew would want to start right away.

"We'll start tomorrow. I don't want to wait too long not knowing what Scarlett is going through. If we're done, Jet you can head up and give Matt his medicine; I need to have a word with Andrew," Ari explained. knowing that they needed to get the wolf in line.

Dawn and Raven both exchanged a look before climbing to their feet muttering that Andrew was in trouble. Vincent followed their lead running off to his room not wanting to earn Ari's wrath. Jet chuckled at the others' reaction. "Take it easy on him, we'll need his help too tomorrow," he warned before climbing to his feet, collecting the potion, and heading to Matt's room.

Andrew climbed to his feet grabbing a bottle of water from the fridge waiting for Ari's lecture. He drummed his fingers on the table waiting for her to yell at him recalling her comment from earlier.

Chapter Fifty-Three

Ari watched for them all to disappear letting out a sigh as she glanced over at Andrew. "I'm not going to lecture you, clearly words mean nothing to you, and I have enough on my plate without wasting time on things that won't work. I want to know what is wrong with you Andrew. You don't care who you hurt so long as you obtain your goal. You could have killed Matt; do you realize that? Do you even care that you put someone's life in danger? That I'm terrified of you because you almost murdered me on the eve of the full moon thinking I was Matt, why do you hate him so much?" Ari asked, wrapping her arms around herself for comfort.

Andrew frowned and understood her fear around him now. "Ari, I'm sorry, I wasn't just mad at Matt that night, they were all teasing me, and I let my anger consume me. I would never try to hurt you after all you've done for me," he confessed, wondering if she would even believe him. "Usually after a full moon I disappear for a few days in the woods until the animalistic rage leaves and this time with the curfew in place I couldn't. I had no idea that Matt's injuries were that severe, but you're right it doesn't excuse my actions," he added, wondering if she would ever feel safe in his presence.

Ari was quiet studying his aura grabbing her locket. "I believe you and I accept your apology, but it may take some time for me to be comfortable around you again when it comes to the full moon. I'm not the only one you need to say that to though throwing an injured man across the room will do that to their injuries. I'm not sure why you and Matt are at odds but for the time being you need to call a truce. Scarlett is missing and it will take all of us to bring her home," Ari warned, not voicing her fears that they may already be too late.

Andrew rubbed the back of his neck knowing that she was right, but he didn't want to apologize to Matt. "I will take your advice under advisement, but I can at least agree to a truce, for now," he groaned, hearing Jet return seeing him pause in the entryway.

Jet crossed the room placing his hand on Ari's shoulder seeing how tense she was. "Sorry to interrupt, but I was able to administer the potion without any problems and then he went back to sleep," he announced, seeing that Andrew had tried sneaking out of the kitchen. "Let him go, you said your piece, and he at least agreed on a truce, though care to join me outside?" he offered, seeing that she needed to relax.

She nodded her head, following him outside. "I wanted to tie him to the wall and start waxing off all his fur. I don't get how someone can cause pain to others and feel no remorse for it. The only thing he's sorry about is scaring me but when it comes to Matt it's like he gets enjoyment out of it. How is Matt doing?" she asked, taking a seat under the tree he had created.

Jet moved sitting behind her letting her rest against his chest massaging her shoulders. "I would have paid to see that though you didn't tell me about the scare, was it when you were closing the cage?" he asked, seeing her nod in agreement relaxing under his touch. "His fever finally broke but aside from that his magic hasn't fully restored but the potion should help," he replied, unsure what Andrew's issue with Matt was.

"That's a relief, I was worried about the fever causing him trouble but now he should fully recover given time. I didn't want to admit it at the time, how terrified I was at having a werewolf enraged and charging at you isn't something you can get over easily," she admitted, relaxing under his touch.

Jet sighed wondering why he wasn't in charge of the task. "Are you willing to teach me the spell, so you don't have to do it, at least until some time has passed?" he offered, understanding that it must have been scary knowing her only safety away from him could burn her.

Ari frowned thinking over the idea. "I could but I don't know if you can perfect it in time before the next full moon. Don't make that face. I trust your magic and your skills. I just doubt your speed when it comes to casting. You know if I didn't fear your safety, I would teach it to you," she replied, knowing he wasn't happy with the news.

Jet played with her hair tugging it lightly not offended by her answer. "I wasn't making that face because of your answer, it makes sense, I just want you to be safe. Can I at least be down there with you when you cast it?" he offered, trying to think of a better solution.

Ari laughed turning onto her back to glance up at him using his lap as a pillow. "I know but until you get your casting speed up you can't be down there with me. I may just put him to sleep and have him carried down into the cell. I don't think I can trust him to be awake before the moon rises," she explained, knowing that he was concerned but she wouldn't put him in harm's way.

Jet continued to stroke her hair seeing that she was content. "Tomorrow is going to be a stressful day, though the others acted like once you leave the manor you'd act like a caged bird and fly away," he teased, hoping that they'd find clues to where Scarlett had been taken.

Ari bit her lip not denying his comment. "If I did, would that be a sad thing? I don't mean fly away but not come back to the manor straight away. I was wondering if you could show me around, I grew up inside these walls. I would love to see something new for a change," she admitted, blushing slightly at her confession.

Jet laughed amused to see her cheeks flush more. "I would be more than happy to escort you around the city, though do you have any objections to riding on a motorcycle? That way Vincent can take the others in the jeep then we can meet them back once we finish?" he suggested, thinking of a few things they could check out. *I wonder if Ari realized she just asked me out on a date,* he thought, a sly grin on his face.

"I've ridden a few times on Matt's when I was helping him tune it up, but it's been a while. I take it you know how to drive one though I don't think Vincent will mind. Should we ask him to bring a leash for Andrew?" she asked, smirking at her own joke.

Jet laughed trying to picture putting a leash on Andrew. "Yes, it's fun to race Matt in them, although a harness would provide more control. I believe they're made for children. Vincent seems to have bounced back quickly from his encounter with Simon, or at least hiding it," he replied, surprised to hear her make a joke wondering if she would try to make a harness to make the others laugh.

Ari tapped a finger to her lips thinking over the suggestion. She raised her finger in the air writing out equations as though considering the offer. "I don't think he's hiding it. I checked his neck when we had the meeting and it appears to be healed. I did go into his room and added some lavender and honey to his body wash to help with any remaining discomfort. Do you think if I made it Andrew would wear it if I made it appear as a jacket?" she asked, thinking that the others would enjoy it.

"Physically sure, that's the beauty of his immortality but he seemed distraught as if he feels as guilty as Matt over what happened," he replied, seeing the thoughts tumbling in her mind. "A cunning trick though Raven would have to swear she got it for him, so he'll not suspect anything," he warned, amused by the concept.

"Why would he feel guilty he was knocked out before the fight even started, so it's not like there was much he could have done to help with the situation. That's not a bad idea and I'm sure Raven will agree to it. I think she's over her crush seeing how Andrew will never return her feelings," she replied, thinking of the perfect way to design it.

"Yes, but if he had been present during Matt's fight with Simon, he could have helped Matt win. Think of it as survivor's remorse, your head is full of different scenarios of what happened and how it could have been different," he replied, seeing her thinking of the design. "Andrew will still trust her judgement since he sees her as a friend," he added, feeling sorry for Raven.

"Is that what occurred to you after waking up in the mine? Sorry it just appeared as though you were speaking from experience. I think he won't consider it being a prank from her because he knows I'm not comfortable being near him so I would ask someone else to give him the item for me," she explained, moving her finger to draw on his stomach

Jet squirmed trying to swat her hand away. "Yes, I felt guilty being the only one to make it and still not sure how because no one should have survived being buried underneath that much rubble," he remarked, reaching for her hand clutching it in his.

Ari frowned feeling bad for upsetting him. "You have magic that could have awoken and protected you during the blast. I'm not sure seeing how there's not much about you before the blast that you can recall or that I was able to discover. There wasn't a file for you in the government database," she explained, giggling wondering if he was ticklish moving her other hand to his chest.

Jet coughed trying to hide his laughter seeing she had figured out he was ticklish. "I know sensing magic brought me to where you and your brother was, but I can't explain what happened in that mine… it claimed so many good men, yet I was spared," he admitted, sighing at feeling both hands on his chest underneath his shirt.

Ari chuckled seeing that she had found his weak spot as she continued her assault. "I don't have any answers for you besides thinking that magic was the cause, though don't be saddened that you survived. Everything occurs for a reason Jet," she admitted, sitting up to kiss him on the cheek to cheer him up.

Jet bit his lip trying hard not to laugh seeing that she was enjoying his torment. "Being kept busy and our lessons have helped but some days my mind wanders back there trying to recall more," he admitted, pushing her to the ground trying to pin her hands by grabbing her wrists.

Ari laughed struggling to break free afraid he would get revenge. "Have you tried meditation? It could help open up your mind to the memories that were before the accident," she suggested, squirming trying to break free.

Jet smirked causing vines to sprout wrapping around her wrist before lifting her shirt to tickle her ribs. "I recall earlier that we were allowed to use magic in our games," he teased, grinning in glee at hearing her laugh.

Ari shrieked in alarm trying to break free. "Cheater, you know this means war?" she asked, trying to get out through laughter making vines appear to attack Jet's stomach.

Jet's smile faltered seeing the vines appear on either side of him to attack him. Laughter spilled from his lips trying to hasp out a plea for her to stop. "I'm sorry I even started it. Must you win every game?" he wheezed, trying to catch his breath.

Ari laughed making the vines stop giving them both a chance to catch their breath. "I can't help it. I guess it's my competitive nature, I don't enjoy losing though it was a good effort on your part," she teased, giving him an innocent smile.

Jet laughed, rolling his eyes not believing her. "I like learning new things about you, though maybe every once in a while, you can let me win?" he suggested, laughing at seeing her shake her head no to his proposal.

Ari pretended to consider it before shaking her head no. "If you want a win, you'll have to earn it yourself Jet, though good luck on beating me," she teased, climbing to her feet dusting off the back of her pants. "Care to work on some magic?" she asked, pointing to the tree.

Jet climbed to his feet dusting the dirt from his pants. "I thought that's what we were doing but in a fun way," he replied, excited to practice his magic with her.

Ari smirked amused by his comment. "I guess you have a point though in that case we should try working on your barriers," she teased, summoning a vine to lunge at his stomach once more.

Jet closed his eyes taking in a deep breath trying to concentrate on the task. He kicked off his shoes letting his feet brush the soil before whispering the chant he had used before. A stone pillar shot out from the Earth forcing the vine to collide with it. He summoned two more on either side of it adding moss webbing before panting from the effort.

Ari slowed the vine down knowing that Jet wasn't as quick with his spells as hers. "Impressive, you've improved since our last encounter though you left your back exposed. You're not starting to feel caved in, are you?" she asked, giving him a chance to catch his breath.

Jet smiled flattered by her compliment shaking his head no. "I was thinking of adding on to what I started making a ring around myself so I wouldn't feel enclosed, but I was trying to keep up with you and need to pace myself," he admitted, wondering if there was a better strategy he could use.

"I realize this which is why I slowed down the speed of my spell to give you enough time to prepare for it. Your method will work, we just need to work on your endurance and casting speed. You can try going for runs in the morning," she suggested, allowing the vine to sneak behind him and smack Jet on the butt.

Jet cried out in alarm laughing at feeling the vine smack his butt. "I usually go for a run at sunrise but maybe I can resist the practice drills I did for the military. They had us run five to ten miles a day to help get us in shape, though what would help with increasing my casting speed?" he asked, taking her suggestions under advisement.

Ari laughed at his reaction. "Target practice can help; I can set up targets out here for you to use. It will help with aiming and pop up targets will help with speed as well. Fighting each other will help seeing how my spells are cast at a quicker rate, though the spells we use will be harmless," she suggested, making the vine smack him once more.

Jet laughed a sly grin spreading out on his face. He gripped the vine and tried a spell changing it into a burst of cherry blossom petals falling to the ground. "There, now you can stop using it as a whip, though is offensive magic performed the same way as defensive magic?" he asked, bending to pick up one of the flower petals placing it in her hair.

Ari laughed, taking the flower from him using a clip to hold it in place. "Yes, though the intent is different. You cast the spells with the intention of hitting an item or person with it. Some use the idea of causing harm or pain while others see it to prevent harm from occurring to others," she explained, walking over to his stone barriers poking them with her finger returning them to simple soil.

Jet nodded in agreement thinking that her explanation made sense. "Care to join me in the morning for a run, it will be a stressful outing given what you're searching for," he suggested, knowing he always felt energized after a run.

"Sure, why not it would beat running laps in the backyard though you'll have to lead the way seeing how it's your course. It may be stressful but who knows maybe we'll get lucky," she mused, poking him in the ribs before running inside. Jet laughed chasing after her.

Chapter Fifty-Four

Scarlett's eyes flickered open feeling a cold caress slither down her arm. She shivered lashing out trying to push the shade away. Two shades moved to stand beside her, gripping her arm. The tallest one, removed the bloody piece of cloth and bent, pressing its cold lips against her flesh. It grazed its teeth along the long red gash reopening the wound. Scarlett gritted her teeth, blocking out the pain letting her thoughts fill with images of Matt.

"That's enough. We have to pace ourselves or fear of bleeding her dry," Simon announced, approaching them placing more logs to rekindle the dying fire. He moved to stand in front of her, holding a goblet of water in both hands. He frowned seeing her turn her head once the goblet touched her lips. The shade adjacent to him grabbed her other arm. Simon pinched the bridge of her nose forcing her head back.

He poured the water into her mouth watching it spill down her chin and onto her shirt. "You could have made that easier for yourself, my pet. Mortals can't last long without water, or risk withering to dust," he warned, pulling his hand away.

"You can't blame me for being suspicious of anything you give me," she hissed, coughing, and gasping for air. The wind howled throughout the cavern.

"This is twice now you've thought ill of me, and twice I have tried convincing you otherwise. I'm not sure what the other slayers have said to make you doubt my intentions," he pleaded, handing the goblet to one of the shades.

"Just accept that it will keep happening. You'd be delusional to believe I'd ever trust you. You made me choose between my freedom and Matt's life. Others may view such a trade as kidnapping," she hissed, watching the shades place the goblet on a small wooden table.

Simon frowned, placing a plank of wood on the fire. He added fish and mixed berries wrapped in twigs. "I thought by agreeing to spare the mongrel's life in exchange for your company was a fair trade," he replied, turning the meat as the fire seared it.

Scarlett let out a bitter laugh watching the orange flames flicker over the flank of meat. "Don't insult both of our intellects with such pathetic lies. I did what I thought was best. I knew that if I gave you what you wanted, then you would grant me at least one request," she replied, watching his lips upturn into a frown in the yellow glow of the fire.

Simon remained silent turning the wood as the meat cooked. "You have a point there. I was surprised to learn how strong your feelings were for the mongrel. You condemn me for being a monster driven by selfish desires, yet you ignore his enact nature?" he hissed, removing the slab of meat, and adding it to two plates piled high with roasted vegetables.

Scarlett watched Simon hand the plate of food to his shades before approaching me. "You're trying to argue that if I can love Matt then by the same logic, I should love you?" she spat, hearing the chains around her arms jingle. She glanced up watching his fingers slide around the bolts that tethered her restraints to the wall behind her. He grasped both chains in one hand and tugged sharply.

Simon grinned, slipping one arm around her waist, pulling her close against his chest. "The thought had crossed my mind, though we can discuss it over dinner," he whispered, nipping at her earlobe playfully. He dragged her closer to the table watching the shades fill a second glass of wine for him.

How sad, he has the delusion that he can impress me with chivalry; as if one kind gesture can erase my feeling of him? she thought, feeling the cold granite bench brush against her legs. She glanced down watching him wrap the chains around each leg tethering her to the bench. She cringed feeling his icy fingers trail up her inner thigh.

Simon paused knelt in front of her fighting the urge to rapture his poor victim. No, as hard as it is to fight it, I can't give her any more excuses to fear me, he thought, climbing to his feet. He gripped her chin gingerly in both hands tilting her head up and brushed his lips tenderly against hers. He pulled away and moved to stand behind her pushing her closer to the table.

Scarlett reached for the glass of wine placed in front of her taking a long sip to cleanse the bitter taste from her lips. "I see, you still fear I'll try to flee if given the chance?" she sneered, setting the glass down, rubbing at her wrists subconsciously.

"As promised, we can discuss things over dinner. You still treat me like the raving monster, driven by the quench of your blood," Simon replied, taking a sip from his glass. He arched an eyebrow hearing laughter in response.

"I haven't been left to believe otherwise. You claim to be a gentleman yet devour my blood every time you're given the chance. Even worse, you let your minions feast upon my flesh like vultures," she sneered, pushing the plate placed in front of her away in disgust.

Simon rested his chin in his right hand regarding her words carefully. "The shades are an extension of myself and only aim to please me. Many times, I've struggled against the thoughts of animalistic desires and rapturing you in my arms," he confessed, taking in a shallow breath. "But alas, I will bide my time until you push away any lingering thoughts of the mongrel," he hissed, taking another sip of his wine.

Scarlett's eyes widened in horror realizing what he was implying. I took one last sip of my drink before tossing the liquid in Simon's direction. "Admit it, you're jealous that my heart belongs to someone you deem unworthy. I would rather die than offer myself to you," she screamed, placing both hands underneath the table forcing it to turn on its side. The plate and glasses clattered against the cavern floor.

The shades surrounded the table turning it right side up while Simon climbed to his feet. He closed the distance between them. He grabbed her right arm tearing the bloody bandages aside and sank his teeth into the wound. Scarlett whimpered pushing against his chest with her free hand. A shade stood to one side grabbing the hand and raked its sharp nails up her arm lapping up the blood hungrily.

Simon pulled his lips away from her flesh beckoning the shade to follow suit. "Forgive me, in my moment of weakness, I prayed on you like a fallen doe. In your outburst you caused the wound to reopen and your blood is so delicious," he drawled, wiping his mouth against the back of his right hand. He accepted a black scarf from one of the shades and placed it over the wound securing it tightly in place.

Scarlett glared at Simon, pressing her hand over the thin gash shade had created. "It seems like my words struck a nerve. Like I said, you can't force me to respect you even with fear. Just return me to my restraints and stop pretending to be the hero. Matt will come for me in time, and when he does, I'll enjoy watching your demise," she hissed, watching him warily.

Interesting, despite the pain I've caused her she remains defiant. I will succeed in breaking her spirit, and then we shall see how easy it is for her to deny my wishes, he thought, gripping her chin in both hands forcing her to tilt her chin up meeting his hungry gaze.

"One would think you were smarter than this and would try using your brain before speaking. Even if you are my pet, I strain to keep my anger in check," he warned, brushing his lips over hers.

He grabbed her hair, pressing her lips harder against his, biting down on her lower lip, breaking the skin. He sucked in the small droplet of drop hungrily. His eyes darkened before pulling away, laughing at feeling her fists push against his chest. *How amusing, my pet believes she is a match against me given her present predicament*, he thought, watching the shades sweep up the broken glass.

"How many times do I have to remind you, that I don't belong to you?" she screamed, spitting at his feet. "Despite all your efforts, I'll never be yours, nor will I fear you. Face, it. You're nothing more than a monster." She hissed, wiping her mouth with the back of her palm.

"You think I'm a raving monster, but I have restrained myself. There are violent ways of breaking your spirit. I had considered it, but making love isn't worth it when your heart beats for the mongrel," he replied, turning his back to me beckoning for the shades to release my legs from their restraints, dragging me once more to the back of the cavern. My back slammed against the cold granite while my wrists were shackled in chains above my head.

Hot tears stung her cheeks dispelling the frustration coursing through her veins. I see, so since he didn't rape me, I should see him as a chivalrous knight. Can I lie to him and tell him my feelings for him have changed? Even if I convinced him of the lie, I could never forgive myself, she thought, shuddering at feeling the cold caress brush away the tears. Scarlett closed her eyes returning to the memory of being held in Matt's arms protected by the swirling snowflakes cascading around us.

Chapter Fifty-Five

Matt sat up in bed quickly, a scream caught in his throat as he stumbled falling out of bed trying to free himself from the blanket that was wrapped around him. He ran a hand through his hair trying to bring his breathing back under control. He groaned hearing faint laughter in his head seeing that his demon was back as he held a handout in front of him to form a ball of ice.

He whimpered letting go of his power seeing a ball of slush in his hand. "I wouldn't do that if I were you, I used my powers to heal your wounds the rest will take time." His demon warned in amusement.

Vincent stirred hearing a scream before hearing a thud above him. He groaned, tossing the covers aside, rubbing the sleep from his eyes. It still looked dark outside as the sun began to peek out from behind the horizon. Picking up a pair of sweatpants from the floor before heading upstairs. He knocked on Matt's door before poking his head in. Crossing the room, he helped untangle the sheet from Matt's legs helping him back onto the bed.

"Thanks, sorry if I woke you, I know it's probably still early," he groaned, sitting on the bed resting his head back against the headboard. He glanced out the window seeing that the sun was just rising as he glanced down trying not to blush as he pulled the blanket over his lap realizing he was only in his boxers.

Vincent snickered seeing Matt desperately reaching for the blanket to cover up his lap. "You never mustered the strength to get dressed," he teased, seeing a pair of slacks thrown in the corner. "I can give you a hand if you ask nicely," he teased, enjoying the opportunity to tease Matt.

"You're enjoying this way too much. though that would explain why I barely have any recollection of yesterday. All I recall is waking up and interacting with you and Jet, I just don't remember what we discussed though can you help me put some pants on?" he asked, seeing Vincent's amusement annoyed he couldn't shut him up by throwing a snowball in his face.

Vincent nodded in agreement grabbing the slacks before sitting on the edge of the bed helping Matt pull them on. "You slept a lot; Ari was worried about the fever you had. She said it was slowing down your recovery, but you seemed better once it broke," he replied, seeing the melted puddle of snow on the ground. "Was that directed at me because if so, you missed," he teased, sensing that Matt's magic had yet to return.

"No, I created that before you came in here to evaluate if my magic has fully returned, which clearly it hasn't. It hurts to summon my magic I guess that means no snowballs in the face for you when you're being a brat though thanks," Matt mused, grateful for Vincent's help knowing things would have been awkward if one of the girls had come across him instead.

Vincent frowned thinking it was a better question for Ari to answer. "It must not be a total loss if you were able to summon something despite the pain, doesn't you demon have any helpful insight?" he asked, aware it was linked to Matt's magic.

Matt groaned, placing his head in his hands. "Right, because it's been so helpful in the past. He claims he used up his energy to heal my wounds and that I should leave him alone unless I want him to take control again," he replied, knowing how much damage the demon could cause when it wasn't contained.

Vincent smirked, deciding not to argue with Matt thinking it had helped by healing his wounds. "You seem to be in better spirits compared to yesterday, though will you be joining us in the search?" he asked, knowing Matt would want to help search for Scarlett.

Matt glared at Vincent before arching an eyebrow. "What search, you mean for Scar? I would say yes, but I think that will be up to Ari seeing how now she's in charge until I recover," he admitted, though he doubted she would agree to the idea.

Vincent smiled innocently seeing that he was getting on Matt's nerves. "Yes, but your company will help make the search more enjoyable. You know Andrew will seek glory for whatever clues we find," he groaned, not wanting to babysit the wolf.

Matt chuckled understanding Vincent's request. "I feel you though after our last encounter I'm not so sure that's wise, but it would be smart for me to go with you guys. I can show you where the fight broke out instead of being forced to search the entire area," Matt advised, wanting to help find Scarlett.

Vincent nodded in agreement thinking that Ari may still refuse the request. "That's not a bad argument, I'll pass it along to Ari when she returns. She went on a run with Jet just a few minutes ago," he remarked, recalling Jet's excitement when he had shared it with him the night before.

Matt chuckled thinking that it was about time. "I see someone is eager to take in her new freedom, though knowing Ari she'll have a surprise in store for Andrew seeing how he's been a jerk to everyone recently," Matt replied, closing his eyes briefly hearing movement on the floor below them.

Vincent laughed, seeing Matt trying to go back to sleep. "I would be too after being caged in one place all that time," he replied, letting Matt rest before venturing downstairs. He snickered, overhearing Jet and Ari's conversation.

Jet led the way into the kitchen offering Ari a glass of ice water before taking a seat at the table to catch his breath. "I hope the trail wasn't too boring. I didn't want to go too far and end up on the highway, though there are a few different trails we can explore," he advised, surprised that she had been able to keep up with him.

Ari laughed taking the offered glass before taking a seat beside him. "Really so when will the goofy look leave your face, will that be when I decide to make you eat my dust? I told you I run laps in the backyard, yet you have this idea that the run would be too difficult for me to complete. Good morning Vincent, care to join us?" Ari asked, seeing him standing in the doorway.

Jet noticed Vincent nod in agreement moving to make a fresh pot of coffee. "I wasn't implying that it would be too difficult, I was just hoping to beat you in our race, then again it's been a while since my training," he admitted, surprised to see Vincent up so early.

Vincent watched the coffee drip in the pot impatiently, covering his mouth as a yawn escaped it. "It sounds like you both had fun, though I had an early wakeup call from Matt. He was trying to evaluate his powers and fell out of bed," he admitted, informing Ari of his request.

Ari frowned thinking over Vincent's words. "I don't think that's a wise idea, we may get some unwanted attention if people see us helping him into the park since I doubt, he has enough energy to walk on his own. Add to the fact his powers have yet to return he would just be hurting himself in the process," Ari admitted, thinking of how to inform Matt without upsetting him.

Jet noticed Vincent sigh before turning to make pancakes for breakfast. "I understand Matt wants to help by saving us time in finding where the fight took place, but I agree with Ari. If he recovered further, she might have changed her mind. Besides, Ari should be able to focus on Matt's magic to find the location," he added, seeing that Vincent was disappointed by the answer.

Ari joined Vincent at the stove, helping him by making eggs. "I know you would rather have Matt then Andrew keep you company but that's just not the right choice now. Even if Matt were healed if we got a lead what would prevent him from discovering where it ended? I have a gift for Andrew that may entertain you," she admitted, thinking that Vincent would enjoy using the harness.

Vincent arched an eyebrow hearing Jet laughing hysterically at the mention of Andrew having a present from her. "Given Jet's reaction, I'm almost afraid to ask what you have in store," he replied, seeing Jet had snorted water out of his nose.

Ari laughed seeing Jet's reaction to her comment. "There's nothing wrong with giving Raven a jacket as a gift for Andrew. The fact there's straps and a chain which will be revealed with a special phrase is just an innocent bonus." She admitted. not wanting to say it aloud in case Andrew was near.

"I have to admit, I'm a bit envious, I want a jacket designed by you Ari," Vincent whined, seeing that her and Jet were sharing a private joke. "What time do you want us to leave for the park?" he asked, not envying her to be the one to give Matt the sad news.

"Let the others wake up first though I can create a jacket for you Vin just not the one I created for Drew unless you're a fan of bondage. I'll give Matt his meds and let him know he'll be staying here with Raven and Dawn," Ari explained, finishing the eggs as she put them in a bowl before placing it on the table.

Jet carried his glass to the sink moving to fill the tea kettle with water seeing Vincent cooking bacon and potatoes. "That's kindly generous of you to offer is this a hidden talent I wasn't made aware of?" he teased, seeing that Vincent was ecstatic with her answer,

"I just started. I'm not very good at it yet though I made a shawl and the jacket for Andrew so I'm starting to get the hang of it. Most of it is enchanted with runes so I hope that's all right Vin," she explained, sending a text to the girls letting them know there was breakfast for them.

"I find that hard to believe, I haven't seen you fail at anything since you've been here," Vincent protested, laughing at seeing his compliment making her blush. Jet smiled glad to see Vincent was as excited as himself to see her creation.

"Ah, Vincent is sucking up to you, maybe you should reconsider your gift," he teased, seeing Dawn and Raven enter the kitchen both still dressed in their pajamas. He poured Ari and himself a cup of tea handing Ari hers before taking a seat at the table. "Good morning ladies, I hope you slept well?" he asked, seeing Raven head toward the coffee pot failing to hear his question.

Ari took her cup, thanking him before making herself a plate once Vincent had set the rest of the food on the table. "I don't think Raven's up for conversation until she has her coffee, though what novel are you reading now Dawn?" she asked, seeing the girl set a book by her plate before helping herself to the food.

Dawn giggled seeing Raven adding sugar to her coffee before taking a seat beside Dawn. "I started reading Emma, another romantic Jane Austin novel," she replied, ignoring Raven groaning in protest hoping that Ari wouldn't ask what it was about.

Ari hid her face behind her teacup hiding the face upon hearing it was another romance novel. "I'm sure it's a fascinating read for those who enjoy those types of novels. I left the keys to the files on my desk if you wish to continue your project with a beginner's guide to herbology for Raven," she explained, finishing her meal as she put her plate in the sink before fixing a tray to take upstairs to Matt.

Dawn snickered seeing Raven's face fall at the mention of having a text to read as well. "Raven it's not as dry as you fear and your studies have to start somewhere," Jet reassured her, seeing her offer him a weak smile. "I'm going to go see if Andrew is up yet so we can get going soon," he replied, finishing his tea before seeing Andrew enter the kitchen from the backyard.

"It seems like the good little doggie smelled bacon and came running," Vincent teased, earning a low growl from Andrew in return as he made himself a plate.

"Shut up, isn't it a bit early for a child to be awake?" Andrew sneered, getting up to fill a glass with ice water sitting beside Dawn. Vincent rolled his eyes, starting to clean up his mess getting a second cup of coffee.

Ari coughed amused by the bickering between them. "I'm going to go give Matt his meds and then get ready. Raven can you meet me in my room when you're done, I have a favor to ask of you," Ari asked, taking the tray before disappearing upstairs.

Raven glanced at Jet wondering if he had some insight on what it was. "Don't be alarmed, you're not in trouble. She has a gift for you," he remarked, laughing at hearing Dawn swoon excitedly before Raven climbed to her feet placing her dishes in the sink before disappearing to Ari's room excited to receive the surprise.

Dawn dove back into her book waiting for Raven to return and share what the surprise was. "I didn't hear Ari mention that it was a gift, just that she needed her help with something," Andrew noted, seeing Jet shrug his shoulders pretending not to know what it was.

Chapter Fifty-Six

Ari entered her room amused that she had tricked Matt into taking his meds knowing the man wouldn't be awake until they had left for the park. She took a quick shower before entering her room seeing Raven waiting for her.

"Hey, I wasn't expecting you up here so quickly give me a few minutes and then I'll give the item to you," she explained, heading toward her closet to pick out an outfit.

Raven apologized telling Ari to take her time wondering if she had a special outfit picked out for the day. "I'm sure you're excited, you finally get to explore the city with Jet once we're done at the park," she teased, wondering if Jet had planned the day out already.

Ari laughed nervously playing with a strand of her hair. "Yes, but also a bit nervous Jet made it clear it was a date and well I've never been on one before. I just don't want to do something wrong and mess things up between us," she explained, slipping on a pair of black slacks and a light blue tunic adorned with butterflies. She was drying her hair with the towel as she walked over to her dresser picking up two items. "So, this jacket is for Andrew, I was hoping you could give it to him, so he'll wear it. Once on all a person has to say is mush and when touching it will make a lead and harness appear. The other is for you a way to help in your learning," she explained, holding out a small dragonfly pin.

Raven moved, helping to pull Ari's bangs back into a braid leaving the rest down. She stared at the pin holding it in her hands admiring the details etched in silver. "It's a beautiful pin, thank you, though what does it do?" she asked, amused by the prank in store for Andrew knowing he would be annoyed by the command.

Ari took the pin pricking Raven's finger before pinning it to her shirt. "Sorry, it needs a bit of blood to activate. I know how much you hate to study so this will help. Any text you hold all the key facts will be highlighted for you and will be translated if in another language. It's a tester so let me know how it works," she explained, walking over to her desk picking up her locket to put on.

Raven cried out in alarm seeing the drop of blood disappear from the pin. "An interesting trick that will save me a great deal of torment. Another generous gift given to me when I haven't earned it. Don't let today make you nervous, Jet cares greatly for you," she advised, excited to evaluate the pin out.

"Sorry, you'll learn that all magic comes with a price. I hope you're right though good luck with Matt today; he won't be happy that he was left behind and that I tricked him into taking a nap," she explained, grabbing a small green messenger bag throwing it over her shoulder. "You don't have to earn gifts from me Rave, you're my student now and I wish for you to succeed," she explained, heading for the door.

Raven frowned, understanding that Matt would be furious when he learned the truth. "I'm sorry, it's something I'll have to work on. I'm not used to getting things without having to earn it, good luck in your search," she replied, thinking she would send Dawn up to deal with him once the others left.

Ari frowned, not pleased by this as she paused in her steps. "Why do you think you have to earn gifts? Shouldn't a person receive items to assist them in life or to show a token of friendship?" she asked, wondering where this idea came from.

Raven sighed, fidgeting with her hair, staring down at her feet. "Just a rule that was beaten into me because of my parents. I was taken in because Matt felt sorry for me and saw something redeemable in me, but I don't see it, at least not yet," she admitted, knowing it was wrong to think that way.

Ari moved forward bringing the girl into a hug. "No one should feel that way and I'm sorry I didn't notice it sooner. Matt took you in because he knows you have potential but remember you have yet to come into your power. so, who knows what you'll be able to accomplish," Ari noted, before letting go.

Raven returned the embrace offering her a weak smile. "It's easier to hide something that can leave you vulnerable than to share it with others and have it used against you," she admitted, thinking she should take Ari's advice to heart.

"I would disagree, but I know that there are some people in the house that would use your weakness to their advantage. I will give you the same offer I gave Dawn, that if you need to talk my door is always open," she advised, before heading for the stairs to meet up with Jet.

"In time, if I come to accept it instead of being ashamed, I wouldn't care who knew," she admitted, following Ari back to the kitchen to share what she had gotten with Dawn.

She noticed Andrew heading to his room to collect what he needed before leaving. She grabbed his arm holding the jacket out for him.

"Wait, I found this in my room and figured it belonged to you," she lied, seeing him try on the jacket seeing her smile letting out a low whistle.

Satisfied with her reaction, Andrew decided to keep the jacket on until they reached the park.

Ari noticed the jacket as Andrew walked past them, heading for the car. She pulled out her phone, texting Vincent the code word but asking him to wait until they were at the park. "Well we're off, I left a few vials on my desk in case Matt needs them before we return. Text me if you guys need anything," she suggested, heading out the door walking over to where the bikes were kept.

Jet offered her one of the helmets before climbing onto the bike. "The guys already left wanting to get gas first," he explained, swinging his legs over the bike holding out his hand to help her. He hit the switch to open the garage door feeling Ari grip his hand positioning herself behind him. "Let me know when you're ready and hang on tight," he advised, feeling her lean against his back wrapping her arms around his waist.

"I'm ready, though I texted Vin the command word for the jacket, so don't be surprised if he uses it before we get there," she whispered, tugging the helmet on before climbing on, wrapping her arms tightly around his waist waiting for him to hit the gas.

Jet laughed thinking that Vincent would test the command before they reached the park. He jump-started the bike laughing at feeling her grip tighten as the garage door shut behind them. "You can relax, I'm not going to let you fall," he warned, approaching the highway weaving around the other cars grinning feeling her loosen her grip resting her head against his shoulder. As they entered the park's parking lot, he snickered seeing that the jeep was already parked.

Ari waited until they had stopped removing her helmet. "Sorry, I'm used to riding with Matt and well he's not known for being careful on the bike though I enjoyed the ride. Do you think the boys are already in the park?" she asked, placing her helmet on the seat before heading for the entrance.

Jet removed his helmet as well following Ari into the park hearing Vincent laughing. "If you would just be a good doggie, I'll let you off the leash," he teased, holding the restraints seeing Ari and Jet entering the park. "Hey guys, I was just taking Andrew for a walk until you arrived," he announced, waving to them hearing Jet laugh.

"Remind me to thank Raven for tricking me into wearing this thing, though don't think I don't know the spell is your handiwork, Ari," Andrew groaned, waiting for them to approach sighing in relief as Vincent released the harness and it disappeared until the command was given again.

Ari laughed ignoring his glare. "I created the entire thing, but I knew that you wouldn't wear it unless Raven gifted it to you. Now be a good little mutt and sniff out Matt's magic or would you rather mush over there?" Ari asked, laying her hand on Andrew's shoulder making the harness appear again.

Jet doubled over howling in laughter joined by Vincent as Andrew crossed his arms over his chest. "You're the gifted one, use your magic to track him," he growled, enraged by what she had done.

"Andrew, the longer you resist the more opportunities we get to tease you, like what happened at the gas station," Vincent warned, hearing Andrew sigh in defeat bending low to the ground sniffing the dirt searching for the residue of magic.

"Wait, what happened at the gas station?" Jet asked, seeing Andrew clench his jaw, hearing Vincent recall the humiliating story.

"There was a cute girl at the cash register and was flirting with Andrew. When she saw I was buying beef jerky I used the command and Andrew knocked over a display case," he explained, ignoring Andrew flipping him off still amused by the incident.

Ari reached a hand up wiping away the tears of laughter. She waited until Andrew was out of range before commenting. "He has a point; I can locate Matt's magic, but I figured this way would be more fun. I'll take over if he turns up empty," she admitted, before walking after the werewolf enjoying the view.

Andrew sniffed the ground once more getting closer to where the wide oak trees lined the perimeter of the park. He waved to Ari beckoning her to where he was kneeling on the ground. He waited until she reached him followed by Jet and Vincent. "The scent is faint so you may still need to use your magic," he advised, trying to follow the scent but the trail ended.

"Thank you, Andrew. You saved us time having to search the entire park, even with the aid of magic natural elements from the terrain and humans passing through the park can interfere," he explained, clapping Andrew on the back hearing Vincent applauding.

Vincent reached into his pocket holding out a stick of beef jerky to Andrew. "Good boy, here's a treat for being such a good boy," he teased, frowning trying to wave the jerky teasing, yet Andrew was trying to ignore him.

Ari stood beside him chanting a small spell before touching the ground. She poured more magic into it as images appeared playing out the battle before them. It ended with two images running through the trees heading for the mountain path. "Wow, I knew Matt was powerful, but I never thought he would go that far. He almost killed himself before Simon even fed on him," she muttered. letting the spell drop shuddering at what she had seen.

Jet knelt beside her and placed his hand on her shoulder overhearing the comment she had whispered to herself. "What's wrong. What did you see?" he asked, gripping her arm helping her to stand up dusting the dirt from his pants.

Vincent popped the treat in his mouth seeing that what Ari had seen had rattled her. "You saw a glimpse of the vamps' powers? I thought I could manage it, but I never saw him coming," he admitted, shuddering at recalling the encounter.

Ari gave Vincent a weak smile knowing how he was feeling. "I saw the fight and what limits Matt had to go to just to have a chance against the vampire. How are we to overcome his shades they not only give Simon blood and energy, but they can be created so long as there's darkness and everything creates a shadow." She groaned, as her eyes wandered to the path wondering if they even found the vampire's hiding spot would they be able to defeat him.

Andrew noticed her gaze drift off toward the park's exit wondering if she could sense which direction to go search next. "Did you see which way they went once Simon took Scarlett?" he asked, seeing that she was hesitant to share more information.

He failed to see Jet close the distance between them until he rested his hand on his shoulder and whispered the command. "Don't be a fool and rush into something we're not prepared for. I know we can't afford to wait for Matt to recover, but to face Simon and his army of shades we may need his help," he advised, gripping the harness tightly.

"I know they went into the mountains we can start searching but I don't want to be up there searching and running into the vampire. I say search for an hour or two before calling off the search for the day? I feel like we're letting Scarlett down, but I don't know if we can defeat him," she admitted, not wanting to admit that if they came across Simon only her magic and Vincent immortality would survive the encounter.

Vincent took the harness from Jet not trusting Andrew to race off and search on his own. "I don't think we're letting her down, we're trying to be cautious. I tried facing his shades and despite being made from shadows, they are incredibly fast and strong. I don't want to face them again without being prepared," he warned, ignoring Andrew's dirty look, clearly not happy with his answer.

"Vincent let him go, perhaps allowing Andrew to search ahead will uncover where they went. I know they went into the mountains but that could also be a rouse to lead us into a trap." Ari explained, walking back toward the main fighting spot kneeling down to brush the snow away revealing the earth underneath. She pulled out a sheet of paper before drawing allowing the elemental magic to guide her hand.

Jet watched her brushing the slush that was snow aside touching the wet soil to draw. "What are you hoping to gain from Gaia that she hasn't already shown you?" he asked, waiting for her to finish curious to see what she had sketched.

Ari finished the sketch blinking a few times to clear her vision, her iris going from black to its normal color. She glanced down at the paper biting her lip in concentration. "I'm not sure, but I have these runes in a book back at the manor. I don't think we'll gain anything else here unless we wish to explore the mountain paths," she offered, climbing to her feet placing the paper in her bag dusting off her pants as she walked over to where the others were standing.

Jet nodded in agreement watching her put the drawing away. "Do you want to return to the manor to investigate what it means? We can always postpone our other plans?" Jet asked, seeing Vincent waiting for her orders, wondering what to do next.

Ari shrugged her shoulders thinking of what they should do. "What do you guys think, do you wish to look around some more or return to the manor? My research can wait. It will take me a few hours to translate them," she explained, unsure what they should do next.

Vincent shared a look with Jet before coming to a decision. "Go explore the city with Jet, you deserve some fun. I'll go chase after Andrew and return to the manor," he suggested, knowing that Ari was stressed out.

Ari smiled, kissing Vin on the cheek as thanks before grabbing Jet's hand and heading back toward the bike. "So, where are we heading or is it a surprise?" she asked, putting her helmet back on waiting for Jet to get on.

Jet laughed seeing Vincent give them a thumbs up as Ari led him back to the bike. He put his helmet back on. "I figured I would take you to the local tea shop first where I like buying our tea from, but the second place is a surprise," he teased, swinging his legs over the bike before offering her his hand.

Ari laughed, climbing on behind him. "I like that idea though I always thought you just bought the tea online. I could use a cup after our little adventure," she admitted, wrapping her arms around him resting her head back on his shoulder. Jet laughed nodding in agreement racing out of the park's parking lot.

~~*

They drove for a few miles passing a gas station before arriving at a small white stone building surrounded by a mossy patch of grass, with white picnic tables and a black brick sign reading Gray's Café. He pulled to a stop helping her off the bike offering her his arm. A customer exited the café holding the door open for them letting the smell of cinnamon waft out into the air.

Ari nodded her head in thanks to the man holding the door open before stepping inside. The smell of exotic spices filled the air as she took in the small café. One wall held an assortment of tea bags and tea sets for sale as a few tables were set up inside. The other part held the counter showing an assortment of sweets. "I can see why you enjoy the place though should I be surprised if they know you by name?" she teased, as they approached the counter.

Jet smirked opening his mouth to reply when a blonde girl no older than five darted from behind the counter wrapping herself around his leg. He laughed hearing a stern voice warn to leave Jet alone. Jet knelt holding a flower out to her. "Emily, I would like for you to meet my friend Ari, this is her first time here. Do you think you can give her a your?" he asked, laughing as she took the flower glancing up at Ari before taking her hand.

A young woman in her thirties emerged from the storage room behind the counter hearing her daughter ask if Ari was a nickname. "I see you brought a friend, though sorry about Emily. I couldn't find a sitter this morning," she confessed, wiping her hands on her apron covering a blue button-down shirt over black slacks.

"Don't worry about it, Cassie, it seems she is enjoying playing the role of tour guide," he teased, placing a small pot of Green tea and some scones before rescuing Ari directing her to a table before Emily ran back behind the counter.

Ari laughed entertaining the little girl by pointing out what the different tea bags were known for, "I was right, though they seem very fond of you though how long have you been coming here?" she asked, pouring them each a cup of tea adding a small amount of sugar to hers.

Jet nodded in agreement adding milk and sugar to his thinking of the answer. "I was buying teas online like you had suggested but grew unhappy with the product and found a review of this café and have been coming ever since, so the last four years," he replied, taking a bite of his scone.

"Wow that's impressive, though I can see what makes you keep coming back. The owner seems very friendly. Emily seems to be attached to you and here I thought you were not a fan of little girls," she teased, knowing how he had a good relationship with Dawn.

"When they're that young they are easily bribed with pretty trinkets, every year on her birthday I have crafted her a doll since she lost her father in the war. It's nice that I can offer her some sort of peace even if it's temporary," he admitted, refilling his cup.

Ari laughed amused by his answer as she broke her scone apart to see what was inside before popping a piece into her mouth. "I'm glad you were able to offer her some fond memories though you are an excellent carver so I'm sure they're works of art. Should we invite her over for tea?" Ari asked, seeing the little girl peeking at them from behind the counter.

Jet blushed, flattered by her compliment before waving the girl over. She glanced up at Cassie, laughing before walking her over. "I apologize for Emily if she's bothering you. We're accustomed to seeing Jet visiting us by himself," Cassie admitted, bringing them a fresh pot watching Emily climb the booth perching herself next to Jet.

She stole the other half of Jet's scone popping it into her mouth. "It's nice to see him with someone so pretty and kind, though are you his girlfriend?" Emily asked, glancing over at Ari expecting an answer.

Ari smirked, pouring herself another cup before grabbing another teacup, filling it with tea for the little girl, adding cream and sugar. "It's all right though Jet has a little fan base going on though I don't mind sharing. Am I his girlfriend? I'm not sure perhaps you should ask Jet that question," she replied, sweeping her fingers before resting her head on them watching his reaction.

Jet's flush darkened as he stared down at his tea avoiding Ari's glance hearing Emily laugh. He took a sip of his tea before glancing up to catch her eye. "I know we are good friends and I care for her a great deal, and would hate to make her feel pressured to make that decision," he admitted, hearing Emily groan at not getting a clear answer drinking her tea before being called back to the counter by Cassie. "It seems she wanted a yes or no answer, though I meant what I said," he added, reaching out for her hand.

Ari allowed it using her other hand to finish her tea. "I know and I feel the same way but at the same time I've been wondering if there's more to being friends? I would hate to ruin what we have and risk losing a friend and student," she admitted, voicing aloud how she had been feeling the last few days.

Jet frowned resting his free hand on his chin taking in her concern. "We can explore it later. I'm not going anywhere. I have learned a great deal from you and would hate to see it squandered," he admitted, finishing his tea excited by the next destination he had to show her.

Ari frowned not commenting on the thought that passed through her head. "Well seeing how we're both done with our tea, should we head to the next place you have in mind?" she inquired, as she climbed to her feet thinking that she would be venturing back to the store enjoying the café.

Jet nodded in agreement waving to Emily and Cassie holding the door open for Ari. He walked with her back to the bike. "I knew you would enjoy the café. It has a very welcoming vibe to it, though our next destination is a bit of a drive. It's located on the outskirts of the city, but I think you'll like it," he admitted, seeing that her mind was elsewhere.

Ari smiled taking the helmet before climbing on behind him. "You were right, I can see why you would keep coming back here after your first visit though I don't mind the drive," she admitted, seeing that he wasn't going to give her any hints.

Jet smiled positioning himself behind the bike. "I'd be happy to bring you back here anytime you'd like," he replied, kick starting the bike merging back onto the highway following the signs out of the city. He turned down a dirt road slowing down his speed before pulling to a stop. The dirt path led down a hill wrapping around a mossy trail. He climbed off the bike taking her hand. "I believe this used to be a park but got abandoned, but that's not the surprise I have in mind," he teased, thinking of what awaited them at the end of the trail where flat boulders lead out to a waterfall.

Ari laughed climbing off the bike taking in the site around them. "Why would anyone abandon a place when it can offer such peace and serenity though is there a source of water at the end of the path? I can hear water runoff though it's faint," she admitted, allowing Jet to take her hand.

Jet grinned, not surprised that she could hear the water runoff. "Yes, there is a water reservoir, but I think with the construction of the highway the place just became forgotten," he admitted, taking her hand as they started to walk down the hill. "I like to think of it as my hidden oasis. I had a flat not too far from here and my curiosity got the best of me," he admitted, guiding her through the fallen tree logs making their way toward a pillar of steppingstones. He slipped her arm through his remembering that the stones were slick as they continued to a small canopy of vines that lead to a waterfall.

"I see so are you going to show me your flat seeing how neither one of us brought any swimwear? Do you take everyone here or only special people?" she teased, allowing him to lead the way as they walked through the vines impressed by the waterfall.

Jet laughed glad to see that she admired the waterfall. "Yes, if you follow the hill adjacent to the waterfall there's a small cabin, though I've never taken anyone here afraid they wouldn't appreciate its beauty, though Matt knows of its location," he confessed, amused by her second question.

"Well now I know where he disappears to when Matt wants alone time, though I may start using it as well; seeing how spells are most powerful when cast in nature. Do you come out here a lot?" she asked. removing her shoes before dipping her feet into the shallow pool of water.

Jet nodded in agreement slipping off his shoes as well. "I haven't been here in a while it's usually when I can't sleep, and meditation fails or when I need a break from the others. Your training has kept me quite busy," he admitted, sighing in relief as he kicked the water lightly not intending to splash her.

Ari laughed feeling the water hit her face. "I understand there are some evenings where I spend the night outside in the orchard when I'm restless or like you need an escape from the others. Don't get me wrong, it's nice to have a large group of people to depend on; it just sometimes I feel as though none of them can give me the intellectual challenge and I don't include you in that," she explained, kicking the water back at him.

Jet laughed feeling the chilly water hit his face. "That must have been frustrating, wanting to escape from the manor and not having anywhere to go. What about Matt, he seems wise, I'm sure he can offer you a challenge?" he asked, amused that he was exempt from her statement.

"I would say yes when you're able to find him. He likes to give me a project and when I look up, he's disappeared. There are a lot of times where I want to talk with him but he's either helping someone else or isn't in the manor. At first, it was frustrating but over time I grew used to it. Sometimes I would test it I would create portals to places I wanted to visit only for the magic to prevent me from going through but seeing them helped calm me since in a way I was still somewhere else," she explained, tucking her hair behind her ears.

Jet bent rolling up his pant legs before taking her hand to where one edge of the pond brushed up against a thick tree log. He took a seat swinging his legs in content. "I can't say I blame him with the demon and his connection to the spirit realm, I'm surprised he spends any time with us," he teased, thinking of the spell used to create the course.

Ari followed him, taking a seat beside him. "I wonder that as well but it's easy to see that he cares a great deal about all of us; otherwise why bring us to the manor instead of living his life alone. I think he wants to help us but at the same time wants to ensure he keeps control over his emotions. I don't blame him from the little I've seen his demon is a jerk," she admitted, thinking that she was impressed with Matt's mental control.

Jet laughed nodding in agreement. "So, I've heard. But a powerful entity not to underestimate. We can head up to the cabin if you get cold it has a fireplace," he advised, resting his head against her shoulder.

"I agree after seeing the display in the park, but I think if it were up to Matt, he would be happy if he no longer had the demon as company.

We can head up there before sunset, I don't think it's wise to be outside at night," she admitted, not in a hurry to return to the manor.

Jet nodded in agreement, smirking, realizing that would force her to spend the night with him. "Luckily for us, I always keep the place stocked with non-perishables, though I don't think Matt would complain with that option once Scarlett was rescued," he replied, closing his eyes, inhaling her scent, feeling relaxed in her company.

"You mean if she's rescued? I'm starting to have doubts we can save her in time. Matt's out of the picture and the only person I can picture aiding us is a member of the undead," she admitted. leaning back against the tree staring out at the water.

Jet frowned seeing that she had shared his concerns. "Scarlett said that the vamp that runs *Sângele Vampirului* is family, maybe we can convince him to help?" he suggested, thinking that they could call the bar and try persuading him to help.

"You're referring to Donovan? Scarlett revealed he was married to her sister, though I wondered why he wasn't at the park with them. They were at the bar before heading to the park, so wouldn't he have tagged along? Not to mention, vampires are territorial; other vampires usually stay away unless they see an opportunity to steal a location from another blood sucker," Ari explained, thinking they could call the bar later when it was open.

Jet nodded in agreement drumming his hands on his knees. "Another question to ask the vamp when we speak to him, though Dusk will be setting in an hour, we should start heading up the hill," he offered, climbing to his feet, offering her his hand.

Ari took his hand climbing off the log as they headed for shore to collect their shoes. She decided to carry hers enjoying the earth on her bare feet as she allowed Jet to lead the way. "I feel that we may have a couple of questions for him depending on how the conversation goes though do you think he'll talk to us?" she asked, knowing that the vamp could hang up on them.

Jet shrugged his shoulders unsure of the answer. "It all depends on his mood; I'd gather if he had fed, he may take pity and answer some of our questions. I hope you enjoyed our outing, there are a few fun places to visit once it's safer to travel at night," he remarked, guiding the way up the hill as the trees cleared to reveal a small red brick cabin.

"I would like that, seeing how I enjoyed the places you have taken me to so far and there are a few places I would like to take you to as well once this danger has passed," she admitted, as they entered the cabin, taking in the simple decorations.

Jet grinned, guiding her to the sofa as his eyes adjusted, moving around the room to light a few candles. Yellow candlelight filled the room illuminating the warm colors of the room. "I can give you a tour if you'd like though it's not much," he admitted, extending his hand to her after removing his shoes.

"I would like that though I'm sure it's great despite the spartan design," she noted, taking his hand once she placed her shoes next to his motioning for him to start the tour.

Jet smiled taking her first through the living room and into the kitchen, working their way through the kitchen into the small washroom and finally the master bedroom. "I can sleep on the sofa if you'd like the bed," he offered, heading back into the kitchen placing a kettle of water on the stove.

"We can share the bed. I trust you to keep your hands to yourself, and besides it's your home if anyone should take the sofa it should be me. Was this yours or Matt's doing you did say he comes here sometimes to be alone?" she asked, pointing to the snowflake swirls around the mantle.

Jet's cheeks flushed accepting her decision wanting to be respectful. "I believe it was Matt's doing I haven't done any decorating in a while," he admitted, hearing the kettle whistle pouring the hot water into two mugs adding Chamomile tea before adding it to a tray with a milk saucer and sugar cubes.

Ari snickered seeing Jet's blush at her comment. "I figured as much I just wanted to make sure I noticed it gets left behind when he uses his magic. That was part of the drawing I traced in the park. I think the other belongs to the vampire. I think if I can translate it, I'll have Simon's magical signature," she explained, thanking him as she took her teacup from him.

He led her back to the sofa, setting his mug on the coffee table. "Do you think the magical signature is time sensitive? I'm not sure when the last time Matt was here and what would make him use his magic," he remarked, excited by her concept not wanting her to get her hopes up.

"I believe Scarlett hinted that he disappeared before they were to meet up on the night she first ran into Simon. Magic is time sensitive and will disappear over time but depending on how powerful the spell it can last for a long time. The barrier is a good example, I only had to renew the wards once a year and since I created the spell my magical signature can be located within it if one knows how to locate it," she explained, taking a sip of her tea.

Jet stared down at his tea realizing the topic flooded his braid with a horde of questions. "Can you learn a person's magical signature, or does it change each time a spell is crafted?" he asked, aware that the knowledge could be a powerful tool.

"The signature remains the same every time, the trick is locating the signature and identifying it. You must look deep into the magic and see what is hidden within. It's easier to find a symbol tied to the person and then explore the symbol though it's not as easy as it sounds. I know what to look for with Matt's a snowflake with a wolf howling inside the magical circle. You can also hide your signature if you wish to cast a spell without being discovered," she explained, curling up on the sofa with her teacup.

Jet climbed to his feet setting his cup down as he turned the fireplace on ensuring there was enough firewood. "I think you managed to make it sound more complicated," he teased, reaching for a pen and a pad of paper underneath the coffee table sketching what she had explained to him when describing Matt's signature. "Does it look like that?" he asked, seeing her nod in agreement. "I can see how you can tell it's Matt, though what does mine look like?" he asked, flipping to a blank sheet of paper.

Ari laughed amused by his response. "I was trying to simplify it for you. It's easier to see the main element if you can't locate the person's signature," she explained taking the notepad from him. She sketched out a large oak tree adding details to the branches and leaves on the knot of the tree she drew a medal of honor molded in the shape of a leaf.

Jet stared at the image in awe unaware that his signature reflected his tie to Gaia. He glanced up seeing that she was watching his expression. "Thank you, this should help with meditation and having a way to picture the magic building within me, do you know what your signature is? He asked, tearing the page free to fold up to place in his pant pocket.

"No, at least not the entire thing but that may be due to part of my magical source being hidden from me. I know what the outer circle looks like, but the core is a blank slate. I thought recreating the barrier would reveal it but if it did, I wasn't able to decipher it." She explained, taking the pen drawing a butterfly each wing she wrote in a different element since they lacked colored pencils.

Jet studied the drawing intrigued by how it represented all the elements. "You said that when you learned where you came from, that you geared your magic being tainted, but butterflies are pure. Some even believe that they can represent angels," he replied, snickering at seeing her blush.

Ari blushed using her hair to cover her face. "Nice try, but the outer circle shows our connection to the magical world. It's the inner circle that's important; it shows the part of magic that's connected to our souls. So, since both of yours is earth does that mean I get to call you the green man?" she teased, not wanting to focus on dark thoughts.

Jet raised both hands defensively reaching for his cup. "It's better than being called a tree hugger," he replied, glad to hear his answer had made her laugh. He finished his drink, setting it down before gently brushing her hair out of her face. "A valiant effort, and I'm going to keep trying until it works," he whispered, kissing her cheek before entering the kitchen to refill his mug.

Ari took a sip of her drink setting it down on the table waiting for Jet to return. "I don't know I was considering Pan, but I didn't want your ego to get too big. I think tree huggers are more a hippie that pretends to be one with nature due to special drugs," she admitted, waiting for Jet to sit down.

Jet laughed bringing his cup and a fruit tray with cheese and crackers. "What do you mean, anytime you offer me a compliment you're risking the chance of inflating my ego. Though ready to try calling the bar?" he asked, wanting to get it over with.

Ari reached for the plate grabbing a piece of cracker and cheese to pop into her mouth before pulling out her phone. She dialed the number waiting for it to stop ringing before putting it on speaker. "Good evening, if you are calling to check availability, we are still currently closed." A male voice rang out on the other end of the line.

Ari swallowed hearing the note of boredom in the man's voice. "Is this Donovan? We were hoping to ask you a few questions we're friends of Scarlett's," Ari explained, before the man could hang up the phone.

Jet frowned, not surprised that she hadn't received the answer she was hoping for. He grabbed a slice of apple and cheese reaching for his phone. "I may have a way to get a message to him," he advised, dialing the number receiving the same monotone recording. "Can I speak with Michael?" he asked, surprised not to hear the phone hang up before a long pause before another male voice came on the line.

"Hello, Michael here, how may I help you?" Michael answered, taking the phone from Donovan, leaning against the bar. Jet offered the phone to Ari knowing that he would respond to hearing a female's voice.

Ari rolled her eyes, not amused. "I think your partner hung up on me before I could say anything. I have a few questions, but it's not associated with the bar. Do you guys know Scarlett?" she asked, moving to lean against Jet so he could be included.

Michael poured himself a shot of gin, glancing over at his brother, watching him return to his room. "Yes, she has been here frequently and was here recently with her boyfriend," he answered, aware that the girl was either a slayer like Scarlett or her friend.

Ari laughed, catching the note of annoyance. "I take it Mathew rubbed you guys the wrong way. He can be a bit overprotective at times. I was wondering if you noticed them leave and why you didn't join them knowing that there was another vampire after her? Aren't vampire's territorial?" she asked. putting the phone on speaker reaching for some of the fruit.

Michael refilled his drink, choosing his words carefully, not wanting to earn his brother's wrath. "I was under the impression that they had spent the night here until dawn," he replied, becoming aware that he had neglected to inform her of why his brother had been absent.

Jet reached for the pad of paper. See he was willing to spill his guts for a pretty voice; he wrote showing her the paper knowing he would get smacked for teasing her.

Ari laughed before smacking him playfully. Be nice Jet, most guys usually act that way, she wrote back, "No, they left during the night heading for the park to help an innocent and were ambushed by Simon. Scarlett was taken and Mathew was left close to death for us to discover. I know a small amount of vampire law, so I find your actions a bit confusing," she admitted, since how they were acting didn't match her research.

Michael processed the information wondering how his brother would react. "There was an incident at the bar and Donovan was poisoned, he was given the antidote but it left him weakened," he admitted, flinching at hearing wood being broken indicating that Donovan had overheard his rambling thoughts angered by the news.

Ari winced thinking of the few items that could poison a vampire. "Well that explains my theory about why Simon wasn't prevented from invading your area or has been dealt with though there's not many cures for a blood blossom besides surgery to remove the flower which usually kills lesser vampires. If he survived that would make you both noble blood which means you both have a unique gift correct?" she asked, trying to not get excited by the new information.

Michael groaned hearing her excitement over the science behind the remedy. "The poison was a drink mixed with the flower petals, so I don't think he had to extract the flower. He performed what you would think of a blood transfusion cleansing the blood of the toxin," he explained, rubbing his temples getting a headache from thinking too much.

"A blood transfusion; I wasn't aware vampires could do that without losing control due to their natural bloodlust. Wouldn't the scent of blood drive you to drink despite the source? That explains Donovan's actions but why didn't you go after Simon?" Ari asked, hearing the vampire groan in annoyance on his end of the phone.

Michael banged his head against the bar hearing his brother laugh at hearing the frustrated thoughts swirling around in his head. "Listen, lady, I shared more with you than my brother was willing to, but you're boring me to tears. We have an excessive supply of blood from the hospital, as you know we don't feed on humans," he explained, refusing to provide insight on their gifts to a stranger.

Jet snickered hearing the frustration in the man's voice tapping to what he had written earlier claiming he was right. That may be all we get out of hum, he lacks enough intellect to comprehend your mind, he wrote, adding a winking face feeling a throw pillow hit his chest.

Donovan chuckled entering the bar seeing his brother slump against his seat. "Give me the phone Michael unless you enjoy the mental torture. It's clear that they will hound you for answers," Donovan teased, as the phone was thrust into his chest before Michael bolted for his room. "Forgive my brother despite his age he has the intelligence of a mere child. May I inquire who I am speaking with?" he asked, taking his brother's seat at the bar.

Jet couldn't help but laugh hearing the echo of a door slam in the background. "It seems you wounded your brother's ego, though like Mathew, we are slayers hoping to seek answers regarding what happened to Scarlett," he answered, placing the pillow back on the sofa.

"I gather as much given the pattern of the conversation though are all slayers so thorough with their research on the supernatural?" Donovan asked, trying not to insult the girl. "What can I aid you with as my brother pointed out they were here, and we assumed they had returned home by morning light," he explained, removing the phone from his ear to cough wiping the blood from his lips before placing the phone back against his ear.

Ari blushed darkly understanding the insult. "Better to be overinformed than dead, not all slayers are immortal or born with unique gifts. It's clear why you are unable to fight Simon now, but why didn't you prevent his blood lust when the bodies first appeared? Why allow a stranger to hunt in your home?" she asked, knowing she was pushing it, but she figured it was the best way to gain answers.

Jet arched an eyebrow surprised that she had asked him that, wondering what she was trying to gain. "Be nice we called him hoping he would help us find Scarlett, no need to anger him," he warned, afraid her question had offended him.

"I heard from Michael's end of the conversation; she was kidnapped by Simon, correct. What makes you think I will be any help in locating her? Even if I had a way, why would I be inclined to help you knowing how your slayers treat my kind?" Donovan asked, seeing that the girl was bold a trait Scarlett had as well.

Ari frowned glancing over at Jet. "I don't think you're like your kind otherwise why stop drinking human blood knowing the drawbacks you will face. I know you care about Scarlett and despite your condition will go to save her. All we're asking for is a lead to go on. We went to the park and were met with a dead end," she explained, seeing that the vampire was quiet considering her words.

Jet reached out for her hand squeezing it tightly seeing that she was getting frustrated. "You're free to decline helping us. It will just slow down our search. The more troubling fact is defeating Simon and his army of shades. Matt nearly killed himself trying to protect Scarlett and was severely injured," he added, trying to persuade Donovan to help them.

Donovan sighed knowing that their leader was either too wounded or worse bitten to be of any aide. "If I had known they were going to his hunting ground I would have tagged along and offered my assistance. Inform me of what strengths your group contains. I know where to find Simon, but I won't reveal it if it means I'm sending mortals to their doom," he admitted, knowing that the shades would be the hardest to put down.

Ari smirked, seeing that they had gotten their way. "Our leader is a half snow demon but like Jet said is too injured to be of any help. There's also a werewolf, an immortal, and two spell casters. Those without any abilities are being left behind for their safety," she explained, sticking to just the basics.

Jet offered her a high five relieved to see they had convinced Donovan to help them. "With your aide do you think we stand a chance against Simon? His shades are relentless and can just offer him more blood if we manage to weaken him," he noted, thinking of what Ari had said when informing him of the struggles Matt had faced.

"That depends on two matters: your group reaching the area and myself being cleared of this poison. I take it one of you knows how to create a portal that would give you passage, and the light would keep the shades at bay. Shadows are a bit difficult even though I have trouble locating them and they take little effort for Simon to create," Donovan explained, laying his head on the cool bar beneath him.

Ari frowned, pulling the paper from her pocket, turning to a blank side before writing down a set of numbers. "I know how to create portals and there's a combination that would create a continuous circle of light, but we'll need you at perfect health. I know you may not like this, but couldn't you just drink human blood as a quick cure? We can get you

E.L. SUMMERS & L.N. FROST

some from the local hospital?" she suggested, only to hear the dial tone on the other end before she hung up the phone.

Jet stared down at the numbers she had written before taking the phone from her resting it on the coffee table. "We gained more information than we thought seeing as how we assumed, he wouldn't want to talk to us," he replied, seeing that she was lost in thought. "What are the calculations for anyway?" he asked, finding a way to distract her.

Ari allowed him to take the phone glancing down at her notes. "Formulas figuring out the area and depth of the portal and how long it takes for each person to pass through. I can add in the light spell but casting both will leave me open for an attack," she explained, sketching a small scale of the circle writing different runes on the outside of the circle.

Jet watched her focus on the drawing to work out the details in her head. "You were able to hold the portal one longer than I expected when the spell was interrupted for the training course, would the portal be the same?" he asked, noting the runes she had sketched around the perimeter of the circle.

Ari frowned yet knew he was right. "It helps that I knew the area, this time I'll be creating the portal to an unknown location. I would just have felt better if the vampire has already been there, if my landing were off, he could be used as a distraction," she explained, placing the paper on the table before moving to rest against him.

Jet sighed, shifting his weight to lean against the side of the sofa to pull her against his chest. "We have yet to learn where the location is, perhaps Vincent and Andrew had some luck searching near the park. In either case, we can travel during the day and try getting a better sense of the area. If you're more confident in the spell there's less chance you'll leave yourself vulnerable," he suggested, stroking her hair gently.

"I'm confident in the spell. It's what's waiting on the other side that has me worried. I can manage the shades but what are we going to do about Simon? I really wish Donovan were there, I fear he's the only match for Simon," she explained, closing her eyes relaxing under his touch.

Jet continued to stroke her hair understanding her anxiety. "Yes, Matt was the only match for hum, though Donovan said he would aid us against Simon, so what are you really worried about?" he asked, wondering what was troubling her.

Ari sighed glancing up to meet his eyes. "I fear that we have already failed in some way. That regardless of the outcome Scarlett will be lost to us." She admitted, having a feeling of dread that she couldn't shake.

Jet kissed her forehead trying to wash away her fears. "That's to be expected we don't know what Simon is doing to Scarlett now or within the time it takes to get there," he whispered, slipping his arms underneath her waist scooping her up and lifted her up carrying her to the bedroom seeing that the fire would die out shortly.

Ari laughed wrapping her arms around his neck resting her head against his chest. She let him place her on the bed before crawling underneath the covers. "Care to join me?" she teased, understanding something clearly at last flush appear on his face.

Jet smiled relieved he had gotten her to laugh. He sat on the edge of the bed before blowing out the candle. Slipping underneath the covers he wrapped his arms around her waist. "I hope that despite the darkness you fear you were able to enjoy your newfound freedom," he noted, reaching up to brush the stray strands of hair out of her face.

Chapter Fifty-Seven

Donovan's shadow flickered in a blur of yellow light blocked by darkness; in his long strides along the large bay windows, listening for his brother's return. His mind flashed back to the last time the melancholy feeling washed over him, was Isabel's death. His thoughts were interrupted by the gentle knock on the doorframe.

"Donovan, are we opening the bar for the evening?" Shiva asked, standing in the doorway watching his restless movements.

"No, I have more important matters to contend with. I'm sure the mortals can manage another night without their spirits and entertainment. Lock the place up before coming upstairs," Don explained, collapsing to his knees coughing spitting up blood. If only I could be rid of this plague, then I could track down Michael's location, he thought, seeing her nod in agreement returning to the bar.

She wiped down the empty stools and bar before stepping outside to sweep the entryway. Her foot kicked a damp cardboard box. Leaning the broom against the door frame, kneeling to inspect the parcel. A white piece of stock paper was taped to one side with a note regarding Donovan's urgent attention. Smelling the blood contained inside, she wrinkled her nose gingerly picking up the box cradling it against her chest.

She kicked the door behind her once she stepped inside, turning to lock the door. She reached Donovan's room again. "Donovan, this was addressed to you, from Simon, it said it was urgent you opened it," she warned, placing it on the coffee table, seeing drops of blood had outlined her path and had also stained the hem of her dress.

Shiva's thoughts turned to concern seeing Donovan's startled reaction to the contents of the parcel. "Donovan?" she called, seeing him place his head in both hands. "Donovan, what's wrong? What did he send you?" she pleaded, seeing him clenching his teeth in anger.

Shiva climbed to her feet reaching her hand out to comfort him, recoiling in fear at seeing him bare his fangs in rage. "Who was responsible for this act of brutality?"

Don growled, groaning in annoyance hearing her relentless demand of questions.

Shiva took a step back careful not to stumble into the coffee table. She turned to carefully lift one of the folds of the cardboard up to glance inside. Horrified by the bloody head that greeted her, she closed the box collapsing to her knees, grasping the edge of the coffee table as tears streamed down her cheeks. "Donovan, I'm sorry for your loss—" she whispered, wiping away her tears failing to see his shadow close the distance between them until he gripped her throat pushing her across the room. She cried out in alarm, slamming her back against the door. Before she could move, he was in front of her digging his nails into her shoulders pinning her to the wall.

Shiva squirmed under his grip trying to push him away, yet he laughed driving his nails deeper into her flesh. "Why are you taking your anger out on me, it's not my fault," she pleaded, seeing him bare his fangs in response.

"He spent all his time with you, if anyone could have stopped him from embarking on a fool's errand, it would have been you. All you had to do was smile pretty and spread your legs to gain his attention," he hissed, extracting his nails, taking a step back, licking up the blood.

Shiva tore two strips of fabric from her dress wrapping it around the puncture wounds blocking out the pain staring at him in disgust. "I know you are grieving over the loss of your brother, so I'm going to overlook your crude remark. He deserves a proper funeral," she protested.

Donovan let out a bitter laugh as a coughing fit consumed him. "I was being honest, why should I listen to you after all the harm you have caused me?" he sneered, wiping the blood from his mouth with a handkerchief.

Shiva wrapped her arms around herself pressing her back against the wall. "You don't think if I could have stopped him, I would have? He said he was going on a supply run," she whispered, hearing him groan in agony as another coughing fit consumed him.

He told Scarlett he had a cure, yet it's taking too long. If he fed on human blood would that speed up the process, but Michael swore they never fed on humans, she thought, interrupted from her thoughts at hearing him let out a bitter laugh.

Donovan pinched the bridge of his nose staring at the box as her stream of desperate thoughts added to his throbbing headache. "If your insufferable train of thoughts are supposed to comfort me, you're sadly mistaken," he hissed, debating on how to manage his brother's remains. "The herbal remedy is taking too long. I would never break my promise to Isabel, but I would never forgive myself if I let Simon take away the last of my family," he whispered, glancing out the window admiring the moonlight.

Shiva glanced up at him, her brows furrowing confused by his remark. "I want to help you, you've lost enough people you care for—" she pleaded, climbing to her feet seeing his hand extended out to her.

He pulled her close before tugging the bloody scrap of fabric free. Ignoring her protests, his fangs dug into her flesh drinking in her warm blood savagely. "Wait! What are you doing?" she cried, using her free hand to try and push him away feeling him take a step back collapsing onto the sofa once more pulling her down with him. "Stop it, you're going to kill me, for what a feeble human? What about your promise to Isabel?" she pleaded, feeling her blood rub freely down her arm staining the sofa.

Donovan watched her arm rise weakly trying to push his mouth away from her arm but had already lost too much blood. "Don't flatter yourself with false delusions of humanity, we're not humans just animated corpses," he sneered, releasing her arm to wipe the blood from his mouth as she closed her eyes trying to regain her strength. "Interesting, it seems your blood is helping to speed up my recovery," he noted, laughing at seeing her eyes widen in fear trying to roll off the sofa. She managed to fall on the floor before Donovan leaped on her, sinking his fangs into her neck as blood from the wound on her arm bleed freely. He continued to drink before she went limp in his hands crumbing into a bloody mess of blood before he rose to his feet relieved to see that the coughing had stopped.

Chapter Fifty-Eight

Ari entered the manor, pausing mid step before letting out a sigh, placing her bag on the kitchen table. Hearing a door close, she grabbed the kettle, filling it with water. "I take it all was well while we were gone. Did your search in the park turn up any leads?" she asked, placing the kettle on the stove.

Vincent moved behind her hearing the water in the shower turn on above them. "The harness was a wise restraint to use on Andrew. Once we started to get close to the caves, he lost control and tried running off without me. He ventured through a few caverns without results but we gained an insight of the layout, they were all the same," he explained, hoping the information would be helpful, grabbing an apple before taking a bite out of it.

"I figured he would lose control if he caught Scarlett's scent, was there any more altercations between himself and Mathew? I have the vampire's magical signature and can open a portal to his current location. It will take some time to figure out the correct size and length of the portal given that it's to a place I have yet to visit," she explained, pouring the water into a teacup adding a tea bag of Earl Grey to the cup.

Vincent grabbed a pencil from a mug on top of the fridge and a memo pad sketching out a blueprint of the caves they explored. "Not that I'm aware of, every time he and Matt were in the same room he goes for a run. Will this help with your portal given a better sense of the area besides going there yourself?" he offered, seeing her frustration, seeing her admiring the blueprint.

Ari studied the drawing biting her bottom lip. She pulled out a marker from her bag writing half runes and drawing circles on the paper. "That will work once I have the rest figured out though it may take me a day to get the runes stabilized. How were things here, anything interesting occur?" she asked, taking a seat at the table tucking the paper into her bag.

Vincent stared at her in puzzlement deciding not to ask too many questions seeing that she had it managed. "Raven felt confident once she was able to brew another batch of meds for Matt, and I think it went to her head," he remarked, chuckling. "She tried brewing a potion to increase one's luck and it blew up in her face," he admitted, thinking it was wise to distract her by helping quiz Dawn on what she had learned with the archives.

Ari chuckled in amusement thinking she would visit the girls before checking up on Matt's recovery. "I hope for her sake it was just a blow up and that there was no backlash or bad luck lingering over her. I take it you gave her a warning about how I told her that she was not to experiment without being supervised?" she asked. trying hard not to laugh thinking of what could have occurred.

Vincent finished his apple holding up his hands defensively. "Um… yeah about that, she was being supervised by me. I thought it would help to have luck on our side, and she made it seem so easy," he protested, tossing the apple core away keeping a safe distance from her not wanting to get smacked.

Ari sent a glare in Vincent's direction seeing him keeping space between them she sighed before lashing out using her magic to smack the back of his head with a rolled-up dish towel. "Of all the times to be stupid and ignore the limit amount of time I spent teaching you the laws of magic, you thought it was safe to experiment with fate? I thought Andrew was an idiot, but it appears I was wrong," she mused, hitting him once more before climbing to her feet heading for Raven's room.

Vincent cried out in alarm rubbing the back of his head, "Ouch, that's no way to say thank you, it came from good intentions," he yelled, calling out to her as she exited the kitchen wondering why she was so upset. "I don't get why she's made, it didn't even work anyway," he groaned, retreating to his room.

Ari rolled her eyes thinking of a good hex to use on the moron to get the lesson through his thick head. Sighing, she knocked on Raven's door before entering the room. "I heard from a little bee that you were brewing items not on your list. Don't worry I place the blame on Vincent and not you," she explained, closing the door behind her.

Dawn glanced up hearing the approaching footsteps before burying her head back into her studies. Raven frowned seeing that she had been right to question Vincent's request. "I tried talking to him out of it, stating that I wasn't comfortable brewing the potion without your permission, but he swore it was harmless," she admitted, relieved to hear that she was going to punish Vincent.

"To be fair, he lied stating he had seen you brew it before and that if she mastered the medicine for Mathew then there was nothing to fear," Dawn interjected, keeping her head buried in what she was studying.

Ari nodded, taking a seat on the edge of Raven's bed. "Dawn, please pay attention, I wish to talk to both of you. Hopefully, this never occurs again," she warned, waiting until she had both girl's attention. "The medicine I left in your hands Raven due to it being a simple healing remedy one I knew you would be capable of brewing. In magic, a person should never experiment with free will. Luck falls under Lady Fate and she is not kind to those who travel in her domain. Death is another master that should be respected though love can be bended at times depending upon the situation. What Vincent did was wrong, and you are lucky that nothing bad occurred from the potion," she explained. checking them both over to ensure they were safe.

"We're sorry Ari," they apologized in unison. Dawn bit her lower lip closing her book giving Ari her full attention.

"We didn't mean to worry you, we wanted you to come back reenergized, though how was your time with Jet?" Dawn asked, trying to cheer Ari up.

Ari gave them a smile knowing that they regretted their actions. "It's all right I don't blame you just next time text me before you follow Vincent's or Andrew's ideas, since neither one thinks things through." She mused, a light blush appearing on her face thinking of the previous evening. "It was a nice evening. I got to see Jet's home away from home and we spent the evening talking," she explained, deciding not to give away too many details.

They both swooned, laughing at seeing her blush deepen. "So, you spent the night together?" Dawn asked, trying to pry more details from Ari about her evening with Jet.

"Dawn calm down. It seems it was a nice get away when things have been chaotic here, though at least you have an oasis when you need it," Raven interrupted, seeing Dawn smirk seeing that she had been caught in her agenda.

Ari laughed, climbing to her feet. "We did share a bed together, but we didn't go pass kissing. I'm going to go check up on Matt before working on the portal," she explained, knowing that her comment would tease Dawn.

"Yes! One of them finally made the first move," Dawn squealed, making Raven laugh teasing her for being a romantic before returning to quizzing her.

~~*

Ari entered Matt's room trying not to shiver feeling the arctic breeze hit her bare skin. Walking over to the bed she sat on the edge, seeing that Matt was watching her actions. "You're awake and here I thought you would be sleeping. Did you have fun with the girls?" she asked, helping him move into a seated position.

Matt nodded his head in thanks waiting until he was resting against his headboard. "It was all right, the girls kept me company. Dawn had a lot of questions about the files and Raven had questions about magic. Did you find anything?" he asked, watching her movements.

Ari pulled his shirt up seeing that the bandages were gone. "Not much was discovered though I now have the vampire's magical signature. How did you survive that battle? I saw the entire fight Mathew' how are we supposed to win when you were brought to the brink of death?" she asked, feeling Matt reach out for her arm pulling her closer.

Matt moved pulling Ari into a gentle hug. "Arianna, you are all stronger than you believe. Stop fearing your magic and embrace it. Know that you are powerful enough and that the others will support your decisions. I'm sorry, I forced you into a role of a leader without giving you a choice. The others have always sought out your support and now they will look to you for guidance in areas I usually cover," he explained, running his fingers gently through her hair.

Ari sighed as they sat in silence before she pulled away. "I should go work on the portal though the girls will be staying here. I don't think they'll be much help in the fight. You're not coming with Matt, even with your wounds healed can you even cast a snowball or get up for that matter?" she wondered, poking him in the ribs before leaving the room. Matt glared after her summoning a glob of snow to throw at her only to growl seeing that she had been right in her assessment of his recovery.

Chapter Fifty-Nine

Simon stormed toward the north-east corridor of the cairn where a wooden coffin resided. A wall of boulders and rocks aligned the front of the coffin blocking it from explorers wandering through the cave. *I don't know how much longer I can remain patient with my pet. Nothing I do seems to weaken her defiant spirit. Yes, I get she spared the mongrel's life because she loves him, but she doesn't have to love me just respect me and my wishes,* he thought, opening the lid of the coffin.

He glanced over his shoulder toward the direction he had come from. "Be gentle while watching over her. Even if she refuses my desires, she is still human," he warned, climbing into the coffin letting the black velvet caress his skin before one of the shades slid the lid close, snuffing out the faint orange glow in darkness.

~~*

The sound of birds chirping in the distance stirred Scarlett from her pleasant dreams. *Damn, I didn't want the dream to end. Like any fairytale, my prince had slain the beast and we were riding off into the sunset on his motorcycle*, she thought, rubbing the crust from her eyes with the back of her palm.

She sucked in a long breath letting out an exasperated sigh, noticing the shades standing guard. *Why does it always feel like they're undressing me with their eyes*, she thought, casting her gaze down at her feet. "You can tell Simon, that his antics of trying to break me are getting old. Matt is on his way to rescue me from this dank cavern," she hissed, spitting at the feet of the closest shade in disgust.

An eerie howl filled the cave as two shades drifted closer toward her. "I'm not afraid of you, you're not real," she screamed, kicking at the two shades that appeared closer to her.

One of the shades cold fingers caressed her cheek, moving to the crook of her neck, sweeping her hair away from her shoulder. Scarlett squirmed twisting her neck to the side. The second shade gripped her chin in both of its hands. Their icy lips pressed against hers.

The first shade's lips brushed against her neck causing the hair on the back of her neck to stand on end. Steam rose from the white cross on her collarbone. That's what they get, she thought, a smug smile dancing across her lips.

The first shade hissed lashing out with its fingers digging their long nails into my shoulder. A sharp pain raced down my arm, feeling my warm blood coating the shade's fingers. I whimpered feeling its sharp teeth bite down upon my flesh, lapping the warm blood hungrily.

The shade lips traveled once more up her arm, kissing her cheek, before grazing her right earlobe in between its teeth. What are they doing? she thought, feeling their icy fingers caressing her thighs slowly moving up her backside. No… there's no way I am enjoying this. Am I? she thought, hearing a soft moan escape her lips. Their hands moved up her arms untying her restraints.

The second shade grabbed her wrists with one hand pinning them around their neck. Their lips pressed against hers even harder forcing their tongue in between her lips. A cold sensation swept through Scarlett, numbing each inch of skin the shades caressed. "Please, just leave me alone. You've had your fun, now it's time to stop," she pleaded, hearing the eerie laughter exchanged between the two shades.

The shades took both of her hands, biting each finger and sucking on it lightly sending warm shivers down her spine. Oh, god. They're not going to stop until they break me, she thought, feeling her hands drop limply by her waist. The second shade swept her legs out from under me.

Scarlett cried out in pain, slamming her chin against the cold granite falling on her stomach. She tried kicking them away desperately trying to crawl toward the exit. The second shade grabbed both of her legs, while the first grabbed a chunk of her hair. The first shade slammed the back of her head against the cold granite. An eerie laugh filled her ears while her vision blurred.

Her eyes widened in fear feeling the metal restraints locking around both ankles. Darkness enveloped her while their nails tore away at her clothing. Just when I thought this nightmare couldn't get any worse, she thought, lifting her head up to slam it against the cavern floor until she lost consciousness.

Chapter Sixty

Ari took a deep breath clearing her mind of all thoughts focusing on calming her magic. She made her way to the backyard finding a clear area before opening a bag of white sand. She drew a large circle before adding in the rune she had seen at the park using black and red sand to fill in the gaps. She held her magic at bay knowing that a touch of magic would open the portal before they were ready.

"I'll take care of transportation and the shades, but the rest will be up to the rest of you. I can activate it once you guys are ready," she explained, feeling a shadow fall over her.

Jet stood off to one side watching her sketch the rune with her hands. Andrew and Vincent were standing in the kitchen window, each carrying a bag full of weapons and supplies. Vincent watched from the bay window waiting for Jet to give the signal for them to join them. "When we get there, will the portal remain open, or will you have to open a new one?" he asked, knowing the spell would be exhausting for her despite taking on the shades.

Ari paused glancing up at him. "The portal will be more like a doorway and can open on both sides with a simple phrase. You only need to be standing on the portal to be taken to and from the area, though the portal will remain open for a few minutes after the phrase has been spoken. I set a few defenses near the house in case anything unwanted slips through upon our return," she explained, adding blue sand to add in her own magical rune to the portal before climbing to her feet.

Jet nodded in agreement seeing that she was satisfied with her creation. "There's no harm in taking precautions, though is it ready?" he asked, getting a simple nod as an answer before waving the guys out into the yard, seeing Andrew following Vincent.

"Explain to us again, why this is a safe way to get there? Won't we be walking right into a trap?" Andrew asked, still uncertain of the plan.

Vincent smacked Andrew on the back of the head earning a snicker from Jet. "When has Ari ever steered us wrong? This way we won't waste time getting there before nightfall, though will the vamp be joining us?" he asked, referring to Donovan.

Ari walked over to the side putting on her cloak picking up her staff. It was made of dark cherry wood covered in runes as the top held the shape of a raven. "We could go the normal route, but it will take longer, and Simon will be attacking long before we reach him. This way, we can catch him off guard. As for the vampire I'm not sure though I hope he aids us seeing how much he cares about Scarlett," she explained, standing in the portals center as she waited for the others to join her.

Andrew arched an eyebrow at hearing her answer. "With all those shades at his command, how can we catch him off guard?" he asked, fidgeting with the strap of the duffle bag that hung over his chest.

Vincent rolled his eyes grabbing Andrew's arm pulling him toward the portal. "Jet reassured us that the portal will work, bringing us to the exact location of where Simon is," he groaned, growing impatient as they waited for Ari to activate the portal.

Ari smiled wrapping both hands around her staff. "I would advise closing your eyes, the light may be too bright when I activate it." She warned, using one hand to pull her hood up as she waited for them to get settled. Taking a deep breath, she reached out to the magic simmering beneath their feet. "Glac linn," (Embrace us.) she whispered, knocking the ground with her staff once allowing it to rest in front of her. Her staff lit up with energy as the raven opened its beak letting out a cry as energy stretched out from under their feet creating a golden ball of light before they disappeared.

~~*

The shades moved aside watching their master approach as they scattered, moving to guard the entrance to the cave. Scarlett was curled up in a fetal position sobbing hysterically, unaware that the shades had abandoned her. The chilly draft numbed her pain as she clutched her eyes thinking of Matt wondering if he would come to rescue her from her prison.

Simon grabbed her arm pulling her up to her feet, grinning as a high-pitched wail escaped her lips. He laughed watching her eyes widen in fear, desperately trying to push him away. He laughed harder as he scooped her up in his arms carrying her back to her shackles. "I'm sorry, my shades disobeyed me by releasing you from your chains. I can't be too mad at them, they offered me a delectable delight," he marveled, licking his lips in delight.

Scarlett spat in his direction watching his gaze linger over the bits of flesh revealed by her torn clothing. She hung her head ashamed that she hadn't been able to fight back. "My patience is wearing thin, I had hoped Donovan would come by now to attempt to steal my prize away," he remarked, a heavy sigh escaping his lips removing the spittle from his cheek. Seeing the sun sink behind the clouds as the horizon changed from orange to violet. He instructed the shades to watch her before venturing to gather more firewood now that Dusk had fallen.

Chapter Sixty-One

Donovan sat in the remains of the living room coming back to his senses taking in the damage he had caused in his grief. "This is why I never partake in human nourishment. Even after a millennium their blood still acts like a drug coursing through my veins. Forgive me brother, your life was sacrificed due to my faint sense of morality, but you shall be avenged." He whispered, glancing at the box sitting on the table. Sighing he allowed the backdrop of noise to envelope him trying hard not to stumble from the overwhelming sounds.

Frowning he tried to focus searching through thoughts until he came across the voices he was seeking. A low growl escaped his lips hearing Scarlet's fearful thoughts mixed with Simon's lustful ones. Moving quickly, it only took him a few minutes to leave the bar to enter the cave seeing the shades look at him in confusion. Reaching out his hand, he grabbed one by the throat cutting off its air supply. He waited a few minutes knowing the pain would gain Simon's attention.

Simon dropped the bundle of firewood he had been carrying and closed the distance between them. He clapped his hands together in a mocking fashion. "I was wondering if the poison had taken you or my offering had driven you mad. The ward on Scarlett's neck prevented me from turning her, and had considered draining her but it's not as fun with an audience," he drawled, glancing in Scarlett's direction seeing that her eyes were still clenched tight rocking back and forth.

Donovan dropped the shade walking towards Simon. "Why? You could have sent my brother on his way; you had no reason to kill him. Is the entire world nothing more than a game to you?" he sneered, glancing over at Scarlet in concern.

Simon rolled his eyes amused at hearing the heartache in Donovan's voice. "I had considered it. He thought he could earn your praise by defeating me, yet he was nothing more than an annoying pest buzzing in my ear. I took pity on him offering him a chance to flee and he squandered it," he explained, laughing at seeing Scarlett open her eyes at hearing a familiar voice, a hopeful expression flickering across her face.

"Liar, do you expect me to believe you when your mind speaks of a different matter? Do you think recollecting on his decisive moments is a wise decision given the mood that I am in? Many would choose their thoughts and words carefully when staring down death," he mused, removing his jacket before kneeling in front of Scarlet gently wrapping it around her shoulders checking her for injuries.

Simon opened his mouth to retaliate but remained silent allowing Donovan a chance to mend to the girl. A slow smile spread across his lips recollecting the gift the shades had given him aware that it would infuriate Donovan.

Scarlett flinched startled to feel soft silk wrapped gently around her shoulders. Inhaling the familiar scent of limes and copper she opened her eyes offering Donovan a weak smile. "You came to rescue me?" she pleaded, her voice cracking, hoarse from screaming.

Donovan sighed deciding to ignore the vermin. "Yes, though I apologize for my late arrival. Perhaps if I have acted on instinct rather than emotions you would not be in such a fragile state. Can you stand or shall I carry you?" he asked. allowing his power to keep the shades and Simon at bay.

Scarlett noticed the fury in his eyes wondering what had happened to upset him. "You're here now, that's all that matters," she whispered, pointing to the shackles chaining her to the wall. "You might want to remove these first. They're not silver, so you should be able to break them," she added, seeing that the shades were trying to ambush Donovan.

A bitter chuckle escaped his lips taking note of the chains. "Forgive me, I was so rash in securing your safety I overlooked your imprisonment. One moment little butterfly and you shall be free," he whispered, reaching a hand up easily breaking the chains around her wrists and ankles. He ensured she was free before placing one hand under her knees and back lifting her gently before climbing to his feet.

Scarlett muttered a thank you slipping her arms around his neck, comforted by the gentle embrace. She frowned seeing Simon step in front of Donovan blocking their path. "Did you honestly think I would let you leave with her? Your pathetic brother stood no match against me, what makes you think you do?" he sneered, lunging toward Donovan trying to take Scarlett from him amused at seeing her recoil in fear.

Donovan growled quickly reaching into his pocket pulling out a dagger before throwing it at Simon seeing the blade slice through Simon's arm. "Take that as a warning, I will prevent you from harming her again. Besides, there is a good possibility you will have other company in a few moments. I wonder will you remain standing once the dust has settled?" he mused, seeing an orb of energy appearing out of the corner of his eye.

Simon hissed feeling the silver blade slice through his skin. A river of blood streamed from his forearm before discarding the blade in disgust. Simon rolled his eyes, failing to believe Donovan's words. "An amusing theory, the only flaw in your statement is that the one person that opposed a threat to me would become my puppet if he were to come here," he gloated, started to see Scarlett push against Donovan's chest. He tried to lunge at Simon aware he was referring to Matt.

Don cursed using more force to keep her pinned against his chest. "Not now, his jest is to only anger you, your pet wolf is not among the minds gathered," he explained, already past Simon heading for the glowing light.

Chapter Sixty-Two

Ari opened her eyes taking in the cave seeing the darkness closing in on them. Tightening her grip on her staff, she sent out tentacles of light from the circle seeking out the shades. She gave in to her magic not seeing the shadows mix with the light creating small shadow ravens.

Simon lunged after Donovan amused to see that he had lit a fire in the girl with his statement. He bent collecting the fallen dagger and lunged at Donovan's back, only to stagger backwards as the shades cried in unison paralyzed by the blinding light.

Scarlett sighed in relief feeling her shoulders slump comforted by his words. Thank you, the last thing I wanted was to see him plagued with nightmares of being used to fight against the other slayers. *Can you tell how many are here?* she thought, her voice too hoarse to speak mesmerized by the ring of bright light.

Donovan hissed feeling the dagger dug into his left shoulder. "There are four in total, a woman and three men. I think it would be best to allow one of them to watch over you until Simon is dealt with," he explained, trying to ignore the pain while moving toward the light.

A small smile fluttered over Scarlett's lips understanding why the cavern was flooded with bright light. I'm sorry if Ari's magic is causing you pain, but at least now Simon will surely be defeated, she thought seeing Andrew step forward a low growl emitted from his chest. Please, don't let him watch over me, I want to help. She protested, seeing Andrew reaching for a rapier he had tied to a scabbard at his waist.

Donovan glared seeing the mutt reach for the sword. "Remove your hand unless you wish to be neutered? Where are the other gentlemen, I doubt you of all people can keep her safe," he snapped, walking past the werewolf impressed by the level of spell work cast by Ari.

Vincent appeared behind Andrew laughing at hearing Donovan's witty retort. "I think neutering him would help relieve some of his anger," he replied, glancing over his shoulder once his eyes had adjusted to the light. He frowned seeing that Jet was hesitant to leave Ari's side. "I can take her off your hands. Jet wants to stay back with Ari anyway in case she becomes exhausted from the magic," he explained, aware that if the vampire drew too close to the circle the light would burn him.

Don gave a simple nod handing Scarlett over to him. "Is it possible for the witch to take Scarlett to a haven? Now that she has been returned to you what reason do you have to stay?" he asked, turning to watch Simon to ensure he was occupied with the attack.

Andrew let out a bitter laugh amused by the arrogant statement. "If you haven't forgotten there's a horde of shades, what makes you think you can take them all on and Simon alone?" he sneered, removing the rapier from his scabbard, and lunging towards the shades.

Vincent laid Scarlett on the ground next to where Jet was standing beside Ari. He watched Andrew charge at the shades in glee fueled by the rage after seeing the damage they had caused Scarlett. "The safest way back is through the portal and I don't see Ari letting us use it to take Scarlett to safety," he advised, drawing two swords from his back to follow Andrew's pursuit.

Donovan watched them run into the fight trying hard to focus his hearing on the thoughts of every person in the cavern. He reached up trying to tug the dagger free only to hiss realizing it was too deep to get a grip on it. Sighing, he turned his back on the trio inside the circle seeking out Simon among his shades, pulling out another dagger.

Simon laughed watching the slayers combat the countless waves of shades. The blinding white light continued to grow slowly filling the cavern with light. He tried moving deeper into the cave to seek refuge ignoring the anguished cries of the shades as the light weakened them. He ducked seeing a dagger sail through the air nearly miss his forehead, as he ducked letting the blade embedded into the wall behind him. "How amusing, you think those pathetic slayers will hold back my army? How long will their efforts last before they cave into exhaustion?" he demanded, reaching for the blade behind him.

Donovan walked toward Simon reaching for another dagger. "I'm not sure though from the looks of things you may end up being slain before they reach the limits of their powers. I'm impressed, who knew a mortal held such power," he explained, closing in for the kill. He paused mid-step catching a thought filled with fear as the lights flickered.

Ari paid little attention to the others knowing that they could manage their own in the fight ignoring the cries as the shades were killed either by her magic or their weapons. She gave a small smile seeing Scarlett being handed over to Jet by the vampire, relieved that she was safe. She turned her focus back to the spell making it reach every corner of the cave, knowing that it would trap Simon in its coils. She gasped feeling a tug on her energy as a few more soon followed. Fear gripped her heart realizing what was the cause.

"Jet remember how I claimed my magic would keep them at bay. It turns out the shades feed on other things besides blood. The little devils are feeding on my magic," she explained, trying to keep the fear out of her voice trying to push the light into the far reaches of the cave faster before exhausting her magic.

Jet placed a protective circle around Scarlett seeing that she was lost in her own thoughts overwhelmed by the pain the shades had inflicted upon her. Climbing to his feet he reached for his athame, slicing his palm with the blade before kneeling beside Ari drawing the rune for power hoping to offer her strength and refuel her magic. He ignored her protests watching the flickering light grow, as he focused on drawing power from the Earth redirecting it to Ari.

Ari glanced over at Jet frowning at his actions. "Jet, I don't think that's smart. I'm going to need your aide when this fails seeing how the vampire is taking his sweet time killing Simon," she warned, closing her eyes focusing on the magic that made up the shades trying to prevent them from feeding on her spell.

Jet bit his lower lip thinking over her warning, aware it was unwise to go against her. "I don't think he's taking his time; we don't even know if they're evenly matched or if one has the advantage. Isn't that why you're trying to take out the shades?" he asked, thinking if he kept the spell going it would tip the scales in their favor.

Chapter Sixty-Three

Simon tilted his head back to laugh seeing Donovan hesitate. He felt a surge of energy course through his veins. He lunged at Donovan closing the distance between them, pushing him up against the granite wall behind them. The power caused the cavern to shake as chunks of granite rained around them in a cloud of dust.

Donovan screamed in pain feeling the dagger being buried up to the hilt into his back. He gritted his teeth against the pain using one hand and grabbed Simon's wrists while the other reached for another dagger slamming it with force into Simon's ribcage giving it a quick twist before yanking it free repeating the action to Simon's left rib cage.

Simon growled trying to swat the dagger away, but it was too late. He staggered back, spitting blood in Donovan's direction. He tried laughing but started coughing, gritting his teeth to ignore the pain. Simon bared his fangs trying to beckon Donovan to attack him wanting their duel to be finished so he could reclaim his prize. He licked his lips savoring over the taste of her blood trying to provoke Donovan.

Donovan smirked seeing Simon stumble hoping the bastard would choke on his own blood. He tossed the handle to the side knowing that the blade was buried under Simon's skin. He frowned wishing he had another weapon besides his throwing daggers. "Please, I have grown up with a child stuck inside a man's body. Do you really think such thoughts will get me to react? Even with your parasites you still struggle for an advantage," he sneered, seeing a hunter fighting the shades nearby. He could tell it was the wolf as he reached behind him yanking the sword out of the man's hands knowing he could fight the shades with his bare hands. He lunged toward Simon aiming the sword at Simon's lungs under the broken ribcage.

Andrew growled in annoyance feeling his sword be tugged free from his hands, kicking a shade away with ease. *How smart, come to your enemies' den unprepared, yet this is the bloodsucker we're supposed to protect?* he thought, gritting his teeth, feeling a shade bite him before using his claws to tear out its throat.

"I'm not sure why you're complaining, mongrel, aren't you used to acting like a wild animal during your hunts. If I recall you took down an entire nest oh wait that's right those vampires were not trying to harm you," Donovan growled, knowing that the wolf could hear him striking out again at Simon.

Simon grabbed the sword holding it with both hands with ease, still high with power thanks to Ari. Simon spit the blood at Donovan's feet in revulsion. *Don't feed on the wolf, he tastes like dirt and sweat, feed on the girl,* he thought, driving Donovan back a few steps with brute force. "That mongrel slaughtered your family, yet you spare his life in return, why?" Simon demanded, baffled by the sentiment.

Andrew blinked startled by the question understanding Donovan's sardonic response. His mind raced with thoughts and questions about that day, questioning if he had made a mistake, merely following orders to keep the mortals safe from monsters.

Donovan bared his fangs slamming Simon into the wall behind him. "Do you think I willingly let that bastard wonder away freely? If I were not so focused on ending your existence Simon, my hands would be around his throat instead of yours. An argument for another time since you will learn that your mind games have no effect on me," Don gritted through his teeth wrapping a hand around Simon's throat squeezing with all his strength.

Andrew jumped over a shade he had kicked to the ground to avoid being bitten again. "You don't mean that, you're supposed to be on our side?" he groaned, catching the sword Vincent had tossed him flinching at hearing a familiar scream fill the cave.

How endearing, my little pet found some strength and is trying to aid you, how sweet. What will you do, focus on ending my life or flee to protect hers? He thought, gasping for air, trying to bide himself some time to recover.

A wave of magic vibrated throughout the cave before the barrier fell, snuffing out the circle of light casting the cavern in pitch darkness. Scarlett could hear Jet groan in effort slipping his arms around Ari seeing that the strain of holding up the barrier had exhausted her. Picking up the aflame, she staggered to her feet seeing that Jet was focused on tending to Ari. She ignored his protests to stay within the protective circle and charged into the nest of shades surrounding them.

Her thoughts flickered to Donovan afraid that he had been wounded in his duel with Simon, allowing it to fuel her swift attacks ignoring her stiff aching muscles. I nearly lost Matt to that monster, he can't take Donovan too, she thought, using her forearm to wipe away her tears trying to maneuver in the darkness.

Ari cursed feeling her knees buckle underneath her feeling Jet's arms wrap around her protectively. She bowed her head allowing her hair to hide her face knowing there were tears running down her face. They were losing the battle she could see it wouldn't be long before the tide was turned against them. A spell appeared in her mind, yet she knew the set-up time would cost them. "Jet, can you place me in the protection circle and help the others? There's sun orbs in my bag that can create light for you guys," she explained, not wanting Jet to be too close to interrupt the spell, since she could still feel the bastards feeding on her magic.

Jet nodded in agreement using his palm to gently wipe her tears away. He gently lowered her into the circle Scarlett had been in, kissing her forehead gently. "Don't be too harsh on yourself, you got us here safely and tried to aid us in the fight. The rest is up to us," he replied, taking the orbs from her hearing the scream vibrates throughout the cavern as he activated one of the orbs, smirking at hearing the shades hiss in pain.

Ari gave him a weak smile in return waiting until he was far enough away to cut off the trickle of magic coming from him. "Norms, please let me be wrong, let the morn only claim the undead tonight," she whispered, closing her eyes before opening them knowing that the darkness had swept within. Taking a dagger, she cut a crescent moon into her left palm before placing it on the ground outside of the circle.

"Hecate, bandia na gealaí dorcha agus na draíochta a thugaim ort. Cuidigh liom le do chuid draíochta agus treoraigh mo lámh sa tasc atá romham. Banna leis an maidin agus fáil réidh leis an ngalar seo ó mo veins. Beidh mé mar óstach uafásach duit go dtí go ndéanfar an tasc," (Hecate, Goddess of the dark moon and magic I call upon thee. Aid me with your magic and guide my hand in the task before me. Bond with the morn and rid this disease from my veins. I will be your humble host until the task is done.) she whispered, closing her eyes, and focusing on her breathing. She could feel the magic run through her veins knowing that over time it would turn to fire burning every shade and their master from the inside.

Donovan kept his hand wrapped tightly around Simon's throat hearing the scream, yet he knew running to her side would allow Simon a moment to escape. He raised the sword to behead Simon only to scream in pain, feeling the magic lash out striking against his back before the cavern was bathed in darkness.

Simon choked out a hoarse laugh seeing pain flicker across Donovan's face causing him to drop the sword. "Just when I thought you would strike the final blow, fate has smiled upon me and given me a second chance," he gloated, spitting in Donovan's face hearing the shades cry out in agony being poisoned by Ari's magic.

Donovan glared at Simon gritting his teeth fighting the urge to collapse to the ground. He blinked a few times forcing the black spots away from his vision. He had lost control over his powers being assaulted with thoughts as he tried to regain control keeping his hand around Simon's throat. His left hand fumbled into his pocket trying to force trembling fingers around a dagger ignoring Simon's mocking thoughts. He placed more pressure against Simon's throat feeling the man struggle to break free.

Grasping the hilt, he pulled the dagger free stabbing Simon in the heart before cutting off his head letting the body drop to the ground in disgust. His knees buckled underneath him curling in on himself fighting the urge to fight off the lure of unconsciousness to escape the pain. Footsteps approached yet he ignored them not seeing a reason to focus now that Simon was dead.

Vincent sighed in relief watching the remaining shades dissolve in the blinding light emitted from the orbs Jet had released. He smirked watching Donovan stab Simon in the chest before the head rolled to the ground near his feet. He closed the distance between them seeing the man's knees buckle. Vincent sheathed his sword slipping his arms underneath Donovan preventing him from collapsing. "You did it! You slain the monster," he exclaimed, wondering if Donovan was still conscious.

A cry of pain escaped his lips feeling the man's chest brush against his back sending a wave of white-hot pain through his body. His body tensed reminding him of the dagger still lodged in his back. "Sorry I lack your enthusiastic rejoice at Simon's demise. I merely need a moment of rest. Could you by chance remove the dagger?" he requested, feeling the man gently lower him to the ground tearing another grunt of pain from his lips.

Vincent frowned, failing to see the dagger buried in Donovan's shirt, yet noticed the drops of blood splashing the ground at his feet once he had moved him. Vincent grimaced pushing the clothing away to grasp at the hilt tugging it free causing blood to splash his hands. He apologized once hearing Donovan cry out in alarm. "Would it help if you fed? It looks like you lost a lot of blood," he remarked, at a loss on how to help Donovan.

Donovan sat there gasping trying to gain control of his thoughts waiting for the pain to die down. "Perhaps, but that is of little concern to me now. Where is Scarlett? I heard her scream during the mists of battle," Don asked, tearing off what remained of his shirt ignoring the pain from his back. The skin would be hot to the touch covered in blisters and patches of raw skin from the witch's earlier spell.

Vincent blinked his eyes drawn to the boiled flesh flinching wondering how the man could endure that much pain. He frowned registering the question as he craned his neck trying to peer into the darkness. "I had hoped to leave her in safe hands with Jet, but he may have been more concerned of Ari once the spell faltered," he remarked, hearing Andrew calling out to him for help.

Chapter Sixty-Four

Once the shades had faded away Andrew began calling out for Scarlett wondering where she had disappeared to. Sniffing the ground for her scent he wrinkled his nose greeted by the overwhelming smell of sweat and copper. He dug through the loose piles of fallen rocks and debris finding her limp body pinned against large chunks of rocks. Stricken by panic he tossed the rocks aside calling out for Vincent making his way to her afraid to move her. Andrew brushed the dirt from her face brushing his lips gently over hers, hoping the sensation would wake her.

"How gross would it be to wake up and have a sweaty, dirty dog licking at your face?" Vincent teased, making his way to Andrew seeing him kneeled at Scarlett's side, noticing the broken blade lodged in her ribs. Andrew rolled his eyes, turning to glance at Vincent wondering if they should try removing the blade despite the risk of causing internal bleeding.

"Don't be foolish, I doubt a Neanderthal would have the surgical knowledge to remove the blade without killing her. Do you not have a healer in your merry band of killers?" Don asked, following Vincent to where the wolf was standing. He moved the wolf to the side placing her head gently in his lap running his fingers gently over her neck searching for a pulse.

Andrew tried to step forward but was stopped by Vincent. "Don't let your ego get in the way of saving Scar. Fetch Jet and inform him of the situation," Vincent ordered, hearing the growl Andrew had sent at Donovan after seeing him cradling Scarlett in his arms.

Andrew rolled his eyes but nodded in agreement hoping that Jet could help her. "Can you detect a pulse? You'll have to forgive Andrew, he came here with the sole purpose of rescuing Scarlett," he replied, hoping she was still hanging on.

Don gave a weak chuckle stopping at the pain the action caused. "His intentions were quite clear, instead of seeking out her injuries, his first intention was to steal a kiss from her. I'm surprised your so-called leader hasn't murdered him yet for his boorish behavior," he mused, feeling a faint thump under his fingers. He placed a hand over her mouth, checking her breathing. "She's alive but just barely my guess is that she was caught in the rocks after being assaulted by the shades though why did you flee from safety," he asked, more to himself checking her for other injuries.

Jet approached overhearing Don's comment, sighing in relief to hear she was still alive. "I'm sorry, last I saw she was resting, and Ari needed my help keeping up the spell," he announced, informing Vincent that Andrew was with Ari. "Simon drained her of a lot of blood already, and if the blade broke side she could bleed out," he noted, seeing how deep the hilt of the dagger was buried into her ribcage.

A groan escaped his lips hearing this thoughts race in panic. "Calm yourselves, I find no blame in your actions. I was merely speculation to myself. If you remove the blade, I can heal both the wound and Scarlett, though the act may appear barbaric in your eyes," he explained, closing his eyes to gather himself for their reaction.

Jet nodded in agreement taking in a deep breath through his nose before letting it out solely. "Surgically removing it would prevent infection but if we wait too long it could break down and cut a major artery," he explained, aware that Vincent would protest his idea. Jet rummaged in his bag finding a lighter and another dagger. He also removed a small vial of alcohol wiping down the blade and the area of skin surrounding the hilt.

Vincent glanced away as Jet sliced through the layers of skin before instructing Donovan to reach for the hilt and gently pulling it toward him until it was removed. He worked quickly trying to finish out the shards of metal hoping that he found them all. He pushed the folds of skin together before stitching the wound close before letting Donovan take over.

Donovan bit into his left wrist deeply with his fangs holding his bleeding wrist over the open wound helping it close quickly as Jet stitched the wound close before bringing it to Scarlett's lip. He held it there for a few minutes watching his blood pool in her mouth forcing her to swallow it. He pulled away, licking his wrist to close the wound, shutting his eyes tightly and ignoring his need to feed. He waved a hand for Jet to check her to see if it had worked. He could barely hear Jet's thoughts let alone his words. He could feel his body falling backwards against his will knowing that he couldn't prevent the darkness from taking him.

Vincent glanced away repulsed by the action yet knew it would offer Scarlett a fighting chance. He glanced back at Scarlett seeing that the vampire had passed out. "Vincent, I need you to stay with Ari in case she wakes. I need Andrew to return to the manor and fetch the jeep," Jet ordered, aware that Ari was in no condition to summon the portal.

Jet watched Vincent nod in agreement conducting the order. He placed his index and middle finger against Scarlett's neck sighing in relief at hearing the steady pulse. Donovan saved two lives today, since Matt would never forgive himself if he lost her, he thought, waiting for Andrew to return with the jeep.

Ari stirred awake hearing faint voices above her, yet their words were muffled to her ears. She groaned trying to open her eyes fighting the lure to go back to sleep. It took several tries as her eyes opened blinking to bring the world back into focus. She wrinkled her nose seeing that with her senses returning the scent of copper reach her mind realizing that there was blood on her face.

Vincent sat beside Ari wondering when she would wake, He smirked hearing her groan trying to sit up, resting his hand gently on her chest. "Hey, sleeping beauty, I have a face wipe for you, but didn't want you to wake up to me touching you," he admitted, taking the wipe and gently removing the blood from her face. "It seems the magic you used came with a hefty price?" he asked, hearing her mumble in agreement.

She gave him a weak smile allowing Vincent to help her sit up resting against his shoulder. "Sometimes in dire situations you call upon spells that are usually frowned upon. I'm sure Jet will lecture me later though are the others all right?" she asked, wincing being reminded of the cost of the spell.

Vincent stroked her hair gently noticing the bags under her eyes. "Andrew left to get the jeep so we can return to the manor," he replied, glancing out toward the direction he had come from wondering if Jet and Donovan had any luck saving Scarlett.

Ari frowned despite relaxing under his touch. "That's smart. I doubt I have enough magic to light a candle yet alone activate a portal. Was someone seriously injured during the battle?" she asked, seeing how Vincent had avoided her question.

Vincent sighed nodding in agreement seeing that she wanted an answer. "Deeper in the cave, Jet and the vampire are with Scarlett. She got swept up into the fight," he admitted, tightening his grip on her chest gently seeing that she wanted to go investigate it for herself.

She sat up straighter, moving to stand only to collapse back against Vin as a weak scream came from her lips for her efforts. "How bad?" she asked, taking a few deep breaths to calm herself and force the bile back down.

Vincent frowned; aware she may react to the news. "You still need to rest, see this is why I didn't want to tell you," he protested, hesitant to share what shape Scarlett was in.

"It would have been better if you had just told me, the way you're acting I thought the norm was coming for her," she muttered, glancing up only to see him pale at her words. "Vin take me to her please?" she asked, seeing that she couldn't move on her own.

Vincent cursed shifting his arms underneath her legs, picking her up bridal style. In a few quick strides he reached the area where he had left Jet with Scarlett. Jet glanced up seeing Vincent set Ari down next to him. "Sorry, Jet. I tried to keep her away, but she wanted to see what state Scar was in for herself," he admitted, not wanting to be yelled at.

Ari buried her face in his neck blinking back the tears of pain feeling him put her on the ground as she rested against Jet's shoulder. "Sorry, I just—I thought the worst had happened, given how Vin was acting, though what happened," she explained. glancing over both Scarlett and the vampire seeing that Jet had moved him so that he was resting on his side next to Scar.

Jet reached his hand up gently wiping away the tears wishing he could take her pain away. "Andrew found Scar unconscious and buried in some rubble. When we got to her, we noticed a dagger was embedded into her ribcage. With Donovan's help, we were able to remove it and extract the broken shards," he explained, before Vincent interrupted adding how Donovan had offered his blood to increase the healing process.

Ari took in a few shaking breaths to calm herself. "That's good vampire blood has healing properties in it though why is the blood sucker out cold? Has Scar woken up since you tended to her wounds?" she asked, leaning into Jet's touch wanting to sleep but she was worried about Scarlett.

Jet frowned, seeing that Ari had asked the question that was troubling him as well. "He was badly injured as well, likely more from your magic than from his duel with Simon," Jet replied, smirking at hearing a soft yawn escape her lips. "That was a powerful spell I'm surprised you're still awake," he teased, glancing over at Scarlett checking her pulse once more.

Vincent smiled noting how concerned Jet was for Ari. "I offered him my blood as payment for saving Scar's life, but he refused," he noted, thinking it would have grossed him out, but it was the least he could do for Donovan.

Ari glanced over Donovan's body taking in his injuries. "A wise choice he would have drained you dry trying to recover from those wounds. I take it either he was used as a shield or was caught in it by accident. It was a twist on the blood poisoning spell, which I wouldn't recommend you playing around with," she muttered, curling up on Jet's side feeling him comb his fingers through her hair.

Vincent sighed in relief hearing his phone vibrate in his pocket. "Andrew is on his way back with the jeep, though should we try moving her?" he asked, not wanting to jar Scarlett's injuries nor leave the vampire while he was unconscious.

Ari bit her lip thinking over his question. "It should be safe to move her and our medical supplies are back at the manor. The vampire may be a problem; the wards are modified but I'm not sure if they would let him through," she admitted, yet knew that he needed help.

"Andrew can help Vin get Scarlett and you inside the manor. I can stay with Donovan and ensure he gets treated," Jet explained, mentally preparing the argument Andrew would have of helping Donovan. "I worry that even if he can get past the wards it may strain the injuries he obtained from your magic," he added, seeing Andrew enter the cave.

Andrew let out a bitter laugh having overheard the request. "You're kidding, right?" he sneered, hearing a heavy sigh escape Jet's lips.

"Don't be a child, he helped save all of us from Simon and his shades otherwise we might not have made it out alive," he protested, holding up his hands silencing Andrew's bitter remark. "All I need you to do is help get him into the jeep," he added, moving out from under Ari to help Vincent gingerly pick up Scarlett before climbing to his feet. He bent down to pick Ari up, feeling her rest her head against his shoulder.

Andrew gave him a mock salute before picking up Donovan and slinging him over his shoulder, making his way to the jeep. Jet heaved a sigh of relief, feeling Ari squeeze his hand gently. Vincent followed them excited to leave the cave. Vincent climbed into the passenger seat. seeing Jet sitting in the back with Ari passed out beside him. He turned in his seat, watching the others seeing Andrew toss the vampire in. trying not to wince at hearing a bone snap. "Are you trying to kill him a second time Drew? You know he can't hurt you when he's out cold?" Vin asked, once Andrew had slammed the trunk before climbing into the driver's seat.

Andrew rolled his eyes. turning the key in the ignition and started to drive toward the highway. "Sometimes I forget my own strength, though he'll recover and just assume it was caused by Simon," he protested, ignoring Jet's mocking laughter before continuing to drive back to the manor.

Vincent instructed Andrew to stop outside the gates letting Andrew carry Scarlett inside before helping Jet carry Ari inside wanting her to keep sleeping. He grabbed the supplies for an IV drip and a few blood bags they had kept for emergencies. He returned to the jeep opening the trunk inserting the IV drip into Donovan's right arm before connecting it to the bag of blood. He leaned against the jeep wondering how long it would take.

An hour passed before Vincent switched the empty bag with a second one before a low groan was emitted from Donovan as his eyes fluttered open. He glanced around in confusion trying to figure out where he was. He moved into a sitting position hissing as he put pressure on his left arm cradling it his chest seeing that it was broken. "How are the others?" he asked, hearing the man's thoughts wander to those other than the condition of Scarlett.

Vincent jumped startled by the sound of Donovan's question having dozed off while leaning against the jeep. "The others are worried about Scarlett. She still hasn't woken since we left the cave. Ari and Jet are resting, though you can thank Andrew for the broken arm," he replied, surprised to see that the bones hadn't recovered.

A weak laugh escaped his throat. "That's fair seeing how I threatened to end his pathetic existence. Her body just needs time to recover from the ordeal," he explained, closing his eyes resting his head against the backrest behind him. "I had internal injuries and severe blood loss from the blast. They are more critical than a broken bone though they should heal in time," he muttered, catching the quick glance of concern.

Vincent nodded in agreement hoping that Donovan was right. "I can't help but fear Simon's defeat springing forth more vampires for us to deal with," he groaned, wondering if the next would be more powerful than the next.

"Your fear is valid, but I doubt another would be foolish enough to claim my territory. I will be venturing home to dissolve any illusions another vampire may have of this area and to claim justice. Simon killed my brother and I wish for his creator to tremble in terror before meeting his demise. Being a council member will not save Dameon from my wraith," he admitted, knowing that he would return to visit Scarlett.

A flood of questions evaded his mind, yet he merely nodded feeling sympathy for Donovan. "I would hate to be the victim of your wrath after witnessing you taking on Simon. How far do you have to travel to reach your home?" he asked, fighting back the other pointless questions.

Donovan groaned reaching a hand up to rub his temples. "I was wrong when I thought only Scar had a curious nature, though I would appreciate it if you didn't shout your thoughts. I will be journeying to Transylvania to the castle of Count Dracula, where my mother rules all vampires in his passing," he explained, waiting for the next horde of questions.

Vincent blinked baffled by the remark yet recalled the ability the group had discussed Donovan possessing. "I'm sorry, there's a lot she chose not to share with us about you. That is a long journey to make after an intense battle," he remarked, wondering if he would inform Scarlett of his trip.

Donovan sighed, opening his eyes once more to glance at Vincent. "No apology is needed, though there is still plenty I have yet to share with her. I will be leaving in a few days once I have my personal affairs in order," he explained, still trying to think of a way to break the news to her.
"Good luck, you know she'll want to go with you, especially after hearing that you had lost your brother," he warned, not sure how Donovan would break the news to her.

Donovan sighed but nodded his head in agreement, knowing that Vincent was right. He glanced over his shoulder, seeing that the car was parked in front of a manor. "I take it we are in front of your dwelling. If you wish to venture inside you may. I will be fine on my own," he suggested, glancing over at Vin finally noticing the IV and the bag of blood arching an eyebrow at it.

Vincent nodded in agreement, seeing Donovan admiring the manor. "Sorry about that, I knew you needed blood and feared you might drain me dry," he explained, helping Donovan remove the IV seeing that it was empty.

He laughed softly, taking the offered hand before climbing to his feet. "Your theory would have been proven right and then I would be no worse than that bastard, Simon. I will be retiring to my establishment. You can inform Scarlett of my location when she awakes," he explained, climbing out of the car, nodding his head in thanks.

Vincent wished him good luck before going back into the manor. He paused, turning around seeing that Donovan was already gone. He returned to his room, collapsing onto his bed.

Two hours had passed before Scarlett woke, feeling bile build up in her chest. She rolled onto her side, releasing the vomit, and watching the sun rise from the kitchen windows. She closed her eyes, trying to block out the sun, wondering if she was getting an infection from her injuries.

Matt ran his fingers through Scarlett's hair. Jet had informed him of the events of the battle before heading to bed. Hearing retching, he pulled her hair back, waiting for her to finish. "Are you all right?" he asked once she was done.

Scarlett whimpered, wishing the pain would fade, focusing in on the familiar voice. She closed her eyes using her shirt to wipe the bile from her mouth. She reached out for his hand curling up against his chest resting her forehead against his shoulder. She bit her lower lip fighting back the tears. "It feels like everything inside is on fire," she gasped, feeling his fingers stroke her hair gently.

Matt frowned, placing a hand on her forehead seeing that she had a fever. He kept his hand there knowing that the cold would help break the fever. He moved to pull her lip away from her teeth only to wince seeing in horror two small fangs sticking out coated lightly in blood. He stared at her in horror trying to figure out what was happening to her. "Calm down, fool, she's not a vampire. She's only half turned," his demon called out in a mocking tone. Keeping one hand resting against her forehead, he combed the other through her hair luring her to sleep.

About the Authors

Emberly Lily Summers is native to Baltimore, MD and has been writing for the last ten years. She writes poetry, paranormal romance, and urban fantasy. Her inspiration comes from nature, the fantasy and paranormal literature, classic musicals such as The Phantom of the Opera and Wicked and of course, her favorite music ranging from showtunes to punk rock. Emberly also loves reading about magic, mythology, faeries, witches, and dragons.

She hopes to inspire creativity and imagination to others with her writing. She started writing poetry and short stories inspired from her favorite authors before enduring longer stories sparked by dreams, mythology, fantasy, and even paranormal. She has had several poems featured in *Maryland's Best Emerging Poets 2019* by Z Publishing and *Fae Thee Well: An Anthology* and *Rogues and Rebels: An Anthology* both published by Dreampunk Press.

Luna Nyx Frost is a native to Baltimore, MD and has been writing for the last twenty years. Her inspiration mostly comes from nature, ancient history, and classic literature. Luna has also looked up to the magnificent work of poets such as Edgar Allen Poe and Emily Dickens. Her passion for writing and reading doesn't stop at sonnets and novels. She has also read many works by Shakespeare and fables by The Brothers Grimm. Luna has also been intrigued by the great ancient civilizations awakening her mind and wanted to author stories that took form in her mind.

After publishing her first book. *Sherwood Asylum: A Book of Poetry*, she has had other poems featured in anthologies such as *Maryland's Best Emerging Poets* by Z Publishing and in *Fae Thee Well* by Dreampunk Press.

Made in the USA
Columbia, SC
21 October 2020